WICKED FOX

WICKED FOX

KAT CHO

putnam

G. P. Putnam's Sons

G. P. Putnam's Sons
an imprint of Penguin Random House LLC, New York

Copyright © 2019 by Katherine Cho.
Penguin supports copyright. Copyright fuels creativity, encourages diverse voices,
promotes free speech, and creates a vibrant culture. Thank you for buying an authorized
edition of this book and for complying with copyright laws by not reproducing, scanning,
or distributing any part of it in any form without permission. You are supporting writers
and allowing Penguin to continue to publish books for every reader.

G. P. Putnam's Sons is a registered trademark of Penguin Random House LLC.

Visit us online at penguinrandomhouse.com

Library of Congress Cataloging-in-Publication Data
Names: Cho, Kat.
Title: Wicked fox / Kat Cho.
Description: New York: G. P. Putnam's Sons Books for Young Readers, 2019.
Summary: After eighteen-year-old Gu Miyoung, a nine-tailed fox surviving in modern-
day Seoul by eating the souls of evil men, kills a murderous goblin to save Jihoon, she is
forced to choose between her immortal life and his.
Identifiers: LCCN 2018057954 (print) | LCCN 2018061139 (ebook) |
ISBN 9781984812353 (ebook) | ISBN 9781984812346 (hardback)
Subjects: | CYAC: Supernatural—Fiction. | Murder—Fiction. | Soul—Fiction. |
Animals, Mythical—Fiction. | Seoul (Korea)—Fiction. | Korea—Fiction.
Classification: LCC PZ7.2.C5312 (ebook) | LCC PZ7.2.C5312 Wic 2019 (print) |
DDC [Fic]—dc23
LC record available at https://lccn.loc.gov/2018057954

Printed in the United States of America.
ISBN 9781984812346
1 3 5 7 9 10 8 6 4 2

Design by Dave Kopka and Suki Boynton.
Text set in Adobe Caslon Pro.

For my mom and dad, Kello Katie and David Young Cho.
You taught me what love looks like.
사랑해요. 보고 싶어요.

1

GU MIYOUNG'S RELATIONSHIP with the moon was complicated, as are most relationships centered around power.

Her muscles vibrated with anticipation as she balanced on the edge of the roof. The moonlight made her skin itch, like a string pulled too tight. She breathed deeply to steady her speeding heart, and the stench of rotten trash filled her nostrils.

Her mother told her to be grateful for the power of the moon. It gave her strength, but sometimes Miyoung resented being strong.

Miyoung scanned the roads below. The streetlights were burnt out and had probably been so for a while. Miyoung didn't mind. She saw as easily in the dark as most did in broad daylight. In her opinion, the broken lights only helped the aesthetic of the buildings. Cracks spidered across the crumbling facades, decorated with blooms of mold. Perhaps a more optimistic soul would see a strange beauty in the pattern, but not Miyoung.

She pulled out her phone and dialed one of the two numbers saved in it.

"Did you find him, Seonbae?" Nara asked as soon as she picked up.

The way she stuttered out *seonbae* made the respectful title sound suffocatingly formal. As if she were speaking to an elder twice her age, instead of Miyoung, who was only a year her senior. But Miyoung knew the younger girl used the title for multiple reasons, one being that two weeks ago her name hadn't even been Gu Miyoung.

"I tracked him to the same alley. He's been coming here all week—just haven't figured out which apartment he goes into."

"I've been trying to use the phone location app," Nara said helpfully. "It says you're right on top of him. Or is that your location? Click on your GPS."

Miyoung wanted to tell Nara to stick to communing with the spirits, but instead she swiped her screen and turned on the tracking option.

"Wait, now there are two of you." Nara fell into muffled mutters. Miyoung rolled her eyes to the heavens as she held her tongue. It wouldn't help to yell. Nara was nervous by nature, a side effect of her ability to see ghosts since birth.

Plus, Miyoung knew Nara meant well. But Miyoung didn't need good intentions; she needed a target.

To stop herself from pacing, she sat on the edge of the roof and let her feet dangle over the six-story drop. Gaining the high ground allowed her to stake out the area as well as her prey.

Still, she'd only seen him from a distance, going on the vague description from Nara.

Miyoung closed her eyes and counted to ten to settle her nerves.

Before her lay the cityscape of Seoul. The skyscrapers of Cheongdamdong, a mecca of entertainment and glamour, the home of fashion and K-pop. The soaring height of 63 Building, a symbol of the modernization of the capital city, sitting sentry beside the Han River. And the lights of Namsan Tower, where lovers and tourists went to see the world at their feet. Miyoung sneered at her own worn sneakers, dangling over a trash-filled alley.

"What is he doing here?" Miyoung mumbled, mostly to herself, but Nara answered.

"The spirit says he goes there every night. Her death was too violent." The other girl's words became morose. "She needs justice before she can pass to the afterlife."

Miyoung wasn't sure if what she did was justice. Still, it was better than nothing. And if she had to kill, she might as well help a few wayward ghosts settle their grudges.

Not for the first time, Miyoung wondered whether putting all her faith in Nara's spirits was a bad idea. She couldn't feed without the power of the full moon. No, that was a lie. She *wouldn't* feed without it.

The full moon increased her senses, opened her up to energy, allowed her to absorb it without ripping a man apart. So if she didn't feed tonight, she'd have to wait another month or . . . she'd have to become a monster. She almost let out a laugh because she knew that even though the prey she chose were vile men, it didn't mean she wasn't a killer.

Still, she wouldn't give in to her more base instinct, the one that wanted her to tear into flesh. To uncover the energy kept deep within every living creature. To drink that energy from a man without the need of the moon to channel it. No, she'd take it as gently as she could and pretend that she was a benevolent murderer.

She'd failed this task only once, and she'd refused to feed any other way, even when her mother begged. The only time she'd ever refused her mother. Miyoung's body began to weaken within a week and didn't recover until she fed at the next full moon. That's why her mother had her rules, one of which was *Never miss a hunt.*

But Nara was a gifted young shaman, able to contact spirits across the country. And no matter where Miyoung moved, Nara had found victims for Miyoung each full moon without fail. A useful ally to have.

"Seonbae?"

"What?" Miyoung asked, perhaps too gruffly.

"Be careful tonight. Many households banished evil spirits this month during Sangdalgosa. They might be wandering."

Annoyed, Miyoung stood so she could start to pace again. "I'm not scared of a few spirits."

Miyoung glanced down at the sound of a door squeaking open. She made out laughter and music from inside before the door swung closed, some kind of underground club. A man emerged. He was short and thick, his balding head pale white under the bright moon. She recognized the tattoo peeking through the wide collar of his shirt, an oversized spider he probably thought made him look tough but just accented his aging body in all the wrong ways.

"Got him. I'll call you back." Miyoung hung up as she stepped off the roof. She landed lightly on the ground, creating a cloud of dust and stink.

The man stumbled drunkenly and Miyoung kept pace with him. As she moved out of the shadows, muscles flexing as she prepared for the kill, he dropped a soju bottle he'd been carrying. Cursing, he sneered down at the shattered glass. Miyoung hid herself from sight. It was a knee-jerk reaction, but unnecessary. It didn't matter if he saw her. He would tell no one of what happened tonight except other spirits.

She was so caught up in her musings that she didn't notice

when he started walking again, down the narrow streets, leading to where civilization gathered. She cursed herself for waiting. Another of her mother's rules: *Find somewhere private for the kill.*

The salty smell of boiling jjigae and the charred scent of frying meat surrounded her in smoke and steam. Bare bulbs hung from the corners of food stands. Their harsh light distracted the eye from the run-down, cracked plaster of the buildings beyond.

She'd just moved here and she'd already decided she didn't like it. She'd lived in Seoul before, among the soaring skyscrapers of Gangnam, or in the shadow of the old palace in Samcheongdong. But this new neighborhood was neither brand-new nor significantly historical. It just was. The air was filled with the scents of spicy tteok-bokki and savory pastries. Her mouth watered despite her disdain for the greasy food.

The man paused to stare at dehydrated ojingeo. The legs of the dried cephalopods twisted, brittle enough to snap off at the slightest touch, hard and fragile at the same time. It was a dichotomy Miyoung often pondered. If someone cut out her heart, it would probably be a twisted chunk of brittle meat like the ojingeo.

The man broke off one of the eight legs and stuck it in his mouth.

"Ya!" shouted the ajumma manning the food stand. "Are you going to pay for that?"

Miyoung sensed a fight brewing and didn't have the patience to wait for it to resolve itself. So she broke her mother's final rule: *Don't let anyone notice you when you're on a hunt.*

"Ajeossi!" She slid her arm through the man's. "There you are!"

"Do you know him?" The ajumma looked Miyoung up and down.

"Of course, sorry about that." Miyoung put down a crisp orange bill. "I don't need change."

"Whozit?" The man squinted at her through bleary eyes as she led him away.

Miyoung grimaced at the heavy stink of soju on his breath.

"It's been so long. You were childhood friends with my father." She turned them onto a less populated road. Trees loomed at the end of the street, a perfect cover.

"Who's your father?" His eyes rolled up, as if searching his brain for the memory.

Miyoung almost said, *Good question*. She'd never met the man. So she built him out of her imagination as she started up a dirt hiking path. Trees rose around them, sparse at first, then thickening as she led him deeper into the forest, winding away from the road.

"You went to middle school together. I met you a few years ago. You came to our house. My mom made japchae." Miyoung used any random detail that popped into her head. She wound through the trees toward the more secluded trails.

Her plan to take him farther was ruined as he finally took in their surroundings. "Where are we?"

Miyoung cursed.

"What is this?" The man yanked his arm away, spun around, and ran, clearly disoriented or he'd know he was headed farther into the forest. It almost made Miyoung feel pity for the old fool. He barely made it a dozen steps before she caught him by the collar. He yelped, struggling to free himself.

She shoved him against the trunk of an ash tree, wrapping her fingers around his thick neck. She tasted his distress as she siphoned some of his gi—the energy that emanated from all living things. The energy she stole to be immortal.

"What do you want?"

Instead of answering him, Miyoung pulled out her phone.

Nara's face filled the screen, a classic oval with pale skin and a brush of bangs. Her eyes wide with concern. There were bags under them, a souvenir of the past few sleepless nights she had stayed up to help Miyoung stake out her prey.

"Did you catch him?"

Miyoung turned the phone toward the frightened man. The sight of it pulled him out of his shock. His eyes took in Miyoung's form: an eighteen-year-old girl with long limbs, dark hair, and a heart-shaped face. He visibly relaxed, lulled into complacency by her pretty looks. It only made Miyoung pity him more. Foolish man didn't know beauty was the best camouflage for a monster.

"Is this him?" Miyoung ignored the man's lurid stare, far too used to the look.

"Yes."

Miyoung nodded and hung up.

"Who was that?" The man's demand was rough, fed by agitation and the belief that he was not truly in danger. Her prey always made this mistake, every month like clockwork.

"She's a shaman," Miyoung answered because it didn't matter what she told him and because, despite her morbid intentions, Miyoung was a proper Korean girl taught to respect her elders.

"Some quack fortune-teller?" the man spat out.

"People have no respect for the old ways anymore." Miyoung clicked her tongue with disappointment. "True shamans do more than tell fortunes. They can commune with the spirits. As in the dead. As in the girl you killed last month."

All the color leached from the man's face. "How do you know?"

"Don't you regret what you did?" she asked, as if the question was rhetorical, but she hoped for a sign of repentance.

As always, she was disappointed.

"Why should I be sorry? It was her fault." The man's face became bright red. "She should have kept quiet. I only tried to make her stop screaming."

"Then you've made your choice and I've made mine."

She felt the moon, heard it whispering to her, telling her to feed.

Miyoung let her energy flow, let part of her true form free.

The man gasped.

They wove behind her, nine tails made of moonlight and dust.

In this last moment before she took a life, she had a need to be her true self. No more lies or false facades. She'd show these men what took their lives in the end.

She gripped the man by the shoulders, letting his gi fill her until her muscles vibrated. The moon urged her to let go, to allow her baser instincts to take over. If she ripped out his liver, the process would be over in seconds. But Miyoung couldn't bring herself to do it. And so she watched him die slowly, yet painlessly, as she siphoned his gi bit by bit. As simple as a person falling asleep.

While she became full, the man deflated like a balloon losing air. She loved the energy filling her, even as she hated herself for being a monster.

"Why are you doing this?" The man's voice became slurred.

"Because I don't want to die." She watched the light fade from his eyes.

"Neither do I," he mumbled just before he lost consciousness.

"I know," she whispered to no one.

2

THE PC ROOM was hot with thirty running computers, though only three stations were occupied. It was stuffy and dark and smelled like the shrimp chips and instant noodles sold as snacks.

Ahn Jihoon loved it. He clicked with nimble fingers, his left hand glued to the hot keys, his right hand sweeping the mouse over the screen.

"If we don't leave now, we'll be late," Oh Changwan said, his hands waving like anxious butterflies with nowhere to land. He'd long since logged off after losing his own game.

"Then we'll be late." Digital armies marched across Jihoon's screen.

"I can't be late again." Changwan frowned. It highlighted his exaggerated features. His ears were too big and his nose too long. A puppy who hadn't grown into his looks yet.

Jihoon knew being late wasn't Changwan's problem. His problem was being timid and having a family rich enough to care. As the eldest son, he held the weight of the Oh name on his shoulders, which was only doubled by wealth. It didn't sit well on Changwan, who was prone to anxiety and merely mediocre at anything he tried. It made Jihoon grateful he'd been born poor.

"Changwan-ah, you always worry about the future instead of enjoying what's happening now. You need to learn that life isn't worth living if you're not having fun." Jihoon narrowed his eyes, searching for the final tower on his opponent's base. He found it with a triumphant grunt, and the screen announced victory in bold green letters hovering over his Protoss army.

"Great, you won. Time to go?" Changwan asked.

Jihoon stood and shrugged on his navy-blue uniform blazer.

"Changwan-ah, no one likes a nag."

Changwan scowled and Jihoon added a friendly smile. One that said he meant no harm but knew he spoke the truth. He wielded his grin like a weapon, a crooked tilt of his lips that revealed deep dimples. When he used it, few could stay mad. It worked, as Changwan gave a reluctant smile.

Outside, Jihoon took a deep breath, inhaling the smell of car exhaust and simmering oxtail from the seolleongtang restaurant down the street. He swung an arm around his friend's shoulder as they walked in and out of the sun that peeked between the tall buildings.

"Is it me, or does the morning always smell fresher after the thrill of victory?"

"It smells like someone needs to clean their fish tanks." Changwan scrunched his face at the seafood store. Jihoon followed his gaze to one of the giant glass aquariums, the bulging eyes of a flounder stared back.

The city bus pulled up, and Jihoon slapped Changwan's shoulder cheerfully. "Come on, don't want to be late."

They were late.

By the time they reached the school, the front gate sat closed, a signal that class had started without them. Jihoon helped boost

Changwan over the side wall before climbing up himself. He miscalculated the distance and his pant leg caught.

"Aissi!" Jihoon grimaced at the long rip in the calf of his beige pants.

He'd had a growth spurt the past year, making him the tallest in his class. It also made him unintentionally clumsy.

The school was a U-shaped building with long narrow hallways, lined on one side by classrooms and on the other by wide windows facing the inner courtyard and sports fields. The building was old, and there was no central heat to warm the halls in the brisk fall chill.

They snuck into the back of the classroom with ten minutes left in homeroom. The teacher, Miss Kwon, was still addressing the class.

"I'd like to remind everyone that now is not the time to slack off." She zeroed in on Jihoon. "Next year is your third and final year of high school. It's our job to prepare you. And your job to learn."

"Yes, Sunsaengnim," the class chorused.

"That's it for today," Miss Kwon said.

The class president stood. "Attention. Salute."

"Thank you," the students chorused as they bowed in unison.

Instead of leaving, Miss Kwon walked down the aisle and knocked on Jihoon's desk. "If you come in late again, it's detention."

"Yes, Sunsaengnim." Changwan bowed so low, his forehead smacked his desk beside Jihoon.

"Saem, you say that like spending more time with you is a punishment." Jihoon accompanied the words with a lazy grin.

Miss Kwon fought the smile that eventually bloomed across her face. "I'm serious, Ahn Jihoon."

"So am I," Jihoon replied without missing a beat. He widened his smile so his dimples flashed.

Miss Kwon let out a soft chuckle despite herself. "It's my last warning," she said before exiting the classroom.

As soon as she cleared the back door, the peace of the room erupted into the chaos of kids jumping up from their seats to join their friends.

Changwan shook his head. "I don't know why teachers let you talk like that."

"It's because of my charm and good looks."

"It's because he's so ridiculous, they have to laugh or else they'd scream." Lee Somin stepped up to the boys' joined desks. She was 158 centimeters of attitude packed in a petite package who'd known Jihoon since they were in diapers.

She glanced at the kid sitting in front of Jihoon. "Get lost."

The boy scurried from his chair like a startled rabbit.

Jihoon took in his best friend. Somin dressed like a handbook for how to break dress code: her uniform shirt unbuttoned to reveal a graphic tee beneath; her nails painted black. Her hair was different again. Somin's look changed with the seasons, a girl who could never make up her mind. It gave Jihoon whiplash, but he also hated change. It took too much effort. Today her short hair was dyed bright red, and she looked as fired up as her locks right now.

Jihoon flicked a hand across a flaming strand. "What punishment did the vice principal give you today?"

"I had to kneel in front of the school this morning. Again."

"You had to know you'd get in trouble for it," Jihoon pointed out.

"You're one to talk," Somin retorted. "What are you going to tell your halmeoni if you get detention and the school calls her again?"

Jihoon's easy smile disappeared at the thought of his grandmother's reaction. Then he dismissed it. Concern took too much effort.

"You should care more. The school year is more than half over," she said with a pointed look at the changing leaves of autumn outside. Jihoon usually loved fall because it meant winter was right around the corner and then school would end. At least until it annoyingly started up again in March.

"So?" Jihoon asked, though he knew what Somin was going to say.

"So next year is our third year."

When Jihoon gave her a blank stare, she continued, "Our senior year and suneung exams. You're the bottom-ranked student in the second-year class right now."

"Someone has to be last when there are rankings," Jihoon pointed out.

"Why is everything such a joke to you?" Somin asked.

"I'm not joking. I just—"

"Don't care," Changwan and Somin chorused.

Jihoon shrugged with a rueful smile. He knew everyone thought he was an affable guy with nothing much going for him. That's how he liked it. The less people expected from him, the more they left him alone.

Somin was the only person in the whole school who continuously believed in Jihoon no matter what. Something he graciously forgave her for, due to their lifelong friendship.

"One of these days you're going to find yourself in a situation even you can't talk your way out of," she said.

"When that day comes, should I take a page from your book and punch my way out?" Jihoon mussed her hair.

Somin slapped his hand away. "Like you could. Look at those weak sticks you call arms. The only time you lift your hands is to shove food into your mouth or wipe your butt."

Changwan cringed. "Somin-ah, not very ladylike of you."

"And when did I ever claim to be a lady?" Somin tilted her head. A tiger eyeing her prey.

"Never." Changwan lowered his eyes.

As his friends continued to bicker, Jihoon laid his head down to take a nap.

o   o   o

It was so late the sun barely lit the streets when Jihoon climbed the hill toward home, past the forest bordering town. The woods were welcoming during the day, frequented by hikers and families seeking a bit of nature in the bustling metropolis. At night, however, the branches looked more crooked and the leaves shivered from invisible beasts passing. Jihoon grew up beside this mountain forest, and he'd never dared set foot inside after night fell. A by-product of fables his halmeoni used to tell him of goblins and ghosts coming out at night to eat bad little boys.

"Late again, Jihoon-ah." An old woman sat outside the medicinal wine store. Everyone called her Hwang Halmeoni. She was the oldest person in the neighborhood and claimed she'd stopped keeping track of her age years ago. Last she knew, she was ninety-two.

"It was a long day." Jihoon gave her a wink.

"Studying or playing?" Hwang Halmeoni's smile was knowing. She sat on a low wooden deck and peeled garlic into a bowl. The scent stung Jihoon's nostrils.

"Playing." He grinned. "Always."

She clucked her tongue, popping a piece of raw garlic into her mouth. Jihoon hated eating it raw, though his own halmeoni said it was good for his health. Still, when Hwang Halmeoni held out her hand, he dutifully accepted a peeled clove.

"When are you going to make me the happiest man on earth and agree to marry me?"

Hwang Halmeoni chuckled, her eyes sparkling. "Your silver tongue is going to get you in trouble one day."

"It already has." Jihoon winked again. "Many times over."

"Stop stalling. You have to go home and answer to your halmeoni."

Jihoon sighed because she was right. He bowed and crossed the dark street toward his halmeoni's restaurant and slipped silently into the second-floor apartment. He toed off his sneakers and placed them neatly beside his halmeoni's worn shoes. A small form raced down the hall with a high-pitched yip.

"Dubu! Shhh." He tried to quiet the tiny ball of fur. She ignored him and jumped onto his legs for the requisite petting.

Jihoon winced as a door opened.

"Ahn Jihoon!" his halmeoni yelled. "I was about to send the police to search all of Korea."

Jihoon folded in a bow of apology.

His halmeoni had been pretty once. Proof lay in the old black-and-white photos on her nightstand. Now worry and age lined her face. A small woman, she only reached Jihoon's shoulder, but he withered in the face of her anger.

"Halmeoni, you shouldn't get worked up. Your high blood pressure, remember?"

"Where were you?" she asked sternly.

Jihoon didn't bother with empty excuses. "You know where."

Halmeoni clicked her tongue in disapproval. "You are such a smart boy and you waste your brain on those games. I'm not asking you to get into a top-three SKY university. I just want you to go to college. Your mother got married right out of high school. That is why she was helpless without your father."

Jihoon shook his head at the mention of his parents.

"I don't need to go to university to help out in the restaurant," Jihoon said. "Or maybe I'll become a famous gamer and buy you a mansion. Either way, I just want to stay here with you, not go to a fancy university."

His halmeoni frowned and changed tack. "I went to see a shaman. She said your soul is being shadowed by something."

"You should stop giving your money to those people. They're a bunch of scam artists. The only spirits they talk to are in a bottle." Jihoon mimed throwing back a shot.

"She said you'll soon see darkness. Don't you know what that means?"

Jihoon shrugged and walked into the kitchen to avoid the conversation. Whenever his halmeoni went on one of her rants about his soul, his stomach churned.

He hoped she wouldn't get the idea to exorcise him again.

"If you keep staring at the computer, you'll ruin your eyes." Halmeoni followed him into the kitchen. It wasn't a long trip. The apartment was as small as a postage stamp.

"I can't lose my vision or else I won't be able to look at your beautiful face." Jihoon gave one of his lazy grins and Halmeoni's lips twitched. She fought back the smile and gave him a glower instead.

"Don't try to sweet-talk me. You think I'm a fool who'll fall for pretty words?"

Jihoon wrapped her in a tight hug, engulfing her in his long arms. "I'd never think that. My halmeoni is the smartest woman in the neighborhood. Maybe all of Seoul."

Halmeoni gave him a resigned huff and a stern pat on the back before wriggling out of his embrace.

She took his hand and placed a yellow paper in it. Bold red symbols stood out against the bright background. He recognized it as one of the talismans she hung inside the front door.

"What is it for?" Jihoon held it with two fingers like it was a rotten banana peel.

"A bujeok from the shaman for warding off evil. Keep it with you."

"This is ridiculous."

"You say I'm smart, so do as I say." Halmeoni folded his fingers around the paper.

He finally conceded and stuffed it into his pocket. "Fine."

"Good boy." She patted his rear in approval. "Now eat your dinner before it gets cold, and then take the dog out."

o o o

Twilight had become full night by the time Jihoon led Dubu out for her walk. Clouds covered the moon, so the road was lit only by lamps, which lengthened the shadows along the asphalt.

The angle of the street sloped so steeply, the buildings leaned to stay straight. Land was at a premium in the city, but Jihoon's neighborhood retained its quaint short buildings, winding around crooked roads so narrow that cars had no right to be on them.

The dog, no higher than Jihoon's calf and white as the moon, had no interest in going to the bathroom. She stared down the dark road with her ears perked.

"You going or not? If you have an accident inside, you'll have to answer to Halmeoni."

Dubu let out rapid-fire barks and took off so quickly, she wrenched the leash from Jihoon. With a curse, he ran after the dog, almost falling down the steep street.

Jihoon stopped in front of Hwang Halmeoni, who was still peeling her garlic. "Have you seen Dubu?"

"She ran past barking like a samjokgu. I think she was heading toward that little playground." Hwang Halmeoni held out a peeled clove and Jihoon accepted it, though he still hadn't gotten the garlic smell off his skin from earlier.

The playground sat at the base of the road, adjacent to the first line of trees.

"Dubu!" Jihoon yelled, hoping she'd hidden in the plastic jungle gym.

No such luck, as her barking answered him from the woods.

Jihoon whistled, hoping it would be enough to gain her return, but she didn't emerge.

Misty clouds hung heavy in the sky. He didn't like the idea of going into the woods when even the light of the moon was absent. A shiver ran down his spine and goose bumps rose on his skin.

Jihoon clicked on his phone light, squared his shoulders, and entered the woods.

"Dubu, come on, girl," he yelled loud enough for his voice to echo back.

At night, the shadows became a menacing gray of shapes reaching for him. Ghosts and monsters shifted in his peripheral vision.

It didn't matter that he'd stopped believing in those things long ago.

Night and darkness made a believer of everyone.

Something pulled his sleeve and he spun around with a shout an octave higher than he would like to admit. Jihoon half expected to see a leering dokkaebi with rotting teeth and malicious intent, story monsters used to make kids obey their parents.

It was a branch.

He laughed to release his jitters.

A shape darted past and his laugh became another yelp.

"Dubu!" Jihoon took off after her. He was going to wring that dog's neck. He'd go to the pet store and buy an exact replica of Dubu. His halmeoni would never know the difference.

Jihoon tried not to twitch at every noise or rustle of leaves. He kept his eyes straight ahead, refusing to glance into the shadows surrounding him.

He finally caught up with Dubu and scooped her into his arms. She wriggled, clutching something in her teeth. Jihoon hoped to the heavens it wasn't a rat. She dropped it, and he jumped back in case it was still alive.

With a fair bit of embarrassment, Jihoon realized it wasn't a rodent but a shoe. More specifically, a girl's sneaker.

"Oh, good. This is exactly what I needed. I'm so glad we went into a dark, terrifying forest to find this."

Wandering back through the woods with a wriggling Dubu in his arms soon revealed that Jihoon was good and lost. He couldn't even find a hiking path to give him some semblance of direction.

In his arms Dubu's body vibrated with a low growl. Nervously, Jihoon glanced around, expecting to see some wild beast approaching. But there were only shadows and trees.

It seemed Dubu was reacting to nothing, or perhaps a wayward squirrel had scurried past. Then Jihoon saw one of the shadows by an old oak shift until he made out the shape of a lurking creature. The beast growled, an echo of Dubu's. Jihoon clamped his hand around the dog's muzzle to quiet her. At first he thought the animal was warning them away, until he realized it faced the opposite direction.

As he stepped back, his ear adjusted to the sounds. They weren't growls. They were words.

"Wait . . . Fox . . ."

Before Jihoon absorbed this new fact, Dubu shook her snout free of his grip and let out a tirade of barks.

When the hunched figure turned, the light of the moon slanted over its face.

Jihoon gasped.

Its features were distinctly human, with ruddy, rounded cheeks and a hooked nose. Still, Jihoon knew this was no ordinary man. It stood, revealing a stocky build with biceps as wide as Jihoon's thighs.

"S-sorry." Jihoon couldn't stop his voice from shaking. Something about this creature pulled him back to a time when he was a little boy cowering under his sheets.

"A human. Wrong," it said. The rumbling voice sounded like gravel scratching under metal.

Dubu launched herself out of Jihoon's arms. She tumbled against the dirt-packed ground, then surged forward. The beast swatted the dog away like a fly. With a yelp of pain, her small body slammed into a tree before crumpling into a limp pile.

Jihoon hurried toward Dubu but found his path blocked by the creature.

Stay calm, he thought. It's what they always said to do when you're faced with a predatory animal. And Jihoon had no doubt that this creature, despite its human features, was a wild thing.

"Look, I don't want any trouble." Jihoon kept his voice low. "I'm just going to take my dog and leave and not talk about this to anyone."

In the blink of an eye the creature attacked, and a beefy arm hooked around Jihoon's neck. It smelled like overripe fruit and body odor—not a good combination.

Bristling whiskers pressed into Jihoon's forehead as the beast sniffed him. Jihoon tried to strain away, but the grip around his neck was too strong. The harder he struggled, the tighter the stranglehold became.

Jihoon imagined dying alone in the middle of the forest. How his halmeoni would worry. How his body would be found days later, bloated and unidentifiable.

"Ya!" A voice shouted behind them.

The beast whirled so quickly, Jihoon's head spun.

When everything settled, he blinked in surprise. Jihoon couldn't decide if he was imagining things because of lack of oxygen or if a girl really stood there. If she was real, she couldn't have been older than Jihoon's eighteen years. Her eyes were sharp and her lips peeled back from her teeth. It made her look as wild as the creature choking him. She was slim and tall, perhaps a head shorter than Jihoon. Her feet moved into a fighter's stance, pulling his gaze down her long legs. She was missing a shoe.

"Let him go, dokkaebi saekki-ya." She spat in the dirt.

Puzzle pieces clicked into place, like finally remembering a word that had hung just out of reach. The beast holding Jihoon looked like the stocky, hunched goblins in his halmeoni's stories. Except dokkaebi didn't exist.

The dokkaebi let out a bellowing laugh. "Take him from me, yeowu."

The girl's eyes flared.

Jihoon knew this was an uneven match, but he didn't have the courage to tell the girl to leave.

She grabbed the dokkaebi's thick thumb and with a quick jerk twisted it off.

The beast wailed in pain. His arms loosened, dropping Jihoon.

Fear made Jihoon's muscles weak as he fell to his hands and knees, wheezing to pull in precious air.

There's no blood, Jihoon thought as he dry-heaved. *Why is there no blood?*

In fact, the thumb cracked off like a piece of porcelain snapped from a vase.

The creature hunched, cradling his injured fist. His face was now so red, it clearly reminded Jihoon of the crimson-skinned dokkaebi in his old children's books.

Jihoon stood on shaky legs, the girl now between him and the dokkaebi, the thumb still in her hand. She squeezed her fist closed until her knuckles cracked. White powder flew from her palm. The dust wove in and out of the light as if the girl had cast a spell. Then Jihoon realized the clouds covering the moon had parted. It lit the scene with a silver pallor. Everything that had once seemed ominous now softened to the haze of a dream. The shadows shifted. A glow of shapes coalesced around the girl in a wide fan.

No, not a fan.

Tails, as bright and pale as the moon.

She looked like a warrior queen, fierce and unforgiving. And as untouchable as the ghostly tails dancing behind her.

Memories flooded Jihoon of Halmeoni reading him fables from the yellowed pages of her books. Stories where foxes lived forever. Where they became beautiful women to entice unsuspecting men. Where those men never survived.

Now he understood why the dokkaebi had called her *yeowu*—fox.

"Gumiho," Jihoon whispered.

The girl's head whipped around, her eyes bright as fire.

Jihoon knew he should fear her, but instead he felt a strange fascination.

The clouds reclaimed the moon, making the shadows bleed. The darkness took over until Jihoon couldn't see a thing.

He wanted to convince himself it had all been a trick of the light. He almost could as his eyes adjusted and he saw the girl, now tailless without the moon.

The dokkaebi let out a guttural growl and charged.

The girl met the goblin head-on. It pushed her back, her feet digging divots in the ground.

Jihoon never tore his eyes from the fight as he bent to scoop up Dubu's limp form. She seemed too light in his arms, but he saw her small chest rise and fall with relief.

Mere meters away a battle played out that Jihoon thought he'd only see in his video games. A dokkaebi versus a gumiho. A goblin versus a fox. The two were so evenly matched that any ground gained by one side was soon lost again.

Jihoon started to flee, then stopped. He couldn't force himself to take another step. What kind of person would he be if he abandoned the girl after she'd saved him? Not the boy his halmeoni had raised.

Already annoyed at his conscience, he called out, "His right side!"

The girl glanced over, the distraction enough for the dokkaebi to sneak under her guard. The goblin twisted her around, choking her in a headlock.

"His right side!" Jihoon repeated.

If dokkaebi and gumiho were real, then maybe his halmeoni's other tales were real. The ones that said dokkaebi were good at wrestling but weak on the right.

The girl's eyes lit with understanding, and her lips pursed in new determination. She leaned all her weight to the right, but the dokkaebi had heard Jihoon's advice as well. It pulled out a strip of gold paper decorated in red symbols—a bujeok—and placed it over the girl's heart with a meaty fist. She screeched, pain etched in the piercing sound. The talisman stuck to her like a fluttering badge.

Her legs shook and she started to lose ground. The dokkaebi's arm tightened and her eyes widened, showing fear for the first time. At this rate, she'd lose more than ground.

Jihoon was not a brave boy. So he was already regretting his half-formed idea as he put Dubu down. He took two deep breaths, clenched his teeth, and took off in a sprint. He barreled headfirst into the dokkaebi's right side, under the arm that held the girl. The three tumbled to the ground together.

Bodies collided. Limbs grappled madly. The girl twisted until she sat atop the dokkaebi, whose meaty fist looped around her slim neck. Its other gripped Jihoon by the hair.

"Kill the fox," the dokkaebi kept repeating. "Kill the fox."

Despite her predicament, the girl didn't struggle. She wore the calm look of one who had complete control. Perhaps she'd become delusional from pain and lack of oxygen.

The girl placed her hand against the dokkaebi's heart, her long fingers splayed across his chest.

The beast jerked. The hand holding Jihoon tightened until he felt the sharp pain of hair being ripped from his head. Jihoon let out a yelp and gritted his teeth as he tried to pry open the thick fingers holding him.

The dokkaebi's legs flailed as if the girl were choking him instead of the other way around. Her eyes were unblinking, dark, and depthless. Sweat beaded over her pale skin.

Around her, shadows danced, like smoke caught in a vortex. The phantom tails wove through them.

The atmosphere thickened, the autumn chill replaced by sweltering heat. There were waves in the air, the kind that rose under a hot summer sun.

The dokkaebi's fists tore at more of Jihoon's hair. The heat and pain combined to blur his vision, as white dots danced before his eyes. He watched them coalesce into ghosts that raced through the forest. He watched them fly away and wished he could join them.

Wait for me, he tried to shout. One stopped. A girl? It glanced back at him before sprinting into the darkness.

The howls of the dokkaebi echoed through the trees. The goblin convulsed—leaves crunching and dirt flying—until its body jerked in a final death throe like a fish flopping on a deck.

The smoke dissipated. The girl's tails faded. The air cleared.

She sat upon the dokkaebi as calm as a child perched on her favorite reading chair. Her hand was still spread over its chest. Then the beast's body began to crack, fissures racing along its ruddy skin.

The dokkaebi imploded into scattered dust as the girl stood.

"You killed it," Jihoon sputtered.

"I saved your life." She stepped over the particles of dead

dokkaebi until she loomed above Jihoon. "Make sure I don't regret it. You will tell no one about what you saw tonight."

He nodded furiously.

She frowned at the bright yellow paper still plastered to her chest and tried to rip it free. With a hiss of pain she snatched her hand away.

Jihoon stood and reached for it. But she retreated from him, her lips twisting in a snarl.

He held up his hand, palm out. "Can I help?"

She watched him carefully but didn't move as he reached for the bujeok. The talisman came away as easy as plucking a leaf from a tree. As he wondered what magic had let him remove it when the girl, obviously much stronger than he was, could not, the bujeok dissolved in his hand.

The girl lurched forward and Jihoon barely caught her as she fell. The momentum sent them both falling to the ground.

She convulsed like a person being electrocuted. Foam spilled from her pale lips as her eyes rolled back.

Jihoon wasn't sure what to do. He'd heard once that if someone was having a seizure, you should put something between their teeth. And while he debated his next move, she stilled.

"Hello?"

No reply.

He leaned in to check her breathing.

She rocketed up, slamming into his forehead as she gagged. Jihoon fell back as something bulleted toward him. It hit him on the cheek before rolling away, and the girl crumpled into an unconscious heap again.

Jihoon, lying in a pile of leaves and dirt, turned his head to glance at the object. It was a bead, small and opalescent as a pearl.

Sitting up, he reached for it—then almost dropped it as it pulsed against his palms. His hand trembled as he recognized the pattern of the steady *thump*, like the beat of a heart.

A silver line speared from the pearl, a thread connecting him to the girl's heart.

Jihoon's fingers became numb so quickly, it seemed as if the warmth had been leached from his skin. And the thread pulsed, growing brighter, thicker. A wave of fatigue overtook Jihoon. He almost fell back to the ground when the girl's eyes flew open, zeroing in on the bead.

Jumping up, she snatched it away. A growl rumbled in her throat. A terrifying, beastly sound. The rage that twisted her face wiped away the clouds of fatigue from Jihoon's brain and replaced them with fear.

She retreated so fast she was a blur. Leaves spun and branches cracked as she sprinted into the trees.

With nothing but the sounds of the forest for company, Jihoon was suddenly aware he was all alone again. And still lost.

A rustle pulled a yelp from him. Then he relaxed again as Dubu limped over and flopped into his arms with a whimper. Jihoon, hands shaking, pulled her close and buried his face in her fur.

HAVE YOU EVER wondered where the gumiho came from as you lay awake fearing the full moon?

Some say the first gumiho came from the land to the west, traveling down the peninsula to settle in the mountain forests they preferred. Some say the first true gumiho arose in Korea before the country claimed the name. That tale begins as Prince Jumong—the Light of the East—founded the Goguryeo Kingdom.

There lived a fox, already over five hundred years old, who watched the activities of humankind with curiosity. She was strong and sleek, and hunters coveted her beautiful pelt. No matter how fast their bows, they were never able to catch her. Even Prince Jumong, the grandson of the water god Habaek, renowned for his hunting skills, could not catch her. Out of one hundred arrows shot, he hit his target one hundred times, until he came up against the fox.

She wandered into Prince Jumong's hunting grounds every day. Her reasons were not quite known. Some said she loved the prince. Others said she liked to mock him with her presence. But who can truly know the motivations of the ancients?

After she'd lived for a thousand years, the fox had gathered an exceptional amount of gi.

Through this energy she transformed herself into a human. A beautiful woman loved by any man she met, but never for long.

So she walked the earth alone, not quite human, but not quite beast.

A fox who loved the mortals she mimicked.

Until she could not love them anymore.

3

JIHOON WAS DREAMING. *He knew this even though there was nothing to particularly signal this. It was just an overwhelming sense of knowing.*

The forest was silent as he wove through trees made silver by the moonlight. Fog obscured the forest floor, so he couldn't make out his own feet. For all he knew, he floated above the ground, as his steps made no sound. In fact, nothing did. No rustling of leaves from wind or birds. No snapping of twigs from scurrying creatures. No noise of any kind broke the complete stillness of the woods.

He'd never been aware while dreaming before, but it had been a strange night all around, so what was one more weird thing to add to the pile? He remembered hearing someone say that if you could lucid dream, you could make yourself do things, like breathe underwater, or fly. He mused over it a moment, then took two running steps before leaping into the air . . . and falling to the ground with a thump. *Twigs and leaves dug into his cheek as he fell on his face.*

"What are you doing?"

He jerked up to stare into the empty forest. Then he stood and looked down the path. Nothing. When he turned back, she stood there. Her eyes hooded by shadow. Her arms folded. Her tails fanned behind her.

At the sight of her, the woods came alive again. The whistling of wind blew at her long hair. Leaves crunched as he took a step back. And the call of a far-off bird echoed dimly as he stared at her.

"What's happening? Why are you here?" Jihoon tried not to stutter.

"This is a dream, but how you got here I'm not sure. It's worrisome."

"What's that supposed to mean?" he asked, but she didn't answer.

Her head cocked to the side, her eyes lifting to the moon as if listening to a faraway call.

Then, without warning, she yanked him behind a clump of thick bushes.

His yelp of surprise was muffled by her hand.

"She'll hear," the girl whispered. There was steel in her voice.

Her words were enough to keep him silent. Hadn't he just learned to believe in monsters?

Every movement of the woods became a threat. The howl of wind through branches. The snap of twigs as creatures skittered. A rustle to his right. A flash of pale movement.

"Was that—?"

The girl shushed him and held up a thin arm, pointing to their left.

A lithe shape lurked among the trees, almost invisible. Its graceful movements made no sound, like the mist of fog sifting through the forest. It had a sharp snout and pointed ears, thick red fur, and bright eyes. And behind the fox wove nine tails.

The gumiho paused, her head perked up, eyes tracking toward their hiding place. Jihoon held his breath. The fox stepped forward when a crack echoed from farther in the woods. She took off toward the sound in a flash.

Jihoon finally exhaled and glanced at the girl. She let a handful of stones drop in a rain of thuds.

"Who was that?" Jihoon asked.

"My mother. She doesn't like humans."

"And you do?" Jihoon rose, and the movement made his head spin.

"I don't hate them," she conceded. "Though it's worrisome that you're here."

"You said that before. What does it mean?" The forest tilted to the left, then to the right, like the sway of a ship on the sea. He felt like he was being pulled somewhere he didn't want to go and tried his best to hold on to this place, this dream.

"Why did you pick up my bead?" she asked.

"Your bead? You mean that pearl?"

"Why were you in the forest tonight?"

My dog, he tried to say, but bile rose in his throat instead of words.

"Did you know I'd be in the forest? What did you want with my bead?" The girl's voice sounded garbled, like it was processed through a synthesizer before reaching his ears.

"What's happening to me?" Nausea rolled through him, thick and sticky, as the surrounding trees did tight pirouettes.

She watched him curiously. "When the body wants to wake, it doesn't matter what the mind desires."

"I'm waking up?" Jihoon asked. "Then why do I feel so funny . . ."

Before she could reply, the forest floor fell from under Jihoon's feet.

He dropped into darkness, his screams absorbed by the earth as it swallowed him.

4

MIYOUNG WOKE SLOWLY from the dream. It took her a moment to realize she wasn't in the forest but in her new bedroom. In a wrought-iron bed piled high with pillows. Large windows beside her bed let in the moonlight. She glanced at the clock and the bright numbers glared back at her: 3:33 A.M.

The memory of the dream clung to her like a film of grease covering her skin. Forest and mist and that boy. She rarely dreamed, and when she did it was never quite so vivid. It felt as if he'd walked into her mind. *It's worrisome.* She'd said it in the dream and she thought it now.

She'd heard tales of gumiho who could walk the dreams of their victims. Driving them slowly mad before ripping out their livers. But she'd never done it herself, never thought it was a skill gumiho still possessed. Perhaps they didn't. After all, she hadn't meant to share a dream with that boy. Maybe she was just thinking about that boy and her subconscious had gotten out of hand. It made sense that she'd be stuck on thoughts of him; after all, he'd been there when she'd lost her bead . . .

Miyoung turned onto her side and pulled open her nightstand drawer until the bead rolled gently into view. It shone so bright, she wondered if it emitted its own light or merely reflected the moon's.

She stared at the stone—a *yeowu guseul*—a fox bead. Myth said every gumiho had one, but she'd never given them much thought. Nara sometimes went on about them, comparing them to the human soul.

Maybe Miyoung should have listened more to the shaman's harebrained theories. They were varied and long-winded, so Miyoung had ignored most of them. She remembered the shaman warning that if a human ever gained control of the yeowu guseul of a gumiho, he could command her to do his every bidding. And there was the story of a gumiho who lost her bead but still fed, slowly becoming more and more of a demon.

Closing her eyes, Miyoung rolled the stone across her palm. It sparked along her skin like static electricity. Or residual energy. It didn't feel like the gi she'd absorbed from that ajeossi. That had been bitter and stale. This tasted fresh and bright. The boy? But she hadn't fed from him. Why would his energy be in the bead?

But she could guess the answer. He'd touched it, held it directly. And it had absorbed his energy. She'd felt a boost of energy that had woken her, disoriented on the forest floor. Had the bead transferred a bit of his gi to her even when it wasn't inside of her?

If he had known what power he held . . . but he obviously hadn't. And she had it now; it was safe. Or as safe as it could be like this.

She didn't know why she'd been driven to save that boy. But his actions afterward confused her more. How he'd stayed. How he'd charged the dokkaebi after knowing full well the danger.

Miyoung squeezed the bead in her hand. The boy was not what she should worry about right now.

She needed to figure out a way to reabsorb the stone. She might not know much about the myths that surrounded a yeowu guseul, but she knew its proper place was *in* a gumiho. Already she felt an emptiness in her, like a puzzle piece ripped from her middle, leaving a gaping hole.

Climbing out of bed, Miyoung padded her way down the hall toward her mother's room.

The shower ran in the master bathroom. Steam sat heavy in the air, so thick it almost choked her. It lit a panic that she calmed with deep breaths. Ever since Miyoung could remember, she'd been afraid of water. A phobia so deep she refused to even take a bath. Her mother despised any sign of weakness in her daughter, so Miyoung did her best to keep it buried.

The water was turned off and Yena stepped out of the shower. Through the curtain of steam Miyoung saw the crisscross of white scars on her mother's bare back.

Miyoung once asked about them, and Yena said it had been humans. Done when she was too young and too weak to heal fully. Miyoung sometimes wondered if they'd scarred more than her skin.

As the mist dissipated, Yena wrapped herself in a robe. And she was back to being perfectly stunning. She was tall and willowy, with jet-black hair and dark eyes to match.

Everyone who met them said Miyoung looked exactly like her mother.

Miyoung always said thank you with a ninety-degree bow. After all, Yena was the epitome of beauty. Her perfection made men regret the time they spent on blinking.

"Miyoung-ah, what are you doing?"

"I needed to talk to you." Miyoung tried to think of how to explain her unsettling dream in a way that wouldn't reveal her mistake.

"Is it about Monday?"

Miyoung blinked. "Monday?"

Then she remembered. Her new school.

"I'm okay. It'll be like every other school. I'm used to it." It was true. Miyoung was the perpetual transfer student. Never somewhere long enough to lose the label.

"It's a good school, though this neighborhood is not as nice as our old one. But of course we couldn't stay there after your . . . indiscretion." The way her mother said it, with a tinge of blame, made Miyoung purse her lips. As much as she hated to move, they were often forced to relocate because of one of Miyoung's mistakes. And Yena's irate mood each time reminded Miyoung that her problems were a burden on her mother. Perhaps it was not smart to reveal her latest mistake so soon after her last.

"I'm sorry, Mother. I didn't mean to do it and the girl survived." *Excuses, excuses, just useless excuses.*

"But you still almost exposed us by losing control with a human. And in broad daylight."

"I was just trying to get her away from me! She wouldn't stop pushing me, so I pushed back—" Miyoung cut off with the sinking realization that her words echoed the ajeossi in the forest. *It was her fault . . . She should have kept quiet. I only tried to make her stop screaming.*

Miyoung hated how much she had in common with the evil she hunted.

"I don't need your excuses," Yena said, breaking into Miyoung's thoughts. "Just do what I say and everything will be fine."

"Actually, there's something I need to tell you."

"I know what you're so worked up about and it's fine." Yena waved away Miyoung's concern. Not the reaction she was expecting.

"It's fine?" Miyoung couldn't stop the gallop of her heart. Was it not that bad, revealing her identity to a human and losing her bead in the process?

"I didn't mean to—" Miyoung began.

"Don't lie to me, daughter. I know you siphoned your last victim again. You still can't go for the quick kill."

Miyoung almost let out a sigh of relief. So Yena didn't know about the boy or her bead.

"I don't mind doing it the slow way." Miyoung could have given a dozen excuses. Her way there was less mess, less screaming, less blood. But she knew those weren't the real reasons and so did Yena.

"Your desire for human approval is why you're weak." There it was, her mother's disapproval of the half of Miyoung that was human. The half that came from her father.

"It's hard to live among them and not care," Miyoung muttered.

"Living among humans is a necessary evil. If we want to feed every month, then we must be where the food is."

Miyoung winced at her mother's choice of words, but she nodded. "And if one of them knew what we were?"

"Then we'd take care of them, of course. Their mortal lives are so easily ended." Yena said it so flippantly that Miyoung's heart stuttered. Could she have killed that boy? Snapped his neck and left his remains to rot? The thought made her shiver. But maybe that was her problem. She wasn't ruthless enough.

"What is it?" Yena asked, her eyes shrewd.

"I'm just feeling off," Miyoung said. "This place is so unfamiliar and having to hunt so soon after moving."

"It couldn't be avoided," Yena said sharply. "You refuse to hunt without the moon."

"I know." Miyoung wondered how to broach the subject she really wanted to ask about. "Actually, I noticed a few books while I was unpacking. One of them was about fox beads."

Yena gave a short laugh. "Those fairy tales? Things humans made up to tell their children. There's no such thing as a fox bead."

Miyoung frowned, her hand clenching in the pocket of her robe where that mythical object rested. Could it be that in her mother's hundreds of years she'd never actually seen or felt her own bead?

"Miyoung-ah, I'm tired. It's been a long night. No more talk of fantasies and what-ifs."

"Yes, Mother." Miyoung felt defeated.

"I worry sometimes that I let you have too much freedom with your dramas and shows." Miyoung's heart sank, fearing a new rule or restriction about to be declared. "Don't let those fantasies warp your brain. You have to stay alert always. We must protect each other. It's only the two of us against the rest of the world."

Miyoung nodded. The words were something Yena often said, as easy as any other parent would offer a comforting hug. But Yena didn't hug. In fact, she rarely touched Miyoung at all.

"Mother?"

"Yes?"

Miyoung tried to screw up the courage to tell her mother about her bead and the strange boy in the forest. But she couldn't push out the words.

"Good night."

"Good night, Miyoung."

5

JIHOON OVERSLEPT, WHICH wouldn't usually bother him, except it was Saturday and he was supposed to help in the restaurant.

He shuffled down the hall to look in on Dubu. She lay curled in her small bed. With a low whimper, she tried to limp over.

"Oh, you brave girl," Jihoon crooned, giving her a gentle hug. He still wasn't sure if he was mad at Dubu or relieved she was okay. Probably an even mix.

He'd been up half the night with thoughts of goblins and gumiho. Halmeoni used to tell Jihoon stories about dokkaebi tricking humans and nine-tailed foxes eating the livers of men. Horror stories camouflaged as fables to teach lessons. But those types of stories were supposed to stay in books, not come to life and almost choke him to death.

He'd tried to convince himself last night had been a vivid hallucination. But he couldn't ignore the bruise on his temple, a reminder of the girl's head coming into contact with his. And the strange stone that had come out of her. His fingers still tingled from it, like it had sucked out his very energy.

When Jihoon shuffled down the rear staircase, the sound of the bustling restaurant greeted him.

Voices drifted up from the back room, but he ignored them until the words *animal attack* stopped him in his tracks.

"Thank you for coming to let us know, Officer Hae," Halmeoni said.

"Detective."

"Sorry, Detective Hae."

"We're letting the neighboring apartments and businesses know so they can be on the lookout. It seemed like a wolf or a wild dog came down from the mountain, so be careful."

Jihoon froze, absorbing the words. Animal attack? Like a fox?

"We'll let our customers know," Halmeoni said as the door opened. "Come by anytime if you're in the mood for a good home-cooked meal."

The door shut, and Jihoon heard his halmeoni make her way to the front kitchen.

Jihoon wondered if the animal attack could be connected to that girl.

He shouldn't worry about her. She'd told him not to speak of last night, so it would be easiest to forget it completely.

As he entered the back room, Somin swung through the kitchen door, balancing a tray of dirty plates. Her graphic tee and ripped jeans were covered by the knee-length apron for Halmeoni's restaurant.

"What are you doing here?" Jihoon blinked owlishly at her.

"Your halmeoni said you were sleeping like the dead. She didn't want to wake you, so she called me and my mom. It's a madhouse out there."

There was no accusation in Somin's voice, but his shoulders hunched with guilt.

He'd been helping out in the restaurant kitchen since he was little. He used to sit for hours, cutting the tails off soybean sprouts and pinching closed the shells of dumplings. Now he was glorified waitstaff and delivery boy.

"I was going to call you," Jihoon said, tapping a serving spoon against the counter as he considered his next words.

Somin was always available when he needed a sounding board. And after last night, he definitely did. Since they'd grown up together, Somin had heard all of his halmeoni's fables, too.

But the girl's threat still rang clear in his head: *You will tell no one about what you saw tonight.*

So instead, he asked, "Did you ever believe in dokkaebi?"

Somin thought a moment. She was one to take questions seriously when asked by a friend. "Sure, when I was younger. I heard there's an app now that talks to kids in a dokkaebi voice to scare them into eating their vegetables."

"Not the dokkaebi our parents used to scare us. Real ones."

Somin laughed—the sound grating on Jihoon's frayed nerves— but sobered at his serious expression. "Jihoon-ah, you know dokkaebi aren't real."

"Of course I do," Jihoon said firmly, trying to convince himself more than her.

"You know you can tell me if you're having problems." Somin tilted her head. "Or delusions."

"Ya!" Jihoon protested, throwing the spoon at her.

Somin snatched it out of the air. She'd always been the more athletic of the two.

Jihoon flopped over in defeat, letting his head fall onto the counter. What was the point in trying to figure this all out? He'd never see that girl again. "I need caffeine."

"Well, you're in luck." Somin pulled a packet of instant coffee out of her apron pocket. Jihoon perked up at the sound of the ripping foil.

"You can't find a way to inject it directly into my veins?" Jihoon asked as Somin used the emptied packet as a makeshift stirrer. He took the mug gratefully. The coffee burned his tongue, but he didn't care. "You're a goddess," he said on a sigh of satisfaction. "One day they'll build temples to you. Shrines with your likeness."

Somin chuckled. "Come out front when you're feeling full human."

When Jihoon walked into the front kitchen, Moon Soohyun, Somin's mother, was bickering with Halmeoni over seasoning.

"Mrs. Nam," she said, "if you add too much fish sauce, then it'll overpower the flavor." She gestured wildly with her wooden ladle, and Somin snatched it from her mother's hand before it knocked over a pile of pots.

"I've smacked your bottom with that ladle and I can do it again," Halmeoni said.

"Mrs. Nam, everyone has loved your cooking for years. But even you have to admit you're getting old. When you get old, your taste buds and your vision are the first to go."

Halmeoni tsked. "I don't know why I let you hang around."

Somin's mother grinned. "Because you love me so much."

"I just grew used to you," Halmeoni muttered. "You've been running around this place since you were in diapers with my Yoori."

Jihoon's heart fell into his stomach. He didn't like to be reminded about how his mother and Somin's grew up together. They'd played together, gone to school together, gotten pregnant together. But Somin's mother had stayed and his had left.

"I like your cooking." Somin hugged Halmeoni. "Maybe I'll marry Jihoon-ah, and then I'll get to eat it every day."

Jihoon finally spoke. "Who says I would even marry you, Lee Somin? You know I hate it when other people tell me what to do."

"Jihoon-ah!" all three of them said with varying degrees of affection and scolding.

"Oh, look at our Hoonie." Somin's mom pinched his cheek with a devilish glint in her eyes. He only allowed it because it was her and she knew it. "You're lucky, Mrs. Nam. Saves you money on stepladders with a grandson who can reach the tall shelves."

He held back a laugh.

"Stop teasing him," Halmeoni said.

Somin's mom let Jihoon go, but he wasn't free for long. Halmeoni turned Jihoon's face to examine him. Her eyes zeroed in on the bruise on his temple. "What happened here?"

"Nothing," Jihoon said too quickly. He could only imagine where his halmeoni's superstitions would take her if she knew about last night.

Halmeoni stared at him so hard he practically heard her thoughts. She was deciding if she would push the subject or not. She let it go along with his chin. "I had a dream about a pig last night," she said.

Jihoon looked over to Somin for clarification. She shrugged.

"It brings good fortune. So you two should study hard." Halmeoni swept her ladle between Somin and Jihoon.

"Yes, Halmeoni." They gave twin bows.

"Eat yeot. It'll make the knowledge stick."

"Yes, Halmeoni."

"Here, take this out to table three." Halmeoni handed him a tray of stews, still boiling in their stone pots.

"Then get back in here. I'm going to finish fixing the seasoning in this next dish for table six," Somin's mother said before resuming her bickering with Halmeoni.

Somin gave Jihoon a smile and an eye roll as she also picked up a tray.

Jihoon followed, for once grateful for the chaos that was his life. By the end of the lunch rush, he'd almost completely forgotten about fox-girls and goblins.

WHEN THE FIRST gumiho neared the age of a thousand, the Silla Kingdom joined forces with the Chinese Tang dynasty and overthrew much of what used to be Prince Jumong's Goguryeo. It brought with it the rise of Buddhism.

Nine (gu, 九) was the symbol of the dragon and, therefore, the symbol of the king. It was the symbol of longevity, the symbol of immortality.

Nine nations were to submit to the Silla dynasty. They built the grand imperial dragon pagoda with nine tiers. The largest of its kind in all of East Asia, it symbolized the power of Buddha and Silla.

The fox grew eight extra tails.

Nine tails for power.

Nine tails for immortality.

6

MONDAY MORNING, MISS Kwon quieted the class to start homeroom. As the kids settled, she didn't launch into morning announcements as usual. Instead, she cleared her throat and glanced at something written in her notebook. "We have a new transfer student today: Gu Miyoung."

She gestured to the open door.

The girl moved quietly into the room. That was what Jihoon noticed first.

He half rose from his seat at the shock of seeing her. The dozens of times he'd thought of her over the weekend, he never imagined she'd do anything as boring as attend school. Let alone *his* school.

In the sunlight her face was striking. All angles and planes, a straight nose, and dark eyes framed with long lashes and curving brows. The boys in the room sat up straighter, like they were all puppets with their strings suddenly pulled taut.

"Introduce yourself." Miss Kwon invited Miyoung to step forward.

"My name is Gu Miyoung." She bowed. "My mother and I recently moved to Seoul. Please take good care of me." It was the generic introduction of any new transfer student, but the way she said it held an edge of warning: *Stay away from me.* Her eyes were hard as they swept over the room. Jihoon waited for them to find him. But she didn't even pause when she saw him.

"I think I'm in love," Changwan whispered.

"Stop drooling." Jihoon didn't spare his friend a glance. He was too busy staring at Miyoung, who refused to meet his gaze.

"You may sit by Lee Somin," Miss Kwon said.

Miyoung took her seat, keeping her head down and thwarting Jihoon's attempts to catch her eye.

Miss Kwon finished the morning announcements as the bell rang. As soon as she left, the room erupted into chatter. While the teachers moved from classroom to classroom for each period, the students gained a few minutes of freedom to gossip and eat forbidden snacks previously hidden away.

Jihoon usually used the break for the latter, but this time he pushed back from his desk, stepping toward Miyoung.

He was beat to the punch by Baek Hana.

"Transfer student," Hana said. She was pretty in a traditional way: classic oval face, pert nose, and rosebud lips. Her straight bangs perfectly styled, her pleated skirt perfectly pressed. She reminded Jihoon of a porcelain doll, if dolls had judgmental eyes and sharp tongues. "Where'd you transfer from?"

It took Miyoung so long to answer, it seemed she intended to ignore the question. Finally, she said, "Jeollanam-do."

"The whole province of South Jeolla?"

"Gwangju." Another clipped answer.

"I have cousins in Gwangju." Hana smiled, but it held no kindness. "You're very pretty. Who was your plastic surgeon?"

Jihoon rolled his eyes at the barb. Everyone knew that Hana had begged her parents for double-eyelid surgery; just because they denied her didn't mean she was above plastic surgery. He saw

Miyoung's hands clamp, two tight fists folded together. He wondered if she did that to save Hana from a well-deserved punch in the mouth.

"Do you need something, Hana-ya?" Somin asked, and half the class stopped their conversations. Some settled in for the show.

Hana squirmed under Somin's stare. Jihoon didn't usually find pleasure in other people's discomfort, but he felt a grim sense of satisfaction as Hana's eyes darted back and forth between Somin and Miyoung. She seemed torn between playing with her new target and preserving her own skin.

Hana lifted her chin and Jihoon couldn't help but think she'd made the wrong choice. "I'm saying hello to the new transfer."

"Well, you said it. You should sit before the teacher gets here."

"Sure, whatever." Hana shrugged, a jerky movement filled with nerves. Everyone knew better than to cross Somin.

"I didn't ask for your help," Miyoung said, and heads across the room turned to stare in surprise.

"Excuse me?" Somin asked, and Jihoon got the impression of two powerful forces pushing against each other.

"From now on, keep out of my business." Miyoung's words were low but easily heard in the silent room.

Jihoon watched Somin's jaw flex, like she held back a biting retort. But he knew her. She rarely succeeded in curbing her temper.

It was as if the whole class held their breath, waiting for the thick tension in the air to break.

Instead, the door opened and the math teacher, Mr. Hong, entered.

Jihoon watched Miyoung throughout the class.

She sat a row up and across the aisle from him. Her hand took quick notes as the teacher lectured. He stared at it, remembering how she snapped off the dokkaebi's thumb. He shivered involuntarily.

Jihoon scribbled a quick note and leaned into the aisle, casting a furtive glance at Mr. Hong. The teacher was watching two kids try to solve problems at the board, tapping a split bamboo branch on his palm. He liked to crack it against desks when kids fell asleep, and Jihoon knew that before corporal punishment was outlawed in schools, Mr. Hong would have used it directly on the kids.

"Ya," Jihoon whispered.

Miyoung's hand stopped writing, but she didn't look over. Jihoon tossed the paper. It hit the edge of Miyoung's desk and fell to the floor.

Miyoung continued taking notes as if nothing had happened.

"Ya," Jihoon said again, his voice the urgent gravel of a whisper-shout.

A foot dropped on top of the note, and Jihoon grimaced as the teacher picked it up.

"Gu Miyoung, it seems Ahn Jihoon would like you to meet him after class," Mr. Hong said. It earned muffled laughter from the other kids. "The two of you, follow me outside."

In the hallway, they sat on their knees, their hands raised in the air. A punishment they'd have to continue until the class period was over. Already, Jihoon's arms ached.

"You should have caught it," he said.

Miyoung ignored him, staring straight ahead.

"You *could* have caught it. I've seen your reflexes."

She still didn't answer.

In the sunlight filtering through the windows, she was striking. Almost delicate looking. But Jihoon remembered how fierce she'd been in the forest, effortlessly squaring off against the monstrous dokkaebi.

He tried again. "About the other night in the woods—"

"I don't know what you're talking about," Miyoung interrupted him.

"But—"

"I just moved here. I don't know the area. Why would I be in the woods?" Miyoung's face was set, her eyes clear. She seemed so sure of herself, he almost believed her over his own memory.

He started to speak again.

Mr. Hong tapped on the glass and mouthed, *No talking.*

Jihoon lowered his head and tried to ignore the ache in his shoulders.

The bell rang, a shrill noise that broke the silence and marked the time for gym. It hurt to lower his arms after holding them up for so long. When Jihoon stood, his legs trembled, the pricks of a thousand needles creating a shiver of pain.

As he struggled to his feet, a group of girls descended upon Miyoung, who didn't seem to have any issues shaking off the physical effects of the punishment.

"Your face is so small. You could be a model," one of them cooed. "I'm jealous."

"Your skin is so clear. What foundation do you use?" asked another.

"I don't wear any," Miyoung said, her voice cold and dismissive.

The other girls didn't seem to get the hint as they continued to pepper her with questions.

"Ahn Jihoon." One of the girls zeroed in on him. "Hitting on the transfer on her first day? It's so unlike you."

Jihoon shrugged by way of answer.

"Does Lee Somin know you're crushing on the transfer?" Jihoon glanced over to see Miyoung's reaction, but realized she'd taken this opportunity to disappear.

"Lee Somin knows you're talking about her behind her back." Somin stepped out of the classroom, her arms crossed. The girls jerked upright, like army privates faced with their colonel.

"You should change for gym class," she said. The girls nodded and scurried away.

"Somin-ah, if you keep doing that, no one will ever talk to us again." Jihoon threw an arm around her shoulder in a light choke hold. The movement was more to support his still-weak legs than anything else, but no one had to know.

"Is that a bad thing?" Somin jabbed him in the side so he loosened his grip. "What did you want with the transfer?"

"Just trying to be friendly," Jihoon said. He didn't want to discuss the confusing mystery that was Gu Miyoung right now.

"I don't like her. She's rude."

"You don't like her because she's not afraid of you," Changwan said, joining them.

"No one cares about your opinion," Somin said, and the two began to bicker.

"Come on." Jihoon threw his other arm around Changwan's shoulders, turning the three of them into a unit. "You can work off that extra energy in gym."

7

MIYOUNG WAS EXHAUSTED from fending off the curiosity of her new classmates. She'd grown accustomed to the few get-to-know-you inquiries she always encountered as the new kid in class. But this time was different, more intense. And she laid that blame directly at the feet of one Ahn Jihoon. His stunt with the note had garnered her a lot of unwanted attention, and she was starting to regret saving his useless life.

The large indoor gymnasium echoed with the chatter of her classmates, mingling in small subgroups of friends. Miyoung stood in the back alone. Her normal position.

The gym teacher was an unassuming man with the face of a toad and a name Miyoung didn't bother to remember.

He informed the class that today's lesson would be partner dodgeball. The students' moans bounced off the high rafters.

The teacher handed out five red balls and explained the game. Students made teams of two, with one as the guard, the other as the guarded. Only the guard could touch the ball. If the guarded was hit, they were out. If the two separated, they were out. It seemed unnecessarily complicated to Miyoung.

The kids quickly began pairing up. Anytime someone approached her, Miyoung sent them a glare that stopped them until all the kids were paired except for her and Jihoon, who walked toward her with a rueful smile. Miyoung's frown deepened.

"I guess we're partners," he said, seemingly unperturbed by her glower.

"I can't play." Her annoyance was so thick it choked her. "My foot hurts."

"Did you hurt it when you fell?" he asked in a whisper.

His question confused Miyoung. "I didn't fall."

"Not today, the other night."

Her eyes narrowed as she tried to decide what level of idiotic he was.

"Begin." The gym teacher blew a whistle. The kids spread out, some already squealing in distress before any balls were thrown. The loudest of whom was Changwan clinging to Somin's shoulders.

Jihoon took the front position. Miyoung held on to the hem of his shirt with two fingers. They wove and dodged, Miyoung easily following Jihoon's jerking movements. He stumbled as he dove to the right, avoiding the ball instead of blocking it.

Miyoung jerked back as another ball almost hit her in the face. And she found herself annoyed at the prospect of being one of the first pairs out.

She could practically hear Yena's voice. *No daughter of mine would lose at a human sports game. Especially one as insipid as dodgeball.*

"You have to keep your eyes open. Pay attention to who has a ball," she growled through gritted teeth.

"They're moving too fast."

"Left!" she snapped. He scooted over, barely batting away the ball.

Miyoung felt the beginnings of a headache, and each time she dodged a ball Jihoon failed to block, her stomach rolled. At first, she thought it was anger, until the nausea climbed into her throat.

"Are you okay?" Jihoon asked, glancing back at her.

"Of course." She took deep breaths to slow her rapid pulse. She normally never got sick. Her bead bumped against her leg, like it sought to remind her that all was not normal.

"You don't seem like you're okay."

"Watch it!" She pulled him to the side and narrowly avoided a ball. "Will you pay attention to the game?"

"Is this because of what you did the other night? How you fought that—"

"Would you shut up?" Miyoung's annoyance made her head-ache swell toward a crescendo.

"It's just that you didn't seem well after that either."

"Well, I'm fine now. You don't have to think of me."

"I wish," Jihoon said with a laugh.

"What's that supposed to mean?" Miyoung asked before she could stop herself.

"I don't consider myself a really curious guy, but I can't stop thinking of you." At Miyoung's glare he quickly continued. "Not like that. I just mean, the stories my halmeoni told me were true. It's a bit surreal. I can't seem to stop thinking about it, and then I had this weird dream."

"What dream?" She snapped back to attention, glaring at him so intently he leaned away.

Before Jihoon could answer, the teacher blew his whistle and told them to trade places. Miyoung was now the guard and Jihoon held on to her shoulders. Instead of running around trying to avoid the balls, Miyoung batted them away effortlessly, her eyes never leaving Jihoon.

"What dream?" she asked again.

"We were in the forest together, hiding from . . . your mother?" He ended it like a question, as if asking for approval.

The coincidence in details couldn't be ignored. This confirmed one of her fears. He'd touched the bead, and it had temporarily connected them. This was a problem. What else had he seen in her head?

She closed her eyes against the full-blown migraine pounding at her temples. The pressure was so great she thought her eyes would pop out of her skull.

"I don't mean to pry," Jihoon said, even as his eyes searched her face. He took a step closer, and she held out a hand to stop him. Except her headache threw off her depth perception, and she caught him in the sternum, throwing him back so hard he slid a meter across the floor on his butt.

"No fighting!" The gym teacher blew a whistle and the game play stopped. "Jihoon, you hurt?"

Jihoon shook his head as he stood.

"You're new, right?" the gym teacher asked, approaching Miyoung.

"Yes," she mumbled, seething at the attention as dozens of eyes stared at her.

"Already causing trouble, Transfer," the gym teacher said. "I'm going to have to call your mother."

o   o   o

Waiting for Yena was hell. This was a record for Miyoung, getting sent to the vice principal on her first day of school. She was standing outside of the teachers' office waiting for her mother. If that impending arrival wasn't enough, she was in the perfect location for kids to ogle as they walked past.

They sent furtive glances at her as they made their way back to the classrooms. Miyoung kept still. She knew the best reaction was no reaction.

Parts of conversations drifted over. She heard the words *violent* and *freak*. This was not a good start to a new school. And she was good at gauging that. She'd been in a dozen schools, and each had proven to be the same. Kids, no matter where they lived, just wanted to fit in. And that meant ridiculing anything and anyone that didn't. Fitting in was practically against Miyoung's genetic makeup. No matter how much she'd tried to match a mold, she always popped back out. A fox peg trying to fit into a human-shaped hole.

So she'd stopped trying, choosing instead to keep a low profile. If she managed to stay under the social radar and proved to be uninteresting, the other kids would leave her alone.

But she'd already gained attention. And worse, negative attention. Kids loved gossiping about troublemakers. First strike was what she'd said to Lee Somin this morning. She hadn't meant to, but she'd been so thrown off from seeing Jihoon. And then getting a punishment in front of the whole class, strike two. And strike three, getting into a "fight" in gym class.

There was one common thread through it all: Ahn Jihoon.

She saw him walking up the hall with his friends. The awkward boy named Changmin or Changwoo gave her a quick bow when he spotted her. A mental debate raced across Jihoon's face before he started toward her.

Miyoung narrowed her eyes and gave a small shake of her head that clearly said *Move on.* So Jihoon lowered his eyes and hurried past. Lee Somin followed in his wake, sending a scowl in Miyoung's direction.

The click of shoes approaching could have been anyone, but Miyoung knew it was Yena before she glanced up.

As kids filed toward their classrooms, necks craned. Even teachers stopped to stare. Her mother didn't seem to notice her dozens of admirers. Her cold eyes saw only Miyoung, who was suddenly rubbing sweaty palms on her uniform blazer. Yena was pissed. Miyoung straightened her shoulders and clutched her hands together to hide her trepidation.

Yena swept past Miyoung without a word and into the teachers' office, where the vice principal waited. Miyoung followed behind, head lowered.

The vice principal was a large man who somehow reminded Miyoung of a rhinoceros.

"H-h-hello," the vice principal stuttered, rising from his desk as if he were the one called into Yena's office. His hands gripped at his jacket, straightening it as he gathered his composure. "You must be Miyoung's eomeoni."

A smile curled across Yena's lips, congenial with just a hint of seduction. Miyoung hated this smile even as she spent her nights trying to emulate it in her bathroom mirror. Whenever Yena used it, men did her every bidding, as if a spell had been placed upon them.

"I'm honored to meet such an important man as yourself, Vice

Principal," Yena said, her voice smooth as velvet. Miyoung wondered if this was what sirens were supposed to sound like. "I'm sure you're too busy to be dealing with such trivial things as this." She flicked a hand at Miyoung.

The vice principal let out a giggle that was more suited to a young schoolgirl. It grated against Miyoung's nerves.

"Oh no, it is my pleasure to meet with a parent of a new student. I've always said it's important to make the effort, as our students are all so precious to me." Miyoung had once seen a cartoon where hippopotami danced a ballet, an awkward attempt at looking graceful. The vice principal's posturing reminded her of that strange dichotomy now.

"I'm horrified that my daughter would make a scene on her first day. I must take complete responsibility. After all, when a child is lacking, it's a reflection on their parent." Yena let her lip quiver and blinked her eyes as if holding back tears, but when she opened them again they were clear.

Miyoung almost frowned at her mother's award-winning acting.

"Oh no, Miyoung's eomma, you mustn't think that way. I'm sure that moving so far into the school year must have been a stress on our Miyoung."

Miyoung's eomma? Our *Miyoung*? She scoffed at the familiar addresses and nearly applauded. Her mother's skills were working quickly on the vice principal. He would probably give Miyoung an automatic pass for her whole second year if Yena asked right now.

"Well, I wouldn't blame you if you put my precious daughter on probation for committing school violence. I trust in your good judgment. After all, only an honest and fair man could reach such a venerated position." Yena gripped the vice principal's hand.

A flush spread up the man's neck. "Well, it's only one small mistake, and I hear the kids were playing dodgeball, a very violent game by its nature. Our Miyoung seems like a good girl; I'll let her go with a warning to be more careful. Okay, Miyoung-ah?"

Miyoung blinked, realizing she was being addressed directly. "Of course, Vice Principal," she said, working hard to make her voice sound as sweet as Yena's. Instead it sounded too breathy.

"My dear Vice Principal. You're too kind," Yena said, squeezing his hand. And Miyoung thought he'd faint on the spot.

They walked out of the office together, silence hanging around them so thick, Miyoung thought she'd choke.

Once outside, Yena didn't even glance at Miyoung as she spoke. "You disappoint me."

"I'm sorry, Mother—" Miyoung began, but Yena's hand came up, silencing her. She knew her mother would never hit her, but still she flinched back. But Yena just waved her hand to hail a cab.

"I'll see you back home," Yena said. And Miyoung didn't even think to ask for a ride and risk angering her mother further. She watched as Yena climbed into the car and it sped away.

It was better this way. Miyoung had an errand to run.

o o o

Miyoung stared out the bus window. The air felt close with a coming storm.

Her stomach churned as the bus bumped over a pothole. Ever since the fight with that dokkaebi, she'd felt unsettled. She didn't even know why she'd stuck her nose into it. Maybe because she was so horrified to see the goblin attacking a human boy. Even after she'd taken lives herself, she didn't like the sight of something from the supernatural world taking the life of an innocent. Though Jihoon did his best to make Miyoung feel like he wasn't quite so innocent by annoying her all day. But she knew it wasn't just the fight with the dokkaebi that caused her to feel unsettled. She shoved her hand into her pocket. At her touch, the bead warmed against her skin, adjusting perfectly to her body temperature.

She needed to put it back where it belonged. And for that she needed help.

An hour later, she exited the bus. The streets were crowded and a salaryman bumped her shoulder as he hurried past. Usually Miyoung would ignore it, but at his touch nausea rose up in her. She could sense his energy as if she had the power of the full moon guiding her instead of the sun blazing overhead. She frowned as her mouth watered. What was this? She shouldn't be hungry so soon. She'd just fed.

Shoving her hand into her pocket, she rubbed her bead and knew it must all be connected. Quickly, she turned onto a street that was more alley than road, taking her away from the crowded street. Sandwich-board signs directed patrons to the second and third floors, offering anything from cell phone covers to makgeolli to massages. Miyoung ignored the racks of clothes set far into the road to entice customers to enter shops no bigger than an alcove.

Instead, she entered a small store. Above it, the sign read SHAMAN, 占.

A cloud of incense hit her, heavy and cloying.

The wares leaned in towering piles. Woven baskets created pillars in front of the windows, blocking the sunlight. Tables were laden with incense, fans, and paintings. Copper dishes in their protective plastic were stacked high. Along the wall hung paintings on thick beige paper, creating a tapestry of hand-drawn portraits. Bold reds, dark blacks, bright whites, and deep blues depicted the stern expressions of a dozen noblemen and -women. Miyoung avoided their dark eyes.

"Eo-seo-o-se-yo!" sang out a voice from the back.

A girl emerged. She was short and cute, her hair pulled from her face in a messy bun. Her linen hanbok was wrinkled from work, but it hung prettily on her slight frame. She stopped short at the sight of Miyoung. "Seonbae."

"Nara-ssi," Miyoung replied. "I see you're doing brisk business." She gestured around the empty shop.

Nara pursed her lips but didn't disagree.

"I guess now that you're back in Seoul, you can stop by more often," Nara said. "Reminds me of the old days."

"Yes, well, my mother and I wore out our welcome down south. It was time for a change."

"After you left Seoul the last time, I wasn't sure if you'd ever move back."

"It was bound to happen eventually. Seoul's enormous, the best place to get lost among millions."

An awkwardness hung between the girls because, even after five years, Nara couldn't help but try to reach across the divide that Miyoung continually insisted on creating.

"Is your halmeoni out?" Miyoung asked.

Nara's nervous eyes moved toward the ceiling, and Miyoung figured the old woman must be upstairs in the apartment over the shop. She knew Nara kept their relationship a secret from her halmeoni.

There were stories of the old shaman that had reached even Miyoung's ears. Nara's halmeoni was originally from Jeju, where the practice of shamanism was more common. There were rumors that she'd done away with more dark spirits and creatures than any other shaman in the city. She was definitely no fan of Miyoung's kind. Beings that preyed on humans. Evil things.

"I shouldn't stay long," Miyoung said. "So I'll make it quick. I have a problem I need help with. Shaman help."

"Come with me." Nara led the way into a back room, which was even more cluttered than the front. Books were stacked high, and thick oak tables held the tools of a shaman: scrolls of paper, bronze bowls, and incense.

Nara moved easily through the crowded space. She helped run her halmeoni's shaman shop and knew where everything was located in the nonsensical clutter. She was a shaman who'd received the calling through blood instead of spiritual possession. Shamanism was business and tradition in her family.

As they walked past a large bookcase, Nara let her fingers trail over a framed photo, the only thing clean of dust on the crowded shelf. A man and woman smiled at the camera, a small infant cradled between them: Nara's parents.

They'd died when Nara was a baby. Now shamanism and her halmeoni were all she had.

"What can I do for you, Seonbae?" Nara spoke with a slight stutter. Her eyes shifted as if watching for spirits hiding in the shadows.

Miyoung wondered how so much power could be in such a timid girl.

In fact, the bravest thing Nara had ever done was approach

Miyoung. Twelve-year-old Nara had been a small girl with big eyes and fidgeting fingers. She'd almost failed to get Miyoung's attention, but as soon as she whispered the word *gumiho*, she didn't need to do much else.

Now Nara gave Miyoung evil men to hunt each month, and Nara could give peace to some of the spirits that plagued her.

Miyoung sometimes thought they were a strange pair, two misfits who'd never fit in the worlds they were born into.

Nara watched Miyoung with expectant eyes, waiting for her to speak.

"Something happened after the last full moon." Miyoung hesitated, so used to keeping her secrets close. She picked up a bamboo fan. The mulberry paper was hand-painted with a delicate scene of mountains and forests—a tiger grinned at her as a magpie called to it.

"What happened?" Nara prompted, her eyes wide.

"I ran into a dokkaebi in the forest. He attacked me." She didn't know why she didn't mention Jihoon again. The second time she'd felt the need to keep him a secret.

"Are you all right?" Nara gripped Miyoung's hands.

She pulled free, but not before Nara's eyes blurred. It was the same look she got when she sensed spirits. No amount of poking and prodding would bring her back before she was ready.

Nara swayed, almost knocking into a towering bookcase filled with leather-bound tomes and sand-filled bowls that held the stubs of burnt incense. Then her eyes cleared.

"What did you see?" Miyoung asked.

"I felt something move through me." Nara hummed out the words like a low chant.

"I thought you didn't become possessed by ghosts or gods."

"Not usually. My halmeoni says . . ." Nara trailed off, her eyes lowering to the ground.

Miyoung knew Nara's skills weren't normal, even for a shaman. Her fear of the ghosts that plagued her made it hard for her to control her abilities. Not the granddaughter one would expect of a powerful shaman who'd exorcised evil spirits.

Nara lived with high filial expectations and low familial affection. Something Miyoung knew well herself.

"It wasn't a spirit or a god. It was a feeling. An imbalance. A flash of the sun, then complete darkness." Nara spoke in circles as she worked through the puzzle aloud. "Something gone. Something missing."

Miyoung sucked in a sharp breath.

"What did you lose?" Nara asked, staring intently at Miyoung's face. Then her eyes narrowed, like she was clicking the last mental puzzle piece in place. "Your yeowu guseul."

"Yes," Miyoung said. There was no use in denying it. This was why she'd come here in the first place.

Nara's eyes became wide as two full moons. "Where is it now?"

"Safe."

"If the wrong person gets ahold of it, they could use it to control you." With each word Nara's voice rose with agitation.

"It's safe," Miyoung insisted, and fought the urge to check her pocket.

"Does your mother know?" Nara whispered. She always lowered her voice when the topic of Miyoung's mother came up, a quiet reverence mixed with a healthy dose of dread. As if speaking of her aloud would call Yena forth.

"She doesn't know and she doesn't have to if you can help

me put it back where it belongs." The fox bead felt heavier in Miyoung's pocket, like it knew they were discussing it.

"So you believe me now? That a yeowu guseul is a gumiho's soul. It controls your life and holds your gi."

"I never doubted that," Miyoung said, then added, "in theory. But I've never heard of a person's soul falling out."

"People used to believe a gumiho's bead carried all the knowledge of heaven and earth," Nara said quietly. "But not many know that its true purpose is balance. Without it you run the risk of losing your grip on your humanity."

"What is that supposed to mean?" Miyoung's fists clenched, as if preparing for a fight against an invisible enemy.

"It means that your control over your yokwe side, your . . . monstrous side, might slip."

"Well—" Miyoung's voice broke and she cleared her throat. "That's why we need to put it back right away."

"I might know a way," Nara said slowly. Long, drawn-out words that agitated Miyoung's frayed nerves.

"What is it?" she asked impatiently.

"You won't like it."

"Tell me," Miyoung insisted.

"Can you give me the bead?"

Miyoung took a step back instinctively.

"I didn't think so." The hurt in Nara's eyes almost made Miyoung feel guilty, but she knew she had to protect herself. Even from Nara.

"It might be dangerous for you to get too involved." It was a weak excuse, and from Nara's scrunched expression, the shaman saw right through it.

"If you can't trust me, I can't help you."

"Is there nothing else?" Miyoung asked.

"Nothing I've ever performed before." Nara started to turn away, but not before Miyoung saw the glint of something in her eyes.

"What is it?" Miyoung grabbed Nara's arm.

The shaman hesitated, her eyes darting back and forth, never staying still long enough for Miyoung to capture them with her own. "I don't know if it'll work."

"I'm willing to try anything."

Nara nodded as she pulled a jacket off a crowded coatrack.

"It's not here?" Miyoung asked.

"No, but he's close."

DO YOU WEEP for the battered, empty heart of the gumiho? You should. Though she has often yearned for love, she has always been denied it.

There is a tale that takes place long after the first gumiho had become nothing but myth. And many more had risen to take her place as monsters of the night. Humankind traded stories of their existence like they were fables warning men against temptation. And only a few knew that there lay truth in the terrifying stories.

During this time lived the son of a poor scholar, bright and precocious.

Along the road to his private tutoring sat a Chinese Scholar tree.

All were warned not to stand under the tree at night since the spirits liked to visit it when the moon was high.

One night, the boy walked home long after the sun had set. He spotted a figure under the tree and approached to warn the person of the evil spirits.

As he reached the tree, he realized it was a beautiful girl. She was bashful and shy, yet when he warned her of the spirits, she laughed him off. And every night after, she still stood under the tree and he found himself stopping to speak with her more and more. They spoke of life and love and the philosophy of the spirits.

One day he went with her to a tile-roofed house in the forest. There, she fed him delicious food and gifted him with her love. Though she refused to kiss him on the lips.

Confused, the boy sought counsel from the elder scholars, who told him she was no girl, but a fox in human form. One of the many that plagued the countryside. They told him he was lucky to have escaped her clutches with his life. But since he had her trust, perhaps he could gain something no man had yet possessed.

These fox women had a special stone, called a yeowu guseul. She hid it under her tongue; this was the reason she would not kiss him.

However, if he stole the stone from her, he would obtain infinite knowledge. They urged him to look to the sky at once after possessing it. Then he would know all the workings of heaven and bestow this knowledge on all of his descendants.

The boy accepted the challenge, wishing to know all that heaven knew.

The next night, he met the girl under the tree and professed his love for her. Surprised, the girl returned his words.

"If you love me, then you will give me a kiss," he said.

The girl, enamored by his love, agreed.

Once her lips touched his, he stole the yeowu guseul from under her tongue and captured it in his own mouth.

However, as he ran away, he tripped over a stone. Instead of looking to the sky, he looked to the earth.

It came about that he did not understand the workings of heaven, but only knew the things of the earth.

And all mortals who came after him would only know of earth as well.

8

IF THE ROAD to Nara's shop was an alley, this one was a gutter, only wide enough to move single file. The close proximity of the buildings squeezed out the sun's rays, so the alley sat in constant shadows.

Nara stopped at a wide door made of rusted metal and knocked.

There was no answer for so long, Miyoung assumed no one was home. Then it opened a crack and an eye peeked out at them.

"Can I help you?" The voice was male and suspicious, but also smooth and cultured. Not that of someone Miyoung would expect to live in such a run-down area.

"We need to see Junu," Nara stuttered.

"He's busy, come back later."

Miyoung stopped the door from slamming in their faces. She met with surprisingly strong resistance before she pushed the door open and revealed the boy in all his glory.

Miyoung had thought him a man before but now saw he was barely older than her, perhaps nineteen or twenty. He stood in a silk pajama set. His hair was mussed like he'd just crawled out of bed. Miyoung raised a brow. It was already dusk. She studied the rest of him. He was gorgeous, straight nose, warm brown irises, high cheekbones, and tall enough that Miyoung had to tilt her head back to look him in the eyes. Yet, despite his beauty, she felt an aversion to him, like they were two magnets of the same pole, pushing away from each other.

"I don't like seeing people this early in the day—"

"It's dinnertime," Miyoung interrupted.

"Your point?" The boy sighed and shuffled away before she answered.

Miyoung glanced toward Nara, who shrugged, and they followed through the open door.

It felt like stepping through a portal to another world. Miyoung had expected a shabby room with stained concrete walls and dirt-covered floors like outside. Instead, they stood in a gleaming entryway. The walls were a shining white, made out of a material as smooth as glass. Marble floors were warm beneath their feet as they removed their shoes. Pristine-white guest slippers were lined up neatly, and Miyoung slipped into a pair.

They walked toward the sound of clanging into a kitchen made of granite and steel. The boy held a bag of coffee beans, glaring at a cappuccino machine so new she doubted it had ever been used.

"We need to see Junu. Do you know when he'll be back?" Nara asked, taking the beans from the boy and pouring them into the grinder attached to the machine. It was just like the shaman to step in to help. Her biggest flaw, in Miyoung's mind.

The boy scowled but deigned to hold out his cup to let Nara make him his espresso.

"What do you want from him?" He leaned against the counter in a pose that seemed styled for the pages of a magazine, *Rumpled Pajamas Weekly*.

"We need to purchase something from him. A talisman," Nara explained as she twisted a knob. With a hiss, steaming espresso began pouring out.

"Why would a shaman need to buy a talisman when you could make it yourself?" the boy asked.

"You know I'm a shaman?" Nara stuttered.

"Girlie, you practically reek of ghosts." He gestured up and down at her. "I say that with all the affection a guy can muster before his morning caffeine."

Miyoung started to point out the time again, but gave up. "Can you tell us where Junu is or not?" she asked, her annoyance starting to get the better of her.

The boy accepted the espresso from Nara with a nod of thanks before downing it in one gulp.

"Well, now that he's had his espresso, he's right here." The boy set the cup down and gave Miyoung a wink. She decided she didn't trust this cocky boy.

"You're Junu?" Nara looked incredulous as she gave the boy a once-over.

"Surprised?" He smiled warmly, unperturbed by Nara's shock.

"I just didn't think you'd look like this," Nara said.

Miyoung had never known the shaman to be so blatantly rude, especially to someone senior.

The boy chuckled and flicked an affectionate finger under Nara's chin. "You thought I'd be hairier? Maybe red-faced? Hunched over and smelly?"

"You're a dokkaebi," Miyoung said in an accusatory tone.

"At your service," Junu said, giving a deep bow. Despite the ninety-degree angle, it felt more mocking than polite.

"What kind of dokkaebi looks like you?" Miyoung asked.

"The chonggak kind."

"Those don't exist." Miyoung thought of the tales of bachelor goblins so handsome that lovers fell at their feet. They were rumored to be made for one thing: love.

"Like how gumiho don't exist?" Junu ran a finger over Miyoung's cheek. She balked. Junu grinned. Miyoung glowered. "Or should I say a half gumiho? Your human side is showing."

She gritted her teeth and let out a growl.

"Oh, don't be sour. Your human side is why you're allowed inside my home. I've had . . . unhappy dealings with gumiho in the past."

Miyoung did not like this boy, dokkaebi, whatever.

"We are looking for a talisman," Nara said, pulling the attention of the room back to her. "I was told you could get it for us."

"I am assuming it's no ordinary talisman or else the granddaughter of Kim Hyunsook wouldn't come to see me."

"You know who my grandmother is?"

"It's my business to know things," Junu replied, his eyes sliding over to Miyoung. "Like how I know your mother is Gu Yena, one of the oldest gumiho I've ever had the honor of doing business with. Though this was long ago."

"Was my mother the gumiho you had bad dealings with then?" Miyoung asked.

"Oh no, Yena knows the value of a good deal." Junu let out a laugh before clarifying his joke. "She pays a lot of money. The best kind of client."

"Well, we're here because we need a gui talisman," Nara specified.

Junu's eyebrows rose. "Taoist? Are you trained in the practice?"

Miyoung took an instinctive step back at the mention of

Taoism. There were ancient tales saying some Taoist sorcerers held as much power as the sun god, Haemosu.

Her mother had spoken of the practice only once, a warning never to go near Taoist magic. It hadn't just been disdain in Yena's command, but fear. Anything that scared her mother must be powerful. And dangerous.

"Why are we here for a—?" She paused to collect herself before continuing. "For that kind of talisman?"

"It opens one to receive," Nara said pointedly.

Miyoung nodded in understanding. So it would allow her to open herself to the bead.

"Do you understand the practices of Taoism?" Junu asked, his voice low and serious. A departure from his previous mischievous taunting. "It's not just magic like you seem to think. It's a balance between the ways of heaven and the ways of the earth."

Miyoung didn't like the judgment she heard. As if they were foolish children to be chastised. "Do you have this talisman or not?"

He looked back and forth between the girls, considering, calculating.

"I might have it. How much is it worth to you?" Junu's eyes settled on Miyoung like he knew instinctively who'd be responsible for payment.

"Cost is not an issue; just get it." She shooed him away with her hand, condescension clear in every flick of her fingers. "I don't like spending too much time in strange places."

"Listen, sweetheart, my place is state of the art. My fridge tells me the news, and my stove listens to voice commands."

"Must make you feel right at home, talking to inanimate objects," Miyoung scoffed. In her mind, dokkaebi were one of the only things less human than gumiho. At least gumiho were born; dokkaebi were made.

Junu frowned, the first sign she was getting to him.

He stomped out of the kitchen.

"You shouldn't have upset him. He might not give us the talisman now," Nara said in a nervous whisper.

"He'll give it to us. Dokkaebi only care about money."

Nara chewed at her lip, obviously not as convinced as Miyoung.

"I've never heard of one who worked for their cash, though," Miyoung mused. "What's his deal?"

Nara glanced nervously toward the hallway, then spoke in a whisper. "Rumor is that Junu lost his goblin staff long ago, so he can't summon riches like other dokkaebi."

Miyoung found this fact amusing. Seeing as Junu acted so high and mighty, it was funny he didn't have the most basic tool that most dokkaebi possessed. She'd never seen a goblin use his staff, but it was a common part of all dokkaebi myths. A club that could magically summon whatever they wanted as long as they knew where it was.

"Anyway," Nara continued, "he's pretty industrious, has connections all over the world that can get him anything his clients need, which is lucky for us."

"What exactly does this talisman do?" Miyoung asked.

"It's for a ceremony where we seek the power of gui, the five ghosts. We want to transform your yin and yang energy so you're open to receive."

"And that will let me reabsorb the bead?" Miyoung asked.

"In theory."

"Theory?" Miyoung's voice rose. She didn't like the idea of putting her faith into a theory.

"It's all I have," Nara said, spreading her hands out.

Junu came back holding a manila envelope, not exactly the container Miyoung would expect for a magic so powerful it scared her mother.

"I'd ask what a shaman and a gumiho want with a Taoist talisman, but I really don't care."

"Great." Miyoung reached for the envelope.

Junu whipped it away and wagged an infuriating finger at her. "Uh-uh. Payment first. A million won."

"A million won?" Miyoung sputtered out.

"Don't have it? I'll also take it as a hundred yen, a thousand US dollars, your first-born child. Don't accept bitcoin yet, but I hear it's growing in popularity."

Miyoung ignored his sarcasm and pulled out her wallet reluctantly. It wasn't that she couldn't spare the cash—she had plenty—it just felt like the dokkaebi was unfairly inflating the price. From Junu's self-satisfied smile, she knew her guess was right.

"Fine." Miyoung slapped the bills on the counter. She put out her hand for the envelope, but Junu held on to it while he counted the cash.

Once satisfied, he held out the talisman. Miyoung resisted the urge to yank it from his hold and instead took it delicately, giving a nod in lieu of a full bow. She hoped the disrespect was clear.

"Good doing business with you. Come back if you need anything else. I hear there's Western magic that uses eye of newt."

"Har-har," Miyoung said, her voice as flat as a fallow field.

"Thank you." Nara bowed low, her manners too strong for her own good.

"Let's go." Miyoung stomped past the shaman and into the

entryway. She shoved her feet into her shoes so hard they almost hurt.

Junu sauntered after them as Miyoung opened the front door. It caused a dozen bujeoks plastered around the entrance to flutter. She eyed them. "Do you deal in talismans often?"

Junu gave her a curious look. "It's a popular item among my clientele. Why?"

"What about dokkaebi?"

"What about us?" Junu asked, his eyes narrowing.

"Do you sell them to dokkaebi?" Miyoung asked, thinking of the hulking beast in the forest. It had to have gotten the bujeok from somewhere.

Junu's eyes darkened at the question and his lips pursed. "I don't reveal the identity of my customers. A service you'll benefit from as well."

"Come on, Seonbae." Nara tugged at Miyoung's sleeve, holding the door open. Miyoung sent Junu one last glare before the door closed between them.

Miyoung sneered at the rusted metal. "I think I prefer the snorting, hunchbacked ones."

"I don't like any of them," Nara said with a shudder. "Why were you asking him about bujeoks?"

Miyoung answered with a question of her own. "Do many dokkaebi have things like talismans? Is that common?"

"Junu is the only one I've heard of. Most dokkaebi wield a more basic magic like their staffs. They have no need of shaman bujeoks."

"Well, the other night, when I lost my bead, that dokkaebi had somehow gotten his hands on one." Miyoung rubbed her hand against her chest, remembering the searing pain.

"If he got it here, I'm sure Junu won't talk. He has a reputation for his discretion."

"It doesn't matter." That dokkaebi was dead, and whatever evil intentions he'd had died along with him. Miyoung needed to concentrate on returning the bead to where it belonged.

"What do we do now?" Miyoung asked as they reached the main road again.

"We wait for the full moon."

"That's not for weeks!" Miyoung complained.

"I'm not experienced in Taoist practices. I don't want to take any chances. I want to use the power of the full moon."

Miyoung acquiesced. "Fine."

"Everything will be okay, Seonbae. Trust me." Nara started to reach out, and Miyoung took a step back. "If anything happens in the meantime, please call me."

"What do you think could happen?"

The younger girl sighed, obviously used to Miyoung's suspicious nature. "I just mean if you need me, I'm here." Nara bowed before making her way home. "Take care of yourself."

Miyoung bypassed the bus stop on the main street, choosing to walk instead to clear her head.

The bead tapped against Miyoung's side. Her own version of a telltale heart, mocking her with its beating presence.

DO NOT BE FOOLISH enough to think all magic is the same.

Though shamans were long the spiritual leaders of the people, other practices came to take their place.

Long after the rise of the gumiho, Taoism arrived to the Land of the Morning Calm in the midst of Jumong's Goguryeo. A practice taught by the mountain sages, but an influence that reached the throne. Taoism trained the Hwarang of Silla and taught discipline of the mind. A discipline that some thought could transcend death.

Yi Hwang was a Confucian scholar and a gifted Taoist who could wield magic. As a man of discipline, he chose to use his powers sparingly. Still, tales of his deeds traveled across the land. He saved a disciple from a ghost. Extended the life of his nephew. Foretold the crisis of a descendant who wouldn't be born for nine generations.

He was so renowned he was called upon to restrain another Taoist master, the geomancy expert who served King Seonjo and who did not use his Taoism for good.

They said Yi Hwang's eyes were so intense they could make a child fall from a tree.

They said he could speak to beasts.

They said he swallowed a fox bead to gain its magic.

Perhaps this was when foxes started fearing the Taoists.

9

JIHOON ZIPPED THROUGH traffic on the small scooter. A flag on the back flew the name of Halmeoni's restaurant.

The moped never hit over forty kilometers per hour and was always five seconds away from dying. A deathtrap on two tread-bare wheels. Really, Jihoon wondered why his halmeoni had such little regard for his personal well-being.

He prayed it wouldn't break down as he veered around a large bus spitting out exhaust.

Here the neighborhood had given in to chain stores. Doors swished open to let customers out. Blaring pop songs followed them. Jihoon bopped along to the beat.

The scooter protested as he turned onto a steep hill, and despite Jihoon's urging, it gave up five blocks from the restaurant. He debated leaving it in the middle of the street, but dutifully pushed the scooter along. His halmeoni wouldn't be happy if he abandoned the piece of junk.

"Halmeoni, your favorite grandson is back," he called, stripping off his jacket as he entered the restaurant. The scents of jjigaes still hung in the air, though the kitchen was closed for the rest of the day like it did every Monday evening while his halmeoni made kimchi and other side dishes for the week.

Jihoon already smelled the pungent aroma of fermenting cabbage.

"I'm up here," she called from the front of the restaurant.

Jihoon found her surrounded by plastic tubs. She'd pushed the tables aside to make space for her work. Some of the tubs were filled with raw cabbage; others held leaves rubbed with bright red paste. Jihoon plucked off one, red as blood, with his fingers. It tasted bitter and spicy, just the way he liked his kimchi.

His halmeoni sat with her plastic-gloved hands deep in a tub of cabbage.

"Jihoon-ah, one more delivery."

"But we're closed. And the scooter's dead." Jihoon took another bite of kimchi.

"Again?" Halmeoni slapped his hand away when he reached for a third piece. "It doesn't matter. You'll need to use the bus. Take those to Hanyang apartments." She gestured to two containers, packaged and tied up neatly in pink satin cloth.

"Why?" Just the name of the apartment complex put him on edge. "Who are they for?"

"Who else do we know who lives there?" Halmeoni clicked her tongue at him. Usually it would be enough to make him stand down, but he held his ground and crossed his arms.

"Why would you be sending her anything?"

"Take them, and be polite," Halmeoni said without looking up.

"Just because she's your daughter doesn't mean you have to take care of her. She has a husband for that."

"Don't speak that way about your mother," Halmeoni said, this time with enough iron to make Jihoon stop arguing.

"She's not my mother anymore," Jihoon mumbled, but he

hauled up the two containers. Outside, thick angry clouds gathered, matching his dark mood.

As Jihoon trudged toward the bus stop, he realized he'd forgotten his jacket. He glanced up the road and decided against returning for it. The heat of his anger was enough to ward off the chill in the air. He reached the main road as an approaching bus stopped with a huff of lung-clogging exhaust.

Dropping into a seat at the back, Jihoon balanced the containers precariously on his knees. Every time the bus bounced over a pothole, they jumped and slammed on his thighs, building his aggravation.

Glaring out the window, Jihoon tried to think of anything but the woman who'd left him. So of course she was exactly where his mind traveled.

He remembered two things from the first few years of his life: hearing his parents' long screaming matches and knowing they didn't love him. After each fight, his father turned to the bottle. His mother turned to her own bitterness. His early life was full of harsh words and quick slaps for anything from crying too loud to being too quiet. When he was four, his father was arrested. His mother immediately filed for divorce and moved them into the small apartment above Halmeoni's restaurant.

Living with Halmeoni had been like finally feeling the sun after a lifetime underground. She made sure he was clean and fed. Gave him toys and clothes. But when Jihoon's mother asked for spending money, Halmeoni handed her an apron and told her to earn it.

When Jihoon was almost five, he was sitting in the kitchen during the dinner rush. He remembered the smell of jjigae simmering on the stove, savory and salty, with just enough spice to sting his nostrils.

Halmeoni sang an old-fashioned trot song from the radio, and Jihoon followed along, butchering the lyrics. But his effort made Halmeoni laugh and it encouraged him to sing louder.

Their song joined the clatter of the kitchen and the shouts of voices in the dining room.

His mother came into the kitchen, her tray full of dirty dishes. Her hair escaped its rubber band to fall into her flushed face, sauce smeared on her sweaty cheek.

Jihoon thought she looked beautiful.

Overjoyed to see her, he jumped up and ran over.

She tripped as he clutched her knees, and the tray slipped from her hands to crash on the floor. A wayward shard of glass bounced up and cut Jihoon's cheek.

"Jihoon-ah!" she screamed. "Why are you getting in the way? You shouldn't be back here." She'd grabbed him, spanking him in punishment. The pain of her palm on his bottom was numbed by his fear.

His tears fell in streams, stinging the cut on his cheek with its salt, but he didn't make a sound. He'd learned in his short life how to cry silently or risk a harsher punishment.

"Yoori-ya," Halmeoni chastised.

"No!" Jihoon's mother swung toward Halmeoni. "I am sick of living like this because of him." She directed an accusing finger toward Jihoon, who had flopped down to cry among the spilled food and broken dishes.

"If he hadn't come around, I wouldn't have married that man. I wouldn't be living like this. I wasn't born this pathetic!"

She stormed out, leaving Halmeoni to clean up the kitchen and Jihoon. A week later she met her new husband.

The memory left a sour taste in Jihoon's mouth. It wasn't one he took out often, but it was one he couldn't quite erase. For a while, he'd wondered if that was when he'd lost her. Maybe if he hadn't been so clumsy. If he hadn't gotten in her way. Then she wouldn't have left.

Jihoon glanced out the window. The streets became wider, the buildings taller. The bus crossed the Han River, entering the opulence and established wealth of Apgujeong.

Jihoon hated this part of town. Not because it was more developed or cleaner. Not because it flaunted its wealth so blatantly that international hit songs had been written about it. Because it was her part of town. The place she went when she'd abandoned him.

Jihoon stood in front of his mother's front door for four minutes before he mustered the courage to ring the bell.

The eye of the camera glared at him. It made him feel like an intruder. He averted his face, afraid he'd be rejected before the door even opened.

"Who is it?" The question rang out, cheerful and bright.

"Delivery," he mumbled.

The door beeped as it opened, a happy trio of chirps.

She wore a bright yellow dress. Her hair was pulled into a short ponytail. A ruffled pink apron decorated her waist. And she held a sleepy toddler in her arms.

"Jihoon-ah." His mother spoke high with surprise.

He stared at the toddler, who blinked at him with curious eyes, his small hand fisted in the collar of her dress.

"Delivery," Jihoon repeated, holding up the containers with aching arms.

She glanced between the two giant bundles, then let out a sigh as she held the door open.

"You can put them there." She pointed at the floor of the foyer. "I'm going to put Doojoon down. It's nap time."

She didn't wait for a reply and disappeared into a side room.

Jihoon stood in the entryway, refusing to step farther without being invited. The apartment was pristine, the living room larger than the small apartment Jihoon shared with his halmeoni. A family portrait hung prominently. A man with a square jaw held Jihoon's mother from behind, and in her arms lay baby Doojoon.

They looked perfect and happy. The way a young family should. Jihoon had never seen a picture of him with both of his parents. Halmeoni said his mother threw them all out.

His mother emerged and gestured at the containers. "What did she send this time?"

"Kimchi," Jihoon replied, but her disdain wasn't lost on him. "Leftovers from the restaurant," he added. He would die before he told her Halmeoni meticulously seasoned it all day for her.

"Doojoonie's appa doesn't like spicy things. Why did she make so much?"

Jihoon clenched his teeth to hold in his frustration. "I delivered it. Don't forget to tell Halmeoni if she calls you."

"Your halmeoni let you leave the house like that? It's about to rain, you don't even have a jacket."

Her tone reeked of judgment, yet his traitorous mind overlooked it. She was worried about him going out in the rain. That meant she cared, right?

"I'm fine," he whispered. If he spoke any louder, his voice would crack.

"Wait there." She disappeared into the back room and emerged with a bag of clothes. She pulled out a long trench coat. "We were going to donate these, but you can have them."

Jihoon glared. The clothes were obviously those of a middle-aged man.

"I don't need your charity."

"Don't be so stubborn. They're name brands."

Jihoon was about to tell her what she could do with her name brands when a door opened down the hall. A halmeoni shuffled out. She wore a floral housecoat, her hair up in rollers. The thin wisps around the curlers were onyx black. A color that only came out of a box. When she spotted Jihoon, she stopped.

"Doojoon's eomma, who is this?" the halmeoni asked.

Doojoon's eomma. The title swam through Jihoon's head. It wasn't new to him. He'd heard many of his friends' mothers addressed as such by neighbors or teachers. But he'd never had the opportunity to hear his own mother called Jihoon's eomma. And now she was Doojoon's eomma. It served to show she really wasn't his mother anymore.

"Eomeonim," she addressed her mother-in-law. "He's a delivery boy. He brought kimchi. I thought I'd make kimchi jjigae with it tonight."

Jihoon almost laughed at her easy lie.

"Kimchi jjigae gives me heartburn." The old woman rubbed a hand over her chest. "When is my son coming home?"

"He should be here soon." Jihoon's mother wrung her hands, her eyes darting between him and her mother-in-law.

Jihoon wanted to laugh, to shout, to punch a wall. So he decided it best to leave.

"Thank you for your business," he said with a bow.

"Wait, young man," the halmeoni commanded, a person used to being obeyed. His manners stopped him from dashing out.

"Here." She held out two green bills.

This time, the beginning of a laugh did escape and he covered it with a cough. He caught the mortified look on his mother's face. Maybe that's why he took the 20,000 won before bending in a deep bow.

As he left, the door closed behind him and locked with a beep.

o o o

Back on the bus, Jihoon rested his forehead against the cool glass, exhausted. His very bones felt tired. In fact, they didn't feel like bones at all, but brittle sticks unable to hold his body up any longer.

He'd wanted his mother to tell her new family the truth. That Jihoon was her son and she wasn't embarrassed to claim him. Yet that wasn't what upset him the most. What he couldn't get over was the sight of her cradling the baby so gently. How she'd glanced affectionately at him. There'd been a maternal love in her eyes that Jihoon couldn't recall from his own childhood. What did that mean about Jihoon that his own mother couldn't love him the way she loved her new child?

When it began to rain, the window fogged. A matching haze filled his vision from the gathering of unshed tears. He blinked them away, refusing to let a single one fall for that woman.

As soon as Jihoon stepped off the bus, the rain drenched

him. His clothes stuck to his skin and goose bumps rose along his bare arms. He thought fleetingly of the bag full of coats. No, he'd rather freeze to death than wear that man's cast-off clothing.

Reluctant to go home just yet, he sat on the bench under the bus shelter.

He pulled out his phone and shot a quick text to Changwan, thinking a trip to the PC room would clear his bad mood. He watched the blank screen, willing it to light with a response. When it didn't, he swiped to his contacts and clicked on Somin's number. It rang a full minute before she picked up.

"Hello?" Somin yelled over the clashing sound of crowds in the background.

"Somin-ah." Her name came out a quiet croak.

"I can hardly hear you. You have to speak up."

"Where are you?" he asked.

"I can't hear you. My mom and I are at Gwangjangsijang. She's eating her way through all the kimbap and soondae in Seoul."

"Somin-ah!" A voice sounded in the background. "Should I get another order?"

"Gotta go, if I don't stop her, my mom is going to eat so much I'll have to roll her home. Text me if you need something." The phone clicked off.

His breath shuddered out as he lowered the phone.

He shouldn't have called Somin. Her mother's voice had been saturated with laughter in the background. Though Somin feigned annoyance, there had been an answering glee in her tone. They were having fun together. Somin didn't need Jihoon's problems bringing her down, too.

His phone buzzed with Changwan's belated answer: **Dad saw my grades. Grounded. -_-**

Jihoon knew he was in a bad place when he felt jealous Changwan had a dad around to ground him. It would all pass, he promised himself. This tightness in his chest never stayed for long.

Restless, Jihoon left the safety of the bus shelter.

He followed the winding streets decorated with yellow speed bumps. A stone wall held in the forest, but branches still reached over the small barrier defiantly.

"Babo-ya, you never hear of an umbrella?"

Jihoon stopped, barely fazed by being called stupid.

He stared at the shiny boots in front of him before he lifted his eyes.

Miyoung stood under the shadow of her umbrella so all he saw were her lips curled into a sneer.

"Excuse me?" His voice was as cold as the rain.

"Who walks around in a downpour with no coat and no umbrella?"

She obviously made a good point but only succeeded in throwing him into a darker mood.

"Just leave me alone." Jihoon walked into the small neighborhood playground to escape. The colorful plastic tunnels looked faded and gray under the overcast sky. The swings swayed lightly, like they'd recently been abandoned for drier ground.

Jihoon flopped down in one. He hadn't expected Miyoung to follow him, but she stood in front of the swing set, eyeing him.

"I think we need to get some things straight—" she began.

"You're worried I'll tell." Jihoon cut her off.

Her fist squeezed tighter around the umbrella handle.

"That's why you're here, right?" Jihoon asked. "You're afraid I'll tell everyone what you are." A voice in the back of his head told him to shut up, to stop poking at the girl who could literally tear out his heart.

Miyoung tilted her umbrella back, her head quirked to the side to study him.

"If I were you, I'd hold my tongue. I've had a bad day."

"Well, join the club," Jihoon said, ignoring the hard warning. It was just the latest in a growing list of bad decisions he'd made that day.

"How did you do it?" he asked, suddenly wanting to know. Needing to know. "How did you kill that thing?"

"The same way I'd kill you if I wanted."

Jihoon gulped, shivering from more than the cold. At least the rain had slowed to a drizzle. "It's true, then? Everything? All of the folktales and kid stories?"

"Probably. It's not my business to catalogue what's real and what's just silly human imagination."

"So why don't you have fox ears. Or a snout? Aren't you supposed to look more . . . foxy?"

"I can't decide if you're brave or dense," Miyoung mused, her tone deceptively casual. Like a predator slowly stalking her prey before the strike. "So willing to make light of me when you know what I am. I could rip out your liver right here."

"Could you?" He'd balled all of his outrage into a fire in the back of his throat and shot it at her.

The snarl twisting her lips only accentuated her beauty when it should have made her frightening. "You're making a mistake if you assume because I saved you before, I wouldn't kill you now."

"You're bluffing," he said.

"What makes you say that?"

"Because you hesitated before you said the word 'kill.'"

Her fingers curled around his neck before his brain registered the movement. She slammed him against the play set so hard it pushed all the air out of his lungs.

"You're pushing me very close to my limit," Miyoung growled.

"I don't care." The adrenaline rush of fear mixed with his anger, daring him to go further. Perhaps if he died, his mother would finally regret leaving him.

"I gave you fair warning." Miyoung's fist shot forward. Jihoon winced as he waited for the impact. Instead, he heard the echo of a *thud* as her hand crashed into the plastic tubing by his head.

He looked at the long cracks running from the large dent two centimeters from his skull.

"Next time I won't hold back."

His legs threatened to buckle when she released him, so he held on to the edge of the slide for support.

"Okay then." His voice was breathy.

"What did you see in the forest?"

"I didn't see much." He thought back. "Just the dokkaebi. Your tails. And . . ."

"And?" She leaned forward. This close, she was stunning, and he blinked at the sight of her, like a man staring into the sun.

"That bead." He barely got the stuttered word out, suddenly feeling like his whole body was made of nerves. Despite himself, he'd searched his halmeoni's old books until he'd found the tales of the gumiho. And one had detailed a fox bead, one that held all the knowledge of the universe.

She hummed deep in her throat. "What did you feel when you picked it up?"

He paused, searching for the trap in her question. When he couldn't clearly see one, he replied, "It felt warm, like it was alive."

"And nothing else?" she asked roughly, like she was already blaming him for something, but he didn't know what.

"Nothing until the dream. It felt real, like it was you, not just a memory of you."

"Gumiho can come to humans in their dreams. It's not unheard of." She flicked her wrist like a dismissal of his concern, as if visiting each other's dreams was as simple as visiting the corner market.

"Are you going to do it again?"

Her eyes were dark as she replied, "No."

He started to push, to demand better answers. But he kept quiet. His halmeoni had instilled enough superstition in him that he knew it wasn't smart for a person to go looking for trouble among things he didn't understand.

"Will you be okay?" he couldn't stop himself from asking. And Miyoung's wide-eyed stare showed she hadn't expected such a question. "Without your bead," he continued, "will you be okay?"

A frown marred her smooth features. "I'll be fine," she said softly, but her voice trembled.

She didn't look like she was fine. Her face looked drawn, her eyes shadowed. But instead he said, "I really will keep your secret. Let's make a deal. I promise not to tell your secret if you promise not to rip out my liver. Call?" He held out his hand.

He expected the hesitation, but not the slight tremor in her hand when Miyoung finally took his.

As she closed her fingers around his, it stilled, as if it had never trembled in the first place. But he knew what he'd felt. She was afraid of him, too. Maybe as much as he was of her.

"You're supposed to say 'call,'" he said with a friendly grin. He felt a need to soothe her worries. "Or else the deal isn't sealed."

She shook her head and pulled her hand free, leaving a smear of blood across his palm.

"You're bleeding." Jihoon grabbed her hand again.

"I'm fine."

"Don't be a baby," he said, digging in his pocket and pulling out a tissue. He clucked his tongue at the blood as he tied the makeshift bandage around her hand. "I don't have anything on me, but you should clean it when you get home. Or else it'll get infected."

"You sound like an old woman."

She watched him so intently with a look somewhere between confused and intrigued. It made his heart stutter a beat.

Jihoon dropped her hand and wiped his suddenly sweaty palms on his pants. "I get it from my halmeoni." He used his rambling words to chase away the sudden awkwardness. "She'd lecture you for an hour about bad habits. When I was younger I used to bite my nails and she'd dip my fingers in goya juice every morning to deter me. Now I think I actually like the taste because it reminds me of her."

"Must be nice."

"What?"

"Nothing," she muttered, gripping her crudely bandaged hand with the other. "I just don't know what it's like to have a halmeoni to fuss over me."

Jihoon blinked at the hint of wistfulness he heard in Miyoung's voice. It seemed so ordinarily human, to wish for family. It made her so much more of a mystery and he couldn't help asking, "Do you have parents?"

Miyoung scowled at him.

"I mean, I thought the myths said gumiho were originally foxes."

"I was born just like you," she said, almost indignantly.

"And your father is a gumiho, too?" He wasn't sure if he'd ever heard of gumiho being anything other than female.

"He was human."

"Was?" Jihoon's mouth suddenly felt dry and he swallowed. "Is he dead?"

"How should I know?" Miyoung mumbled. "I've never met the guy."

"How dysfunctionally ordinary," Jihoon said. Then he thanked the stars gumiho didn't have laser eyes or else her glare would have melted his face off. "Sorry, I didn't mean that the way it sounded. I'm not judging or anything." He began to ramble again as her dark eyes continued to watch him. "I mean, I wouldn't even have the right to judge, I grew up without my father, too. Haven't seen him since I was four."

"Well, humans suck sometimes," Miyoung said. It was not the reaction Jihoon usually got, and definitely not the one he was expecting from her.

He was silent a moment, unsure how to reply. Then he let out a roaring laugh. "Thanks."

"What for?"

"Just for distracting me from my problems by being you."

"You're so strange." Miyoung shook her head. "I should get going."

But she didn't leave. Instead she narrowed her eyes, like she was debating something. Then she held out her umbrella.

"What's this for?" Jihoon asked.

"Gumiho don't get sick. I don't need it."

"Be careful," he said, accepting the umbrella with a grin. "I might start thinking you like me."

She rolled her eyes as she left. Her form faded long before he was able to tear his gaze away.

It's not smart for a person to go looking for trouble among things he doesn't understand, he reminded himself.

But it seemed he wasn't that smart.

10

AS MIYOUNG MADE her way through the forest, unease sat heavy in her chest. Was she a fool to allow a person to roam free while he held her secret?

Yena would just make him fall in love with her. She always claimed that when humans thought they loved, they'd do anything. Miyoung didn't like the idea that love could be manipulated. Yena might be jaded about the human heart, but Miyoung wasn't yet.

Still, Jihoon worried her with his observant eyes, devil-like smile, and glib tongue. It was a bad combination. Someone who knew too much and cared too little.

It felt like he could see right through her lies. Like how she claimed to control their shared dream. It had been as much a surprise to her as it was to him. But she needed him to believe she was more powerful than she was. She needed to scare him into silence. He'd given his word, but she couldn't trust that. Even though she wanted to.

Will you be okay? His question echoed in her head. It had sounded like he truly worried for her well-being. Just thinking about it made her heart ache.

Miyoung squeezed her hands into tight fists and felt the tissue still wrapped around her right hand. It was tied in a neat bow despite the delicate material. She ripped it off, revealing skin that had already healed.

Maybe it would be best to tell her mother everything. Yena always knew what to do. But that might mean Yena would take care of Jihoon by making sure he never talked to anyone, ever again. Miyoung didn't like that Jihoon knew her secret, but she didn't think he deserved to die for it.

And Yena's mood was bound to be severe after her trip to the school. It would be best to keep Jihoon a secret a little while longer.

Miyoung's house sat at the end of the road. The structure was made of glass and wood, open to the nature all around it.

The living room was pristine, not a mote of dust on any surface. They were completely unpacked the same day they'd moved in. There would be no living with moving boxes for Gu Yena.

Glass cases displayed relics from societies past.

Terra-cotta horses, posed for eternity with their regal heads held high. Given to Yena as a token of affection. The man had smuggled them into the country as proof of his love.

A six-pointed crown, dripping with jade beading and gold pieces. A gift to Yena from a cousin of a king.

Long jade binyeo, hairpins with smooth shafts. The ends carved and whittled into intricate maze-like patterns creating delicate vines tipped in lotus flowers. A set of them commissioned by the head scholar at Sungkyunkwan.

A bronze fox leered at her from across the room. Miyoung wasn't sure who'd given her mother this artifact, though she liked to think they had a good sense of humor and a strong constitution. They had to if they had the gumption to gift Yena with such a symbol.

Sometimes Miyoung felt like one of those antiques, something Yena had collected over her centuries of life. And that was Miyoung's problem. How could she compete with thieves and princes and royal scholars?

She felt like she had to be stronger than the terra-cotta, more regal than the gold, and more beautiful than the jade. If she wasn't, would she be relegated to a glass case of her own? Packed away where Yena could remember her fondly from a distance?

Miyoung stuck her hand into her pocket and wrapped her hand around the yeowu guseul nestled there. A new habit she'd already formed.

She made her way to her room. A poster of IU, Miyoung's favorite singer, hung over her bed. Something Yena originally protested. Why idolize singers when there existed real gods and demons? Miyoung had insisted and her mother gave in, one of the only times Miyoung had ever won an argument.

She clicked on the large TV in the corner. The sound of it in the background always helped calm Miyoung's nerves, drowning out the anxious thoughts that swam through her brain. The drama playing was popular right now and halfway through its run. That meant there would be fewer long, angsty looks between the main leads and more confessions of love. The middle of a drama was Miyoung's favorite part.

She'd barely had time to settle on her bed when there came a knock on her door. Without waiting for an answer, it swung open. Miyoung stood and gave a bow of greeting. "Hello, Mother."

"You took a long time getting home."

"I'm sorry," Miyoung said.

"Don't be sorry. Be better."

Miyoung nodded and gripped the hem of her shirt to keep her fingers still. A piece of tissue was still stuck to the side of her knuckle, reminding her of Jihoon carefully wrapping her cuts. She clamped her hands together, hiding the bloodstained tissue between them. She didn't want Yena to find out about Jihoon. Not yet.

Yena leaned forward, peering into Miyoung's lowered eyes.

For a minute, she worried her mother saw through her skull to the secrets she hid. But Miyoung knew that, despite the myths, gumiho who read minds were long extinct.

"Miyoung, who are you?"

Miyoung almost gave a sigh of relief, but instead exhaled deliberately slow. "Gu Yena's daughter," she replied to the familiar question.

"And what does that make you?"

"Smart."

"And?"

"Beautiful."

"And?"

"Strong."

"Good." Yena nodded, satisfied. "You should not let the mortals affect you. My daughter is better than that. And I expect better things from you than getting into petty scuffles with your classmates."

It was said as more of a command than a comfort, but still gave Miyoung strength.

"I'm sorry for causing problems today, Mother."

"I know," Yena said, and left Miyoung alone with only the sound of her drama as company.

11

IF JIHOON EXPECTED Miyoung to act differently toward him at school, he was wrong. She ignored him all morning.

It was an uneventful day, if you didn't count the many times he was distracted by the mere presence of the gumiho. She didn't acknowledge their conversation from the night before. Jihoon found himself wondering whether she'd forgotten all about it. Then he realized that he was acting the same way a lovesick fool would and decided it best to carry on as he normally would, which meant napping through English class and skipping out to play video games. But he'd continued to sit watching the back of Miyoung's head as she scratched out furious notes.

"Don't you think quiet girls are so cool?" Changwan mused at lunch.

Jihoon glanced over to see what his friend was staring at. He shouldn't have bothered. Changwan was looking at a lone Miyoung, sitting in the corner of the lunchroom and resolutely ignoring all the students who tried to approach her. Well, at least Jihoon wasn't the only one she wouldn't talk to.

If loneliness were a flavor, Jihoon could taste Miyoung's like a bitter aftertaste that sat on his tongue. It wasn't just that she refused to engage other students in conversation; it was the way her shoulders hunched. How her face pinched and her hands clenched. As if the very act of socializing caused her physical pain.

After school, Changwan abandoned Jihoon for the new after-school academy his father had signed him up for. Which meant no distracting video games to help him ignore his worries. So Jihoon leaned against the glass of the bus shelter and pulled out a pair of headphones while he debated just going to the PC room alone. He had a good view of the school gates and recognized Miyoung's smooth gait as she exited. Pretending to fiddle with his phone, he watched her slow approach to the bus shelter. He pinpointed the moment she recognized him among the students waiting by the pause in her step. Then she continued forward and took a seat on the bench, never acknowledging his presence.

Jihoon let his head rest against the glass and watched her out of the corner of his eye. She sat staring straight ahead. He didn't know why it looked so odd until he realized everyone had their eyes glued to their phones. Everyone except Miyoung and a group of students chattering at the other end of the bus stop.

"I heard she got kicked out of her last school," said a boy short enough to look like he was still a first year. He had a sprinkle of freckles on an upturned nose and a pointed chin. He reminded Jihoon of devious elves from his halmeoni's stories.

The group shot dagger glances at Miyoung. Their vitriol seemed overblown. Miyoung had only been at their school for two days. What could she have done to warrant such hatred?

"I heard she got kicked out of the last three schools," said a girl as she sucked on a lollipop, clicking it against her teeth as she spoke. Jihoon recognized them as friends of Baek Hana, a crew that used intimidation and rumors to maintain their popularity. Miyoung slumped low in her seat, as if she'd become invisible if she were small enough.

"I heard that's not even her real face." The girl had a slight lisp from the large braces decorating her teeth. They made her lips puff out and gave her a disposition more sour than the cherry lollipop she sucked on. "She definitely got plastic surgery."

"You're totally right. I can see the surgery scar," said the boy.

Fed up, Jihoon pulled his headphones from his ears and held them out to Miyoung.

When she only stared at them, he pushed them into her ears himself. She jerked back at the sudden contact, but he persisted until she wore the earbuds.

Miyoung looked up, perplexed.

He gave her a grin and a shrug by way of explanation. Then went back to leaning against the bus shelter.

She lowered her head, but she kept the headphones in.

The bus pulled up, and the catty clique boarded. Miyoung stood, but Jihoon held her back.

"Let's wait for the next one." He gestured toward the back window where the gossipers glared from their seats. Miyoung didn't reply, but she let the bus pull away without them.

"Why would you wear headphones without music?" She handed back the silent earbuds.

"If I listen to music, I can't hear what other people are talking about."

"So you spy on people?" she asked.

"I don't make them talk about their private life in public."

"Creep," Miyoung muttered.

Jihoon shrugged. "You have a funny way of saying thank you."

"For what?"

"They stopped gossiping. When they think you can't hear, they lose interest."

Miyoung stared at him so long he felt the urge to fidget. "You say that like you have experience with it."

"You say that like you care if I do," Jihoon said as the next bus rolled to a stop in front of them.

Miyoung's lip curled before she boarded the bus.

She took a seat in the back and Jihoon slid in beside her. She scowled, but didn't protest.

"Why did you let those kids talk about you?" Jihoon asked. "You could have taken them."

"If I cause a scene, they'll start to pay more attention to me." Jihoon lifted a brow. It seemed they had something in common, a need for privacy. He tucked that tidbit away to chew on later.

"Thank you." The words were almost lost among the rumble of the bus and the chatter of the other passengers.

"What?" Jihoon asked, leaning closer.

"If you didn't hear, then I'm not repeating it," Miyoung said.

"You're welcome," Jihoon said. "It was no problem. I'm good at avoiding negative attention."

Miyoung studied him, her eyes so dark and direct that he wanted to lean away. "Oddly, I think I believe that."

The pitying look made Jihoon squirm. To combat the nervous tension in his shoulders, he stretched out like he had not a care in the world, draping his arm across the back of the seat in a leisurely sprawl. "So what do you usually do after school?" He gave a cheeky grin that he knew would deepen his dimples.

She didn't answer and slid her eyes toward his hand, almost touching her shoulder. He retracted his arm for fear she'd rip it off.

"I usually go to the PC room," he said. "Do you play L-o-L?"

Miyoung stared out the window, ignoring him.

That just made Jihoon more determined to get a reaction out

of her. "One of my favorite champions is Ahri." Jihoon chuckled. "If you played, you'd get the joke." He leaned in and said in a stage whisper, "She's a gumiho."

Miyoung glared at him. Jihoon grinned. She continued to glower, unmoved by his best weapon. His smile wavered. "Do you really not do anything for fun? Sports? Knitting? Ancient tea ceremonies?"

"I don't do things for fun," she said.

"Why?"

"Why do you care?"

Jihoon shrugged. "Because it looks like you could use a friend."

"I don't need friends," Miyoung muttered.

"Everyone needs friends," Jihoon countered, despite the frown Miyoung gave him.

"Fine, I watch TV, read, eat." She ticked off her fingers for each thing.

"So things you can do at home."

"Things I can do alone," Miyoung clarified, then turned firmly back toward the window.

Jihoon let her end the conversation this time. He figured a smart man knew when to stop poking at a sleeping bear. Or, in this case, a sleeping fox.

o o o

At dinner, Jihoon stirred his galbi-jjim, thick hunks of beef and potatoes swirled in a gooey brown sauce both savory and sweet. He plucked up a roasted chestnut, then let it plop back down into a pile of carrots. Dubu sat beside him, her tail thumping hopefully against the floor, but she knew better than to outright beg. At least not in front of Halmeoni. Unfortunately for the dog, tonight Jihoon was too distracted to sneak her a bite.

He glanced furtively at his halmeoni, then back at his food.

He did this three times before she said, "Ahn Jihoon, if you keep staring at me, I'm going to think you did something wrong."

"No, I didn't. Lately," he added with a wry grin.

"I found this in your laundry," Halmeoni said, pulling out the bright yellow bujeok. "You're supposed to keep it on you at all times."

Jihoon frowned at it, remembering the night in the forest. How that dokkaebi had used a talisman against Miyoung. Slowly he picked up the paper. "Halmeoni, I have a question about those fables you used to tell me."

"Yes?" Halmeoni set her chopsticks down and folded her hands in front of her to show he had her full attention.

"Do you know what made gumiho bad?"

"Where did this come from?" Halmeoni sat back, like someone settling in for a particularly interesting conversation. They sat on the floor at the low table in the living room. Halmeoni's back was to the sofa so she could lean against it.

Jihoon sat cross-legged opposite her, thinking through his words. "Just curious. I remember there was a story about a fox spirit that was good. She helped a monk find enlightenment. I wonder what made the fox turn bad."

"It's not as simple as you're implying." Halmeoni's tone became didactic. "A fox is an animal just like you and me. She does not choose evil or good upon coming into this world."

Jihoon nodded along. His halmeoni liked to take a circuitous route to get to her points, but he always loved hearing her stories.

"According to some earlier stories, the gumiho was, at first, a benevolent creature."

"Then?" Jihoon prompted, unable to help himself.

"Then, as humans tend to, we needed someone to blame for our problems." Halmeoni said this like she was apologizing for a great misdeed. "Men fell in love with gumiho because they were beautiful. Then they blamed their adultery on the creatures instead of accepting their own mistakes. Maybe it happened often enough that it became normal to say gumiho lured men into cheating on their wives. And the gumiho was given a label of evil she didn't deserve. When you're constantly treated as a pariah and labeled bad, you might begin living up to that expectation."

Jihoon frowned into his rice. Was this true of Miyoung as well? She wasn't a bad person as far as he could tell. After all, she'd saved his life. And he'd seen firsthand how cruelly people reacted to her mere presence. Could the harsh words of others turn her into a monster? Had they already?

"What about the liver thing?" he asked. "Where did that come from?"

Halmeoni shrugged as she scooped up rice. "I don't know about that one. It could be a warning not to drink too much, and they added it to the gumiho myth as a two-for-one deal."

Jihoon chuckled at the bad joke, but stopped when Halmeoni grabbed his hand, her expression suddenly sober.

"Jihoon-ah, even though I think the gumiho didn't start out evil, it doesn't mean she didn't end up that way. It's always good to know what you're looking at before it bites you." Jihoon nodded slowly, trying to read if there was a deeper message under his halmeoni's ominous warning.

Then her eyes folded into a smile as she gave his hand a pat and went calmly back to her meal.

The rest of the night, all Jihoon thought about were myths and fables. The lessons they taught and the price they came with.

12

MIYOUNG DIDN'T LIKE being home alone, but though Yena insisted on having everything just so, she rarely spent any time in the house. Perhaps she had more of a need for fresh air as a full gumiho. Or maybe she just didn't like making awkward small talk with her daughter.

The other night as they ate a silent dinner together, curiosity had pushed Miyoung to ask, "Mother, what do you do for fun?"

"Fun?" Yena had said the word like it was a virus.

"Yeah, do you knit? Play games? Read . . ." Miyoung trailed off at the icy glare from her mother.

"What a strange question. I honestly don't know what's gotten into you," Yena said.

"I think I'm just tired." And Miyoung had asked to be excused to her room.

Maybe that was why Yena had texted saying she wouldn't be home for dinner tonight. She probably wanted to avoid Miyoung's "strange questions." And without her the house felt empty, with nothing but Yena's collection of artifacts for company.

Miyoung was so often alone. That was how she started loving dramas. They were always on. The weekend daytime shows depicted family melodrama; the evening prime-time shows often showed more high-stakes stories. And some took on the fantastical. She remembered when she was younger and there were reruns of a drama on. The main character was a nine-tailed fox who fell in love.

She couldn't wait to share the drama with her mother. It reminded her of her parents—a human boy falling for a gumiho girl. She'd never heard the story of how her parents had met, so her heart had filled in the blanks with the soft moments and sweet love that bloomed between the main characters.

When Yena had gotten home, Miyoung showed her the first episode that she recorded. Yena smashed the television set and told Miyoung if this was how she spent her days, then there was no need for a TV at all.

That night as Miyoung cried herself to sleep, Yena came into her room and apologized.

"It surprised me," Yena explained. "And it's wrong. That's not something I want you to fill your head with. It's dangerous to think that's possible."

"But you met my dad. You fell in love with him."

"Meeting your father was a mistake, and it was nothing like that drama. He was a man and men only ever want one thing from us. I was tricked into thinking he could be different. But in the end he abandoned us. He couldn't love his own daughter enough to stay. I don't ever want that for you."

And it was the first and last time Yena had ever discussed Miyoung's father with her.

Tonight, the weeknight dramas weren't holding Miyoung's attention, and she checked her watch. Dinner should have been delivered by now. She glanced at the crumpled menu that had been wedged in their mailbox. She usually didn't order in, but there was nothing in the fridge and she was starving.

Miyoung rubbed a hand over her stomach as it turned and twisted. It was almost painful, but it wasn't as if she'd been neglecting her meals. At least not for food.

The doorbell chimed and she jumped up. She swung the door open and reached for the food when she stopped short. In front of her, holding out a plastic-covered delivery tray, was Ahn Jihoon.

"What are you doing here?" she blurted out, though it was fairly obvious as she saw his delivery scooter behind him.

"I'm working," he said, glancing at the tray he held between them.

Miyoung grabbed it, and if it hadn't been wrapped so tightly, soup would have sloshed out of the metal bowls. She set it on the ground and held out a few bills.

But Jihoon wasn't paying attention to her. He craned his neck back and stared at the vaulted living room and let out an impressed whistle.

"I've never seen inside of here. Too scared to take a peek."

"Are you going to stop babbling and take the money?" Miyoung asked.

"You know they say this place is haunted," Jihoon continued, making to step inside.

Miyoung moved to block, causing him to collide with her.

"What do you think you're doing?" She made her tone icy like she'd heard Yena do when she was displeased.

"Come on, you can't blame me for being curious," Jihoon said with a wide smile that flashed his dimples. "They've been telling stories about this house since I was born. That it once belonged to an old witch whose lover ran away and she placed a curse on it so no one who ever lived here would find love."

Miyoung rolled her eyes, but she folded her arms, suddenly wondering if she felt a chill.

"You're an idiot if you believe in those types of stories."

"Really? And would I be an idiot to believe in stories about gumiho and goblins?" Jihoon asked with a laugh that sounded too relaxed.

Miyoung could tell he had no intention of leaving quietly. It would just be easier to give in than waste time arguing with him.

"Fine, if I let you take a look around, then will you leave?"

"Sure." Jihoon shuffled in and took off his shoes. He picked up the delivery tray without asking and deposited it on the low coffee table in the living room.

Miyoung picked it up and placed it on the dining table.

"Whoa, cool," Jihoon said, staring at the statue of the bronze fox in its glass case. Then he glanced at Miyoung with a mischievous grin and asked, "Relative of yours?"

She held back a retort. Yena always said control was her greatest tool.

"Okay, have you seen enough? Will you go?"

"You're not a very good hostess. You didn't even offer me anything to drink," Jihoon pointed out.

"Well, I've never had anyone over before."

Jihoon stopped his study of the jade binyeos and stared at her. "Really? Never? Not even when you were a little kid?"

"Why would I have people over? As an appetizer for my mother?"

Jihoon frowned at that. "So you never had friends to your house to just hang out?"

"I've never had friends."

"How sad," Jihoon mumbled to himself, and Miyoung was

sure she wasn't meant to hear. Except her great gumiho hearing picked it up. And it poked at her, his pity.

"Well, I'm sure it's hard for someone like you to understand, but people don't necessarily like me."

"Someone like me?" Jihoon asked.

Why was that what he focused on?

"Yeah, the type of person everyone likes."

Jihoon threw back his head and laughed, a boisterous sound that filled the space until it felt just a little less cold. A little less empty. Miyoung blinked in surprise.

"That is definitely not me. A lot of people don't like me."

"That's not true," Miyoung insisted. "I've seen you. Everyone in class likes you. They all talk to you in the halls and greet you."

"They're polite, I guess," Jihoon said with a frown. "But they don't know me."

"So?" Miyoung asked.

"Well, someone can't *truly like* you unless they know you." He said this like it was obvious. "Maybe it's why you've had trouble making friends," Jihoon mused. "Because you never get to know people."

"Well, I'm never in a place long enough for that," Miyoung said dismissively, making her voice and expression cold. She didn't like this conversation; it made her head hurt and her heart squeeze. As if Jihoon were trying to knock at feelings she'd long since buried away.

Miyoung walked to the front door and opened it. The happy chirp of the lock disengaging was in direct opposition to her sour mood.

"You should go."

Jihoon seemed resigned as he walked to the door. "Remember to leave the tray outside when you're done. I'll come pick it up."

"Fine," she said, and slammed the door in his face.

o o o

Miyoung didn't like how Ahn Jihoon talked to her. Like he was her friend. He'd fallen into the casual speech of banmal without her permission. She wondered if he even realized it. But more important, she wasn't sure why she hadn't put an end to it.

She was already in a bad mood and now she was waiting in the seemingly unending line for lunch. She'd dawdled too long in the classroom after the bell rang. Her old class was half the size of this one, so she'd forgotten how intense the lunch rush could be in the overcrowded Seoul schools.

She did her best to ignore the few students who whispered about her. She was an expert at ignoring stares and gossip. But her hearing was so good that it caught a few words, and she noticed that her name was continuously paired with Ahn Jihoon's. It seemed Baek Hana's friends hadn't liked his stunt with the headphones. They thought she and Jihoon had acted too friendly. And the rumors of them dating spread like wildfire.

It worried her. These rumors garnered too much attention. But it was also a departure from some of the harsher rumors she was used to hearing. Ones that called her Ice Queen.

As the kids jostled around her in line, one of them bumped her shoulder. The contact brought with it the taste of something bright, as if electricity raced along Miyoung's skin and strengthened her muscles. She hadn't even realized they were aching until she felt this rush of energy. It was the student's gi. Young and fresh and there for the taking. She almost turned, almost grabbed the boy. Her hands had reached halfway toward him before she stopped herself.

Instead she gripped her palms together so tightly her fingernails dug into skin.

A hunger protested from deep inside. She closed her eyes and took three deep breaths. It was never this bad this soon after her last feeding. It felt like the energy she'd absorbed at the last full moon had not lasted the full month like it usually did. Leaving her hungering for more.

She knew it must be because she no longer had her bead inside. Without the bead to store the energy, it had seeped out of her like water leaving a cloth sack.

She finally reached the front of the line and took one of the metal trays, glad for something to fill her hands. The lunch staff filled each compartment in the tray with food: steaming rice, miyeokguk with its cloudy broth, bright red kimchi, and savory meat. The students seemed particularly excited about the fact that they had meat today.

She could practically taste the excitement in the air. It made her stomach rumble for something other than food.

She exited the line, eager to escape to some dark corner, but the room was packed, barely a seat available. No matter where she sat she'd be squeezed between groups of kids.

Then she spotted Jihoon and his friends. Lee Somin was a prickly seatmate, but at least she left Miyoung alone. And Oh Changwan was a nervous, bumbling boy, but he was always polite to Miyoung. She sighed and walked to their table.

" . . . think it's cool they're dating," Changwan was saying.

"That's just because you want to ogle her up close." Somin

stabbed her chopsticks into a fish cake so hard they clanged against her metal lunch tray.

"Ogle who?" Miyoung asked, though she knew the answer.

Jihoon glanced up. Changwan froze beside him.

"What are you doing here?" Somin refused to meet Miyoung's eyes.

"There's nowhere else to sit," was Miyoung's only reply as she took the empty seat by Somin.

"How are you liking our school, Miyoung-ssi?" Changwan stuttered out, his cheeks burning red.

"It's fine."

"Usually people ask permission to sit," Somin said.

"Why do I need to ask when no one was using this seat?" Miyoung asked, taking a calm bite of rice.

Somin flushed, her cheeks puffing out as if her anger gathered there. Miyoung could almost see it around her, an energy so bright that it made her glow.

Miyoung had never fed off a girl before, but she thought perhaps Somin's energy would fill her to the brim.

"Miyoung-ssi, didn't you want to see where the kids play soccer during lunch?" Jihoon blurted out, pulling Miyoung's attention to him. His eyes were wide as they watched her.

She wondered if he knew what she'd been thinking and guilt tightened her chest. "Sure," Miyoung said, accepting his offer of escape.

She dropped her utensils on her tray and stood. Perhaps her steps were a little too fast to be casual. Perhaps she let her tray drop in the discard pile a little too loudly. But she needed to get out of the room, filled with bodies and gi and temptation. She could barely breathe for wanting all that delicious energy.

The hallway was blissfully empty, and she took in gulping breaths of air.

Jihoon left the cafeteria behind her.

"I wasn't going to do anything to her," Miyoung said as they walked. For some reason she needed him to know that. She needed him to believe it.

"What makes you think I was afraid for Somin? She has a fierce right hook and she's the ace in this school. Never lost a fight."

Miyoung snorted out a derisive laugh. "A human girl could never take me."

"But when you're here, aren't you supposed to be just a 'human girl,' too?"

Miyoung's eyes darted to take in the hallway, searching for anyone who might be close enough to hear, but it was empty.

"Be careful how you speak to me," she said through gritted teeth. "If we weren't in school, you wouldn't be standing right now."

"I never thought I'd be so grateful to be in school," Jihoon muttered, pushing open a door.

"Where are you going?"

"I told Somin and Changwan we were going to the soccer field."

"I thought that was a lie to get me to leave your friends alone."

"I don't like to lie if I don't have to," Jihoon said.

"You said I *wanted* to see the fields," she pointed out. "That was a lie."

"Well, now it's only a half lie." Jihoon pulled her outside.

Her muscles clenched beneath his touch. Never had someone so casually touched her like Jihoon did. Not even her mother.

Her skin was too sensitive from her gnawing hunger, and it made tingles race up her arm.

Pulling free, she took a few steps toward the field below where a dozen boys and girls ran across the grass in a game of soccer. "How do they have enough time to eat and play?"

"They don't. They usually skip lunch so they'll have enough time for a game."

"Why would they do that for something so trivial?"

"To them it's not." Jihoon shrugged as he watched the game, too. "When something's important to you, you're willing to give up a lot for it. This is the only time they have to play."

"I don't understand why kids go through so much effort for such things," Miyoung said. "What will it help them gain?"

"It's not to gain anything." Jihoon laughed. "It's just for fun. Sometimes you need to stop thinking so hard about what you get out of life and have fun."

"Fun is a human luxury," Miyoung muttered, trying to hide her resentment. She hated that she envied these kids whose only worry was whether they'd have enough time for a game of soccer.

"You're part human, too." Jihoon's words were quiet, but they struck deep.

Not because he reminded her she was part human, but because he reminded her that part of her was not.

"I didn't realize we could come out here for lunch," Miyoung said. It was a good place to get away from the suffocating crowd of the cafeteria.

"It's getting cold," Jihoon said, glancing at the blazing sun overhead.

"That doesn't affect me," Miyoung said with a shrug.

"Really?" Jihoon asked, fascination too clear in his voice. She wasn't used to someone being so blatantly interested in her.

"Why are you doing this?" she asked, unable to keep the frustration out of her voice.

"Standing here?"

She sucked in a breath, holding it before she said something she'd regret. "Why do you insist on acting out this charade of fake friendship?"

Jihoon's brows knit. "It's not fake. We are friends."

"I don't make a good friend."

Jihoon let out a chuckle. "Well, I'm okay with having a bad friend. So I guess we're agreed." He walked back inside, and she held in a scream of frustration.

"What does that even mean?" she called after him.

He didn't look back and just lifted a hand in a friendly wave as the bell rang for class.

13

MIYOUNG'S DAYS SLOWLY became routine. She was a fan of order. It ensured that there were no unforeseen variables. If she knew what each day would bring, she could better control her world.

However, it felt strange to have a routine while a ticking time bomb sat in her pocket. The yeowu guseul was a heavy reminder that her days were not completely normal.

Jihoon, on the other hand, was completely random. He never did anything consistently. He liked to goof off in class or sleep, but never with any rhyme or reason. More often than not, he'd be in the computer lab instead of class because he went there to play games.

Jihoon had an odd skill for getting away with doing as little work as possible and staying in the teachers' good graces. Probably because he had a wickedly boyish face with an equally mischievous grin. It worked well to get him his way.

She hardly spoke to anyone during the school day. It was one of her top coping mechanisms. Ignore everyone until they started ignoring her, too. The only exception was Jihoon. He would say casual hellos to her in the hallway. Invite her constantly to sit with him and his friends at lunch (the accompanying glares from

Somin would have stopped her if she hadn't already started eating lunch alone on the outside steps).

But the only place she couldn't avoid Jihoon was the bus. It had become a strange part of her routine. He'd always sit beside her, babbling about his day, asking her questions about hers. And when she didn't answer, he'd just keep rambling on.

It was an odd, new experience, to have someone who sat with her, talked with her. And annoyed the living daylights out of her.

She started to recognize his small habits. How he tapped his fingers against any surface, a mindless action. How he accepted everyone and in turn people gravitated toward him. Even Miyoung, though she hated to admit it, was starting to feel more comfortable around him.

Making her way out of the school building, Miyoung scanned the courtyard. Not to look for a specific person, she told herself, but when she didn't see a lanky form with ruffled hair, she was disappointed. Jihoon had been held after class to talk to the teacher. He was a horrible student, almost laughably bad.

Miyoung walked out the school gates, shuffling her feet. She felt oddly reluctant to leave, like being outside of campus meant it would be harder for Jihoon to find her. Which was ridiculous, as the bus stop was within view of the front steps. She settled against the bus shelter.

Two boys ambled up, leaning against the opposite side of the glass. One was tall, with pointed features, like a rat. The other was wide, a lumbering boy. The taller, ratty boy slapped a pack of cigarettes against his palm. They were banned on school grounds, but perhaps the boy felt confident since he stood several meters outside of campus. Miyoung practically felt his stare on her and ignored them both.

She craned her neck to the side to see if Jihoon was coming out of the school.

Instead, Changwan was making his way to the curb.

"Miyoung-ssi." Changwan used the formal title, like his manners overwhelmed the fact that they were peers. It was something she secretly liked, his politeness. "Are you waiting for the bus alone?" He looked around, and Miyoung knew he searched for Jihoon.

"Why wouldn't I be?" Miyoung asked, then realized it was probably a bit harsh. And something about Changwan softened her heart. "Would you wait with me a bit?"

The shy boy blushed, gave a small nod, and sat, keeping half a meter of space between them. She couldn't help it, she grinned. She was used to boys being awestruck by her, but Changwan's admiration felt so innocent.

"He's a good guy," Changwan said.

"Who?"

"Jihoonie. He's a good guy. I know it might seem like he's lazy and doesn't care, but he does," Changwan said. "You've probably noticed I'm not as cool as him or Somin. But they've never once made me feel like I don't belong."

"Are you being a wingman?" Miyoung couldn't keep the amusement from her voice.

"He didn't ask me to say anything," Changwan said quickly. He held up his hands like he'd been caught doing something wrong. "But I can tell he likes you. I'm hoping you like him, too, and if you don't, I'm hoping you'll let him down easy. Jihoon puts up a brave front but he's been through some stuff."

"Been through stuff? Like what?"

Changwan shook his head. "It's not my place—"

"Everyone knows about Ahn Jihoon's criminal father and runaway mother. Makes you wonder what secrets he's hiding that made both of his parents leave him," the rat-like boy said.

Miyoung's eyes tracked down to his uniform name tag: JUNG JAEGIL. Now she remembered him. He was a second-year in a different class. Miyoung had seen him in the halls, bullying first-years, sometimes for lunch money, sometimes for fun. Miyoung abhorred bullies.

Behind him stood the larger boy. His name tag read KANG SEHO. It seemed like Jaegil was the mouth and Seho the muscle—a bully cliché if Miyoung had ever seen one.

"That's none of your business," Changwan said, but his voice wavered with fear.

"You're the one who brought it up," Jaegil said with a shrug. "Trying to impress a pretty girl?"

"That's not it at all!" Changwan sputtered.

"Good, because you should know better," Jaegil said. "Girls don't talk to losers like you, no matter how much money your father makes."

Changwan hunched and Jaegil grinned. He was already reveling in the pain he'd inflicted.

It made Miyoung despise him even more. Maybe that was why she did such an uncharacteristic thing next.

"He's my friend. Right, Changwan-ah?" Miyoung threw her arm around the boy's shoulders.

"Yeah," he stammered, a blush rising over his neck and onto his cheeks.

Jaegil let out a huff, glancing back and forth between Miyoung and Changwan.

A car pulled up to the curb, the windows tinted so black Miyoung couldn't see inside.

Changwan let out a sigh of relief.

"I gotta go," he said to her, not bothering to glance at the two bullies who still loomed above him. "See you tomorrow, Miyoung." He paused, then added the friendly modifier "-ah."

"See you." Miyoung forced a smile as he rushed to the car.

"You know, I could be your friend, too," Jaegil said with a leer.

"I have enough." The smile slid from her face as she turned away, but Jaegil moved with her.

"You want a smoke?" Jaegil stood above her, a cigarette perched between two fingers. She imagined he thought the pose attractive. He'd probably practiced it a dozen times before pulling it out to impress the girls.

A small voice in the back of her head told her there was a way to get rid of Jaegil. To make sure he wouldn't bother her or bully anyone ever again. The hunger gnawing at her had become a constant ache. And it pushed at her, telling her that this boy didn't deserve his life if he was going to use it to cause others pain.

"I asked you a question." Jaegil's tone became insistent, grating at her raw nerves. "It's rude not to answer. Isn't it, Seho?"

"Very rude," the larger boy said. His voice was a mocking baritone.

"I don't smoke." Miyoung laced her words with venom. *Get away from me,* she thought, *before I do something I'll regret.*

Jaegil didn't take the hint. "You sure you don't want one? I usually don't share."

He shoved a cigarette under her nose so she smelled the sour tobacco. She snatched it from his hand as she stood. But before she could make another move, Jihoon arrived and pushed Jaegil back. "Lay off."

"Aw, Ahn Jihoon came to rescue his yeo-chin."

Miyoung started forward, but Jihoon stopped her. "I don't think you want the attention kicking his ass will get you."

Jaegil let out a derisive laugh, and Seho took a step closer. "You think she could beat *me* up? I'd like to see her try."

"Trust me, you really wouldn't," Jihoon said.

"I don't need you to fight my battles," Miyoung said through gritted teeth.

"Let me handle this," Jihoon said.

"I said to leave it alone!" Miyoung's shout echoed off the glass of the bus shelter. Heat nestled in her lungs. It mixed with her ever-present hunger and made her chest feel too tight.

"I guess she doesn't like you that much after all, Ahn Jihoon," Jaegil said with a chuckle.

"Oh, shut up!" Miyoung whirled on Jaegil, and he took a step back at the vehemence in her voice. "I hate guys like you, who think you can bully your way into getting everything you want. And these"—she snatched the cigarettes from his hand—"are going to kill you."

She balled the pack in her fist. The heat that pushed her rage spread, pulsing through her until she couldn't think beyond it. She swung her fist; Jaegil winced, anticipating the blow. Miyoung pitched the cigarettes away, her wrath fueling her. The crumbled ball of cigarettes and cardboard slammed into the window of the mart beside the bus stop. The force cracked the glass, spiderweb fissures growing from the point of impact. Too late, Miyoung realized she hadn't just thrown it, but used her supernatural gumiho strength. In public.

For a few tense seconds, it seemed like maybe the window wouldn't break. Then it did, the falling glass mocking Miyoung with a delicate chorus of tinkling shards.

"Heol!" Jaegil said, his eyes wide as he looked between Miyoung and the broken window.

Her stomach dropped. This wasn't something a normal girl could do—break a solid windowpane with a ball of trash. Her eyes slid to Jihoon, who stared at the broken window with open-mouthed shock. Then the owner of the mart came running out, shouting rapid-fire curses.

"Who did this? I called the police! Who's going to pay for this?"

Hushed whispers sounded from pedestrians who'd stopped to stare.

Miyoung felt the heat of their eyes on her. Burning points into her skin like someone had lit Jaegil's cigarettes and held them to her.

It felt like the world was shattering around her just as the window had.

She tasted acidic bile as her fear turned to nausea.

"Run! Get out of here," Jihoon said.

"What?" She couldn't understand what he meant. Weren't the police coming? Wasn't she going to get arrested? Her identity would be revealed. Her mother would have to clean up her mess, again. Would Yena kill Jihoon when she found out about everything? Her fault, all her fault.

Jaegil and Seho gave shouts of alarm before they took off, the store owner chasing them down the street.

"You have to leave before the police get here." Jihoon shoved her so she stumbled a half-dozen steps away.

She let the momentum carry her, until she was jogging, then running, then sprinting.

14

JIHOON SAT IN a hard chair against a faded beige wall. A dozen police officers sat at desks placed in random jigsaw patterns around the room.

He'd only been in a police station once before, when his mother had dragged him there to shout at the officer who'd arrested his father. A bad memory compounded by his current discomfort. And the cop currently questioning him wasn't helping.

"So tell me again, how did you break the window?" It was a question Jihoon had answered at least a dozen times already.

"A rock." He kept his answers short. Less chance of getting caught in a lie that way.

"Why?"

Good question, Jihoon thought. Why *had* he decided to cover for Miyoung? It wasn't necessarily because he felt protective of Miyoung. Lord knew she didn't need someone to take care of her. Perhaps it was because he knew she'd expected him to do nothing. Jihoon wanted to show her she was wrong. That he cared about her.

Wait. Did he care about Miyoung?

Before he could dwell on that new thought, the officer spoke again. "And the kids that ran. They weren't involved?"

"No."

"Listen, kid. I don't have time for this. You're facing actual charges here."

"I know." Jihoon didn't mean to sound glib, but short answers would do that.

"I am this close to losing my temper." The officer leaned over the desk so spittle flew and hit Jihoon on the cheek.

"Officer Noh, why don't you take a break?" The detective standing beside them had a calm voice and sharp eyes. Those eyes looked like they saw everything. They worried Jihoon more than the officer's wrath could. "I'll finish this up."

The detective's desk was a cluttered mess. Files stacked haphazardly against a box that held a mix of random tchotchkes. Jihoon spotted a Lotte Giants mug, a small wooden frame with a faded picture of a baby, and a large wooden cross with scripture carved into it: "The eyes of the Lord are on the righteous, and his ears are attentive to their cry. Psalm 34:15."

Detective Hae read the file he'd taken from the officer's desk. His square jaw and salt-and-pepper hair reminded Jihoon of the distinguished actors in the period dramas Jihoon's halmeoni liked. He imagined the man wearing the large robes of a noble, yelling about the honor of the country.

"So you broke a window, and you've decided the best response is to be rude to a police officer?"

"It wasn't an active decision," Jihoon said. The detective frowned and he added, "Sir."

"Do you realize you're in a fair bit of trouble?" Detective Hae glanced down at a paper in his hand. "Ahn Jihoon."

Jihoon turned to his manners. "I understand, sir."

"The store owner also says you weren't alone."

Jihoon nodded; something about this detective made it infinitely harder to lie. "No, sir. But I've confessed."

"Yes, you are the one who's confessed." Detective Hae said this in a way that made Jihoon think the man saw right through him. "The store owner wanted to press charges." The detective spoke in a lecturing tone. Jihoon bristled at it, but kept his head bowed in respect. "However, your halmeoni was able to change his mind."

For the first time, Jihoon felt fear. His eyes darted around the police station, looking for his halmeoni with more apprehension than he'd felt at the previous officer's harsh interrogation.

The detective let out a chuckle, which brought Jihoon's eyes flying back to the man.

"It's good to see you respect her. Your halmeoni is quite a woman. It's a pity her reputation might be tarnished by this."

Now tendrils of guilt curled through Jihoon. This wouldn't affect the restaurant, would it?

Then he processed the rest of the detective's words. "You know my halmeoni?"

"I met her on my first case here. She strikes me as a good and strong woman who doesn't accept foolish behavior. I feel like any punishment your halmeoni will give is worse than what we could. Since there aren't any official charges, when she gets here you're free to leave."

Jihoon nodded and watched the door, trying not to fidget.

His phone beeped and he jumped in his seat before he glanced down at the message from Somin: I heard you're at the police station. What's going on?

Jihoon hesitated before typing back. He usually told Somin everything, but this time he couldn't. If she knew he'd taken the fall for Miyoung, she'd have questions he couldn't answer. It felt strange lying to someone who knew he wet the bed until he was seven.

Don't worry, he typed back.

She replied so quickly, he wondered if she'd pre-typed her message: Why won't you tell me? Are you mad at me? Have I done something wrong?

Guilt spread through his chest.

Don't worry, he typed again.

The message bubble floated on his screen so long he wondered what kind of book Somin could be typing. Then it disappeared. No reply.

Detective Hae closed a file with a slap and threw it on top of a dozen others. The precarious stack toppled over. Jihoon bent to pick the papers up when the words *animal attack* caught his eye. The folder was thick, stuffed with dozens of reports, maps, and photographs. The top report looked like a witness account.

Two salarymen out for drinks. Stumbling drunk. One of them decided to hop the wall around the forest and got dragged away by something.

Jihoon's mind raced as he remembered an overheard conversation the morning after he'd first met Miyoung. A detective talking to Halmeoni about an animal attack.

"That's not for you to read." Detective Hae held out his hand for the file.

Jihoon handed over the stack. "I remember you now. You came by the restaurant to warn us about the animal attacks. Did they find out what did it?"

"I can't answer questions about an ongoing investigation."

Jihoon nodded. He didn't need more answers. *Ongoing* meant that they hadn't found the culprit.

"Ahn Jihoon!"

He winced at the sound of Halmeoni's voice, forgetting the report and all thoughts of murdered salarymen. Murder seemed like nothing when faced with his halmeoni's rage.

15

MIYOUNG SLUNK INTO the house, slipping off her shoes, and let her backpack drop from her shoulder in the middle of the room. The clutter would annoy her mother, but she didn't have the energy to carry everything upstairs right now.

She dropped onto the couch, planting her face into the soft pillows. Her eyes burned with tears, and she shoved her face deeper into the pillows to catch them.

She shouldn't have left Jihoon.

He liked to do idiotic things, but that didn't mean she had to let him. He was so infuriating. She punched her fist into the pillows beside her head.

She kept remembering the anxious concern on Jihoon's face as he'd told her to run. It felt odd to think it had been for her. More unsettling was that she'd accepted his help without a second thought. In that moment, when she'd fled, she'd trusted him.

Miyoung rolled onto her back, staring at the great vaulted ceiling. Through the skylights shone the moon, days away from full. It pulled at her hunger, magnified it. So deep and painful she wanted to curl into herself.

At the sound of feet on the stairs, Miyoung sat up quickly. She smoothed out her messy hair and stood.

"Mother, you're home."

"Were you crying?" Yena stood at the base of the stairs, assessing Miyoung with sharp eyes.

"Of course not." Miyoung fought the urge to wipe her hands over her cheeks to search for tears.

"What happened?"

"Nothing." It was the first time Miyoung had blatantly lied to her mother.

Yena stood so still, Miyoung wondered if she'd somehow broken her.

"Is there anything you'd like to tell me?"

Miyoung's heart sped, and sweat beaded against her scalp despite the cool air.

"Perhaps you want to explain what this is." Yena pulled a manila envelope from her pocket.

"It's not what you think." Miyoung tried desperately to think of a way to explain herself without toppling all of the secrets she'd kept stacked away.

"What have I told you about this kind of magic?" Yena waved the envelope like a flag of shame at Miyoung.

"I need it."

"You will tell me what's going on. Now." Yena's command filled the space so there was no room for argument.

"I can't." Miyoung silently prayed her mother would let it go, just this once.

"I'll give you another chance to tell me the truth. Or so help me . . ." Yena didn't need to finish. The disappointment on her face was more powerful than a thousand threats.

"It's my bead, something's wrong—"

"I told you those don't exist," Yena said. "I don't appreciate you lying to me."

Frustration flooded Miyoung's brain. She knew they existed and she couldn't believe her mother, who'd lived for so long, wouldn't also know it. Why would Yena want to keep this from her? "I'm not lying. If you'd just listen—"

The crack of Yena's palm across Miyoung's cheek echoed through the room.

"What have I done to deserve your disrespect?"

"Nothing." Miyoung's words were muffled by the hand she held over her cheek.

Yena lifted her hand, as if to lay it on Miyoung's shoulder, but let it drop instead. "Miyoung-ah, I am hard on you because there is a part of you that is weak. It's my fault, because I was weak once, too."

Miyoung knew her mother was referring to her father. To Yena, the only thing weaker than humans was gumiho who loved them.

"I don't want to lose you." It was the closest Yena had ever come to telling Miyoung she loved her. "That's why I have my rules. I don't take your safety lightly."

"I'll be better, Mother," Miyoung promised.

"I hope you can be." Yena ripped the envelope, shredding it into confetti that fell from her hands.

Something was going on with her mother. Yena knew more about gumiho lore than Miyoung and Nara combined. She had to know fox beads were real. So why would she keep it a secret? What danger had Miyoung gotten herself into that was so bad even her mother refused to acknowledge it?

She'd find out, Miyoung thought as she watched the pieces of envelope and talisman flutter to the ground. She'd fix her mistakes, clean up her mess, and find a way to make sure her mother could trust her enough to tell her the truth.

16

JIHOON PARKED THE newly fixed scooter in front of the convenience store. The chill of the late-fall night made his cheeks red, and he wanted something hot to drink.

To say his halmeoni was upset would be an understatement. But she'd needed to run the restaurant, so it had fallen to Jihoon to retrieve the scooter from the mechanic. The errand gave him a short reprieve from her wrath.

Jihoon lingered at the case that warmed individual cans of coffee, his thoughts on things other than the toasty drinks inside. Turning toward the cold drinks, he caught a glimpse of movement outside.

Like a vision called forth by force of will, Miyoung sat at one of the plastic tables. Her head hung low so her hair covered her face.

Jihoon walked out and settled into the chair across from Miyoung.

"What are you doing here?" she asked without looking up.

"Just considering a nap, figured this would be a good place. You seem to have the same idea."

"You're hilarious." Miyoung's tone clearly expressed she thought otherwise.

"I like to think so." Jihoon leaned back. He noticed a manila envelope under her folded hands. "What's that?"

"Nothing," she muttered, pulling it to her chest before shoving it into an inner pocket of her jacket.

"Just so you know, I didn't say anything," Jihoon said. When she didn't reply, he clarified. "To the police. In case you were worried."

"You shouldn't have covered for me." She sounded more morose than mad. She looked deflated, like a sailboat on a still lake with no air to carry it. Not the Miyoung he was used to.

"It's what friends do."

"Why do you insist on this? I never asked you to be my friend."

"It's not something you ask for. It's just something that is."

"I can take care of myself."

"But you shouldn't always have to."

Miyoung finally looked up, her eyes rimmed in red. She'd been crying.

"What happened?" Jihoon had never seen her distressed, let alone brought to tears.

"Nothing." Miyoung swiped at her dry eyes as she flushed.

"You don't have to tell me anything." Jihoon kept his expression neutral. "I'll just take you home on my scooter. It's getting late."

Miyoung let her head fall onto the table. Jihoon winced at the hard *thud* of her skull against the plastic.

"I can't go home right now. She'll know what I did." Her hands clutched at her blazer. Jihoon heard the crinkle of the envelope inside.

She was making no sense, but she rarely did. Jihoon had learned not to try too hard to figure out the puzzle that was Miyoung. But he also believed he had only two choices when faced with another person's misery: ignore it or try to fix it.

Jihoon stood and retrieved an extra helmet from the scooter, walked back to Miyoung, and dropped it over her head.

"What are you doing?" Miyoung tried to pull the helmet off but Jihoon held it in place until she gave up.

"We're going for a ride. The air might help you clear your head. It usually helps me."

"My mother says men only want one thing from women after dark," Miyoung said.

Jihoon choked in surprise. "Well, that's what your mother thinks. What do you think?"

She blinked as if confused by his question.

"Give me five minutes. If you hate it, I'll bring you right back." He held out his hand. "Call?"

She stared at his palm so long he wondered if she was going to decline.

"Call."

He climbed onto the scooter and clipped his helmet shut as he waited for Miyoung to settle behind him.

"So you've agreed, then," he said as he started the scooter.

"To what?"

"That we're friends for the night. It was in the fine print. All agreements have it." He took off down the road, the sputtering scooter so loud it drowned out any reply.

At first, Miyoung sat rigid so no part of them touched. Jihoon grinned and perhaps took the next turn too sharp on purpose. His grin spread into a full-fledged smile when her arms wrapped around his waist. When she tried to pull away again, he placed a hand over hers.

"Don't be ridiculous," he said. "You have to hold on."

He felt her hesitation before she laced her fingers together.

Her arms tightened as a truck passed a little too close, horn blaring.

"Ease up on the superhuman choke holds," he called back.

"Oh, sorry." Her voice breathed into his ear, sending a spike of energy down his spine.

Their closeness hit him. Not that he didn't know she was flush against him before. But it was all he could think about now. How her chin rested lightly against his shoulder. Her hands splayed across his belly. The curves of her torso leaned into his back.

In his distracted state he almost missed the turn and took it so fast the wheels of the scooter skidded, kicking up dust and smoke that smelled of burnt rubber. But he made it onto the road leading up a steep mountainside.

As the roads climbed higher, Miyoung asked, "Where are we going?"

"Secret."

Jihoon drove until the city lights below dimmed and the stars took over. Stopping at a curve in the road, he parked along the thick shoulder that created an overlook to the city.

Miyoung pulled the helmet off, shaking her hair free. Jihoon was mesmerized by the snaking movement of raven tendrils as they fell across her shoulders, fine silk floating over the pressed uniform blazer.

"Where are we?" she asked.

"Huh?" He blinked and realized he'd been staring. "It's where I come whenever the city is too loud or I just need to think." Jihoon worked on releasing the tension from his body, willing it to sift away with the wind that pulled at his jacket.

The city lay before them, the buildings scattered toward the horizon. Skyscrapers reached toward the heavens, built so high they looked as tall as the mountains beyond. "Ten minutes up here and you'll forget what was bothering you."

"I doubt it," Miyoung said, but she took in the view. "How did you find this place?"

"My father brought me here once." One of Jihoon's only good memories of the man.

"Jaegil said he was a criminal."

The words weren't said with judgment but they still made Jihoon tense.

"He's one to talk. His father isn't a gem either. Everyone knows he works as muscle for one of the local gangs."

"Explains why Jaegil's such a bully." Miyoung sighed at the vicious cycle of violence passed down from parent to child. "When did your father leave?"

The question surprised him. Usually people skirted the topic of his parents' abandonment.

"When I was four. My mother didn't want to raise a kid alone, so she decided the best thing to do was leave, too. They were actually perfect for each other. Always thinking of themselves no matter the consequences." He let out a sigh, rubbing at the knots in his stomach.

"Parents can be selfish," Miyoung mused.

"Are you talking about your father?"

"Why do you ask that?"

"Because you said he left you. I wondered if it bothers you." He hesitated, then added, "Like it bothers me."

She looked out toward the city; her silence seemed to indicate the topic upset her. But then she spoke. "I never met my father. My mother said he left before I was born. So I guess I never had an image of him. I don't even know who I'd be mad at. Like trying to throw darts without a target."

Jihoon frowned. It was strange to imagine. Would it have been easier if he'd never met his parents before they abandoned him? If he could, would he want to give up the few memories they'd left him with?

Miyoung walked to the ledge, her toes peeking precariously over.

"Careful," Jihoon said.

She shot him a dismissive look. "I don't need a boy to keep me safe."

"I don't think you're going to fall because you're a girl," Jihoon said, equal parts chastised and defensive. "I think you could fall because as far as I know, gumiho can't fly."

"It's hard for me to take you seriously when you make a joke out of everything."

"Looking at life with humor doesn't mean I don't take it seriously. You need to be able to laugh at things, even the sad scary stuff sometimes."

"I don't get you."

"You say that like it's a problem for you." Jihoon joined her at the edge, staring out toward the lights that marked the city.

"It's not," she said, so forcefully he thought she was mad at him. "Or it wouldn't be if you left me alone."

"Does it really bother you that much? That I want to be friends?"

"I don't need friends. I belong alone."

"I don't believe you. No one belongs alone."

"Since I'm not really human, I don't care about human concerns. Like being wanted or having friends."

"For a non-human you have very human reactions. You must be a good liar."

She shoved her hands into her pockets. "Lying is how I survive."

"Well, good thing we're up here all alone. So no one can hear if you accidentally tell the truth." His words were light, but even as he spoke he realized how much he wanted to know the real Miyoung. She had so many secrets. Jihoon wondered if that was all that held her together.

"I'll go first," he said. "I don't think you're pretty."

A frown planted itself firmly on Miyoung's face. "I thought you were going to tell the truth."

"I am. Your face is beautiful, but you're empty. You never let anyone see past the surface, because you think that's all they want to see. You're fake and that's not pretty."

"If people saw what I really am, they'd hate me."

"That's not true. I saw you." *And you were beautiful,* he wanted to add, but didn't. He had a feeling physical compliments didn't go far with Miyoung.

"Not all of me," she whispered.

"I see more than you think," Jihoon insisted. "Do you realize you recoil from people in the hallway? It makes the other kids think you're disgusted by them, so they react to that, not to you as a person or gumiho or whatever. How could they when that's all you let them see?"

Miyoung opened her mouth, as if ready to rain a storm of fury on him. Instead, she turned away.

Jihoon wondered if he'd gone too far. Usually, he didn't worry about saying the exact thing on his mind. This time, he felt regret when he saw the hurt flash underneath Miyoung's anger.

"I think there's more to you," Jihoon tried to clarify. "I heard you helped Changwan this afternoon."

"Because I hate bullies."

"See? You're a better person than you give yourself credit for."

Miyoung rolled her eyes. "Stopping bad people doesn't make me a good one."

Jihoon wanted to take her by the shoulders and shake her. "Then why did you save my life?"

Miyoung let out a bitter laugh. "Do you know what I was doing before I saved you? I was sucking out a man's gi."

Jihoon winced, but held his ground. He couldn't be wrong about her. He knew she wasn't evil and he refused to treat her like a monster. "Sucking out his gi? Like a vampire?"

Miyoung let out a frustrated sigh. "It's like siphoning energy. It's slow but it's like falling asleep."

"I knew it," Jihoon said.

"Knew what?" Miyoung frowned.

"It's because you care," Jihoon said. "You would never rip a man apart like that body the police found."

Miyoung was quiet a moment and Jihoon thought perhaps he'd lost her, but she finally replied. "No, that was my mother. I can't do that."

"Was he a bad man?" Jihoon asked. "The one whose gi you took?"

"Why would you assume that?"

"Just something you said." *Stopping bad people doesn't make me a good one.*

"He was bad. He'd hurt someone innocent."

"How do you—"

"Can we talk about something else?" Miyoung interrupted him. "You promised coming up here would make me feel *better*."

"Oh, sure," Jihoon said, cursing himself for pushing things. He glanced out toward the city. "Sometimes when I come up here, I pretend to stick a pin into a place I want to go. Kind of like a 3-D map."

"Okay," Miyoung said with a hum, considering the landscape, then pointed. "There. The Han River."

"The whole Han River?" Jihoon asked.

"Well, not all of it. But I've always wanted to walk along one of those paths by the river, maybe ride a bike, and sit by the water. It must feel good during the summertime."

Jihoon noted the longing in her voice. "You like the water?"

"No. I'm actually terrified."

"Really?" Jihoon asked.

"Yeah, I always have been. My mother once enrolled me in swimming lessons when I was five but I wouldn't even go into the pool. At first I thought it must be part of my gumiho side, but Yena doesn't seem to have any problem with water. So it's just another way I'm weaker than her."

"Why are you telling me this?"

"You said I'm empty. I'm filling in the void."

Jihoon nodded. "I guess we all have our phobias."

"What's yours?"

"Frogs," he answered immediately.

"Frogs?" Miyoung gave him an incredulous look.

"They're slimy and their back legs are disproportionately strong. It's creepy." He shuddered.

That got a laugh out of Miyoung and softened the mood. Exactly what Jihoon intended.

Her nose scrunched, and her eyes became half-moons that sparkled with humor.

"There it is," he murmured. "That's pretty."

Her mouth dropped open, then snapped closed, as if she meant to reply but thought better of it. Her eyes stayed on his, taking his measure. He could almost see the wheels turning in her head, trying to figure him out.

"We should get back," Miyoung said, starting back toward the scooter.

17

MIYOUNG WASN'T SURE if she was prepared to go home just yet. A new talisman was nestled in her pocket next to her bead. Two lies she kept from her mother. Lies she didn't want to think about right now.

Jihoon parked behind a short square building. The savory scent of doenjang jjigae permeated the air. It was a simple dish, but no Korean could smell it and not feel comforted.

"Where are we?" Miyoung swung off the scooter.

Before Jihoon answered, a voice called out. "Have I been replaced, Jihoon-ah?"

Jihoon chuckled and called back to the old halmeoni sitting on a wooden platform across the street. "Never, you'll always be my number one."

"She's a yeowu."

Jihoon and Miyoung both froze, exchanging shocked looks.

"A foxy girl," the halmeoni said with an amused cackle. "Very pretty."

Jihoon let out a relieved breath. "Yes, she is."

They both turned when the back door of the restaurant crashed open.

"Jihoon-ah! Where have you been?" An elderly woman stood framed in the doorway. Her hands were folded firmly across her chest. Her hair was a shock of white. Her face wrinkled in stern lines.

This was not a woman to cross.

"Halmeoni, this is Miyoung. She's a new transfer student in our class." Jihoon pushed Miyoung forward, ducking behind her like a shield.

"What did I tell you about pushing people?" Halmeoni asked, whipping a rag out of her apron and smacking him with it. Her aim was so precise that Miyoung felt the wind from the rag without feeling the sting of it herself.

Jihoon raced around to Miyoung's other side, trying to escape, but his halmeoni followed, surprisingly spry.

Miyoung was fascinated at the display. Usually, when faced with a guest, people were painstakingly polite. Hiding their family drama behind a facade of bright smiles. Not this family. Jihoon's halmeoni beat on him with the rag while he shouted out in protest.

"I swear, Ahn Jihoon, you are enough to age me ten years in one day. First you get arrested and then you disappear all night? Do you want me to have a heart attack?" From her booming question, Miyoung doubted this was a woman who'd succumb to any ailment easily.

"I was detained, not arrested," Jihoon argued, and his halmeoni's eyes narrowed. Even Miyoung was afraid of how she'd reply.

"Later, Ahn Jihoon. I will deal with you later." Halmeoni smiled at Miyoung, a lightning change in mood. "I suspect you're hungry."

Miyoung was surprised by the quick shift from anger to hospitality but she remembered to bow in belated greeting. "No, I'm fine."

"Nonsense, you're a teenager. Teenagers are always hungry." Halmeoni shuffled back inside, giving Miyoung no chance to refuse again.

"Come on." Jihoon pulled Miyoung's arm toward the restaurant.

"I think I should go," Miyoung said, though the aroma from inside made her mouth water.

"Just let her feed you. She'll never let you leave until you eat."

"Are you sure you don't want to use me as a way to delay your punishment?"

"Of course I do, so be a good friend and let me." Jihoon gave her a crooked grin and her heart wavered. She should have corrected him, told him they weren't friends, but for some reason she didn't. It seemed odd that a month ago she hadn't known this boy existed and now she almost yearned for his company.

The cramped restaurant was unimpressive. The yellowing linoleum was cracked; the water filter gave a sad gurgle in the corner. Under a single fluorescent light, a small table was set for dinner. Steaming bowls of doenjang jjigae filled the room with the salty scent of bean paste.

Miyoung's chair rocked a bit on uneven legs as she sat.

When Halmeoni walked out with an extra bowl of jjigae in her hands, Miyoung jumped up and took it to set on the table.

"Good girl." Halmeoni patted her firmly on the rear in approval.

Miyoung froze. She'd never received such casual affection before. And she was woefully unpracticed in how to keep her composure.

"So you recently moved to town?" Halmeoni asked, sitting.

"Yes, with my mother," Miyoung said as she took her seat again.

"And your father? What does he do?"

"He's not with us." Miyoung lowered her head.

"Oh, I'm sorry for your loss," Halmeoni said, her smile sympathetic.

"He's not dead." Miyoung bristled at the assumption. "He just left."

Jihoon's halmeoni continued, unfazed. "Well, dear, sometimes the universe works in odd ways, but family does not always come about through blood."

Unable to find a reply, Miyoung spooned up a bite. Jihoon's halmeoni placed a piece of meat on top. Such a simple gesture. One Miyoung had witnessed in a thousand dramas. One of someone who cared for another. Miyoung shoved the bite into her mouth despite the tightness in her throat.

Jihoon glanced up and met Miyoung's eyes with his, giving her a wide grin. He had kimchi stuck in his teeth. And she hated that it made his goofy smile even more endearing.

Jihoon and his halmeoni moved with such consideration of each other, a lifetime of learned behavior. She spooned some of her meat into his bowl. He nudged the cucumber kimchi closer to her before she reached for it.

Jihoon laid a hand over his halmeoni's as he ate. His thumb moved back and forth over the thin skin of her knuckles. Miyoung wondered if he even realized he did it.

How could two people go from shouting in the street to sharing such a loving meal? They were so at ease with their love. They fought and laughed and adored each other so openly.

Her throat tightened on a wave of emotion, and she choked on her next bite. Jihoon and his halmeoni looked at her curiously. Her eyes filled, and she ducked her head low over her bowl to hide the tears as they fell.

It hurt to see such love when she'd never received it herself. Like picking at a wound after she'd long grown a callus over it. And now it lay open and fresh. A feeling of being so hollow, Miyoung wondered if she'd ever be able to fill the empty space again.

o o o

After dinner, Miyoung offered to do the dishes to escape and organize her thoughts.

A drama played on the small television in the corner as she filled the sink with suds. The sound of an argument between two characters spun out of the speakers to join her bitter mood.

Jihoon pushed through the door with the last of the dirty dishes.

She wanted to tell him to leave. Her pain had translated into annoyance, and he was her main target.

Before she had a chance to banish him, he pulled on the second pair of gloves and started washing alongside her.

Miyoung dug her teeth into the inside of her mouth. As she tasted the copper flavor of blood, she forced herself to relax, trying to let go of her anger with it. She might as well let him help. His hands were already submerged in the water, scrubbing at a giant pot.

"What's it about?" Jihoon nodded toward the television.

Miyoung considered ignoring him, but knew he'd badger her until she replied.

The scene showed the heroine driving down a dark road on her way to sacrifice herself for the man she loved. Miyoung shook her head at the foolishness of martyrdom.

"She's poor and he's rich. His family doesn't want them to be together. I think she's going to get into an accident this episode.

She'll get amnesia or something, and they'll be separated for a while."

"If his family doesn't approve, why do they need to create another arbitrary reason to separate the two?"

"Because it adds drama."

"If you can predict the show, why watch?"

"It's company." Miyoung shrugged.

"Company?"

"When you don't have friends, it's nice to fill the space with noise, even if it's just the television."

"Is that really enough? They're just dramas," Jihoon said as the sound of a car crash radiated from the speakers. The ebb and flow of sweeping music accompanied the slow-motion disaster on-screen. "It's not real life."

"I prefer fictional life. Things in the outside world are too messy." Miyoung gestured toward the cluster of police and emergency workers dealing with the accident. "I need to be in control. It's safer that way."

The hero ran through the mess of cars. He was held back by an officer as he sobbed out the heroine's name. The cameras pulled out to show the enormity of the hero's desperation as his voice joined the sounds of sirens. The next scene held the caption: FIVE YEARS LATER. Miyoung almost wished she wasn't able to predict these shows so well.

"Safer for whom?" Jihoon asked.

Miyoung stared at him as the swell of the theme song surrounded them, lyrics of love lost and hearts broken. An unhappy song for an unhappy story.

"Why does it matter?" she asked.

"It matters to me."

His words shouldn't have caused the skip in her pulse. They shouldn't have shot a thrill of pleasure through her. But they did. For the first time in her life, Miyoung's control over her heart wavered. Or maybe she had never had control over it at all.

"You ask too many questions," she said.

Jihoon sighed in resignation. "I'll walk you home."

o o o

It was drizzling lightly when they stepped outside.

Jihoon asked her to wait while he ran back in for an umbrella.

Miyoung debated leaving, but she waited and wasn't quite sure why. Instead, she stood in the rain, closing her eyes as she let it fall unfettered onto her cheeks. It was cool against her skin and brought the smells of the street to her. Dirt and concrete and leaves.

"It's nice out when it rains." Jihoon's halmeoni stepped out the back door, wrapping her coat around her in a tight hug. She'd tied a scarf over her hair, and it protected her from the drizzle.

"Soon it'll be snow." Miyoung put out her hand to catch the cold droplets.

"Big things always happen at the first snow."

Miyoung waited for Jihoon's halmeoni to elaborate but instead she said, "My Jihoonie, he doesn't make friends easily."

Miyoung glanced over, frowning in confusion. "Everyone at school really likes him." She didn't know why she said it. Perhaps to comfort Jihoon's halmeoni.

"I'm glad. He's kind and sweet, but he doesn't trust easily. Not after his mother left."

Miyoung held her tongue. She didn't want to ask, but she was curious about this story.

"When Jihoon first came to live with me, he was such a quiet child. Sometimes he wouldn't speak for days. It worried me."

Miyoung pursed her lips to hold in a laugh of surprise. She'd never have thought the gabby Jihoon was ever quiet.

"I worry about how he lived in the first four years of his life. And I'm ashamed that I let it go on for as long as it did. I wanted to fix that for them. Him and his mother. But she needed something more. And leaving was the best she could do at the time."

"How is a mother leaving a child a good thing?" Yena might be cold, but one thing Miyoung always knew was her mother would never abandon her.

"Just because something doesn't seem right to most, doesn't mean it's not right for you. You get that, don't you?"

Halmeoni had the same observant eyes as her grandson. It was worrisome to Miyoung.

"Jihoon thinks the best way to live is to keep everyone at a distance. He hides it well, too well. But he sees something in you. It might not seem it, but it's a rare gift he's giving you, his friendship."

"I didn't ask for it." Miyoung felt as if gravity had increased, pushing down on her, a heavy weight she didn't want.

"It's not something you ask for, that's why it's a gift."

Why did these two insist on believing in her? Why couldn't they just let her be?

"I'm not worth it." She closed her fist and the rain in her palm slipped between her fingers.

"That's not for you to decide either."

Was there something in Halmeoni's look that implied she knew more than she let on?

The door behind them opened with a loud clang.

"Halmeoni, you shouldn't be out in the rain." Jihoon rushed

forward to hold the umbrella over her, the same one Miyoung had given him in the playground. Somehow that made her fidget with discomfort.

"Don't fret about me." Halmeoni grinned, patting Jihoon's cheek before stepping to the door. "Walk this girl home." She captured Miyoung's eyes with her own. "You stay safe."

"What was that about?" Jihoon asked as the door closed.

"Nothing," Miyoung lied. Heaven save her from observant humans and their nosiness.

She started down the path without waiting for Jihoon. His shoes slapped against the damp pavement as he jogged to catch up.

Jihoon stood so close his shoulder bumped hers, and Miyoung tried to scoot away.

"Don't be a baby." Jihoon stepped closer again.

"The umbrella is too small."

"Which is why you should be grateful I'm sharing it," Jihoon said.

"It's *my* umbrella."

"I thought it was a gift." Jihoon blinked innocently, an exaggeration that made Miyoung want to laugh. So she frowned instead.

A breeze swept against the umbrella, pushing it back so the moon came into full view. The sight of it made Miyoung's stomach clench. Her hunger was twice what it should be. A reminder that without her bead inside of her to hold the energy, she was losing strength too quickly.

She lowered her eyes to the shining asphalt.

"Does it affect you now?" Jihoon asked, and she knew he referred to the moon.

"I can always feel it." Miyoung tried to ignore the pains running through her muscles like wild horses, a reminder that something was missing inside. She shoved her hands into her jacket, tightening her fingers around the yeowu guseul. It warmed against her palm, a small comfort in the cold. "My mother says gumiho are always women because we gain our power from the moon."

"And what is a man?" Jihoon asked.

"Dinner." She chuckled as Jihoon stopped short, giving her a raised brow.

"Myth says men are the sun and the moon is his wife," Miyoung said. "The moon and the sun both live in the sky but they are not together."

"It's just a fable."

"I live in a world of fables."

"But you live in the human world, too. You go to school. You do homework. You ride the bus."

Miyoung heard a note of frustration in Jihoon's voice, but couldn't decipher why.

"My mother thinks it best I learn to naturally assimilate. What better crash course in the pitfalls of humanity than public school?"

Jihoon gave a hearty laugh, his dimples deepening. The sound of it warmed her.

"Well, it's working. Hating school is as normal as you can get."

"I don't hate school." Miyoung sighed. In fact, she loved it. Learning new things, being able to pretend she could have such basic problems as homework and tests. "But school comes with kids, a lot of them. And gumiho don't do well in crowds."

"Why?"

"In all the old folktales, we lived in mountains, feeding off travelers. There's a reason for that."

Jihoon nodded, and the lack of disgust on his face encouraged her.

"People don't travel cross-country by foot anymore. So we need to be where the people live. But the more people we're around, the more likely someone will figure us out."

"Is that so bad?"

Of course he would ask, but not everyone was like Jihoon.

"My mother knew a gumiho once. She believed we could be honest with those we loved. Perhaps they only feared the myth of the gumiho because they'd only been shown the monstrous sides of us. After all, if they loved us when they thought we were human, shouldn't they love us no matter what?"

"And?" Jihoon asked, leaning forward, curiosity clear on his face.

"Let's just say it didn't end well for that gumiho." Miyoung didn't feel like rehashing the doomed tale. "Crowds can become mobs very easily."

"People get scared when you eat them." Jihoon shrugged. And though the words should have upset Miyoung, they didn't because he said them so matter-of-factly. No judgment, just truth. Patented Jihoon.

"If I don't feed every month, I'll die. Maybe it's selfish to choose myself over so many others, but what choice would you make?"

Jihoon frowned and she knew she'd gotten him with that question.

"You really can't find another way?"

A weight pulled on Miyoung's heart. Of course he'd ask. He was probably afraid of that part of her nature. And she couldn't blame him, though it hurt more than she was expecting. She gripped her bead tighter. "If I stop absorbing gi for a hundred days, I'll die. I trade human energy for my life and for immortality."

"Oh yeah," Jihoon said, eyeing Miyoung. "I've been meaning to ask how old . . ." He trailed off with a conflicted purse of his lips.

"Are you asking me if I'm an old lady in an eighteen-year-old body?"

"Well, since *you* bring it up."

"I'm really only eighteen."

"And your mother?"

"She's older than the country we know now."

"She sounds formidable," Jihoon said with a grin. "No wonder you never have friends over."

She smiled, leaning her head back to glance up at him. She hadn't realized they stood so close. The umbrella left little room between them. Jihoon stood hunched a bit as he held the umbrella low over them both. At this angle, with her chin tilted, their faces were exactly lined up. Eye to eye, nose to nose, mouth to mouth.

He smelled of salt and rain, with just a hint of something smooth beneath. The scent of his skin, sweet like cream. It made it hard for her to think.

Miyoung gave herself a mental pep talk. *You are Gu Yena's daughter. You are strong. You are beautiful. You are smart. You will not be shaken.*

It didn't work.

She wanted to let herself give in to the warm feeling spreading through her belly. It was a sensation she'd never experienced before and all she knew was she wanted to hold on to it a bit longer.

Men only want one thing from us, her mother's voice echoed.

She took a step back, retreating from Jihoon's unblinking gaze. When he looked at her like that, it made her think he saw right through her. Down to all of the secrets even she had never explored. It terrified and thrilled her at the same time.

Her senses went into overdrive. She took another step back to escape the overwhelming energy. A horn blared and she blinked as headlights barreled toward her. Why was a car on the sidewalk?

Jihoon swooped his arms around her, spinning them so quickly, her head continued to turn even as they stopped. The horn blasted as the car sped by, missing them by centimeters.

Jihoon hugged her tightly, his heart jackrabbiting against her ears, her face buried in his chest. She smelled laundry detergent, faint on his shirt. His hand trembled as he stroked her hair. And the white noise finally cleared from her ears.

"—can't believe you wouldn't look where you're stepping, babo-ya."

The shock of the moment blended with the realization Jihoon held her so close that his body heat permeated her skin.

Miyoung sensed his gi below the surface. The feel of it was warmth and weight and comfort. And her hunger reached for it. She yearned to absorb it, to fill herself with it.

She jerked away, pushing Jihoon so hard he stumbled back four steps. Rain plastered her hair to her face but did nothing to cool her heated skin.

"Don't come closer," she said when Jihoon made to step toward her. "Stay away from me."

"Okay." Jihoon held up his hands as if to prove he wasn't a threat. She almost laughed at how ludicrous that was.

"Being around me puts your life at risk."

"So you always say."

She scowled at his flippant tone. "Then why aren't you running?"

"Running takes way too much effort." He gave a cheeky grin.

Miyoung didn't want to feel the tight grip on her heart. The one that told her how important this boy had become to her despite her efforts to reject him. "You said you don't lie, but you're lying now."

"Maybe," he began, low and uncharacteristically serious. "I'm not running because I've had people run away from me."

"You mean like your mother?" It was unnecessarily cruel, but did the job, as Jihoon's eyes darkened and he took a step away. Finally retreating. It was what she wanted, she told herself as she left him alone on the dark sidewalk.

Cold leached into her skin. He body ached. Like the chilled rain sapped all of her energy. But that wasn't the cause of her exhaustion. It was wanting something so badly that walking away took all of her strength.

NOT ALL PREDATORS are monsters. But if you beat them enough, they'll bite.

This was a lesson learned by a small village in the late nineteenth century.

Empress Myeongseong, known as Queen Min, sought to bring modernization to Joseon.

During that time lived a gumiho. She chose to reside in a small town that climbed one of the craggy mountains scattered across the country. Though most gumiho lived a nomadic life, she'd fallen in love with her isolated village and the people in it. So she made it her permanent home.

She learned the name of every neighbor. She played with their children. She helped harvest crops.

She never chose her victims from the humans she lived among, for she'd learned to love them. Instead she traveled far each full moon to feed.

Queen Min embraced the progressive movement. She sought to open Joseon to new ideals, new technology, and new religions.

The gumiho saw hope in this movement. Perhaps, without the dark superstitions previously woven through gumiho myths, she could trust those she loved with her secrets. After all, those that told tales of the evils of her kind also told of the power of love.

And one day, she decided to tell the people her true identity.

She chose to tell the most respected elder first, hoping he would influence the town.

When he turned her away, the village did as well. They came to her home that night with sword and stone. They ripped her small hanok apart. But their blades did not kill her.

She fled, crazed from betrayal and pain. They hunted her, combing the mountains and fields for days before giving her up for dead and returning to their lives. The gumiho was alone and abandoned and broken. And the village went back to harvesting their crops and raising their children. Nothing changed for them after they chased her away, and seeing this, the gumiho's rage consumed her heart.

The next full moon, she came back and visited every home. With a swipe of claw and rip of flesh, she pulled the liver from every villager.

The final hanok was the home of the elder who'd turned on her. As she tore at his front door, shamans emerged, cutting her down with their magic, ripping her soul from her body. And she was cast into the afterlife chased by her own bitterness.

18

THE FULL MOON brought with it a tension that pressed on Miyoung's chest. One that came with anticipation and anxiety. She needed tonight to go well. She needed to find her balance again and she'd convinced herself she would when the bead was back in place.

She trotted down the stairs, not wanting to be late meeting Nara. But she came up short when she saw her mother in the foyer with a suitcase.

"You're going somewhere? Tonight?" *At the full moon?*

"Yes, I have an important trip I can't avoid any longer."

"But I need . . ." Miyoung trailed off. She didn't know what she wanted from Yena, only that she felt better when her mother was around. And tonight was so important.

"I'll be away for a few days, a week at most," Yena said.

"Why?" Miyoung asked before she could stop herself.

"Business." Yena's cold tone was proof that Miyoung had misstepped. Miyoung actually had no idea what her mother's business was, only that Yena had lived long enough to make a lot of money and that Miyoung had never wanted for any material things. That was why, as a child, she'd wondered why her mother still needed to work at all. So one day, she asked Yena why she went away so often, and her mother had replied that she was looking for something. The vague answer was patented Yena. She never gave up anything she didn't want to.

"You will behave while I'm gone." It was more command than request.

"Of course." Miyoung bowed low, staying that way until she heard the door shut behind her mother.

After she watched her mother's cab pull away, Miyoung made her way into the forest. The path to her meeting place with Nara was narrow, the stairs made of worn stone that gave way to dirt and rock.

The moon felt fuller than full tonight, like an overfilled balloon ready to burst. Only, Miyoung was the one that might explode. Her skin itched like a thousand bugs crawled over her body. Her stomach turned somersaults, as if warning her that she was running perilously low on gi. She needed to finish the ceremony and feed. Once she fed she'd feel better.

She found Nara at the base of a gnarled tree that had lost all of its leaves to late fall. The moon peeked through the naked branches to cast twisted shadows on the shaman as she set up an altar. On a small wooden table sat a copper bowl filled with water and a bowl of sand holding lit incense.

"I'm almost ready," Nara said, without looking up.

"Will it be quick?"

"The ceremony will." Nara bit her lip, checking a list of hastily written notes.

Miyoung accepted the half answer. She understood they were both in uncharted territory.

"Sit."

"How did you learn about this ceremony?" Miyoung asked as she sat across from Nara. The question was innocent enough, but it brought sadness to Nara's eyes.

"My mother wrote about it in one of her journals. She loved to study other faiths and beliefs from our history. My halmeoni said it made her a better shaman."

Miyoung noted Nara's grief. The yearning of a girl who'd never known the people who bore her.

"I'm sure she'd be proud of you. Both of your parents would." It was a generic platitude, but the best Miyoung could come up with.

"All I can do is try my hardest to live up to their memory." Determination brightened Nara's face. And Miyoung thought that this Nara with her strong eyes and set mouth was beautiful.

"Let's begin." The shaman took deep breaths, her eyes still glued to the paper in her hand. "Do you have the talisman?"

Miyoung pulled it out, handing the envelope to Nara. The talisman looked no different from the yellow bujeoks Nara made in her own shop.

The young shaman started to chant. Words that called forth the energy of yin and yang. She spoke of clean water and pure form. She chanted about fire as she lit the talisman, letting the ash fall into the water-filled bowl.

When the talisman had burned away, Nara swirled the bowl of water slowly. The ash had mixed with it, turning the water opaque gray.

Nara dipped her fingers in and reached forward. Miyoung jerked back.

"Stay still," Nara commanded, so stern that it surprised

Miyoung. The shaman rubbed her ash-covered fingers on Miyoung's eyelids and forehead.

A dozen questions perched on Miyoung's tongue, but she swallowed them as Nara held out the bowl. "Drink."

The water still smelled of fire and smoke.

"Drink," Nara repeated.

The liquid was warmer than Miyoung expected, as if the flame still lived within the ashes of the talisman. As she sipped, she fought the urge to gag. She couldn't swallow the next gulp, and she coughed so hard she worried she'd vomit.

"You must drink it all." There was urgency in Nara's voice.

The next sip tore at her as she swallowed. Bits of talisman stuck to her innards, scraping against her. She doubled over with the pain. The bowl fell from her shaking hands, spilling in the dirt.

"No!" Nara shouted, scrambling forward. But there was nothing for her to salvage.

Miyoung could barely breathe past the agony. Her insides were alight with bright embers that spread through her organs. "What did you do?" Even her voice scraped her throat, like she breathed fire instead of words.

"You should have swallowed it all," Nara said. Panic laced her voice. "I don't know what will happen now."

Shadows wavered and danced. Miyoung wasn't sure if it was the sway of the trees or her own dimming vision. She stumbled to her feet and almost fell when her legs started to buckle.

"Seonbae!" Nara shouted in alarm.

"Don't touch me."

Miyoung's ears buzzed. Her head spun. Her muscles twitched.

Nara scrambled to her feet. "Seonbae, your bead. Where is it?"

"Leave me alone!" she shouted at nothing, at everything.

Miyoung raced away. Branches scratched at her cheeks. Roots raised out of the ground to trip her. Through some miracle, she kept her footing and sprinted through the forest that had, for the first time, become terrifying to her.

She couldn't see. What was in that talisman?

The shadows chased her. And she knew she couldn't let them catch her.

Miyoung broke out of the trees, bursting into the glare of city lights. She swerved to avoid running into traffic. The garbled sounds of cars and people were making her head spin. So she stumbled until she found a side alley, not caring where she'd ended up. The buildings were cracked and stained, built so close that there was hardly space between the crumbling apartments. Rusted doors hanging on squeaking hinges and bars covering windows. The smell of human stink filled her nostrils and she almost gagged.

A door slammed open; a shouted argument rang into the street. Miyoung kept to the shadows, not wanting anyone to see her in this state. She had no idea what she looked like. What if her tails were visible?

And still as she stumbled along the road, shadowy figures followed her, she could sense them stalking her. They whispered to her. Taunted her as she hobbled with no sense of direction.

Killer.

Murderer.

Monster!

"No," she said in a hoarse whisper. "Leave me alone!"

She stumbled over her own feet, slamming into a trash can and falling with a clatter.

She covered her head with her arms, hoping it would keep the shadows at bay, but a door opened and light slanted over the asphalt beside her. She scurried back, hoping whoever it was hadn't seen her.

"Who's there?" The voice was angry and gravelly, slurred with drink. "Boy! Come out here!"

"Yes, Abeoji?"

Miyoung squinted at the familiar voice.

"Didn't I tell you to put the lid on the trash can securely, otherwise stray dogs would get in?"

"I did." She recognized it now. Jung Jaegil. Which meant the man grabbing him by the collar was his father.

"Well, you obviously didn't!" A *thud* and a grunt. Jaegil crashed into the door frame, his hand covering his cheek where his father's fist had connected.

"Useless boy!" the man said. "I'll do it myself. Need to go out for more beer anyway."

The door slammed shut, taking the light with it. Shuffling steps approached Miyoung.

Here he comes. Ripe for the taking.

Was that her own thoughts? Or those shadow voices? She didn't really care as she realized she was starving. Hunger overshadowed the fear and pain she'd been experiencing seconds earlier.

Boots crunched against gravel and Miyoung's mouth watered.

Can you taste him?

She shifted onto her feet, crouched beside the toppled trash cans.

Rip him apart. It's what you were made for.

A boot collided with her shoe.

"Wha—"

She didn't give him a chance to finish the word. Rising from her hiding place, she grabbed him by the throat. His eyes bulged in surprise. They were already bloodshot from drink, his face ruddy from a long life lived the wrong way.

He's scum, she told herself. *He beats his son. He's a bad man.*

She squeezed his throat as he clawed at her hand. She could already taste his gi before she opened herself to it. Siphoning so quickly that he let out a scream of agony. She'd never taken energy so fast before. She never knew she could cause someone pain like this.

"Abeoji?" The door opened again and Jaegil stood there, looking out into the darkness.

And Miyoung froze. What was she doing? This wasn't another one of her criminals and murderers. He was just a drunk. He was someone's father.

She dropped the man, now unconscious, but she saw his chest rise and fall. He was alive.

She slunk away, turning the corner and taking off in a sprint.

I didn't mean it, she told herself. *I'm not a monster.*

Yes, you did. Yes, you are.

Miyoung spun around at the voice. Had someone seen her?

"Hello?" she called into the night.

Shadows danced in her vision, dark shapes that twisted and turned.

"What are you?" she shouted.

The shadows converged, becoming columns of smoke filled

with faces. A tornado of spirits, all the men whose lives had been taken by Miyoung.

They accused her with their eyes. Their gaping mouths emitting a chorus of screams.

The ghosts of her past had finally broken free from her mind and swirled around her. Was this her punishment for living through death? She covered her ears with her hands to drown out the warbling sound of their voices. And when that didn't work, she ran.

TO KNOW WHY the fox was cursed with a murderous fate, we must go back to the first gumiho.

A symbol of wood and tree, the liver feeds the fire that is the heart.

Everything in the body passes through the liver. It detoxifies the chemicals and metabolizes drugs. The liver is the only organ in the human body that can regenerate itself.

This process involves a lot of gi.

The fox did not begin by eating the livers of men.

As with any tragedy or curse, it came about because she loved.

When the first gumiho came to be, she lived off the gi she had gained over her long life.

Though in her later years she grew weary from her travels. She wished to settle in one place, to find a true home. It was then that she met two very different men.

One was a sansin, a mountain god, who would visit her every night to profess his love.

However, she had given her heart to a mortal man and wished to become human for him.

The sansin claimed to know of a way for her to become fully human. He offered the knowledge to her as proof of his love.

He told her to eat a hundred livers of a hundred men and absorb their gi. If she did this in a hundred days, then she would get her wish.

The fox did as she was told, devouring the livers of a hundred men.

On the hundredth day, she visited the home of the man she loved.

He awoke to see her washed in the light of the moon.

He cringed in fear of her. For she wasn't human, but half woman–half demon. Her nine tails wove around her as symbols of her true form. Her soul was now shrouded in shadows, a sign of the evil deeds she had committed.

He denied her love. The gi she'd devoured fueled her despair and she lashed out, killing him in a blind rage.

Heartbroken, she went to the sansin.

He gazed upon her with cold eyes. "You shunned my love. Now you are cursed to roam the earth as a demon. You feasted on the livers of men and you have lost your soul. The gi from those men will make you live forever as a yokwe, a monster, a beast. No mortal man will ever love you. And all who come after you will be cursed with the same fate."

So the fox became a woman, and the woman became a demon.

And she lived forever as a gumiho.

19

JIHOON STOOD OUTSIDE the pristine white door for ten minutes before he gathered the courage to ring the bell.

No one answered.

He glanced up. It was just as beautiful and haunting as the last time he was here, to deliver food to Miyoung.

And he wouldn't be here now except Miyoung had been absent from school since the last full moon. It had been a long week of thinking of Miyoung. Of worrying about her. Of remembering that night in the rain. That night, by the side of the road, drenched, he'd been tempted to kiss her. He'd wanted to see if she'd taste like rain. He suspected it was more likely she'd taste like lightning.

He knocked again to no answer. He had started back to his scooter when the door opened.

Miyoung looked gaunt, like she'd lost ten pounds in the last seven days. Her eyes were covered with oversized sunglasses, and her hair was gathered in a messy bun that didn't hide the fact that it was tangled with knots.

"Miyoung-ah?" Jihoon reached for her.

She jerked away, her breath coming in short, quick gasps.

"Are you real?" she whispered.

"What?" Jihoon asked, moving closer. Now he could see her shoulders shook.

Miyoung cleared her throat, and her voice came out stronger this time. "Jihoon." She took a deep breath like his name had anchored her. "What are you doing here?"

"I was worried?" he said it like a question, knowing that Miyoung wouldn't like it.

"I'm fine. I actually have somewhere to be." She made to move past him, but he blocked her path.

She was shaking so hard, he was surprised her teeth didn't rattle with the movement.

"What's going on? Does this have to do with that bead?"

Miyoung hissed out a breath and tried to shove his hands away. Surprisingly, she failed. What had happened to her strength?

"I don't need you to worry for me," Miyoung insisted.

"Tell me how I can help you."

"No one can help me," Miyoung whispered. "I'm cursed."

"What does that mean?" Jihoon asked, but a taxi rolled up the drive and Miyoung jogged to it.

"Go home, Jihoon. Nothing I do is your concern." She slammed the door closed, and the taxi took off, spraying pebbles in its wake.

20

MIYOUNG BANGED ON the rusted metal door, grateful for the narrow alleyway and its ability to block out the light of the sun. Her sunglasses weren't able to hold off her throbbing headache. And, unfortunately, they only protected against UV rays and not ghosts that danced in and out of her vision.

These ghosts had plagued her for the past week. Demons of her past, men who'd sinned in life, and now, as specters, taunted her with threats.

Cannot wait till your soul joins us.

You kill to live; how is that any different from what I did?

Your sins are all that sustain you in life, and when you die, your punishments will be severe!

Miyoung knocked harder, trying to drown out the whispers.

"Okay! I hear you!" a voice shouted from inside a second before the door opened to reveal Junu's annoyed glare.

"Of course it's you." He scowled. "I'm going to have a talk with that shaman. I'm starting to wish she'd never brought you around here."

"What was it?" Miyoung asked, ignoring Junu's snarl as she stepped into the foyer. And suddenly, the ghosts were gone. She spun around, searching for them. "Wait, what's going on?"

"Okay, you're going to have to ask a full question. These half inquiries are not making any sense." Junu still held the door open as if hoping she'd change her mind and leave.

"What was that thing you sold me?" Miyoung asked.

"A talisman," Junu said slowly, as if she were a child.

"I know that. What does it do?"

"Did you use it?"

"Maybe," Miyoung said vaguely, unsure if she wanted to share too much information with the dokkaebi.

"You did. And now you're seeing ghosts. And you're wondering why they haven't followed you into my home."

Miyoung didn't reply.

"It's this." Junu pointed to a golden talisman hanging by his door. "It's a protection of sorts against unsavory things. I thought it was broken since you're here."

"Har-har." Miyoung rolled her eyes. Her nerves were frayed from a week living with the faces of her victims, following her no matter where she hid. She pulled out her wallet and her fingers trembled. She gripped them together until they stopped. "How much?"

"For the joke? Free." Junu gave her a saucy wink.

"The talisman." She refused to react to how he'd purposefully misunderstood her. "How much for it?"

Without waiting for an answer, Miyoung pulled out all the cash in her wallet. Junu eyed the money, but didn't take it.

"Why did you need the first talisman?"

She glared at him, refusing to answer.

"If you tell me, I'll give you this one." Junu pointed to the yellow strip of paper fluttering in the wind.

"I lost something. I needed to put it back where it belongs and Nara said that talisman would open my energy to it."

"Unless what you lost was ghosts, I don't think your shaman was telling you the full truth."

Miyoung hated that Junu spoke her own suspicions aloud. "Is that really all it can do? Open my mind to seeing ghosts? Nothing else?"

"Well, all things can be . . . shifted," Junu mused. "But it's far too dangerous to try such a thing without the proper skill and direction."

Miyoung sighed. She'd been a fool to think she had a handle on things. And now she was paying the price.

"What could a gumiho lose that would cause her to risk such a thing?" Junu asked as he studied her.

"It's none of your business."

"You can't blame me for being curious."

"I didn't come here for a game of twenty questions. I came here for that talisman."

Junu held up a hand, and it took all of her control not to snap off one of his fingers. His eyes widened with understanding. "How does a gumiho lose her yeowu guseul?"

Miyoung shouldn't have been surprised he guessed so quickly. She'd already figured out this dokkaebi was smarter than an average goblin, and twice as annoying.

"I don't know, but we're about to find out how a dokkaebi loses his left hand."

Junu lifted the appendage in question in surrender. Then pulled down the yellow slip, gave it to her, and plucked the money out of her grip.

"Nice doing business with you. No need to eat this one. Just keep it on you. It'll lessen the presence of spirits."

"Lessen?" she asked.

"It won't completely protect you from the ghosts. My home has other charms that magnify the effects, but they're too bulky to carry everywhere. Whether you like it or not, you are now the proud new owner of the gift of sight."

"Oh goody."

Miyoung pushed back out to the alley. The crash of the door exacerbated her headache, but the ghosts were gone. Or mostly gone. There were still shadows that flew in her peripheral vision, but they no longer swept tauntingly past her, and their whispers were silenced.

The buzzing in her pocket made her jump. For a moment she thought one of the ghosts had broken past the charm to shake her. She pulled out her phone and frowned at her mother's number.

"Hello?"

"The school called me." Yena's voice dripped with displeasure. "They said you haven't been in class all week. You know how I despise being contacted by your schools. Is there something I should know?"

"I just didn't feel like going," Miyoung said lightly, hoping the tremor in her hands didn't transmit to her voice. "When will you be home?" Now her voice did shake. She was tired and scared, and she needed her mother.

"I still have business to take care of. It'll be another two weeks at least."

Miyoung swallowed back a sob.

"You'll return to school tomorrow." Yena delivered the edict and hung up without giving Miyoung a chance to reply.

21

SCHOOL WAS TORTURE. Well, more intense torture than normal.

Miyoung sat across the aisle, face worn, purposefully ignoring him. But at least she'd come back to class. Jihoon made note of her sallow skin and sweaty brow. It worried him. She'd told him gumiho couldn't get sick. So what was making her look so pale?

Jihoon stewed over it as he walked back from the school store with Changwan, arms loaded with snacks. Then he stopped short, noticing Miyoung walking down the hall. She saw him, then swerved right, entering the girls' restroom. Obviously avoiding him.

"She's still ignoring you?" Changwan asked.

"What are you talking about?" Jihoon failed miserably at playing dumb.

"Everyone knows." Changwan shrugged. "There's a bet about when she'll break up with you."

"You can't end something that's never begun," Jihoon said as he positioned himself to wait outside the bathroom. "Here, take my snacks back to the room for me, will you?"

Changwan took the bags of chips and candy, wished his friend luck, and continued on to class.

"What are you doing out here? Being a perv?" Baek Hana stuck her nose in the air as she pushed open the door.

"Last I checked, this wall was open to the public."

Hana rolled her eyes and let the door close in his face.

Another two minutes passed before Jihoon gave up, annoyed. What was he doing? Waiting out here just to get yelled at or ignored, or worse.

He had started to leave when he heard a shout from inside. He pushed open the bathroom door in time to see Hana shove Miyoung so hard she slammed into the tile wall.

"Must be nice to have a rich mom who can pay to fix your mistakes," Hana said. "Even when those mistakes are attempted murder."

Miyoung didn't answer. Her head hung low so her hair curtained her face.

"Ya! Did you hear what I said?" Hana shoved Miyoung into the wall again; this time her head cracked against the tile. "My cousin lives in Gwangju. When I sent him your photo, he said he knew you, but you had a different name. Did you change it because you tried to kill that girl?"

Somin stood in the corner, drying her hands calmly. She acted as if nothing was amiss in the small bathroom.

"What are you doing?" Jihoon asked. All three girls glanced up at him.

"Oh shut up, Ahn Jihoon. I know you have a thing for her." Hana sneered. "Has she told you about why she got kicked out of her old school? She's an attempted murderer."

Still ignoring the scene, Somin threw her paper towel in the trash. Jihoon whipped out a hand to stop her. "Somin-ah, I'm disappointed in you."

"What?" Somin's eyes widened.

"You should have stopped this," Jihoon said.

"You have no right to judge what I do," Somin retorted. "Not when you're obviously keeping secrets from me and shutting me out!"

Jihoon didn't know what to say to that, but he didn't get a chance to reply as Somin shoved past him and stormed out.

"You should leave, too, Hana. If you don't want me to tell Miss Kwon what I saw."

Hana huffed indignantly, but she still slunk out, avoiding Jihoon's eyes as she left.

Jihoon inspected Miyoung for injuries.

"Are you hurt?" He tucked her hair aside to see her face.

She shoved his hands away, like a petulant child refusing a parent's care. "I wouldn't have hurt them."

"I didn't stop them because I was afraid of what you'd do. I did it because they were wrong."

Miyoung's eyes darted to the side nervously.

"Don't worry, she won't come back," Jihoon reassured her.

A small whimper escaped Miyoung's throat, and her shoulders began to shake. Her eyes moved right and left like she followed invisible shadows he couldn't see.

Jihoon frowned. He worried the blow to her skull had confused her. Could gumiho get concussions?

"It's true." Miyoung's voice broke on the words.

"What's true?"

"That girl. She thought I stole her boyfriend. He dumped her because he thought he was in love with me, stupid human boy." Her expression soured. Still a flash of heat burst in Jihoon's chest, the fleeting embrace of jealousy.

"She wouldn't stop bothering me after that. She turned the whole school against me."

Jihoon kept silent. He knew she needed to get her story out. His halmeoni always said things like this were better out than in.

"I got too emotional. I just wanted her to leave me alone. She was so close and I could hear her heart beating. I pushed her only to get her away from me. She shouldn't have followed me over that bridge."

"What happened to her?" Jihoon asked, trepidation thickening his words.

"She survived," Miyoung said. "I don't murder innocents." She eyed him, her face pinched in defense. It spoke volumes. It told him no one had ever taken her side.

"So it was an accident." He breathed a sigh of relief.

"If it wasn't, would you be here still? Would you even talk to me if you thought I hurt an innocent person on purpose?" Miyoung's voice rose.

Jihoon hesitated. "I don't know," he admitted. "But that's not the case."

"That's your problem. You want to be friends with the noble monster, but you forget that I kill to survive. I'm not a good person," Miyoung said. "I never pretended to be." Her voice cracked in desperation.

"I don't forget," Jihoon said. "I just know there's more to you than that."

"Don't say that." Miyoung's voice echoed angrily off the bathroom walls. "You don't know! You don't know what I've done. Stop pretending like you do."

"I know I don't like it when people bully you. Even when the person doing the bullying is yourself."

Jihoon had come to realize Miyoung cared, about everything. She was someone who killed to live, but she had a soft heart. It must have torn her apart that her very existence caused pain for others. And knowing that, Jihoon hurt for her even as he didn't know how to help her.

"I can't stop seeing them." Her voice trembled. "They remind me of what I've done."

"Who?" Jihoon asked, desperate to understand her, convinced if he could, then he could finally help.

Miyoung huffed out a breath, tears brimming, but she never let them fall, so complete was her need for control.

Her phone buzzed and she glanced down at the text. Then without another glance at Jihoon, she pushed past him and out the door.

22

WHY DOES AHN Jihoon have to be so frustratingly understanding?
Miyoung thought.

Her phone buzzed again. Another message from Nara.

I'm outside your school, please can we talk?

Miyoung raced down the hallway despite the warning bell telling students to return to class. She couldn't go back right now. Her head was pounding with the start of a migraine and though she refused to acknowledge them, the shadows of phantoms still swirled around her. If she stood too still for too long, she could just make out their whispered words.

Murderer.

Monster.

Yokwe. Beast.

The yeowu guseul swung in her pocket as she walked outside. It felt like the beats of her life were being tapped away every time the bead thumped her side.

With the front gate locked, she had to climb over the side wall. With any luck this would get her out of school and help her avoid Nara.

But there was no such luck. As her feet hit the pavement, she heard the shaman's voice calling her, "Seonbae!" Nara jogged up to her, slightly out of breath.

"What are you doing here?"

"You're not answering my calls."

"We have nothing to talk about," Miyoung said, turning to walk up the street.

"You shouldn't be shutting me out," Nara said. "I can help you."

Without a word, Miyoung walked through a random doorway that led to a narrow staircase beside a dented elevator. The sign beside it gave a directory for the building: a cell phone store, a noraebang, and a small rooftop café.

"Where are we going?" Nara asked.

"Somewhere we can talk in private," Miyoung said. Inside the elevator, she pressed the button for the third floor.

"A noraebang?" Nara asked, confused.

Miyoung didn't reply as the elevator deposited them into a cramped lobby. Bright neon lights flashed against mirrored walls. A small concession stand offered anything from assorted snacks to soda to alcohol. A handwritten sign boasted they had the newest K-pop songs for karaoke. Miyoung approached the man sitting behind the counter, which was coated with some sticky substance.

"Can we get a room for an hour?" Miyoung asked.

He glanced at Miyoung and Nara's school uniforms, then shrugged and quoted the room price in a lazy drawl. It seemed he didn't care about truancy as long as they paid.

The room smelled like stale beer and soju, but it was private. Miyoung picked up the giant square controller and indiscriminately picked a song. Loud trot music blared out of the speakers. Music of their parents' era, or at least Nara's parents. Miyoung doubted Yena ever listened to music. The lyrics to "Love Battery" danced across the screen, accompanied by generic scenes of flowers and nature.

Miyoung turned to Nara. "Talk."

"These spirits," Nara began, glancing around. Miyoung refused to follow the girl's gaze, refused to acknowledge the ghosts that haunted her. "You can see them now, can't you?"

"Did you do it on purpose?" Miyoung asked the question that had been gnawing at her.

"I live with the curse of seeing ghosts, why would I wish that on anyone else?" Nara said, tears forming in her eyes.

Miyoung let out a sigh as the uncertainty lifted. Of course Nara wouldn't mean her harm. "What went wrong?"

Nara shook her head. "I'm sorry, Seonbae. I just wasn't skilled enough to redirect the energy of the talisman. I shouldn't have even attempted it. I just wanted so badly to help." She gripped her hands together as if she were praying for absolution. Or begging.

Miyoung knew she should reach out; knew she should comfort the shaman with her forgiveness. But she couldn't.

"Can you get rid of them?" she asked.

"Maybe if we perform a protection ceremony? I think there's a kut."

"Nara, I don't think one of your shaman dances is enough for this."

"You'd be surprised, and if you gave me the yeowu—"

"No, I'm not giving you the bead. I'm going to tell my mother about it. I should have told her a long time ago."

"Are you going to tell her about what we did?" Nara whispered, her fear palpable.

"No. I've never told my mother about you and I won't now. Don't worry."

"Okay," Nara said. "Just remember that I'm here."

There was a request in Nara's voice, like she was asking Miyoung to believe in her.

The loud instrumentals faded away. The room was silent as Miyoung stared at the shaman. And the phantom whispers began again. Miyoung reached for the remote to queue up another song and drown them out.

"They're not new," Nara said.

That surprised Miyoung into meeting Nara's eyes. "What?"

"These ghosts, they've always followed you. The ones who were too bitter to move on. You're their unfinished business. I'm sorry I never told you. I thought it would be too big a burden."

Miyoung's hand shook, and she balled it into a fist. She knew Nara spoke the truth, that she had kept this from Miyoung to protect her.

"These ghosts are my problem," Miyoung said. "They're my burden."

"You don't have to do this alone."

"Yes, I do."

"I wonder," Nara said, "why you can't seem to trust anyone. Is it your mother?"

"My mother cares about me. I'm all she has."

"She forces you to be alone because she doesn't trust the world. But she had hundreds of years to make that choice. Did you really have a choice at all?" Nara's sad eyes entreated Miyoung. But if Miyoung admitted the truths in Nara's observations, she'd be giving up on the facade of control she'd worked so hard to build.

"I like being alone," Miyoung said. But she heard the lie in her voice. No matter how good she was at lying to others, she could never master the skill of lying to herself.

23

JIHOON HALF EXPECTED Miyoung to be absent again at school the next morning. When he saw her dark hair curtained around her slumped form, he couldn't hold back the smile of relief.

Other kids sat in small whispering groups, their eyes tracking to Miyoung. He sighed and hoped the rumors of their "relationship troubles" would die down soon. It was taking everyone longer than normal to get over this gossip.

A shuffle of activity by the back door of the classroom drew his attention to Baek Hana.

She was hunched over, cradling a heavy object in her arms. Her friends rushed over, speaking in hurried whispers. One pulled out her phone and positioned herself in the corner, a prime viewing spot.

Hana homed in on her target with a leer.

Miyoung sat with her head down, scribbling notes, oblivious.

Jihoon sprinted down the row as Hana held up a large jar, goo already dripping. Jihoon grabbed Miyoung, cradling her under his body. Mung bean paste slid cold down his back, into his collar, down his shirt.

"Ya!" Hana yelled. "What's your problem, Ahn Jihoon?"

The room was silent in the aftermath, kids staring at the spectacle.

Hana still held the jar, unpoured mung bean paste sitting in the bottom. Jihoon yanked it away in case she got any ideas. "Get out of here before I call the teacher."

"Why are you protecting her?" Hana asked. "Is she really your yeo-chin?"

"Yeah, she's my girlfriend. So lay off."

The room paused, like no one knew how to react. It was the first time Jihoon had ever made the claim aloud.

Miyoung stood up suddenly. The force banged her chair against the desk behind her. She glared at Jihoon, her eyes dark, unreadable. Then she swung past him and out of the room.

24

MIYOUNG SHIVERED AS an early winter wind swept into her jacket. She sat on the steps beside the sports field, watching the kids who braved the cold to play soccer. The cold was a weirdly effective tool against the ghosts that still swung in and out of her peripheral vision. Like it slowed them down. She shoved her hand into her pocket and wrapped her fist around the talisman she'd bought from Junu. It helped ease the incessant buzzing in her ears.

She didn't even glance up as Jihoon sat. He pulled out a banana milk and held it toward her.

Miyoung looked at it with a frown, feeling a sense of déjà vu from when he offered her a pair of headphones.

"I have two. It's a waste if you don't drink one," Jihoon said.

She tried to reject it, but he wrapped her hands around the banana milk, holding them cupped between his. The warmth of his palms seeped into her cold skin.

She carefully took the bottle and watched Jihoon warily as he picked up his own.

"Are you going to finally tell me what's wrong?"

"I'm not used to trusting people with my secrets."

"Well, I know most of them already." Jihoon shrugged. "Seems like we could ignore that, or you could just take advantage of a willing listener."

He was right. Jihoon knew more than anyone, even Yena. "It's my bead," Miyoung confessed. "Ever since that night, I've been getting sicker. And when I tried to fix it, things got worse. The men I've taken gi from." For some reason she couldn't say *killed*. "They've come back to haunt me. I always thought if I ever died I'd be faced with them, but they've come calling early."

"Died?" Jihoon asked. "I thought you'd only die if you stopped feeding for one hundred days."

"We can still die all the normal gruesome ways. Stabbed through the heart, beheaded, good old-fashioned burning."

"Are they here now?" Jihoon glanced around, as if he expected a mul gwishin to be standing behind her, draped in a dripping white nightgown with dark hair hanging over her face. His tensed shoulders relaxed when he saw nothing.

Miyoung realized the buzzing in her ears was gone, like for a second talking to Jihoon had chased them away. Or maybe he'd just distracted her for a blissful moment. Either way, she didn't want to lose this slight reprieve.

"Does it hurt?" Jihoon asked. "Not having the bead . . . inside?"

"I'm hungry all the time," Miyoung said. "Sometimes I feel like the part of me that wants to hunt will come out any second."

Jihoon swallowed, but he squared his shoulders and scooted closer to her, until she felt the heat of his body against her side. "Can I help?"

"You are," she admitted. "By being here, you're a pretty good distraction."

Jihoon smiled and tilted his head to look at the sky. "I can see why you sit out here. It's nice to get some sun."

Miyoung leaned back, too. "It's easier if I sit out here. Away from temptation. Too much gi is in that cafeteria. Plus if kids are going to use food as a weapon, I shouldn't go where all the ammunition is."

Jihoon glared toward the windows of the lunchroom. A few students peered down at him and Miyoung curiously, like people staring at animals at the zoo.

"You should go inside before they get ideas about covering you in flour."

"I don't care what they think." Jihoon gently turned her gaze from their spectators. "And neither should you."

"I can't wait for the day you realize you should run away from me."

Liar, a voice said in her head.

Everything felt like it was shifting, creating a break in her shields, a crack in her heart. She had to be strong, but a part of her started to doubt this was strength. Why did she think depending on others meant she was weak? Because Yena said so?

Nara's words echoed back to her. *She forces you to be alone because she doesn't trust the world. Did you really have a choice at all?*

They were silent as they finished their milk. "Thank you."

"For what?"

"For trying to protect me from Hana. And for lying and saying I'm your girlfriend. I know you hate lying."

Jihoon faced her. "Then maybe we should make it the truth."

His words scared her because she realized she wanted to say yes. "Listen," Miyoung began slowly, trying to find the right words. "I never knew people like you existed. Someone who could know so much about me and still want to know me. It's scary. I'm not used to people liking me."

"What's so wrong about me liking you?" Jihoon asked.

"There's nothing wrong with it, except it's making me want you right back and I know I can't have you."

"Why not? I'm right here. Do you still not trust me?"

"It's not you. My mother and I never stay in one place long. I always make a mistake eventually. People are already suspicious of me now that Hana's told them what happened at my last school."

"What if you didn't leave this time?"

"We will," she insisted.

"Okay, but let's just imagine, what if you didn't?"

She didn't want to play this game that already made her heart ache, but she gave in because that was his power. He made her want to hope. "If I didn't leave, then maybe we could go on a date?"

"Yeah?" He smiled and that damned dimple folded in his cheek. She wanted to kiss it, place her lips right on top of it. And because of it, she pinched her lips tight, as if she thought they'd go rogue.

"What kind of date?" Jihoon asked.

"I don't know," she mused, using the guise of thinking to settle her speeding heart. "Namsan?"

Jihoon let out a laugh, then stopped when he saw her frown. "Namsan Tower? That's kind of a cliché, don't you think?"

"I don't know. I've never been," Miyoung bit out, suddenly embarrassed. She started to turn away.

"Okay, okay," Jihoon said, grabbing her shoulders so she faced him. "We'll go to Namsan and I'll buy you one of those giant hot dogs with the fried potato around it."

"And an ice cream," she said. And then she realized that she was really starting to hope that they could go on this ridiculous, cliché date. "The bell is going to ring."

"Okay, but don't forget that you owe me a date now," Jihoon said, letting her shoulders go. And her skin felt suddenly cold where his palms had been.

"Sure, when we can be two regular human kids, we'll go on this date."

"Good," Jihoon said with a smile.

The bell rang and Miyoung stood quickly, rushing to make it back inside. Her chest was hurting, like something was pressing against her ribs. Or as if her heart was swelling because it was suddenly so full. A feeling she was so unused to, it hurt.

25

MIYOUNG STARTED BRINGING a change of clothes every day. As predicted, the favored attack of the kids was food. Miyoung could make a whole Chuseok meal with the ingredients she'd been plastered with.

She was lucky Yena was still away. It gave her privacy to stew in her humiliation.

Miyoung walked toward class after gym. It had been a particularly harrowing hour of avoiding flying objects that "accidentally" slipped out of kids' hands. Which wouldn't have been such a problem if her balance wasn't constantly thrown off by the ghosts that plagued her. It was almost like they'd coordinated with her human bullies to bombard her all at once.

And she couldn't forget Nara's words. The ghosts weren't new. They'd been following her like flags of shame ever since she stole their lives to prolong her own. They were her punishment.

The late bell rang, letting her know that the extra-long shower she'd taken to avoid the other kids after gym class had been a mistake.

She was hurrying down the hall when an arm shot out, blocking her path. Miyoung glanced up at Jung Jaegil. She could make out a fading bruise over his right eye and remembered his anxious face as he searched the dark, dirty road for his father. Guilt pricked along her skin.

"Get out of my way," she said, adding steel to her voice. "I'm late."

"We're all late." Jaegil gestured to himself and Seho, who stood behind him.

"I don't have time for this." Miyoung tried to walk around Jaegil, but his friend blocked her path.

"I heard you've got a record," Jaegil said with a laugh. "I never thought there'd be a kid worse than me in this school."

Miyoung tried to push past him again, but he slammed her back so hard her shoulders hit the wall with a *thud*.

It's what you deserve after what you did to his father, a ghostly voice whispered. And she didn't know if it was one of her phantoms or her own thoughts.

"Something about you bothers me," Jaegil drawled out. He pushed forward. She smelled orange juice and shrimp chips on his breath. "How did you break that store window?"

"I told you to get out of my way," Miyoung warned. She could feel her control breaking.

"What do you think you can do to make me?" Jaegil ran a finger down her cheek.

Miyoung slapped it away.

Jaegil's eyes flashed, a rage she could recognize. The look of someone who'd been battered by life. And she wondered if Jaegil was more a kindred spirit than she wanted to admit. After all, they had both given in to their violent natures. Jaegil lifted his hand. A windup before the strike.

Then his body flew away from hers, sliding across the tile floor.

Somin stood between them like a shield protecting Miyoung from the dazed bully on the floor.

"Ya, Lee Somin. Nappeun gijibae!" Jaegil yelled as Seho rushed to his side. A door down the hall opened, and a second-year teacher poked his head out.

"What are you kids doing out of class? Who's your homeroom teacher?"

Jaegil and Seho took off, well-practiced in the art of escape.

Somin and Miyoung were not as lucky.

o o o

The disciplinary conference room was a stark square space with white walls and half a dozen desks. The teacher sat them back to back with sheets of paper to write apology letters.

Miyoung stared at the blank page. She made small black dots with her pen, unable to form a coherent thought.

"If you're going to stand up to a bully like Jaegil, then you better be prepared to follow through with your fists," Somin said behind her. "Guys like that only respond to brute force."

Or you could kill him, it's what you do best, a taunting spirit said in her ear.

"Leave me alone." Miyoung spoke to her blank paper.

"What?"

"I said stop worrying yourself about my personal business."

"Sure," Somin said, her tone flippant. "I always conduct my personal business in the *public* hallway."

Miyoung finally whirled around. "I didn't start it."

Somin was already facing her, straddling the chair backward, her uniform skirt bunched over her gym pants. She poked a finger into Miyoung's forehead. "Ah, there's that fighting spirit."

Her heart-shaped face was mischievous and watchful. The type of girl Miyoung would definitely have avoided in the past.

"Do you know how to land a punch?" Somin glanced at Miyoung's hands. "You look like you'd break your wrist on your first try."

"I can punch," Miyoung mumbled.

"Didn't look like it," Somin said.

"Why do you care?"

"I don't." Somin crossed her arms. "And I do. I just hate that Ahn Jihoon was right."

"Excuse me?" Miyoung asked, confused.

"When he said I should have stopped Baek Hana in the bathroom. I'm just as much to blame as she is for bullying you. I'm trying to say I'm sorry," Somin said. She sounded more annoyed than apologetic.

Miyoung couldn't seem to digest the words. Someone apologizing to her felt so foreign.

"It's fine." Miyoung shrugged off the girl's kindness.

"It's not," Somin said. "With all of the rumors Hana is spreading, you know how mean the kids can be. I'll teach you to fight. It's the fastest way to get them off your back."

"They're not rumors. I pushed that girl off the bridge."

It felt good to say the truth—freeing. Was this why Jihoon did it all the time?

Somin looked Miyoung up and down, taking her measure. "Was it on purpose?"

"Why does it matter?" Miyoung asked.

"It matters to me."

Miyoung sighed. "No."

"Okay," Somin said. "Well, the offer still stands if you want it."

It was not what Miyoung had been expecting. "Why would you do that when I told you what I did?"

"We all make mistakes. My mom says we should always get a second chance. How else will we make up for them?"

Somin's words made an uncomfortable flush rise in Miyoung's chest.

"I heard Hana tried to make you into a walking bindaetteok," Somin said.

"Such a waste of good food," Miyoung muttered.

Somin snorted out a laugh.

"I heard what Jihoonie did, too. He better not get hurt because of you or you're dead."

"Do you like him?" Miyoung blurted out the question before she could stop herself.

"Of course I do."

"You know what I mean," Miyoung said, annoyed at herself for starting this conversation. What did she care how Somin felt about Jihoon?

"He's just my friend, nothing more. I love him like a brother. He's my best friend. How else could I hate him so much half the time?"

Miyoung let out a bitter laugh. "Is that what being a friend is like? Then I have a hundred friends here."

"The kids are just jealous because you're so pretty and you don't care what any of them think."

Miyoung almost admitted how wrong that was, how she cared too much what everyone thought of her. Instead she asked, "Will you make up with Jihoon?"

Somin's brows disappeared under her choppy bangs. "Is that concern I hear from the Ice Queen?" She let out a chuckle at Miyoung's look of disgust.

"Come on, you have to know that's what the kids call you. You're so frosty, I wonder if you have an icicle stuck up your—"

"I get the picture." Miyoung couldn't quite hide her smile. "And yes, I'm concerned. Despite myself. A little bit."

Somin grinned. "Wow, I feel so unworthy of such words of deep affection." She laid a hand on Miyoung's shoulder and gave it a squeeze. "The good thing about friends is that even when they fight, they still care about each other."

Somin turned back to her paper and began writing.

Miyoung took a moment to clear her tight throat before doing the same.

26

MIYOUNG AND JIHOON started regularly eating on the steps.

It looked like rain on Friday, but they still walked out to the courtyard at lunchtime, wrapped tightly in puffy winter coats. Miyoung slowed as she approached their normal spot.

Ugly red paint smeared the faded concrete: MURDERER; PLASTIC GIJIBAE; GET OUT OF OUR SCHOOL!

She moved toward it, fully intending to sit despite the fact that the paint was obviously still wet.

"Wait!" Jihoon said. "One minute, okay? Wait for me to come back."

Jihoon sprinted away without waiting for a reply.

As Miyoung stared at the angry words, the door behind her opened again.

Somin stood in the doorway. "What are you doing out here? It's freezing."

"I'm . . ." Miyoung trailed off before she could think of what to say. But it didn't matter. Somin spotted the graffiti and let out a few choice curses that made Miyoung's brows rise, impressed.

Before either girl could speak again, Jihoon returned. Water sloshed out of the bucket he carried, two mops and a few rags awkwardly gripped in his other hand.

"What are you doing here?" Jihoon asked Somin, and the hard tone annoyed Miyoung.

"Oh, can you two quit already?"

Somin and Jihoon both stared at her, but no one was more surprised than Miyoung at the outburst. Then she realized she didn't feel sorry for saying it. In fact, it felt good.

"You've known each other your whole life. Do you know how special that is? If you're going to throw away your friendship, then fine, that's your choice, but it's not going to be because of a fight that involves me. I didn't ask for any part in this."

Somin and Jihoon were quiet a moment, probably shocked into silence, or perhaps neither wanted to be the first to speak.

"I'm sorry for giving you the cold shoulder," Somin finally said.

"I'm sorry for keeping secrets," Jihoon said.

"Well, I guess I should trust that they're important if you're keeping them from me."

Jihoon smiled and the tightness around Miyoung's heart loosened.

"Sooo." Jihoon stretched out the word. "Does that mean you've missed me?" Before Somin could avoid him, he grabbed her in a headlock.

"Ya!" she yelled.

He refused to release her. "Admit you missed me."

Somin punched Jihoon's back with a wide swing of her fists.

He let her go with a grunt of pain. "Ow, that hurt!"

"That's the point," Somin said, still hitting him.

As Miyoung watched, a pressure built in her, like the bubbling of a carbonated beverage with the lid closed tight. And she'd been shaken and shaken. Days of bullying. Weeks of imbalance. Now she was faced with the surreal sight of Somin and Jihoon slapping at each other like kids. Because, Miyoung realized, that was what they were, kids free to be as ridiculous as they pleased.

The pressure pushed its way out, bursting forth in a snort of laughter. Everyone stopped at the sound, but no one was more shocked than Miyoung herself.

"Are you laughing at my pain?" Jihoon asked.

"I find the sight of you getting beat up very amusing," Miyoung said between hiccups of laughter.

"He's not getting beat up by just anyone," Somin countered, suddenly defending her friend.

"Yeah." Jihoon slung his arm around her shoulder in solidarity, their previous fight completely forgotten. "I'm getting beat up by Lee Somin. Her fists can make whole nations fall."

He lifted one of her petite hands as proof.

Three sets of eyes stared at the tiny fist. Then they all flopped over in laughter. Miyoung's abs ached, her head felt light, but it was a good feeling. A cleansing one, like she'd emptied out a dark sludge that had clogged her gut for days.

"Ya! Are you guys hiding from me? I was waiting in the cafeteria for you," Changwan said, his arms crossed as he stood in the doorway.

"Changwan-ah, since you're here, you can help us clean," Jihoon said, reminding Miyoung of the graffiti.

"You don't have to," she said, embarrassed by the harsh red words.

"Of course we will." Somin scowled at the block letters sprawled over the concrete. "Only cowards do things like this."

Changwan nodded and accepted one of the mops. No questions, no pitying eyes. Just acceptance and a willingness to help. It was strange for Miyoung to feel that kind of automatic support.

The three friends exchanged taunts and laughter as they cleaned, claiming there were multiple spots missed or that some-one was slacking off.

Strange that something that could have been another dagger to her confidence instead turned into something so nice.

They did this for her. They were happily cleaning to erase the cruel words directed at her.

She wondered if it could have always been so easy to have friends. And regret sat heavy on her heart for all the time she'd wasted being alone.

27

SUNDAY WAS THE full moon. The house sounded strangely quiet as Miyoung moved through her room, pulling on jeans and a sweater.

She felt oddly calm. No matter what, things would be settled tonight. Yena would be home before night fell, and Miyoung would tell her the truth.

If she was careful how she worded it, conveniently kept out any mention of shamans and talismans, her mother would find a way to fix it.

And then she'd find a way to tell Yena she wanted to stay here, permanently. A true home. With real friends.

Her phone rang and Nara's number lit the screen. Miyoung hesitated a second before answering. "I don't imagine you're calling just to say hello."

"It's the full moon tonight." Nara sounded tense.

"I've heard rumors about that."

"If you want to do something—"

"I'm telling my mother. I don't need your shaman rituals to solve this."

"Shaman what?" At the crack of Yena's voice, Miyoung spun, dropping her phone with a clatter.

Yena watched Miyoung calmly from the doorway as if she'd

asked about the weather. But Miyoung saw her mother's clenched fists, nails digging divots into her skin.

"I can explain." But could she? It seemed so hard to gather her thoughts in the face of her mother's fury.

"I trust you to do what I ask."

"I do."

Yena's eyes flared. "I also expect you to tell me the truth."

She walked to Miyoung's desk, opened a drawer, and pulled out papers, letting them scatter to the floor before yanking the next drawer out. A search, like Miyoung was suspected of a crime.

"I've told you never to talk to shamans." More papers scattered to the floor, joined by notebooks and pens. "They are enemies of our kind. They only seek to hurt us or worse."

"Mother."

Yena halted her with a glare.

"I don't explain all of my rules because there are things in this world that are hard to explain, even to people like us." Yena pulled out the last drawer and let the contents fall, then dropped the wooden drawer as well.

"But everything I do is for you. Everything." Yena pulled Miyoung's school blazer off the back of her desk chair and emptied out the pockets. The talisman fluttered to the ground, like a yellow flag marking Miyoung's guilt. Yena picked it up between her thumb and forefinger, her face contorting with disgust. "And this is how you choose to treat my trust."

"Please!" Miyoung begged.

It didn't matter; her mother's face had closed. With slow, deliberate motions, Yena tore the talisman in half. A spark speared through the golden paper. Miyoung watched the power of the talisman break free and scatter in the air.

Not even a second passed before the shadows rose, bleeding onto the walls.

"What has gotten into you?" Yena said as the shadows behind her stretched and congealed, becoming menacing shapes.

"I'm sorry," Miyoung stuttered, blinking so hard white lights burst behind her lids.

"Tell me," Yena said as the looming shapes rose above her, arms reaching out to embrace her.

"Mother!" Miyoung shouted. But the demons moved right through her mother, and Yena didn't bat an eye.

Miyoung wanted to sob. She'd made a complete mess of her life and had only pretended everything could be righted. After all, lying was Miyoung's best skill, and it turned out she'd finally learned how to lie to herself.

"I'm sorry," Miyoung said, and she didn't know whether she was apologizing to her mother or to the ghostly faces of her victims.

"What have you done?"

Miyoung backed away from her mother's wrath and the ghosts behind her. A gang of threats she couldn't handle. The ghosts bared their teeth, hatred clear on their faces. Their eyes black holes, but filled with accusation nonetheless. "Leave me alone."

"Don't use that tone with me," Yena snapped, her nostrils flaring in barely contained rage.

The ghosts danced across the air, like they swayed along to her mother's fury. They surged forward.

"Get away!" Miyoung screamed, and swung out. Her nails scraped her mother's cheek. Red slashes welled with beads of blood across Yena's pale skin.

"Miyoung!" The roar filled the room and cleared the desperate fear from Miyoung's mind. She blinked as she finally focused on her mother. The ghosts had receded, and she stared down at her hand, smeared in her mother's blood.

"I didn't mean to." Her voice wavered back and forth between distress and apology. "I was trying to fix it, Song Nara said—" She clamped her lips tight, realizing her mistake.

"Song. Nara." Yena said each word slowly. "The shaman you were speaking to is named Song Nara?"

Miyoung nodded meekly.

Without a word, Yena spun on her heel.

"Wait!" Miyoung called after her. "Where are you going?"

But Yena didn't reply as she stormed out.

With fumbling fingers, Miyoung dialed Nara's number.

"Nara, if I give you the bead, can you guarantee you can fix this?"

"Yes, I think I can, Seonbae."

"Tell me where to meet you."

28

JIHOON USED HIS Sunday afternoons for one thing: gaming.

It was his happy time when he didn't have school and his halmeoni gave him a reprieve from helping out in the restaurant. He booted up the ancient computer in his apartment and debated whether it was worth it to put on real pants to go to the PC room for a better internet connection. He pulled out a pair from the pile of folded laundry his halmeoni had left for him. A yellow paper fell from the pocket and he sighed. Even when he left the bujeok in the wash, she meticulously saved it and placed it neatly back in his pocket. He started to shove it into a drawer, then stopped. Of all people, he now knew this stuff wasn't superstition, so he stuffed it into his jacket as he shrugged it on.

The sound of his front doorbell confused him at first. Hardly anyone came upstairs when the restaurant was open below.

The yellow bujeoks around the front door fluttered as he opened it.

Detective Hae stood on the other side.

"Detective. Are you looking for my halmeoni? She's downstairs."

The detective's shrewd gaze took in Jihoon's rumpled clothes and sleepy eyes. "I'm actually looking for you. Your neighbor, Mrs. Hwang, told me you were out by the forest a few weeks ago."

"When was that?" Though Jihoon knew already.

"It would have been about two months ago."

Two months ago. When Jihoon first met Miyoung. When he saw her kill a dokkaebi.

Jihoon's mind raced. Should he lie? Half truth, he decided. Easier to tell the truth even if it wasn't full. "I don't remember every night I'm out in the neighborhood, but I'll try to help if I can."

"Do you remember seeing anything strange?" Detective Hae asked.

"What do you mean?"

"Just anything." The detective was being equally withholding.

"No, the neighborhood is pretty quiet after dark."

"Did you hear anything from the forest?"

"Like hikers?" Jihoon asked.

"Like anything." Detective Hae watched Jihoon so closely he felt if he blinked the wrong way, the man would file it away.

"I don't really notice things."

The detective sighed. "It's about that file you saw at the station. That man disappeared two months ago. We found his *body* last night." The detective emphasized the word *body*, watching for a reaction.

Jihoon kept his expression blank by running through his last gaming battle strategy in detail.

"Sorry, I can't help you."

"Listen." The detective hesitated, then continued. "It's going to sound odd, but I think this is a pattern. There have been other similar attacks."

"Similarities? Like what?" Jihoon asked.

"That's sensitive information," the detective replied, but Jihoon didn't need to hear—he had a good idea. Men missing, turning up without their livers, men who looked like they had been attacked by a wolf . . . or a fox.

"But I'm fairly certain there will be another attack and soon. Now, are you sure you didn't see anything?"

"Yeah, I'm sure." Jihoon set his mouth in a stern line like he'd seen his halmeoni do before.

Detective Hae dug into his pocket, pulling out his card. "Well, if you do remember anything, then let me know."

Jihoon accepted it, making sure to keep his fingers steady.

This detective was getting in way over his head. Miyoung wasn't the only gumiho wandering the city, and from what she'd said, Yena was ruthless. Jihoon's eyes shifted to the bujeoks fluttering inside the door. He remembered the one the dokkaebi had used against Miyoung that first night. How it had weakened her.

"Wait," Jihoon called out. He felt foolish, but what if the detective got hurt and he'd done nothing? So he pulled down a talisman and held it out.

"A bujeok for protection?" Detective Hae asked.

"You know what it is?" Jihoon lifted his brows in surprise.

"My wife used to be obsessed with this stuff."

"You should take it. Seems like you have a dangerous job."

The detective chuckled and patted Jihoon's shoulder. It felt strangely paternal and Jihoon stepped back in sudden discomfort.

The detective gave a final nod. Jihoon folded into a bow.

He leaned heavily on the door after he closed it. He tried calling Miyoung. She'd made him promise to use her number for emergencies only. Jihoon figured this classified as one.

She didn't answer, and he cursed as he pulled open the door again and hurried out.

o o o

Jihoon ran up the hill toward Miyoung's house. He hesitated at the end of the long drive and glanced at the sky, darkening with dusk. But he steeled himself before starting down the path.

A movement in the trees halted his steps and he froze until he recognized the uniform blazer of his school. Miyoung.

He doubted she had decided it was a good time for a casual hike. She was preparing for a hunt, and if that detective was out patrolling, Jihoon didn't want to think of what could happen.

"Miyoung!" he called, but she was either too far away or ignoring him.

He hurried after her, wondering how she could move so fast without making a sound.

The path was narrow, filled with large roots and craggy rocks. The steep slope tired Jihoon quickly. He wondered if it was physically possible for a person to cough up their lungs, but truly didn't want to find out. So he took a short break, leaning against a tree. Up here, the height was dizzying. And the city lay so far below it looked like a toy replica. His break lost him precious time, and when he turned back toward the path, Miyoung was nowhere to be seen.

"Gu Miyoung," Jihoon shouted. No answer. Not that he'd really expected one.

"Miyoung-ah, if you can hear me, answer," Jihoon called. His shouting startled something that rustled the underbrush and he skittered back, stepping over the ledge.

He was pulled back onto the path to fall in a heap. Miyoung

stood over him, her arms crossed. From the look on her face she wasn't just displeased, she was pissed.

"What do you want?" she asked.

"They—" He broke off when his voice wavered. He stood, brushing away the dirt that clung to his pants while he tried to gather himself. "They found a body in the woods," he said finally.

Her expression was unreadable.

"A man who disappeared," Jihoon continued. "They suspect something, they're looking for the culprit, they think they'll attack again."

Miyoung nodded, the only sign she heard him.

"There's a cop asking questions."

"Just because he's poking around doesn't mean he knows anything." Miyoung frowned.

"Maybe you shouldn't be out tonight."

"You need to leave this alone. It's not safe out here for you." Her hand went to her belly; her eyes darted back and forth as if they saw something he couldn't. And her skin had taken on a strangely green pallor.

"Are you okay?"

"Go home." Miyoung didn't wait for his reply. She retreated back into the woods.

She'd seemed distracted. If she was distracted, that meant she might make a mistake. Jihoon didn't give himself time to think; he pushed through the branches, following Miyoung deeper into the forest as the sun waned.

29

AS SHE MADE her way through the forest, the first flake fell onto her cheek, melting against her skin.

Big things always happen at the first snow. Halmeoni's words rang in her head. But they sounded like a warning to Miyoung now.

She ran her hands over the rough bark of trees as she walked. It wasn't to help with balance. She was light on her feet on the craggy terrain. But she liked the physical connection with the flora around her. It gave her comfort, anchored her, when she felt like she was wavering. And she needed all the support she could get tonight.

Her phantoms swung through the trees, dancing from branch to branch, trying to break her resolve.

She ran her fingers through her tangled hair. It stuck to her temple with dried sweat despite the cool winter air.

Nara stepped into Miyoung's path, stopping her short. The young shaman wore a colorful hanbok, the bright colors a sharp contrast to the grays and browns of the bare trees around them.

"Oh, Seonbae," Nara murmured, pity saturating her eyes as they shifted around Miyoung, taking in the spirits. "Come, the moon is rising." She grabbed Miyoung's arm, her fingers digging into skin.

"Your instructions weren't very clear."

"We needed a place with the right energy." Nara pulled hard on Miyoung's arm, so she had to stumble after the shorter girl.

There was a space of earth cleared out below a great oak tree that still held on to a smattering of leaves.

A long altar sat beside the thick trunk, littered with trays of fruit, chestnuts, and rice. Copper bowls held sand and incense. Candles flickered, lighting the faces of a dozen paintings, each staring at Miyoung with dark eyes.

"Light an incense." Nara held out a long stem.

Miyoung obeyed.

Nara picked up a bronze cup and held it out.

Miyoung glanced inside, half expecting the concoction of water and ash from before. It was wine.

"It's to help cleanse you," Nara explained. "We need to connect to the gods, and you need to purify before we can do that."

"Nara, I want to believe this will work, it's just that last time . . ." She trailed off, and the shaman nodded with understanding.

"You're not sure if you can trust me after what happened last full moon."

"This is my life we're messing with," Miyoung said.

"I can't make promises, Seonbae. And I don't think this will work if you don't trust me."

Miyoung hesitated. Considered turning around and walking away. But the hunger in her gut made her whole body ache. And she remembered the mistrust in her mother's eyes. So she took a sip, letting the bitter alcohol sit on her tongue before swallowing.

"I need this to work, Nara," Miyoung said, handing back the cup. "I've let my mother down. I can't go back until this is fixed."

"If your mother did something to you—"

"Let's stop talking about my mother," Miyoung insisted. "Can you do this or not?"

Nara's face smoothed and she straightened her shoulders. "I can do this."

Miyoung nodded, clutching the fox bead so tightly in her pocket she thought she'd crush it. "What're you going to do now?"

"I'm not going to do anything," Nara said. "My halmeoni is."

An elderly woman walked into the small clearing. She wore a traditional hanbok cinched high over her ribs, the satin skirt a wide bell. Instead of the bright colors that usually made up a hanbok, hers was pure white.

Miyoung almost backed away. This hadn't been the deal and the stories about Shaman Kim echoed in the back of her head. They mixed with Yena's warnings. Maybe she shouldn't be trusting these shamans. Maybe she should just go home, find Yena, and beg her forgiveness.

"This is her?" Nara's halmeoni asked, and her gaze seemed to trap Miyoung in place.

"This is her," Nara replied. "Gu Miyoung."

"Gu. Mi. Young." Nara's halmeoni repeated each character of Miyoung's name like she was dissecting it. "I'm Shaman Kim."

Miyoung gave a bow, her manners taking over because her mind was too busy debating her decision to come here. She didn't know anything about Shaman Kim except that she had exorcised more dark spirits and creatures than anyone could count and she hated anything she deemed evil. Miyoung knew that her kind fit that category. She was like a deer trusting a hunter to pull an arrow from her side.

Shaman Kim turned to her granddaughter. "Where is it?"

Nara looked at Miyoung expectantly.

She couldn't pull her hand out of her pocket where it clutched her bead.

"If you don't want my help, then I'm wasting my time."

"I just . . . I need reassurances," Miyoung stuttered out, her voice weak.

"There are no guarantees when it comes to this kind of practice. But I can get rid of your ghosts," Shaman Kim said. "I assume you'd like that."

Miyoung nodded.

"And if you'd like me to reunite you with your yeowu guseul, we'd need that, too."

Miyoung nodded again. Then with a deep breath she held out her bead and dropped it in Shaman Kim's waiting hand.

She shivered. Suddenly ice cold.

Miyoung glanced at Nara, seeking some sort of comfort, but she watched Miyoung coldly, as if she were a stranger. Was it because of Shaman Kim's presence? Did Nara so fear her halmeoni that she'd pretend she and Miyoung weren't close? It hurt even as Miyoung recognized this was what she'd always done, kept space between her and Nara.

"Sit," Nara's halmeoni commanded, and Miyoung obeyed.

Shaman Kim pulled out a bujeok and wrapped it around Miyoung's yeowu guseul. The old shaman's eyes captured Miyoung's. The look was not particularly kind, and Miyoung wondered again whether she was a fool to trust this old woman.

It was too late. Nara pulled a janggu onto her lap, the hourglass-shaped drum decorated in bright reds and blues that matched the girl's hanbok. She struck the instrument, a heavy beat that reverberated through the forest.

Despite her age, Shaman Kim moved gracefully in long, reaching movements. Her feet took slow, measured steps. Her arms folded and twisted into a kut, a shaman dance. Her long sleeves shot out, an extension of her body.

As the kut progressed, the moon rose.

The air became heavy. The smell of incense thickened.

Miyoung coughed to clear her throat, but it didn't quite work.

Nara caught her eyes and mouthed, *Open yourself.*

Miyoung stilled and tried to release the tension in her shoulders. She didn't know how to open herself, but she figured part of it was to relax.

The smoke of the incense wove in the wind. Wisps breaking off to become ghostly shapes. It coalesced, becoming the face of one of Miyoung's past victims. A man she'd caught killing dogs in an alley on a full moon. His gi had tasted heavy and salty.

Then another, the face of a man who'd used his money to buy his freedom after driving drunk and plowing into a family of four; the whole family had died. And Miyoung sent the man to meet them in the afterlife.

More faces formed in the smoke, breaking free to swim around her. A macabre montage of her victims. Vengeful eyes of the dead spinning and spinning around her in a crowd of accusation.

Miyoung yanked at her collar, trying to pull in air. Shaman Kim's eyes found her. Held her as the woman twisted and spun. Her graceful dance becoming sharp, jerking motions.

The beat of the janggu reached a frenzied crescendo, and Miyoung's heart matched it beat for beat.

Release the unclean spirits. The voice wasn't her own, but that of the shaman, whose eyes never left Miyoung.

I can't breathe, Miyoung thought. It felt like the hands of the dead were clamped against her skin, their cold fingers holding her throat closed.

Death holds you. It covers you.

She clawed at her own neck. Trying to tear a path for oxygen to enter her body again.

The gold-wrapped bead in the shaman's hands seemed to glow, bright as fire. A twin of the flames that shot through Miyoung's veins. She tried to crawl, thinking to snatch the bead back, but she could barely sit up.

She tensed against the pain until her back arched in reply. Heat enveloped her, fireworks trailing through her bloodstream.

I'm sorry. I'm sorry, she tried to say, but couldn't get the words out.

She twisted in torment, her body moving along with the jerky dance of the shaman.

And in her wavering vision a darkness seemed to spread, like a black hole opening in the forest. It pulled at the ghosts that surrounded her, devouring them. Their protests became a piercing wail.

Then the darkness pulled at her, like it sucked at her very soul. Like it sought to pull that piece of her free from her body. When she opened her mouth to scream, no sound would come.

Something burst through the trees, a large shape that looked clumsy and shambling next to the graceful dancing shaman: Jihoon. He raced forward, pulled Shaman Kim around, and yanked the bujeok-covered stone from her hands. He dropped it with a yelp, blisters decorating his palm with angry red welts.

Though the dance had stopped, the lightning shooting

through Miyoung didn't cease. She lurched up. Her legs threatened to buckle. Her heart ached.

She craned her neck, gasping for air, and saw the full moon bright in the sky.

Using the last of her strength, she ran.

30

JIHOON DROPPED THE fox bead and stared at the burns on his palm, like he'd pulled a lit ember from the shaman instead of a stone.

The stunned face of the old woman almost had him bowing instinctively in apology. Then Miyoung raced into the trees.

Jihoon took off after her, calling for her to wait. She didn't listen, and by the time he'd left the light of the clearing behind, he'd lost her.

Away from the candles in the clearing, Jihoon realized the moon wasn't breaking through the thick canopy of the forest. Everything looked the same to him. And he was beginning to realize he was alone in the woods on the full moon.

A cry pierced the quiet rustle of the trees, and Jihoon's heart jumped to lodge itself firmly in his throat.

He recognized the cadence. It was too jerky to be the howl of the wind and too tormented to come from an animal. A person crying.

Jihoon found her below a tree that grew in gnarls and twists. Bending in on itself before turning back to reach toward the sky.

Miyoung curled into herself, her limbs folded tight to her body in a strange mirror of the warped tree. She buried her face in her knees.

And waving around her in the dappled light of the moon were nine ghostly tails.

"Miyoung-ah." Jihoon approached slowly, stumbling over roots and rocks.

He inched forward, the way someone would approach an injured animal.

Miyoung's hands fisted in her hair, pulling at the ebony strands so hard, Jihoon worried she would tear them from her scalp.

Jihoon closed the rest of the distance between them. He tried not to stare at the swaying tails. One skimmed against his arm. Jihoon didn't know what he'd expected, but the soft brush of fur made goose bumps rise along his skin.

"I'm so tired," Miyoung mumbled. "I'm so hungry."

"Miyoung-ah?" Jihoon said again.

A shudder stormed through her body. And her muttering halted. The very air of the clearing stilled, like the forest was holding its breath.

She lifted her head, a slow turn and tilt. Her dark eyes captured the moon and she let out a guttural growl.

Jihoon found himself flat on his back. Miyoung crouched above him.

Saliva pooled around her mouth. It dripped from her lips and fell on his cheek.

She lowered her face until it was centimeters from his. Her eyes were dilated, her lips curled into the pleased smile of a predator.

"Miyoung-ah!" He tried to push at her, but she didn't budge. "Gu Miyoung!" He repeated her name, hoping it would remind her of who she was.

She leaned on his shoulders so rocks pressed painfully into his back.

He couldn't move any of his limbs. So he did the only thing he could think of. Rearing up, he bit Miyoung on the shoulder.

She howled in pain. Her grip loosened.

Flipping onto his belly, Jihoon scurried away.

Miyoung recovered too quickly. Her hands wrapped around his knees. Her teeth found the meat of his calf. They cut through cloth and flesh. Jihoon screamed, a high shriek that echoed through the woods.

He kicked and clawed as she rolled him onto his back.

"I'm starving." The words vibrated her whole torso as she pinned him to the ground again.

Jihoon couldn't move and she crouched lower, her heavy huffs blowing his hair.

"Miyoung-ah." Jihoon pushed every plea, every desperate note he could, into the word.

She stopped. Her brow furrowed.

"Please, it's me, Ahn Jihoon." In desperation, he started rambling. "You hate my jokes and you think I talk too much. You're scared of the water. My halmeoni made you doenjang jjigae. You said you wouldn't kill me. You said you wouldn't." A tear tracked down his cheek.

Miyoung jerked up, her eyes clearing. "Jihoon?"

Then her body began to convulse. She shuddered and fell against his shoulder.

Jihoon pulled free from her weight, crouching over her.

"If you're smart, you'll leave her alone." The shaman girl stepped out of the trees.

Jihoon had a feeling of déjà vu, seeing her face. "Do I know you?"

"What? No." The shaman's voice was sharp.

"Ah," Jihoon replied, but he couldn't let go of the strange feeling.

"You're the brightness," the girl said. "The sun chased by shadows. She's the shadows."

"You don't know anything about us," Jihoon said, moving to block Miyoung.

The older shaman moved out of the shadows of the woods, her eyes hard as they locked on to Miyoung. "We know far more than you think," the halmeoni said.

"Well, I don't care what you think you know. Leave us alone," Jihoon said.

"Do you ever stop to ask yourself if she deserves this loyalty? She's a killer." The girl's voice was a clear bell of accusation.

"Wait, I remember now. Where I've seen you," Jihoon said as recognition dawned.

"We've never met before."

"No." Jihoon drew out the word as he tried to grab on to the memory. A ghostly shape receding into the forest as he desperately grappled with a dokkaebi. "I've seen you before."

"No, you haven't," she insisted.

"You were there when I met Miyoung for the first time. I thought you were a ghost, but you were in the forest when she lost that bead."

"What?" The question cracked through the forest. Miyoung sat up behind Jihoon.

"Nara." Miyoung's eyes held fire as they latched on to the girl. "Tell me what you've done."

But it was the old shaman who replied. "What she must to rid this world of a demon."

31

MIYOUNG DIDN'T KNOW what hurt more, the betrayal that bloomed in her chest or the agonizing flames that still shot through her veins.

"Nara?" When Miyoung stood, Jihoon tried to steady her, but she pushed him off. She didn't want help. She didn't need help.

"It's a long story," Nara said. The words meant nothing. There was no explanation that could dampen the blow even as Miyoung wished for one.

"You should leave," Shaman Kim said to Jihoon, though her eyes never left Miyoung. "You don't need to become involved."

"I don't leave my friends when they're in trouble," Jihoon said.

Now Shaman Kim's cold gaze raked over him. "A smart man would not stand too close to a gumiho on a full moon."

"I think I can make that decision for myself." Jihoon gripped Miyoung's hand, his fingers lacing through hers. His conviction eased the ache that surrounded her heart.

"Nara, why does Jihoon think he saw you that night?" Miyoung asked.

"It wasn't supposed to happen like this," Nara said.

"Did you send that dokkaebi?"

The young shaman frowned, like a child caught in her own lie, and Miyoung's heart cracked.

"Why would you do that?"

"I needed the bead," Nara said, like it was explanation enough, but it only created a dozen more questions that spun so fast Miyoung felt nauseated.

"Well, isn't this a cozy scene?" A form, lithe and sleek, moved out of the shadows. Her steps so light, the leaves beneath her stayed silent. As she stepped into the moonlight, Yena's eyes zeroed in on her daughter.

She glanced at Miyoung's hand, still encased in Jihoon's. Miyoung tried to pull away, but Jihoon only held on tighter.

"I never thought I'd see you again, Kim Hyunsook," Yena said.

"You know each other?" Miyoung looked between her mother and Shaman Kim, then to Nara, who looked surprisingly unsurprised.

What was happening?

With every new revelation, it felt like the world was falling away, piece by piece, until she was left hanging on to nothing.

Jihoon squeezed her hand, a reminder that there was still something to cling to.

"You haven't changed at all." Shaman Kim glared at Yena.

"You have. You've gotten old and ugly," Yena replied, her eyes like daggers. "What are you doing here, Miyoung?"

"She's here because you're about to get what you deserve." The old shaman's voice was filled with a hate that stung Miyoung even though she wasn't the target.

"You're still caught up about that?" Yena flicked her fingers, dismissing Shaman Kim's anger so easily that the older woman glowered. "That happened twenty years ago."

"Sixteen," Nara shouted. "You killed my parents sixteen years ago."

"No." Miyoung's voice came out a croak of surprise. Yena didn't spare her a glance, but Nara did.

"I'm sorry. You were just a path to her." The moonlight on her skin might have been pretty if Nara's face wasn't contorted in rage.

"What are you saying?" Miyoung asked.

"It's not enough to take her life," Shaman Kim hissed. "She took almost everything from us. We will take the same from her."

Yena's eyes flashed and she took a menacing step.

"Stop!" Nara yelled. Clearly a command for Yena but it was Miyoung who suddenly felt rooted to the ground.

"What's going on?" Miyoung asked, trying desperately to lift her feet.

"I have her yeowu guseul." Nara held up her fisted hand, then turned to Yena. "Don't come closer or she'll suffer."

Yena's lips peeled back in a snarl and she took another step.

"Seonbae, break your hand," Nara said.

Miyoung gripped her left hand with her right before she could stop herself, squeezing until she felt the minute crack of bone. She let out a howl of pain but still she held on, crushing her fingers until they were swollen, broken things.

"Stop this!" Jihoon shouted, trying to pry her hands apart.

"Fine!" Yena halted.

"Stop," Nara commanded, and Miyoung let go with a whimper. Her hands fell to her sides and she would have dropped to her knees if Jihoon wasn't holding her up.

"You always told me I deserved redemption," Miyoung said, sorrow thick in her voice. "And the whole time you were a monster, too."

Tears fell in tracks down Nara's cheeks. "I did want redemption for you. Maybe you can find it in the afterlife."

The pain of Nara's words pierced deep. Nara's friendship had all been a lie, a cruel trick to get Miyoung to trust her.

"I guess Jihoon would have been collateral damage, then. If that dokkaebi had killed him, too?" Somehow, that enraged her the most. That Jihoon would have died for Nara's revenge.

"He wasn't supposed to be there. It could have ended quietly, without all of the pain you've felt the past two months."

"Oh, how kind of you, to want to kill me quickly." Miyoung's words were meant to be cold, but she couldn't stop the break in her voice.

Not Nara. She cared about me, her mind cried, denying this new truth.

"The Taoist talisman?"

"The ghosts were supposed to scare you enough to come to us for help."

A flash of movement appeared and Miyoung thought it was those ghosts at first.

"Mother!" she shouted as Yena sprinted forward. Her mother hesitated mid-step, not for long, but long enough for Shaman Kim to scramble back, pulling Nara with her.

The young girl fell to her hands and knees and squealed as she went sprawling. The yeowu guseul slipped from her hand, rolling across the ground. Miyoung was finally released from the hold, and she dove, grabbing Yena's ankle. Her mother kicked out, connecting with Miyoung's broken hand, forcing her to let go. But it had been enough to allow Nara to limp after her halmeoni.

There was no time to think about why Miyoung sought to save Nara. Maybe she needed to prove she was not the monster the shamans painted her to be.

Shaman Kim ducked behind the first line of trees. It seemed

a faulty strategy: The thick trunks did little to hide the woman, and Nara's bright hanbok was like a beacon among the gray trees.

Yena grinned as she homed in on her prey.

Shaman Kim pulled a bujeok out of her sleeve. The red hanja glowed as the woman muttered desperate words.

Yena leapt at the same moment Shaman Kim slapped the bujeok against a tree trunk. Yena was shoved back as if by an invisible wall. Falling through the air to land with a heavy *thud*.

"Mother!" Miyoung ran to her side.

"You will not touch my kin again," Shaman Kim decreed from behind the safety of her talisman. "Come, Nara."

As they fled, Yena shoved Miyoung away in a rage. "You fool! Look what you've done!"

Miyoung opened her mouth to apologize, but stopped at the sound of shuffling to their left. Jihoon stood in the middle of the clearing, now cradling the yeowu guseul delicately.

"Give that back!" Yena leapt up.

Miyoung scrambled after her.

Yena's legs were longer than Miyoung's. Her muscles were quicker. But Miyoung had the strength of fear. She tackled her mother to the ground.

They rolled through dead leaves and grass.

"You will kill him or I will," Yena growled, yanking free easily, as Miyoung had only one good hand. She grabbed Miyoung by the shoulders.

"I can't." Miyoung grimaced as her mother's nails dug into her flesh, drawing blood.

"I told you not to talk to the shamans and you did. I told you not to use Taoist magic and you did. When will you realize that everything I do is for you?" Yena's eyes became wide white orbs, her nostrils flaring.

"Mother, please!" Miyoung begged, tears springing to her eyes. How could she explain that despite all of her mistakes, Jihoon wasn't one? But she couldn't find the words and only whispered again in a dying croak, "Please."

Yena let out a grunt of disgust and pushed Miyoung away.

She charged at Jihoon, claws outstretched.

He didn't move, eyes wide with horror.

Miyoung wanted to yell at him to run. Though it would do no good.

As Yena reached him, Miyoung buried her face in her hands. This she could not bear to see.

Yena let out a howl that ripped through the forest.

Miyoung jerked upright.

Her mother lay on the ground, spine curved in agony. A yellow bujeok stuck to her skin. One meant to chase away demons and evil.

Jihoon stood above her, his left hand still held out.

Miyoung didn't have time to wonder where he'd gotten the bujeok as she watched her mother writhe with pain, her hands fisted so tight they couldn't peel off the debilitating talisman.

Miyoung didn't hesitate. She grabbed Jihoon's arm and ran.

32

JIHOON TOOK MIYOUNG back to his apartment.

She should have declined. She wanted to keep running until the city and all her problems were far behind. But she was too tired.

Tomorrow, she'd figure out what to do about the bead Jihoon had returned to her. Tomorrow, she'd wonder if her mother would ever forgive her. Tomorrow, she'd worry about the mess she'd made of her life.

Tonight, she was too exhausted.

Jihoon unlocked his front door, holding it open for Miyoung to walk through. Neither of them had spoken in what felt like hours. Miyoung wondered if she even knew how anymore.

The entranceway was small, littered with shoes, and barely big enough for both of them to stand. Jihoon toed off his sneakers and bent down to place them neatly beside the shoes lined up by the door.

Miyoung stared stupidly at the knotted bows of her oxfords. Her whole body ached. Just the thought of bending down to untie them hurt. She flexed her hand, still sore, but already mostly healed.

Without a word, still kneeling, Jihoon untied them. She watched as he carefully undid the knots of her right shoe. He pulled on the heel and she dutifully stepped out, resting her hand on his shoulder. She left it there. Holding on to the warmth of him against her palm.

It lent her a balance when her whole world was tilting. Who would have thought such a simple gesture could feel so intimate?

Jihoon moved to her left foot. His fingers danced over her skin, light as air but twice as soft. She took her time stepping out. She wanted to concentrate on only this. On Jihoon's hands pulling on her ankle until it lifted. On his careful fingers holding her heel, sending tingles racing up her calf. Too soon, he was done, taking her shoes and meticulously placing them beside his.

Then he stood until they were face-to-face in the entrance of his apartment. For three breaths neither of them moved. Maybe because once they did they'd have to face the trials they'd just run from.

A series of rapid-fire barks broke the moment. A tiny ball of fluff ran down the hall, making a beeline toward Miyoung. Jihoon scooped the small dog into his arms before she reached her target.

"Dubu, stop it," Jihoon chastised.

"Dogs hate foxes," Miyoung mumbled.

Jihoon took Dubu down the hall. Miyoung heard a door close, muffling her barking.

"Where's your halmeoni?"

"She must be downstairs, closing up," Jihoon said. "Sit. I'll be right back."

She glanced around the living room. A lumpy couch took up the middle of the space. Photos crowded the walls, which were yellowing with age. And there was a stain on the bamboo mat covering the floor.

Miyoung loved it.

She could spend all day looking at this space that measured less than her bedroom, but held so many signs of life.

She glanced at the front door and the bright yellow bujeoks that framed it. She stood halfway out of her seat. Goose bumps rose on her arms.

Jihoon returned, holding a basket filled with random first-aid supplies. He followed her glance.

"Oh, I'm sorry!" He tore half a dozen down in one swipe.

"Thanks," she said, then gestured at the basket. "What's all this for?"

"Your shoulder," Jihoon answered.

"I don't need it. Super gumiho healing."

"I know," Jihoon said with a sigh. It seemed his calm had been a facade as well. Now, with nothing to do, he looked as tired as she felt.

"Give them to me." She held out her hand.

He lifted a brow in question.

"Your leg will get infected if we don't clean it." She gestured toward his blood-soaked pants.

"Oh, it doesn't hurt." He crossed his legs to hide the wound.

"Don't be a baby about it," she said, pulling on his knee. She yanked his pant leg up, and he let out a hiss of pain. The imprint of her teeth was almost a perfect oval in the flesh of his leg.

"Sorry," she muttered. To hide her embarrassment, she got to work, dabbing disinfectant on the gash so liberally that Jihoon yelped.

"Sorry," she said again as she began wrapping the wound.

"It's fine," he said, but his voice was a squeak of poorly concealed pain.

Jihoon stopped her when she started to pack everything away and pulled her to the couch. "Will you be okay?"

"I don't know." Miyoung settled beside him. "A gumiho's bead belongs inside of her, not rolling around in her pocket. Outside of me it's too vulnerable."

"Vulnerable?" Jihoon asked.

"If a human possesses a gumiho's bead, he can control her through that connection. That's why my mother got so angry when you picked it up."

"I would never . . ." Jihoon trailed off, but Miyoung nodded in understanding.

"I should never have let it come to this." She laid her head against the lumpy back of the couch and closed her eyes. "I should have listened to my mother."

"Will she come after you?" Jihoon asked.

Miyoung shook her head. "But she'll come for you because you know our secret."

"I'm not scared of her."

"Then you're a fool."

"Well, I'm a fool who has you to protect me." Jihoon grinned. Miyoung didn't return the smile.

"My mother has lived a long time because she's smart. She will come after you, Jihoon. You need to leave town."

"Is there no other option?" Jihoon asked.

"It's the safest."

"Because it's what you'd do?" Jihoon asked, and Miyoung didn't like the accusation she heard in his voice. "When things get hard you run, don't you?"

"It's the safest option," Miyoung repeated. "For everyone."

"But not the only one," Jihoon said.

"Please, just listen to me. I know better than anyone what my mother is capable of."

And I don't want you to get hurt, she thought, but couldn't bring herself to say it aloud. She had no right to care about him when she was the reason he was in danger.

She slumped down on the couch. Her aching body reminded her she needed to feed or face the consequences.

Everything seemed so desperately ruined, like fine silk shredded to pieces with no hope of repair.

"If she loves you, she'll come around," Jihoon said, breaking through Miyoung's thoughts.

She heard his doubt, but appreciated the effort. Jihoon usually didn't lie, so it was nice that he tried to for her.

"She's the only person in this world who loves me. Now I'm not sure if she can anymore. For Yena, there is no love without trust."

"You're wrong," Jihoon said.

"You don't know her like I do," Miyoung insisted.

"No, not about that. You said your mother is the only person who loves you." His tone was deep. So heavy, it weighed her down.

"Don't." It came out as a plea. She couldn't hear this when her heart had already been so battered tonight. If he did this, she was afraid it would shatter.

"Why not?" Jihoon frowned.

"You can't feel that way. It's only been two months."

Jihoon grinned. Not what she expected. "A lot can happen in two months. You can meet a girl who seems angry and secretive and learn that it's all just a front for a kind heart that's been hurt too many times. I know what it's like to need to hide your bruises behind a mask."

"You don't know what you're talking about. I'm not kind."

Jihoon chuckled. "I know you don't see it, but you're a kind soul. You helped Changwan when he was being bullied. You forced me to make up with Somin because you knew I'd regret fighting with her. And you saved me, multiple times. You're my hero."

Miyoung laughed. "People often mistake gratitude for deeper emotions."

"Fine," Jihoon said, his voice sobering. "Then I'll say it simply."

For the first time in her life, Miyoung felt like the unsuspecting prey. Jihoon's irises were dark. Too dark. Like they'd swallow the world, her included.

"I love you."

Miyoung let out a shuddering breath. Tears fell, hot against her cheeks. Jihoon wiped them away with his thumbs.

"You're such a foolish boy."

His dimples flashed. "I take that to mean you believe me."

"Yes, I believe you."

Jihoon brushed the hair from her forehead. Miyoung held her breath as his featherlight touch ran down to her ear. She never knew an ear had so many nerve endings. Every cell in her body vibrated. And she was no longer exhausted.

He leaned closer.

"I've never kissed anyone before." She squeezed her eyes shut, mortified. Her cheeks burned and she tried to push her hair forward to hide it.

Jihoon stopped her fluttering hands.

She kept her eyes closed as he ran his fingers down the line of her cheek and into her hair. He tucked the strands behind her ears carefully. She waited to feel where his hand would trail next.

His movements were slow, like he wanted to savor this moment as much as she. The small moments that built and built, an intricate weaving maze. Branches snaked into every crevice until it latched on to all of her. And she could no longer hide anything, because now he held it all.

She felt completely exposed. But she didn't pull back. She wanted him to see. This was who she was, without artifice or carefully erected shields. For the first time, there was a person who knew all of her. And accepted it.

He cupped her cheek, his fingers curling through her hair.

The first brush of his lips on hers was so soft, she wondered if she had imagined it. Then came the second, a deeper exploration, but just as quick. The feel of his skin against hers made her fingers tingle and she fisted them in the lapels of his shirt.

When he kissed her the third time, she pulled on his collar, dragging him down so his lips crushed against hers. He gasped at the pressure, but the hands holding her trailed back to cup her neck, until it was unclear who held who.

She tilted her head to deepen the angle. A hum sounded in his throat—a vibration that traveled from his lips into hers and down her spine.

A thousand lights burst behind her closed lids. Energy shot through her fingertips, warming her previously chilled body.

Jihoon's arms wound around her waist, pulling her into his lap.

She'd read books that said two lovers' hearts could race as one. This wasn't true for Miyoung. Her heart chased Jihoon's, speeding in a breakneck sprint to catch up.

She wanted to absorb the feel of his skin, the scent of him, the taste of him. Her heart had been emptied tonight, and she wanted to fill it again with him.

33

JIHOON DIDN'T KNOW when they fell asleep. He jerked upright, suddenly awake.

"What is it?" Miyoung had been curled into his side and blinked owlishly at him.

"I don't know." Jihoon frowned, unsure what had pulled him so sharply from sleep.

Then came a crash from downstairs. He rose.

Miyoung stood as well. "Where's it coming from?"

"The restaurant," he said, stepping toward the back door. "Halmeoni?" he called. No answer.

The surprise he'd felt at waking had been centered in his belly. Now it moved to his chest as anxiety overtook him.

"Halmeoni?" Jihoon shouted, now running.

"Wait!" Miyoung called behind him.

He didn't listen. He raced down the stairs, taking them two at a time.

The restaurant was dark and still. It seemed abandoned, and Jihoon had a moment to wonder if he'd imagined the sound when there was a banging crash from the kitchen.

"Jihoon-ah." Miyoung's voice held caution, but he ran toward the sound.

Jihoon stopped short and stared, unable to process what he saw.

His halmeoni lay on the floor, her apron stained crimson. A stack of plates had rained around her, covering the floor with broken shards.

A shape melted out of the shadows and became long and thin. A beautiful body, hair raven black, and eyes to match: Gu Yena.

"Stupid human," she said a second before she struck Jihoon.

34

MIYOUNG LEAPT TOWARD Jihoon. A yell of surprise caught in her throat so it came out a groan of distress.

"I'm disappointed in you, Daughter."

"What are you doing?" Miyoung's question wavered with her sobs.

"I'm fixing your mistakes, like I always do."

Miyoung stood slowly, making sure to position her body between Yena and Jihoon.

"Please, Jihoon is important to me." Miyoung hardly moved a muscle. It felt like she stood at a precipice. One strong breeze would send her tumbling over the edge or back to safety. The direction of the wind relied solely on her mother's heart.

"You care about him that much?" Yena asked.

"I do." She held on to her mother's considering expression like a lifeline.

Then Yena's sudden laughter deflated Miyoung.

"You've proven your lack of judgment to me, Daughter. First with that shaman and now with this boy. A gumiho does not love. We are objects of desire. We are illusion and beauty that humans lust after. That is why they are easily manipulated."

"You don't understand." Angry tears burned at Miyoung's eyes.

"No, I understand too well. I was foolish like you once, and I've been punished for that lapse in judgment."

The words stung. Did Yena mean to imply Miyoung had been her punishment?

"I'm doing this for your own good." Yena picked up a knife and turned toward Halmeoni. "This woman's death will be on you. You need to learn that there are consequences to your actions. And that there can be no witnesses to them either."

"Please." Miyoung held on to a sliver of hope that her mother would love Miyoung enough to listen.

"No!" From behind Miyoung, Jihoon jumped up and charged toward Yena. There was no time to stop him, no time to warn him.

Yena moved so quickly, it was a flash. She stood, aimed the knife, and let Jihoon's forward motion do the work for her.

The blade slid into his gut so smoothly that Miyoung thought perhaps it hadn't happened. There was no jerk of his body, no cry of pain. He dropped with a dull *thud*. And the blood—so much blood—pooled around him, so thick it was black.

35

MIYOUNG'S SCREAM WAS more of a howl as she dropped beside Jihoon, soaking her knees in his blood.

"I suggest you absorb his gi. End it painlessly for him. Let's forget your mistakes. I'll let you start over." Yena didn't so much as glance at the bodies sprawled over the floor as she delicately picked her way to the door and left.

"Please. Please. Please," Miyoung chanted over and over as she pressed her hands against Jihoon's wound. It did no good, so much blood had already been lost so quickly. She gathered towels, rags, anything to stop the bleeding.

When she pressed her red-stained hand to his neck, she couldn't find the beat of his heart and hers stopped.

"No. No. No." It was her new chant now as she pressed her ear to his chest, hoping to find the pulse of his life inside. It was silent.

Miyoung let out a wailing gasp as she pumped her fists against his heart. Her sobbing shook her body and something fell from her pocket.

Miyoung looked down at the yeowu guseul. Small and plain, sitting on the stained linoleum floor. She picked it up, gripping it tightly before collapsing against Jihoon.

"I'm sorry," she whispered, though the words felt useless and hollow. The bead burned hot against her palm. Miyoung jerked up, dropping it to the ground before it singed her skin.

Jihoon lurched with her, desperately gasping.

"Jihoon?"

He gagged, blood spraying from his lips and splattering her face. His body seized; his eyes rolled back. Blood and phlegm dripped from his lips.

"Wait!" She held her hands against his wound, applying pressure. But it only seemed to make the blood flow faster through her fingers.

"Please tell me what to do," she pleaded, with Jihoon, with the gods, with herself.

"The bead," came the whispered croak.

Miyoung looked at the yeowu guseul with trepidation, suspecting the voice had come from the stone itself.

"Use the bead." Halmeoni crawled over, dried blood coating her scalp.

"Halmeoni," Miyoung said, half in relief and half in desperation.

"Use the yeowu guseul." Halmeoni griped Jihoon's hand, his breathing now so shallow it seemed nonexistent.

"How do you know about the bead?"

"The old see and know more than you think. Please, save my grandson." Her tears fell, running through the twisting wrinkles on her face.

Miyoung picked up the yeowu guseul carefully, the heat so intense it caused her skin to pucker. She almost dropped it, unused to feeling pain from her own bead. But she tightened her grip instead.

Jihoon started heaving as he tried to pull in air.

Miyoung pressed the bead over his heart.

The searing stone cooked her skin as she held it in place. Jihoon twisted against the pain. She moved along with him.

Coughs racked Jihoon. His cheeks and chin painted in crimson.

The bead cooled in her palms, the energy leaching from it.

Miyoung cursed as she applied more pressure.

"Don't die," she pleaded.

Jihoon's body did not listen. He shuddered in the final death throes, his body giving in to its fatal injuries.

"It's not working!" Miyoung yelled, pumping her closed fists against his chest.

Then Jihoon stopped seizing. He stopped coughing up blood. Everything stopped. Including his heart beneath her palms.

"No!" She slammed her hands into his chest over and over. Like she could pump his heart herself.

Halmeoni reached out to stop her. "It needs more energy."

"I'm trying." She opened her hands; angry red welts branded her palms. The stone sat on Jihoon's chest, saturated with blood, his and hers.

Halmeoni took Miyoung by the shoulders. "It needs gi."

"I don't have enough."

"I know. Siphon mine."

"What?" She wanted to ask how Halmeoni could know this, but instead she said, "I've never taken a woman's gi. I don't know if I can."

"Well, I guess we'll find out." Halmeoni took Miyoung's bloody hands in hers.

Miyoung hesitated, glancing at Jihoon's still body.

"Please, quick," Halmeoni pleaded.

Closing her eyes, Miyoung formed the link.

When she pulled at the gi, it pushed back, but she didn't let go and finally it flooded her in a hot wave, as if Halmeoni had pushed her energy toward Miyoung.

The bead heated and Halmeoni guided their joined hands, pressing the stone to Jihoon's chest.

Halmeoni's gi entered Miyoung's body, feeding her hunger. Then it immediately siphoned into the stone. Like a flow of thirst-quenching water hitting her stomach only to be squeezed back out again. She was merely a bridge between Halmeoni's energy and the stone.

Jihoon's eyes fluttered, a roll of movement behind his lids. His chest rose in shallow breaths.

Miyoung tried to close the connection, but the bead pulled at the energy. She was helplessly caught in the current, a waterfall effect that couldn't be stopped any more than one could reverse gravity.

She started to pull her hands free, to break the bond physically, but Halmeoni's hands clamped down.

"It worked," Miyoung whispered. "Stop it now."

"It's not done yet," Halmeoni insisted.

Sweat dripped from the old woman's brow, mixing with her blood.

Miyoung felt Halmeoni's energy waning. A drying well that would soon leave an empty pit behind.

A trail of blood dripped from Halmeoni's nose, splattering onto their joined hands.

Jihoon's eyes shot open. He gasped like a fish suffocating on dry land.

Then he lay still.

Halmeoni collapsed, and Miyoung caught her before her head cracked against the linoleum.

Jihoon pulled in labored gasps, but he breathed.

Silence overtook the ruined kitchen.

And the bead was gone.

36

AT THE HOSPITAL, the police came.

Miyoung should have expected it. The restaurant was a crime scene, blood everywhere. There would definitely be questions.

She stood, hugging her arms around herself in the waiting room as the officer interrogated her.

"Can you describe the attacker?" The cop was young. An officer in a gray button-down and neon-yellow vest. The thick black lettering labeling him as POLICE looked stark, almost angry. Miyoung stared at it instead of at the officer's judgmental face.

"I can't," Miyoung said. It was the truth. No matter what Yena had done, there was no way Miyoung could turn her in.

"Miyoung-ah, what the hell happened?" Somin stormed up, eyes puffy from crying. Changwan trailed behind with the forlorn expression of a lost puppy.

"Please, I'm conducting an investigation," said the officer.

That brought a frown to Somin's lips and even though she backed off, she watched the cop closely.

The officer turned mistrustful eyes to Miyoung. "Now, are you saying you can't remember anything about the attacker? You know it's against the law to hide information in a police investigation." She shouldn't have been surprised at the suspicion. She literally had blood on her hands.

"I don't know." Miyoung lowered her head as three pairs of eyes scrutinized her now.

"Maybe a trip to the station might loosen your memory."

"Is that necessary?" Changwan asked.

"It's my job to ask questions."

"It's your job to catch whoever did this, not to treat a witness like a criminal," Somin said.

"I was only wondering if she's not remembering all the details," the officer said apprehensively.

"Oh." Somin backed up with a fake sweet smile, her eyes still bright as lasers. "Then I guess you're done with your questions now that you got the answer."

"Sure." The officer stuffed his notepad into his pocket. "If you can remember anything, then please let us know." He pulled out his card, handing it to Changwan and no one else. It would have made Miyoung laugh if she didn't still feel like crying.

As soon as the officer left, Somin spun on Miyoung again.

"What happened? Who did this to him?" The anger in Somin's eyes pierced through Miyoung's heart. She hadn't realized she'd grown so fond of this girl. And to see the disappointment and hurt on Somin's face caused Miyoung to falter.

"I can't . . ." Miyoung couldn't finish her sentence.

"But you do know. I can tell you know something you're not telling us."

"I'm sorry."

"I don't need your apologies." Somin stomped down the hall toward Jihoon's room, leaving Changwan to follow slowly.

Miyoung found her voice. "Changwan-ah."

He looked at her with sad eyes. "Can you really not tell us what happened? Not even to help Jihoon and his halmeoni?"

Miyoung shook her head silently.

His face fell and his voice became flat. "You should go home. We'll be with Jihoon tonight."

Changwan left Miyoung alone in the waiting room. She'd never heard such a harsh tone from him. And it was his disappointment that finally broke her.

o o o

Miyoung didn't leave, but she didn't go into the room, giving Somin and Changwan time with Jihoon. Even after they left to visit Halmeoni, she stayed on the uncomfortable chairs in the cold waiting room.

A night-shift nurse gave her a cup of water.

Miyoung accepted it with a nod of thanks.

"You should sit with him," the nurse said. "It helps to have loved ones sit with patients."

"I don't know."

"It's good for loved ones, too. Go talk to him. He can hear you."

She wanted to say she didn't know if she was a loved one, but the nurse's kindness was too much for her to resist.

The sound of machines filled the small hospital room. Jihoon lay so still, Miyoung almost panicked until she saw the shallow rise and fall of his chest.

She sat and gripped Jihoon's hand in her newly bandaged ones. For some reason the burns on her hands weren't healing. And no matter her protests, the nurses had insisted on wrapping her wounds.

"I'm sorry," she said. "For my mother, for your halmeoni. For everything." She gripped his hand tightly until her wounds burned and her knuckles turned white.

"You have to wake up, you have to." Shame blazed through her until she thought it would burn her to nothing but ash.

Jihoon's hand jerked in hers, and her eyes flew to his face. He convulsed so violently that Miyoung jumped back. The machines beeped rapidly, as if screaming at her to do something.

Nurses raced through the door. Miyoung was pushed aside as they pulled the bed rails down.

"You should leave." It was the same kind nurse who'd spoken to her before.

"What's going on?" she asked.

"He's seizing; it can happen after a trauma," the nurse said. But Miyoung was an experienced liar; she knew when someone was only telling her part of the truth.

She retreated to the hall, where her legs gave out as she sank onto a bench along the wall. Something wasn't right. She'd felt an energy in Jihoon, something familiar, something strong.

Miyoung knew now that the bead wasn't gone.

It was inside of Jihoon.

o o o

"He didn't die." Yena sat next to Miyoung in the waiting room. Even though the medical team had revived Jihoon, she hadn't dared return to his room.

"No," Miyoung confirmed.

"What did you do?"

"I used the bead." It wasn't worth lying. Her mother would find out eventually.

"Stupid girl."

"You lied to me." The heat of anger rose up in her, and she

embraced it because if she was angry, at least she wasn't feeling any of the other emotions she wanted to ignore.

"What?" Yena's voice was low and cold.

"You said that yeowu guseuls don't exist. If you'd told me . . . if I'd known—"

"I didn't tell you because I knew you were too immature to know. And I was right because you lost yours and have now put it in that pathetic boy."

The truth of Yena's words deflated Miyoung's anger. And without it, Miyoung felt completely drained.

"What do we do now?"

"I want to rip it out of his chest."

Miyoung twisted to see a look of resignation on Yena's face.

"But you can't do it without hurting me, too, can you?"

"It could damage the bead," Yena confirmed. "I don't care about the boy's life, but I won't risk you."

Miyoung should've been grateful, comforted even. Instead she felt empty.

"You can't be around him," Yena said. "If he holds your yeowu guseul, he holds control over you."

"He wouldn't hurt me. I trust him."

"I don't."

"You're telling me to leave him alone. His only family is dying down the hallway," Miyoung said.

"I didn't kill the old woman."

Miyoung sighed, because her mother was right. The blame for that lay squarely on her own shoulders.

"If I feed, will it hurt him?" Miyoung asked.

"There's no way of knowing that." Yena spoke like a politician skirting the topic. It made Miyoung's suspicion expand tenfold until she had no room for anything else, like air or rational thought.

"The bead is connected to me, even in Jihoon. What do you think will happen to him if I feed and it makes the energy of the bead flare up, too? It could kill him."

Yena shrugged, clearly uncaring of what happened to Jihoon. "Without your bead you have to feed more often and you have to feed directly from your prey's flesh. No more of this sifting energy. It's the only way you can guarantee you'll survive."

"I won't feed."

"What?" Yena's eyes narrowed.

"You ruined Nara's life to feed. You didn't need to kill both of her parents. Did you never think about what it would do to her?"

"I don't check the family status of all of my prey," Yena answered, so flippantly it squeezed at Miyoung's heart.

"I won't feed tonight."

"Why? Because I killed that shaman's parents? Or because of that boy?"

"No," Miyoung said. How could she explain to her mother that she'd always struggled with the idea that others had to die for her to live? How could she explain that she just didn't believe her life was worth more than the lives of her victims? How could she explain that tonight hadn't just hurt because of Nara's betrayal, but because Miyoung could understand why the young shaman had done it all. Revenge for the unjust death of her parents. It was true what the shamans thought. Yena and Miyoung were the bad guys in this story. Their choices had a ripple of consequences that even they couldn't see. And people ended up hurt, like Jihoon.

"Not tonight, Mother. The sun is almost up anyway. Just . . ."

Miyoung trailed off and let her head drop into her hands. "Not tonight."

"Fine," Yena snapped, and Miyoung knew the conversation wasn't done, just on pause until the next full moon. "But if we're to find a way to get that bead out of the boy and back into you, then we need to seek out answers. We're leaving. Today." There was finality in Yena's voice.

Miyoung didn't move, her body still, her mind racing. She glanced up and saw Somin and Changwan walk past the nurses' station. They didn't even spare her a look. Everything she had thought she could have here was gone now. She was a fool to think she deserved anything good in this life.

"Miyoung-ah, did you hear me?"

"Yes," Miyoung finally said. "I heard you. We'll leave today."

37

JIHOON WOKE TO a broken life, but his body was whole. He'd expected some kind of gruesome surgical scene when he lifted his sheet to look, but the bandage was a simple square of gauze over his abdomen.

At first, a part of him was convinced it was just a dream, though he knew better.

Christmas came and went while he was in the hospital. Somin and her mother had visited with presents and silly Santa hats. But it just made him more aware that Halmeoni lay in a coma down the hall. This was the first Christmas he'd spent without her in thirteen years.

Three days after being discharged, he had the first episode. A headache that started behind the temples and grew to a migraine within seconds until the pain became a nauseating wave. He barely made it to the bathroom before he was sick. He didn't tell anyone. But when he passed out at the PC room, he woke up in the hospital.

They called it a seizure.

He'd been scanned and tested and had gallons of blood drawn. Everything showed that he'd completely healed, no blood clots, no tumors. A perfectly healthy boy who kept getting migraines so bad that he'd end up in the emergency room.

He spent New Year's in the hospital. And he wasn't liking this trend of celebrating his holidays in a patient gown. So with Lunar New Year fast approaching, he resolved to stave off the headaches.

It didn't help that bills piled up from the hospital and late rent, and Miyoung never came back. He waited to hear from her, convinced she wouldn't leave without a word. Life couldn't be that cruel, to have his parents abandon him, then his halmeoni so sick she wouldn't wake up, and now Miyoung had left. However, as the days, then weeks passed, he realized he'd been wrong to have such faith. Life wasn't fair. It was a mocking master that yanked at the frail strings of his life until they threatened to snap.

o o o

"You skipped Sunday dinner," Somin said, plopping down beside Jihoon.

He didn't look up from his computer screen. The *click-clack* of gaming filled the air of the PC room.

"My mom is starting to get worried. She might call your mother again if you don't—"

"Fine," Jihoon said. "I'll come next week." He still didn't glance up from the screen.

"Halmeoni will be proud of you when she wakes up."

Jihoon didn't reply but his throat tightened as he clicked through the practice test. It was like a full-time job catching up on years of missed schoolwork. But he'd learned that the tactical mind he used for his gaming was actually pretty good at studying.

"Jihoon-ah, don't you think you should get some decent sleep? And some food?" Somin leaned closer and sniffed, then scrunched up her nose. "And a shower?"

"Don't bother, Somin-ah," Changwan said from the other side of Jihoon, where his screen announced his losing score. "I already suggested a trip to the jjimjilbang. It was a fail."

"Like your father would even let you go to a public bathhouse," Jihoon muttered.

"Jihoon-ah!" Somin chastised, and he knew he must have crossed a line. Somin never took Changwan's side.

"Second year is almost over. Once senior year starts next month, I won't have time to catch up," Jihoon reminded them.

"You need to take care of yourself, too, or you'll burn out." Somin studied Jihoon. She'd changed her hair again this week. It was black and blunt cut at her chin with straight bangs like a porcelain doll. It fit her small build and round face. A face that currently watched him with deep concern.

"You slept at the hospital again last night, didn't you?" Somin picked at Jihoon's wrinkled blazer. "Is it because you're not comfortable at your place alone? You could stay with us. My mom wouldn't mind and Dubu misses you."

"No, my place is fine," Jihoon insisted, his eyes never leaving his screen.

"Is it even your place anymore?" Somin asked. "Your mother is paying the hospital bills. I'm sure she'd help with rent if she knew the landlord changed the lease from long-term to monthly. You know he's trying to kick you out while Halmeoni is in the hospital."

"I don't need that woman's charity." Jihoon closed his eyes to ward off a growing headache. It had been hard enough accepting his mother's help to pay the hospital bills. But Somin had pointed out it was her duty as a daughter and mother to pay for it. But he'd refused to admit he needed more financial help for rent, especially when his mother hadn't even offered to let him stay with her and her new perfect family. She had to know he'd say no, but still she hadn't risked asking him.

Somin turned him by the shoulders so she could look at his sallow complexion. "Jihoon-ah, I'm worried about you."

"You don't need to be. I have everything under control." He fisted shaking hands, stuffing them into his pockets to hide from Somin's eagle eyes.

"Maybe you should call her."

"I told you I'm not calling my mother."

"Not her," Somin said. "Gu Miyoung."

Just the sound of her name made Jihoon's heart ache.

"Why would you tell me to do that? You never really trusted her."

"She keeps secrets. If she knows who hurt you—"

"I told you she wasn't there when it happened. She found us after." Jihoon hated lying to Somin, but it was better this way. Safer to keep her in the dark.

Somin shook her head, her eyes conflicted. "That's not the point. I just think it would be better if you got some kind of closure. You're so sad all the time, Jihoon-ah. I don't like it."

"I'm not sad. I'm just busy." He brushed off her statement.

"Don't let your pride get in the way this time."

"This time?" Jihoon scowled, pretending to read his screen but not absorbing any of the words.

"You think that if you admit you miss people, that means you're weak," Somin said. "But maybe it will help you let go."

"I don't need your amateur therapy," Jihoon said, clicking a random answer on the practice quiz and swearing when it came up wrong.

"I just care about you, Jihoon," Somin said.

That was the problem. Jihoon didn't want anyone to care about him. It only hurt more when they left.

38

THE HOSPITAL WAS a tall gray building with a large driveway leading to the glass entrance. The signs had been changed to wish everyone a happy Lunar New Year. With it would come the end of January and the beginning of winter break. And the one-month anniversary of Miyoung tearing his life apart and leaving him.

"Jihoon-ah, how did you do during finals?" Nurse Jang asked as he approached the seventh-floor nurses' station.

"Third place in the class."

"Your halmeoni would be proud."

Jihoon smiled, a weak impersonation of his old dimple-deep grins.

"Make sure you go home tonight," Nurse Jang said. "Your halmeoni would not approve of you sleeping over."

"Yes, ma'am."

The telltale beat of monitors welcomed him as he entered his halmeoni's room. The second bed sat empty today, but it would be filled again soon enough. They couldn't afford a private room, but usually the other occupants never stayed that long. Though Jihoon frowned as he remembered the harabeoji who'd last occupied the other bed had seemed fairly ill.

"I'm here, Halmeoni." Jihoon lowered the humidifier. He took out a stick of lip balm and lifted her oxygen mask to apply it. "If you don't use this, your lips will get too dry. You hate your skin getting cracked."

He pulled out a sheet of paper from his bag. "I got third rank during the end-of-the-year exams, Halmeoni. You'd never believe it if you didn't see it for yourself."

He spoke with a shred of hope, like this was enough to make her open her eyes for the first time in a month.

She lay still and quiet.

"I know, you're asking why not first," Jihoon said conversationally. "I might be more motivated if you were there to nag me." Still nothing and he let out a dejected sigh.

"Jihoon-ah?"

He turned and spotted Detective Hae. "Ajeossi."

"How is she today?"

"I think she has more color," Jihoon said, though he couldn't be sure.

"She looks good." Detective Hae gave Jihoon's shoulder a squeeze. Though it was meant to comfort, it made Jihoon stiffen. Such a paternal gesture was foreign to him. And the detective had a way of making Jihoon wonder what things would be like if he'd had a father figure in his life. It was useless to wonder, though. Jihoon's father was a criminal and a selfish man. Even if he were around, he wouldn't be like Detective Hae, who was stable and kind.

Jihoon cleared his throat and glanced toward the other side of the room. "It looks like we're getting a new neighbor."

"Yes, Mr. Kim passed away last night. His daughters were talking to the nurses outside just now, poor girls."

Jihoon's mouth became dry. The news of death did that to him these days. A sharp fear that he'd soon be the one whispered about with such pity, a poor boy who'd lost someone he loved.

"He didn't seem that bad off."

"He's at peace now and his soul can finally rest."

"You really believe that?" Jihoon asked. Detective Hae was devoutly Christian. Surprisingly, it had lent Jihoon some comfort in the past month as he tried to come to grips with his halmeoni's condition.

"Sometimes, in life, we cannot find the salvation we need. If so, it can come in death."

"Well, sometimes people shouldn't die so soon. It's not fair."

Detective Hae nodded. Jihoon didn't know if it was agreement or not.

"What are you doing here?"

"I'm still your primary contact for the hospital. They called me when you didn't go to your last appointment."

Jihoon's sigh wasn't directed at the detective, though he was the only one to receive it. When Jihoon was in the hospital after the accident, Detective Hae had taken on the case. Without anyone else to call, the hospital had taken the detective's contact information. Jihoon had never changed it.

"I told you, if they call me, I'm coming down here to check on you," Detective Hae said.

"I know," Jihoon said. "I'm sorry."

Detective Hae had proven to be more than a cop trying to close a case. He'd become personally invested in the attack at Halmeoni's restaurant. Sometimes the neighbors told Jihoon they saw Detective Hae diligently canvassing the area. Jihoon knew the attacker would never be brought to justice, but it mattered that someone cared.

"Jihoon-ah, when a man gives his word, he should keep it."

The lecture was something Jihoon would have ignored a month ago, but he nodded dutifully. "Yes, sir."

The detective was a man with a distinct sense of right and wrong. Follow the law, be a good person, and live a decent life.

"Have you given thought to what I asked you last time?"

Jihoon hunched, averse to the topic at hand. "I did," he mumbled.

"And?" Detective Hae prompted. "Would you like me to try to find your father? It could make it easier to have a parent . . ." He trailed off, knowing it was a sore subject for Jihoon. The detective was good at his job; it had only taken a day for him to find out who Jihoon's mother was and where she lived. But he'd respected Jihoon's desire not to call her and that had gone a long way in earning Jihoon's trust.

"I'll be okay once Halmeoni wakes up," Jihoon said, standing. He wanted to end this discussion. "I'll go to that appointment now." And with a final bow, he escaped.

o o o

The neurology floor was newly renovated, frosted glass bordering the halls and freestanding waterfalls decorating the waiting room.

Jihoon checked in and was immediately brought to the back, where Dr. Choi waited in an examination room. He stood with arms crossed, his square jaw set. The gray at his temples gave him the distinguished look of a man with wisdom. Jihoon suspected it was a carefully cultivated look.

"Mr. Ahn, how nice of you to grace us with your presence." Dr. Choi gave a smile that didn't reach his eyes.

"Do you really think another test is going to tell you anything new?"

"What concerns us is that nothing seems to be working and the seizures have grown more severe," Dr. Choi said, as if lecturing a room on a medical phenomenon. "Don't you want to know what's causing this?"

Jihoon couldn't very well say he already knew. What would Dr. Choi do if Jihoon said, *Well, I do know what's causing them. A couple months ago I fell for a gumiho whose mother put my halmeoni in a coma and probably put a fox curse on me.*

That would wipe the smirk off the doctor's face.

"Fine." He shrugged. What was another brain scan in the grand scheme of things?

The tests told them nothing. And the doctor left him with vague talk of possibly trying surgery if medication kept failing.

Jihoon made his way back to his halmeoni's room and plopped down in the chair beside the bed. Detective Hae had long since left, but new flowers stood on the bedside table. A cheerful sight that Jihoon barely noticed.

"She left without a word," Jihoon said to his halmeoni. "We'll never see her again, so we shouldn't hold our breath. Right?"

He stared at his halmeoni, like he was waiting for an answer. "Right," he agreed with himself.

"It's not like we haven't gone through this before. People have left before. We don't need anyone else." Jihoon laid his head on his halmeoni's shoulder, careful not to put his full weight on her. "We never needed anyone but each other."

Nurse Jang found him asleep twenty minutes later.

WE'VE LEARNED HOW gumiho rose. How they were cursed. How they grew to hate the humans who both shunned and fed them. But there is the story of one gumiho in particular that we must learn.

Long after the first gumiho disappeared from the face of this earth, during a time when the stories had started to become myths . . .

There lived a man with three sons and no daughters. He prayed every day for a daughter to be born. One day his wife came home and presented him with a baby girl.

The family lived happily for years. The wife claimed he held his daughter so tight, she feared the little girl would be crushed by her father's love.

When the girl turned thirteen, the livestock started to die. Soon, the man's fortune began to dwindle from the loss. So he set his eldest son on watch to find out why the cows and horses were dying.

The next morning, the eldest son said, "I saw Little Sister going to the barn. When I checked, the cow's liver had been eaten."

Enraged, the man threw out his eldest son.

The next night, he set his second son to stand guard.

In the morning, he reported seeing his sister slaughter a horse.

"You want to kill your sinless little sister! I no longer wish to lay eyes on you!"

Finally, the man set his youngest son to watch the barn.

The third boy watched his little sister approach the barn, kill a cow, and devour its liver.

However, fearing banishment like his older brothers, he lied.

"The cow died naturally," he claimed. "Then a fox came and ate its liver."

The two older sons wandered the land until they came upon a Taoist master who taught them the ways of his magic. However, they could not forget their family. So they decided to return home.

The Taoist master bestowed upon them three bottles: one white, one blue, and one red.

The brothers thanked him for his gifts and left.

When they arrived home, the house was empty save for their younger sister.

She greeted them happily.

They asked her what had happened, and she told them that their parents and youngest brother had died.

"We are thirsty," the eldest brother said. "Would you please go to the spring and get us water?"

When she left to fetch it, the brothers fled. For they knew she had killed and eaten their parents and youngest brother.

She raced after them, calling for them to return.

They threw the white bottle and it created a thicket of thorns. She broke free and continued to chase them.

They threw the red bottle and it engulfed her in fire, but she continued to race after them.

They threw the blue bottle and it created a river that carried her away in a strong current. They never saw her again.

But this was an important time in the life of this gumiho. For she survived. She grew to hate humans and she birthed a daughter, one we all know as Gu Miyoung.

39

JIHOON'S DAYS NOW started before the sun rose. His new reality left no room for the laziness that had previously ruled his days. In an attempt to pay the rent in Halmeoni's absence, he'd taken on part-time jobs while school was out. His first was delivering newspapers and milk cartons to people's front doors before dawn. He rode a secondhand bicycle, but sometimes the streets were so steep, it was easier to push the thing. The crooked roads he used to love became his enemy as he trudged up and down, up and down.

He worked meticulously to get each order of milk on the front stoops or in the mailboxes along with the daily paper.

He'd taken on the day shift pumping gas for less than minimum wage. The owner claimed it was because he didn't yet have a high school diploma.

Jihoon's fingers froze in the late-January cold since he'd forgotten his gloves. When he raised his hands to blow on them, he smelled the bitter gasoline on his skin. He stared at the white scar in the center of his palm. A souvenir from when he'd snatched Miyoung's bead from Shaman Kim. And every time he saw the puckered scar, it reminded him of that night and all he'd lost.

Night fell before he finished work, bringing with it a starless sky lit only by the full moon. The owner of the gas station ran to catch Jihoon before he left for the day.

"Here." He shoved two triangle kimbap into Jihoon's hands. He was a portly man, stingy and balding. "You've been standing in the cold all day. These are barely expired. Take them."

As Jihoon walked, his eyes traveled to the sky. The sight of the full moon brought a dull ache that ran through his ribs. It was the first full moon since Miyoung had left.

He ate the triangle kimbap on his way to the convenience store, his third and final job of the day. The trek was tiring. His breath created clouds in the cold air that fogged his vision in teasing puffs.

His coworker, Kim Pyojoo, stood behind the counter. "You're fourteen minutes late, Jihoon-ssi," he said. "That'll come out of your pay."

Pyojoo was only twenty and had been working at the convenience store three months longer than Jihoon. He was also the manager's nephew and thought that made him Jihoon's boss. Jihoon didn't care enough to correct him.

"The delivery came in this morning." Pyojoo gestured toward the storage room.

Jihoon rolled his eyes behind Pyojoo's back at the implied command. When he'd first started, Pyojoo had claimed the newest employee was responsible for unloading the deliveries. Jihoon had long since realized this was a lie.

Still he didn't complain as he carried the crates to the front. The task made his arms, which already felt like wet noodles after five hours of pumping gas, ache. He had a low-grade headache that the fluorescent lights didn't help. Plus, it smelled like someone had dropped milk somewhere in the store that was quickly souring. He knew it would be his job to find it.

It took Jihoon a half hour to get all of the crates inside and he stumbled a bit as he set the last crate down. Glad to finally be done with the task as he spread his aching fingers.

"Ya, what are you thinking?" Pyojoo asked.

"What?" Jihoon rubbed his sore shoulder.

"Why would we need ten crates of strawberry milk?" Pyojoo tapped the pile. "So?"

"So?" Jihoon repeated.

"So move them back."

Jihoon's fists bunched. He sorely wanted to use them to punch Pyojoo in his snarky mouth. Instead, he made a point of relaxing each finger until he'd regained his control. He needed this job. It was the only one he could keep hours for after school started again.

So he picked up two crates despite his protesting muscles and clenched his teeth as he heard Pyojoo chuckle at something he read in his comic.

On the next trip, Jihoon stumbled under the heavy load and his elbow cracked against the door frame. Pain lanced through his arm and echoed in his head, like a thin needle shoved into his skull.

His muscles quivered and the crates fell with a crash. Strawberry milk squirted over his pants and stained his shoes pink.

Ringing reverberated through his ears a second before he started to seize.

He couldn't hear or think or breathe.

He could only see—darkness and the moon. The full moon. Mocking him.

40

MIYOUNG WOKE WHEN her body hit the ground.

She trembled so hard her teeth chattered.

Though she'd never felt such pain before, like ice crystals stabbing her veins, she knew why. Tonight was the full moon. The first since she'd stopped feeding. The first since she'd left Jihoon.

Something burned along her skin—the light of the moon shining through the window.

It beckoned her, telling her to come back to its embrace and punishing her because she refused.

Her door opened with a crash. Feet pounding as they hurried to her.

"Pick up her feet." Miyoung recognized the anxiety in her mother's voice, layered under the stern command.

Yena scooped hands under Miyoung's shoulders while someone else cradled her legs.

She was submerged in ice-cold water, and her brain yelled at her to escape.

No, not water.

Struggling against the hands that held her down, Miyoung thrashed, surely soaking those who tried to help her.

"Open her mouth." The voice was deep and male.

Fingers pried at her teeth. Miyoung tried not to fight, but her jaw clenched at the numbing chill of the ice water against her exposed skin, and she bit down until she tasted blood.

They tried again, undeterred by her gnashing teeth. And this time a bitter liquid poured down her throat.

Her body sagged, so exhausted she could barely hold her head up. If the water was going to claim her, then so be it. But it seemed it was too shallow and instead her cheek rested against the cold porcelain side of the tub. As long as she kept her head above the water, she'd be fine. It was a lie, but one she repeated to herself over and over until her heart slowed.

"She won't feed?" the male voice asked.

"Apparently not."

"It's only going to get worse."

"I don't pay you to tell me what I can see with my own eyes." Yena's voice was laced with displeasure.

"She's lucky she's half human. It might be holding off the worst of it. If she doesn't feed, there's not much you can do."

"There's one thing," Yena replied.

"The bead is in Seoul."

"Again, something I know."

A pause. "Perhaps it's time to go back. We've found nothing here and my contacts have run dry."

"Then get more contacts," Yena said.

"That costs money."

A pause. "Take whatever you need from the safe."

"Yes, ma'am." There was the pad of retreating feet, then the soft *click* of the bathroom door closing.

Miyoung finally opened her eyes. The room was a blur of light and haze. White on white, but she picked out the shape of her mother's lips, her nose, and her eyes.

Another wave of nausea spiraled through Miyoung.

"It hurts." Miyoung didn't recognize her own voice, desperate mewls of sound.

"It'll pass soon. You are my daughter. You are smart and beautiful and strong. And you will fight past this."

Miyoung shivered with the cold of the bath and the sharp pains that still radiated through her bones. "I'll be a better daughter."

"Then will you feed?" It wasn't said with anger. Instead a true question.

Miyoung let out a sob instead of answering. It was all Yena needed to hear.

"Do you refuse to feed because of that boy?"

"Yes," Miyoung whispered. "But not the way you think. Before I realized I could care for him, I was able to convince myself I didn't care about anyone. But I do. And if continue to kill others just so I can live, I'll become a monster that I don't want to be."

Yena was silent. So quiet that Miyoung opened her eyes to see if her mother had left. She still sat beside the tub, her face pinched in thought. And Miyoung realized the implication of her words. That perhaps Miyoung thought Yena was the monster she didn't want to become.

"You think you've made a choice this last month, but you haven't." Yena's voice was hard and clipped. "You are waiting, hoping for a solution to come that will give you everything you want."

"Is that so bad?" Miyoung asked. "I don't want anyone to be hurt because of me."

"I thought I'd taught you better, Daughter. I've survived a long time because I've made clear choices. Even if you think they were wrong." Yena stood. "You need to make a choice."

With that, Yena left. Miyoung shivered, but not from the ice bath.

41

WHEN JIHOON HAD one of his episodes—that's what the doctors euphemistically called them—he dreamed so vividly he could
paint a picture if he had any artistic talent.

Sometimes he dreamed of his halmeoni, how content they'd
been with their simple life. He woke from these dreams with a
fleeting happiness that dissipated too quickly.

Sometimes he dreamed of his parents, a fake reality where
they'd never left and loved him the way parents should. He woke
from these dreams bitter about all the things he'd never known
and never would.

This time, he had one of the dreams he hated most, the kind
that made him wake up with a desperate longing. He dreamed of
Miyoung.

*A red thread lit his path. He often dreamed of following a string to
find Miyoung at the end. In the beginning it had been a sunny gold,
but over time it had deepened to scarlet.*

*She sat under moonlight on a bench. Her face turned up. A smile
on her lips.*

"What are you doing?" Jihoon took a seat beside her.

*"Talking to the moon." She let her head rest on his shoulder. It fit
perfectly in the curve of his neck.*

"What about?"

"Just saying hello."

"The moon isn't very talkative," Jihoon replied.

"It's not what it says, but how." She tilted her head back to look at him. "I was wondering when you'd find me."

"It's easy with this." He held up the thread. It faded into the night, dissolving now that its purpose was served.

"A red thread. Are you my soul mate, Jihoon-ah?"

He grinned at the old myth: A red string ties together two fated souls.

"Do you want my heart?" he asked. "It's pretty battered."

"You already hold mine." Miyoung offered her lips to him. He accepted them with a soft kiss, smiling before he leaned back.

Something wet, tasting of salt and metal, dripped down his lips onto his tongue. He dabbed at it and his fingers came away red.

His eyes shot to Miyoung. Blood poured from her nose, making trails down her chin dripping into her lap.

"I can't stay," she said, apology thick in her voice.

"You can't leave," he said. "I need answers."

"Answers?" She looked pale, almost transparent.

"My halmeoni is sick."

"What?" The word sounded harsh as it echoed around him.

"What did your mother do? Please tell me. Please help us."

Jihoon reached out.

His hands clutched air.

She disappeared. And Jihoon was alone, with nothing but the moon for company.

42

MIYOUNG WOKE WITH a start, her heart beating so fast she felt it in her fingertips.

It had been another vivid dream. The kind that made her suspect it was more than just memories and longing. The kind that made her think he was really there. But this time something worried her, and she needed to sift through the already fading dream to find it again.

She sat up, ignoring the protest of her aching muscles. Her body felt stiff, like she'd run a marathon. She reached out for water.

The glass on her nightstand was empty.

The apartment was silent as Miyoung padded down the hall.

Shuffling into the kitchen, she refilled her glass. For the last month she never felt completely full. Nothing could quell the gnawing hunger in her belly. And they'd gone through a lot of groceries as Miyoung ate day and night. But she knew the one thing that would end the hunger was gi.

She gulped down more water, tilting her head back for the last drops when the light turned on.

"Turn it off," she growled.

She watched, annoyed, as Junu opened the fridge, using it to push Miyoung aside.

The light from the refrigerator accented the planes of his face. His clear complexion looked perfect even in the harsh glare.

"You're such a grouch in the morning." Junu pulled out orange juice.

"You're such a jerk always." Miyoung replaced the water. "When are you going to get out of my apartment?"

"When your mother stops paying me to babysit her little darling. Your mother's offers are hard to pass up. What kind of fool would say no to an all-expense-paid trip?" Junu sipped the juice and pulled out a slice of milk bread.

"Ya! That's the last piece!"

"It's the end piece," he said, taking another huge bite. "You hate the end pieces."

"Fine," Miyoung conceded because he was right.

"Bad dream?" Junu asked.

Miyoung didn't answer, which prompted Junu to poke her. "Jihoon?"

"How did you know?"

"I'm good at seeing when someone is heartsick," Junu said with a sly smile.

"Oh, shove it." Miyoung punched his shoulder.

He rubbed his arm indignantly. "Maybe I should ask for hazard pay."

Miyoung frowned. She didn't like that Junu knew Yena and apparently had for decades. It made all of her shady back-alley dealings with him seem worse somehow. But when her mother had needed someone who was good at getting information, someone who had connections in their world, she'd hired Junu. It had made for a tense first week where Miyoung wondered if Junu would bring up the Taoist talisman and Nara. But the dokkaebi seemed to know not to poke that hornet's nest, even as he spent most of his days prodding at Miyoung a thousand other ways.

"Where's my mother?"

"Hong Kong."

"When's she coming back?" Miyoung's voice rose with surprise.

"She's not. We're supposed to meet her when her little angel is back from the brink of death."

"Do you really think I'm dying?" Miyoung asked. It was a question she could never bring herself to ask Yena. But she thought Junu would give her a straight answer.

"Why don't you just feed?"

So not a straight answer, but an answer nonetheless. He also thought she'd die if she didn't absorb gi.

"I can't."

"Humans die every day. But we are too beautiful to deny the world of our faces." Junu shot her a mischievous grin.

Miyoung didn't bother to explain. She knew Junu couldn't understand. The idea that a gumiho could value human lives above her own. He was a dokkaebi. Everything he did was for his own personal gain.

Then she remembered her mother's words. That her decision not to feed wasn't a complete choice. She'd still run away. She was still a coward.

And finally she remembered Jihoon's words from her dream. *My halmeoni is sick. Please help us.*

His halmeoni was alive? Miyoung had assumed she'd succumb to her lack of gi, but it seemed she was stronger than she'd looked.

Still, if she was sick, then maybe the lack of energy *was* affecting her, just slower than Miyoung had assumed. How could someone come back from losing so much gi?

Jihoon's plea rang through her mind over and over. *Please help us.* His desperation had been so thick, it magnified the guilt already clogging her chest.

Miyoung stared out the window at the city of Osaka, just waking up for the day.

"I guess the kitsune angle didn't get us anything," Miyoung said, still watching the cityscape. Bright signs lit the streets as the city waited for the sun to rise. It was beautiful and vibrant, and it wasn't home. "I don't want to go to Hong Kong."

"You want to stay here?"

"I want to go to Seoul."

"You know I can't let you go there."

"If my mother doesn't find a solution, I don't have much time left. Think of it as my dying wish." She wouldn't tell Junu the real reason. That if there was no way to save Miyoung, then maybe she could save another. Maybe this was the best choice. She already felt like a restless ghost. And Jihoon and Halmeoni were her unfinished business.

"Gumiho don't get dying wishes."

"This one does. I don't want to be here or in Hong Kong or wherever else she thinks she can find answers. I just want to go home." Miyoung let her voice lower in a plea, let herself look desperate. What was pride to a dying gumiho?

"There's a flaw in your plan," Junu pointed out. "Your mother would never approve of this."

"That's where you come in," Miyoung said with a sly grin.

Junu laughed, shaking his head. "It'll cost you."

"I assumed." Miyoung lifted a brow, waiting for Junu to debate his loyalties.

The dokkaebi shoved the rest of the bread in his mouth and dusted off his hands. "I'll start packing."

43

THE DOCTORS KEPT Jihoon in the hospital for a few days. They ran tests, took blood, poked, and prodded. No new diagnosis. No new solution. So they discharged him.

Somin rushed around the room, making sure nothing was left behind as Jihoon took his time pulling on his sneakers. It hurt to bend down, but it felt good to be wearing his own clothes.

"He wasn't here that long. There's nothing for him to leave," Somin's mother said.

"What if he forgets his phone?"

"It's right here." Jihoon lifted his cell in the air, sharing a look of mutual exasperation with Ms. Moon.

"What about your charger?"

"Here." Ms. Moon held it up.

This was his friend's coping mechanism. If she could fuss over Jihoon, she would worry less. As Somin checked under the bed for the third time, for what, Jihoon didn't know, Detective Hae walked in.

Ms. Moon straightened in her chair, lifting her hands to smooth her hair. "Hello, Detective Hae," she said sweetly.

"Soohyun-ssi." He greeted her with a nod, and she blushed at his use of her name. It had taken him almost a month to stop calling her Somin's eomeoni. "Jihoon-ah, you look ready to go."

"Ready for a while." Jihoon gave a pointed look at Somin, who opened the bathroom door to check inside.

"Somin-ah." Detective Hae took her shoulders. "The nurses have the instructions for Jihoon's medication, why don't you go get those?"

She nodded, grateful for the task.

"Detective, you're always able to get things in order. It's a remarkable skill," Ms. Moon said. "I would love to have you over for dinner, to thank you. How about tomorrow night?"

Jihoon was grateful Somin had stepped out. Seeing her mother flirt would be awkward; of course, it wasn't fun for Jihoon either.

"I'd be honored, but I have a church event."

"Your faith is admirable," Ms. Moon said. Jihoon let out a snort and received a flick from her.

"I'm free now," Detective Hae offered.

"Free for what?" Somin asked, returning with a packet of instructions.

"Just coffee," Ms. Moon said. "Why don't we go to the café on the corner while we wait for Somin to scour the room one last time."

Somin rolled her eyes.

"All right, but I'm buying." Detective Hae ruffled Somin's hair in affection, and the frown fell from her face. He'd taken to her immediately. Jihoon imagined it was because he missed his own daughter, who lived with her mother abroad.

"Ahn Jihoon?" A nurse stuck her head in. "Oh, sorry, I didn't know your family was here. We just have a few discharge papers we need signed," the nurse explained to Detective Hae, no doubt assuming he was the father in a happy nuclear family. Jihoon frowned.

"Sure," Detective Hae said easily, and he followed the nurse, Ms. Moon on his heels.

"It shouldn't bother you," Somin said, and Jihoon jumped. He'd forgotten she was still there.

"What are you talking about?" Jihoon concentrated on gathering his bag instead of looking at Somin.

"We *are* your family," Somin said.

"But he's not my father. I haven't had one of those for a long time." Jihoon didn't know why he felt so bitter about this except that he'd felt so alone in the last month.

"Neither have I," Somin reminded him. "But I think we turned out okay anyway."

He knew Somin was trying to cheer him up, but instead he felt shame on top of his anger. Somin's father had died when she was still too young to know him. "I'm going to go see Halmeoni before we leave."

Somin gave him a sad smile. "We'll meet you in the lobby."

o   o   o

The room was dark with the long curtains drawn. Halmeoni lay with her hands folded over her belly, probably something the nurses had done. She did look more serene this way.

"Halmeoni." Jihoon took her hand in his. It felt paper light, like her bones were as hollow as a bird's. "I'm all better now. You were worried, weren't you?"

Jihoon's eyes stung at the silence that followed. He didn't like her blank face. She'd been so full of life, scolding him for staying out late or for coming home with bad grades. This version of her, empty and emotionless, this wasn't his halmeoni.

"I'll be back to see you tomorrow. Don't worry about me too much." He gently laid her hand back on the covers, hitched his backpack higher, and left. He didn't go to the lobby, but took the crosswalk that led to the far side of the hospital campus. He hopped on the bus that pulled up just as he walked out to the main road.

44

MIYOUNG WATCHED THE door close behind Jihoon. She'd barely pulled the curtains around her when she'd heard him coming in.

"I know what you'll say," she said as she sat in the wide visitor's chair beside Halmeoni. "I'm a coward. And you're right, but I'm not ready to see him. Not yet."

She picked up the hand that Jihoon had just put down. She thought she felt a spark as she rubbed her fingers over Halmeoni's soft skin. A part of her wanted to believe he'd left it there, a piece of him that she could hold on to. And the rest of her, the smart part of her, knew it was foolish to read into a bit of static shock.

Then she closed her eyes and opened herself to Halmeoni's energy. Not to siphon it, but to measure it. Because Miyoung had a good idea why Halmeoni wasn't waking up.

There it was, weak like a fading star, Halmeoni's waning gi. It was as Miyoung had feared: She'd given so much to Jihoon that she barely had any left. And she was trapped in this unconscious limbo. It seemed Miyoung had stolen a life that night even though she'd failed to kill to feed.

"I'm so sorry," Miyoung whispered. "I never meant for any of this to happen."

"He'd never forgive me if he knew what I did." Miyoung brought Halmeoni's hand to her cheek. "Do you think it's selfish that I'm hoping not to tell him? I don't want him to remember me as a monster. I don't expect you to forgive me, but please let me try to save you. For him and for me."

45

JIHOON'S PHONE BUZZED with messages as he rode the bus. The first came from Somin: What are you thinking?! Leaving alone? I'm never talking to you again, Ahn Jihoon!

Though he'd expected it, he still felt guilty, but if he'd left with Somin and her mother, they'd have tried to persuade him to come home with them. And he wanted to be alone right now.

The next text was from Detective Hae: Stay out of trouble. Call me if you get sick.

Jihoon smiled at the message: Be good, be healthy.

A minute later, Somin's follow-up message arrived: There's soup in your fridge. Eat it or you're dead meat.

He laughed. Somin knew him too well.

The walk up the steep hill to his apartment was not easy, and he almost regretted making the trip alone.

"Jihoon-ah," Hwang Halmeoni called as he approached. She sat on the small deck outside her shop despite the chilled February air.

He sat on the deck. It was an excuse to catch his breath, which puffed out in heavy clouds.

"You look tired." Hwang Halmeoni frowned.

"I'll recover."

"Why isn't that policeman with you? He's handsome."

"Hwang Halmeoni, are you cheating on me?" Jihoon asked, adding a huff of indignation.

She chuckled, a twinkle in her faded eyes. She reached behind her and pulled out a small vial of golden liquid, a thick root suspended in it. "Here. It's medicinal wine, ginger root from Palgongsan."

"I'm not old enough to drink," Jihoon reminded her.

"When I was your age, five-year-old kids could drink wine." She held out the vial, and Jihoon graciously accepted it, bowing low.

"Oh, and there was someone looking for you earlier."

"Changwanie?" he asked.

"No, cuter." She winked.

He frowned, hoping it wasn't more creditors.

o o o

The restaurant's front windows were dark. Chairs turned over, stacked on top of the empty tables. A handwritten sign was taped to the door: CLOSED UNTIL FURTHER NOTICE. If Jihoon concentrated hard enough, he could imagine the scent of one of his halmeoni's jjigaes permeating the air, the clatter of dishes, the laughter of customers. But he didn't. Because the memories stung, knowing he'd always taken that life for granted. Taken his halmeoni's presence for granted.

Bujeoks fluttered along the door frame of the apartment as he let the door swing shut. He took off his shoes and laid them neatly next to his halmeoni's, her favorite pair of worn black work shoes.

Though it had only been a month, it felt like the space missed

Halmeoni's presence as much as Jihoon did. Nothing had been moved but everything felt a little duller. He almost expected to see Dubu come running down the hall, barking her happy greeting. She was better off at Somin's, where she'd get daily attention. Jihoon spent more nights in Halmeoni's hospital room than in the apartment.

"This place is a mess."

Jihoon whipped around as a shape emerged from the dark kitchen.

"Who are you?" Jihoon raised his fists, ready to defend.

"I'm not your enemy," the voice said. It was definitely male.

"If you're not my enemy, then let me see your face."

The boy who stepped forward was barely older than Jihoon. Perhaps twenty years old with a chiseled face and clear eyes.

"Nice to meet you. Name's Junu." The boy grinned a dazzling smile.

"I'd introduce myself, but I don't often meet people trying to rob me."

"Do I look like I'm here to steal from you?" Junu asked.

It was a valid question. The boy looked like he'd walked out of the pages of a fashion magazine. Dark pants and a long wool coat hung off his tall frame. A gold watch peeked out from under his long sleeve. Probably expensive enough to pay off some of the bills stacked on the table.

"Why are you here?" Jihoon glanced toward the couch, where he'd flung his jacket. His cell phone was in the pocket.

"Sometimes I ask myself that. Why do I get myself into these situations?" Junu sat next to Jihoon's jacket, crossing his legs comfortably. "I think it's because of my face. It's beautiful, so people want to be around me. And I'm a sucker for good company." He gave a saucy wink.

Who was this boy?

"I'm a good listener. So people think they can spill their guts to me. It's only a matter of time until they're telling me all of their deepest secrets. You'd think more people would be afraid of a dokkaebi." Junu gave a shrug.

Jihoon jerked back. He stared at Junu with a more critical eye. Dokkaebi were supposed to be as ugly as sin, like the beast he'd seen in the woods. There was nothing similar between that rutting goblin and the beautiful boy that sat in front of him now.

"Why would a dokkaebi be in my house?" Jihoon's eyes darted around, looking for a good weapon.

"Why do you think?" A smile quirked at Junu's lips like he was asking a riddle.

"Yena?"

"Ddaeng!" Junu sounded gleefully. "Wrong gumiho."

Flutters winged through Jihoon's stomach, like dragonflies taking flight.

"Miyoung?" He whispered her name, like he was afraid of hoping.

"She's worried about you."

Jihoon's eyes hurt like he'd held them open too long on a cold day. Then he realized he hadn't been blinking.

"She'd kill me for telling you that," Junu said. "She asked me to make sure you weren't living in squalor. Didn't think you'd be back so soon, but I'm not one to hide."

"Where has she been?"

"Around." Junu flicked his wrist, like that was explanation enough.

Jihoon decided he hated this boy.

"Well," Junu said, standing. "It's getting late. I am starving. Do you think there are still kids at the playground?"

Jihoon's eyes widened in horror, and Junu broke into raucous laughter.

"Oh, the look on your face." He slapped his knee. "Dokkaebi don't eat people. I have a delicate stomach. I must treat my body like a temple."

Jihoon stared at him, speechless.

"I should get going. I wasn't joking about being hungry. Should I get jjajangmyeon or jjamppong?" he wondered aloud as he sauntered to the door.

"Tell her to come herself," Jihoon blurted out.

"Huh?" Junu gave him a curious look.

"If she's so worried about me, then she should come check on me herself." Jihoon gripped the sides of his pants so he wouldn't fidget with the nerves that raced through him.

Junu took a moment to consider the request, then nodded before departing. The door swung shut, fluttering the bujeoks by the door. They'd done nothing to keep the dokkaebi from the apartment, but Jihoon had no time to ponder that as he sank onto the couch. He was starting to get a headache.

46

SHE'D BEEN BACK for weeks and had gained no traction in trying to find a solution to wake up Jihoon's halmeoni. At first she thought she could offer some of her own gi. But she quickly found out she was too weak, and after trying to force the connection she'd barely made it to the sink to vomit. That had been the end of those attempts.

But she had a bigger problem now. It was hard to admit, but Miyoung knew she needed to talk to Jihoon. She'd been putting it off, hoping she could slip in, help his halmeoni, and slip back out again. But she knew she needed access to Halmeoni's hospital room and she couldn't keep sneaking in. Jihoon was always there until visiting hours ended. So she'd taken to sneaking in, waiting him out, and then slipping into Halmeoni's room. Except today a nurse had found her and asked her too many questions. She'd covered by saying she'd lost track of time, but the hawk-eyed nurses had definitely memorized her face by now.

She didn't want the nurse telling Jihoon before she could explain why she'd returned.

That was how Miyoung found herself in her old neighborhood, pacing in front of Jihoon's apartment.

She walked past the small squat building for what must have been the dozenth time that night. The windows were lit in the apartment above the closed restaurant. When she'd first seen the handwritten sign stating CLOSED UNTIL FURTHER NOTICE, she wanted to rip it down.

"You're that yeowu girl." The voice was old and cracked and stopped Miyoung in her tracks. She turned toward the old halmeoni who sat peeling chestnuts outside a medicinal wine store.

"Excuse me?"

"That girl our Jihoonie brought home once. You have secrets, dark ones."

"What?" Miyoung tried to act confused. "I don't know what you're talking about."

The old woman cackled as she peeled another chestnut. This time she held it out and Miyoung took it with two hands.

"Don't try to hide things from someone as old as me. I've seen far too much to be fooled." Her words echoed something Jihoon's halmeoni once told her. "Don't worry, I don't need to know your secrets. I have enough of my own, collected over a lifetime. Though I think yours will come out soon enough. If Jihoonie is the one you want to tell, then you should just bite the bullet. He's a good, kind boy."

"Is Jihoon okay?" Miyoung asked. "I mean, without his halmeoni? How is he?"

"Why don't you ask him yourself?" The old woman gestured down the road and Miyoung saw Jihoon making his way down the street. Just as she was about to take off after him, she noticed another figure. One all too familiar.

"Ya!" she shouted before she could stop herself. A rash move as the girl's head jerked around, she saw Miyoung, and then she took off down a side street.

Despite not feeding, Miyoung was still fast when she wanted

to be. At least she was faster than any human, and she quickly overtook her target. She spun the girl around, black hair swinging to obscure the pale face.

"Song Nara." Miyoung spat out the name. "What are you doing here?"

Nara adjusted her jacket, trying to assert a semblance of dignity. "I heard you were back in town."

Miyoung didn't like the sound of that. Had the shaman been keeping tabs on her?

As if reading Miyoung's mind, Nara answered, "When a dokkaebi and a gumiho come back into town, the spirits talk. I didn't realize you'd grown close to Junu."

"Who I spend time with is none of your business. What do you want? Why are you following me?"

"I'm not following *you*," Nara said. "I was following Ahn Jihoon. I wanted to warn him."

"Warn him? About what?"

"About you. I figured the only reason you'd return was to rip your bead back out of his chest."

Miyoung startled at the mention of her bead. How could Nara know about that? "You don't know what you're talking about."

"The spirits talk. What you did is unnatural." Nara paused, conflict clear in her eyes before she continued. "But it was also brave. You saved Ahn Jihoon's life. I didn't expect that of you."

"You didn't know me as well as you thought you did."

"Perhaps," Nara said, studying Miyoung. "But if you truly do care about him, then you'll leave him alone. My halmeoni still has plans and you should know by now that nothing will get in her way."

"Threats?" Miyoung lifted a brow. "I'm not scared of you."

Nara frowned. "If you ever trusted me—"

"I didn't," Miyoung lied.

Nara pursed her lips, and Miyoung felt grim satisfaction at the young shaman's frustration. "Don't ignore my warning. My halmeoni doesn't forget and rarely forgives. If I know you're back, then so will she."

"That warning is as meaningless as your friendship. You'd never betray your halmeoni like this, and I have unfinished business."

"If you're not here to get your bead back, then why did you return?"

"You think I'd tell you that?" Miyoung scoffed.

"Well, if it was easy to accomplish, you'd have done it already. You even have Junu on your side. Perhaps it's because you don't have a solution for your problem."

"And you do? Are you saying you can take my bead out of Jihoon without killing one of us?"

Nara hesitated. "I can't. I took advantage of a month with a lot of spiritual power when I did it the first time. If I do it wrong . . ." She trailed off, but the implication was clear. Done wrong, it would kill him.

"Then you're of no use to me," Miyoung said, and began to leave.

"I did what I did for my family," Nara called after her. "I thought maybe you could understand that."

Fury filled Miyoung. "Funny that you think honoring your family requires you to kill. You're right; it's something I can understand all too well. I guess that means we're both monsters in our own right and we'll both never live up to our families' expectations now."

The words aimed to wound. Nara stiffened as they hit their target.

"He shouldn't be out tonight," Nara said. "His body has healed from his injuries, but it's still mortal. And the bead gains power from the moon. It could overwhelm him."

"What?" Miyoung asked, annoyance lacing her voice.

Nara frowned, then pointed to the sky, toward the full moon.

Miyoung cursed. How could she be so brainless as to lose track of the time. And now she was out during the full moon. It shone down on her, causing her heart to squeeze and her breath to catch.

"Are you okay?" Nara asked, stepping toward Miyoung, but she held up a hand.

"Don't worry yourself about me," Miyoung said. "And don't get in my way. Or your halmeoni will have another reason to want revenge against my family."

That stopped Nara in her tracks. She gave a curt nod and turned to disappear down the alleyway.

Miyoung glanced back at the moon and rubbed at her chest. She needed to find Jihoon.

47

SENIOR YEAR WAS on the horizon, arguably the hardest year for any Korean teen. And Jihoon found himself hoping for it to arrive faster. He hated the time he spent with nothing but his thoughts. Changwan was away with family for the school break, and Jihoon could only spend so much time at Somin's without being fussed over.

He tried to fill his time by visiting his halmeoni, but after his own hospital stay the nurses had become strict with him and forced him home at the end of visiting hours.

So he found himself restlessly wandering his neighborhood. He'd felt claustrophobic cooped up in his small apartment, where everything reminded him of Halmeoni.

He rubbed a hand over his neck. It itched like sharp pins were pricking at his skin. Glancing up, he took in the full moon and sighed. Of course that was the cause of his discomfort. A regular reminder of his past mistakes.

And Jihoon realized he'd stopped right next to the entrance of the neighborhood playground. Like he'd been brought there so he could be haunted by old memories. He should go back home. He knew it was ridiculous, but just the sight of the moon made his heart ache.

Instead, he found himself turning into the playground, running his hands over the roundabout until it spun in squeaky circles. He remembered riding that merry-go-round as a kid, spinning and spinning until he felt like he was going to puke.

Funny, he'd forgotten that once he'd loved this place. Because now it only represented *her* and how much he'd cared about her before she broke his heart. Sitting on one of the swings, he pushed off, leaning back so all he could see were stars and sky.

Then his heart clenched. His breath shortened. And a face, pale as the moon, appeared above him. He let out a shout and fell from the swing. Dirt and gravel dug into his palms as he scurried to his feet.

He glanced up, half expecting to see a ghost. But what stood there was much worse. Miyoung.

She was as beautiful as he remembered. The moonlight hugged her with its bright embrace. Her skin glowed. Her eyes sparked. Dark hair blew around her pale cheeks in the winter breeze. And behind her was the ghost of her tails. He had a moment to worry that someone would walk by and see, but the clouds shifted and covered the moon and she was just a girl again. But not *just* a girl. She was never just a girl to him.

"Are you real?" he breathed, not quite trusting his mind. It had often played tricks on him in the past two months.

"Jihoon-ah."

He held up a hand to stop her. Her voice sounded clear and smooth, as beautiful as he remembered. It made it hard for him to think.

"It's been a while," he finally managed.

She nodded.

"I don't know why you left and I don't need to know," Jihoon said, determined to stay calm. "But I need your help. My halmeoni is sick." He watched her face carefully. It betrayed nothing of her inner thoughts. "The doctors don't know why she's been in a coma this long. Her brain waves are strong. She has a good heart. I brought in a shaman and she said that there is dark energy in Halmeoni, like she's been cursed."

Miyoung shook her head. "It's not a curse."

"Then what is it?" Jihoon yelled. The act of raising his voice made him light-headed. "If Yena did something to her, I need to know."

Miyoung moved forward.

"Stop!" A heat rose in his chest, like a ball of fire that wanted to break free.

Miyoung halted mid-step.

Jihoon pressed his hands against his temples as dots of light danced in his vision. This was not the moment to get sick. He'd waited over two months for this. He would get an answer to his questions before she disappeared again.

His legs wobbled, and before they dropped out from beneath him he sat on the swing again, trying to regulate his breathing. Sweat beaded along his skin despite the winter chill. He counted to ten, then back again.

"Are you sick?" Miyoung asked, still standing a meter away like she was afraid to approach.

"I'm fine," he murmured.

"Jihoon-ah," she said, and it hurt to hear her say his name in such a familiar way.

"What are you even doing here? Shouldn't you go hunt?" he spat out. "Or are you thinking you have the perfect victim right in front of you?"

Miyoung kept her face blank and it should have worried him.

He was prodding her when he knew better, but she wouldn't physically hurt him. Even now he still believed that.

"I'm not—" she began, then squeezed her lips so tight they paled from the pressure.

Jihoon considered pushing the subject, but knew it wasn't worth it. Miyoung had always done exactly what she wanted. If she was going to hunt or not wasn't his concern. He rubbed his fingers against his temple to ease the throbbing behind his eyes.

"You don't look like you're doing well," Miyoung said.

He hated that she saw him when he was so weak. "You think? My whole life was ripped apart by a girl who said she cared about me, then disappeared. My halmeoni's in the hospital, bills are piling up because the restaurant is closed, and I have a damn migraine. Would you be all right?"

His headache swelled. If it got any worse, he might have an episode. That was not something he needed right now, not in front of Miyoung.

"Do you want me to leave?"

He didn't reply because if he said no, then she'd know how much he still cared. But if he said yes, she might go, and he didn't want that either.

"I don't know how to talk to you," he said instead. "I don't know how to be around you."

"I don't regret it," she whispered.

"Coming back?"

"Caring about you."

48

IT WAS THE first time she'd said the words. And they caught at her throat.

Miyoung watched Jihoon struggle with her confession.

"I didn't want to admit it . . . before." She paused, hesitant to bring up the past, but she had to say it at least once. "You made me feel like I could let go for the first time in my life and that scared me. I've lived my whole life letting fear control me. And I hurt you because I still don't know how to let go."

"And you think now that you've come back and said these things, all should be forgiven?"

Miyoung backed away from the anger in his eyes. The full moon broke partially free from the clouds obscuring it, shining against the swing set. Like a boundary between her space and his.

It called to her, urging her to relinquish control. Instead of pulling the beast from her, it pulled out the words from her heart.

"I never wanted to hurt you."

"Well, you did. I hurt all the time, but I'm too tired to stay angry anymore."

"I'm sorry," she said.

"I *want* to forgive you," he admitted.

Miyoung took a step, her heart spurring her forward into the slanting light of the moon. Pain rocketed through her muscles. As if on cue, Jihoon winced, an echo of her suffering.

It reminded her why she'd returned. And it wasn't for a redemption she didn't deserve. A part of her wanted to peel back the last curtain and reveal what she had done to his halmeoni. It would cure him of his suffering, thinking he could still love her. He wouldn't be so foolish as to believe that after he knew what she had done. But another part of her, the selfish part, kept the secret to herself for now.

I came back to help and he won't let me if he knows what I did, but she knew she was a liar and a coward.

Miyoung took a step back, away from the moonlight, away from Jihoon.

His eyes fell, the hope that lit them dimming to nothing.

"Just go," he said.

"Jihoon-ah."

"I said get out of here!"

His words shot into her, a command she couldn't deny. Said with such force that she knew she couldn't stay if she wanted to. But after seeing the anger in his eyes, she didn't want to stay. And she called herself a coward as she fled.

49

SENIOR YEAR OFFICIALLY began. March used to be Jihoon's least favorite month as it meant the start of a new school year and the end of the short reprieve of winter break. But now school would be a good distraction from all the other places his brain wanted to go.

The first day of school was uneventful, exactly what he wanted, except he couldn't keep his mind off a certain gumiho. It was a blur of teachers stressing that third year was not only their final year as high school students but the most important, as they would be taking the suneung exams.

Senior year also brought with it long nights where third-years would stay up well past midnight to study. A fate he'd always dreaded, but now grabbed on to like a lifeline. It was only at dinnertime that he left the school building to make his way to the hospital and see Halmeoni.

He was exiting the school with Changwan, who was headed to his after-school academy, when a black sports car sped into his path, causing him to jump back or risk being hit.

"Whoa, that car is so cool," Changwan said.

Jihoon frowned at his best friend, so easily won over by a sports car.

He moved to walk around the car, when the passenger door swung open and Miyoung stepped out.

"Miyoung-ssi!" Changwan exclaimed. Then his eyes slid toward Jihoon and he wiped the smile from his face. "When did you get back?" he asked in a more moderate tone.

"Not too long ago," Miyoung said. "It's good to see you, Changwan-ah."

Jihoon didn't have time to stick around for small talk. But before he could take a step, Miyoung moved into his path.

"Jihoon—" she began.

"Let me pass."

"No," she said. "I have something to talk to you about."

"I think I'll just go over there," Changwan mumbled, moving toward the car. Neither Jihoon nor Miyoung acknowledged him.

Jihoon tried to walk around her but the signal changed and he watched as the bus pulled up to the stop across the street.

Frustrated, but not wanting to talk to Miyoung, he took his anger out on the driver. Junu leaned against the hood now, explaining the features of his car to an enamored Changwan. If he were a cartoon, Changwan would have hearts in his eyes and Jihoon didn't know if it would be for the car or Junu. His friend always got a large dose of hero worship when he saw someone he thought was cool.

"You shouldn't be speeding so close to a school. It's dangerous," Jihoon said to the dokkaebi.

"Are you with the police?" Junu drawled.

Jihoon curled his lip in disgust, but then again he shouldn't be surprised that a dokkaebi didn't care about who he hurt.

"Why don't we give you guys a ride?" Miyoung said, obviously noting the longing in Changwan's eyes as he stared at Junu's car.

"Changwan, isn't that your father's driver?" Jihoon said, pointing at a sedate (boring) black sedan parked at the curb. A man clad in a black suit stood beside it, watching them.

"Yeah." Changwan pouted, glancing back at the sports car, then let out a resigned sigh. "Rain check?"

"Sure, Changwan-ah," Miyoung said with a smile. He started to smile back but slid cautious eyes to Jihoon, then set his face into a somber expression.

"See ya," Changwan said, obviously trying to make the words clipped but just sounding nervous before he jogged over to his waiting driver.

"Jihoon?" Miyoung asked, and he realized she was waiting for him to respond to her offer of a ride.

"I'm fine. I'll take the bus." He moved to the curb to wait for the crosswalk signal to change.

"Can we talk first?" Miyoung asked.

He didn't reply, and when she didn't continue, he realized she was waiting for his permission to speak. "What?"

"I came back for a reason."

"I don't care unless you came back to save my halmeoni."

"Well, you're in luck."

Jihoon noted the frustration in Miyoung's voice before he absorbed her words. "Wait, what?"

Miyoung's face was an expressionless mask, giving up nothing. But he noticed sweat beading along her brow. He started to ask her if she was okay. Worry bloomed like bright flowers in his chest before he stomped them down. She wasn't any of his concern anymore.

"Okay, continue," he bit out.

"I came back to help, but I can't do that without your cooperation. Your halmeoni has very little gi."

"How do you know that?" Jihoon narrowed his eyes.

Miyoung pursed her lips, and he knew that answer. She'd been to see his halmeoni without his permission.

But he didn't want his anger to get in the way of things. So he held back from yelling at her. "So what does that mean? Her having very little gi?"

"It means that she doesn't have enough energy to wake up again."

Jihoon didn't like the sound of that. Did this mean his halmeoni would never wake up?

"She *could* wake up again," Miyoung said, as if reading his thoughts. "In theory."

"And what does this theory require?"

"If we could figure out a way to get her gi, then it could jump-start her body and she could wake up again."

"Good, where do we get the gi?"

"I'm still working through that."

"Take it from me," Jihoon said. "The gi."

"No," Miyoung said so vehemently that Jihoon stepped back.

"Why not?" Jihoon asked.

"It can't come from you. You're a boy."

Jihoon frowned, but he remembered something from his halmeoni's books about the yin energy of women and the yang energy of men. It could be true, since so many other things were.

"So you'll let me help?" Miyoung asked.

Jihoon wanted to say yes. He wanted to grab her in a hug and thank her for returning. But something held him back. He remembered Somin chastising him for having too much pride, but he couldn't set it aside. Miyoung's mother was the reason Halmeoni was sick in the first place. And then Miyoung had disappeared instead of facing it. He couldn't bring himself to fully forgive or trust her right now.

"I'll think about it," he said before crossing the road to wait for his bus.

50

"SO YOU LIED to him?" Junu asked as Miyoung climbed back into the car. When she frowned at him, he tapped his ear. "We have super hearing, too."

"It wasn't a lie," Miyoung said. "His energy isn't ideal for his halmeoni."

"But not because he's a boy. It's because of the fox bead nestled all cozy in his chest."

"That's not the problem we're trying to solve right now," Miyoung said, crossing her arms as Junu took off from the curb.

"It's the only problem you should care about," Junu pointed out.

"Do you want to get paid or not?"

"Do you want your dear mother to find out where her darling daughter is?"

Miyoung ground her teeth, trapped.

As if on cue, Miyoung's phone rang and Yena's number lit the screen. She glowered at Junu in warning before she answered. "Mother."

"Daughter, have you started feeding again?" It was always the first question Yena asked, and Miyoung bit back a sigh.

"No, I haven't. But I feel fine."

"Of course you don't. Every day you don't feed you get weaker.

I should never have let you stay in Japan. Maybe it's best if you come meet me."

"No," Miyoung said a bit too loudly. She took a deep breath, then continued in a smoother tone. "I really am fine. Junu is making me that gross juice and I'm drinking it every day. It helps. A lot."

"I've become too soft with you," Yena said as if she was talking more to herself than Miyoung. "I don't know why I let you convince me to leave you behind."

"If you're worried about me being weak, then wouldn't travel be bad for me?" Miyoung took a chance that she could use her mother's own logic against her.

"Fine. But remember you have to answer every one of my calls. If I go to voice mail even once, I'm coming back."

"Yes, Mother," Miyoung said dutifully.

The call ended without so much as a goodbye and Miyoung leaned back, closing her eyes, sapped. She'd lied to her mother. She felt weaker than ever. She couldn't seem to catch her breath these days. And her muscles burned, like they were disintegrating slowly. She'd looked up the symptoms of starving to death and it seemed like her body had reached the stage where it was trying to find energy from less ideal tissues.

"How is Mommy dearest?" Junu asked.

Instead of answering, Miyoung asked, "Do you have any more of that sludge you make?"

Junu glanced at her, and if she didn't know better, she'd have said he looked worried. "I have some at home." And he stepped on the gas, speeding through a red light.

Miyoung didn't have the energy to complain about his horrendous driving.

51

THE FOLLOWING WEEKEND, Changwan dragged Jihoon out against his will to see daylight. He'd been spending too much of his time in the classroom or the hospital, according to his best friend. The forecast actually called for rain, which Jihoon sullenly pointed out.

"You want to go to the PC room?" Changwan asked as they entered a coffee shop.

"Wasn't getting some sun the whole point of coming out?"

"Oh." Changwan looked crestfallen and Jihoon gave in.

"Well, if you want to spend an afternoon getting your butt handed to you, who am I to deny you?"

Changwan grinned and seemed absolutely delighted at the idea of having Jihoon beat him at video games all afternoon. It was enough to snap Jihoon out of his sour mood. He'd been a bad friend lately. Plus, hanging out with Changwan gave Jihoon an excuse to skip another unnecessary summons from Dr. Choi.

Then Changwan glanced over and his eyes lit up. "Hyeong-nim!"

Jihoon glowered as Junu walked up to the counter.

"What a coincidence! Were you here to get coffee, too?" Changwan sounded like a fan greeting his favorite idol.

"It *is* a coffee shop," Junu said with a crooked grin perfectly styled for his face. The counter girl sighed as she replied with a smile of her own. Jihoon wanted to punch the dokkaebi right in the mouth. "Haven't seen you online lately. When are we going to do another round of Starcraft 2v2?"

"You guys have been hanging out?" Jihoon asked, suspicion blooming.

"We ran into each other at the PC room a couple of times," Changwan explained, his eyes darting between Jihoon and Junu. "He's a great gamer. You should see his skills."

"It was a nice coincidence. But it was good luck for me. I love a good gaming partner." Junu gave a sly grin that told Jihoon it had not been a coincidence.

So this was how they wanted to play it? Keeping tabs on him and his friends? Did Miyoung think this would change his mind about her? If so, she was sorely mistaken.

"And how are you, Jihoon-ah?" Junu asked, his address far too familiar.

"I'm fine," he said.

"Can I buy your coffee for you, Hyeong-nim?" Changwan asked.

"Oh no, I'm older, I should be buying for you."

"I insist, Hyeong-nim!"

"Thanks, Changwan-ah." Junu gave an amicable nod.

Changwan beamed. "No problem, Hyeong-nim."

"Just call me Junu-hyeong."

"Yes, Hyeong-nim," Changwan said obediently.

Junu laughed. "You're funny. I like you."

Changwan lapped up the compliment like a starving man given bread. "Thank you, Hyeong-nim. We were just going to the PC room. You should come."

"Sounds fun," Junu said.

"I just realized, I have a checkup with Dr. Choi." Even more tests were better than spending a whole afternoon with the dokkaebi.

"That's a shame." Junu didn't miss a beat. He gave Jihoon a half smile that implied he knew it was a lie. "I thought I could also finally give you a ride in my car. Don't think I forgot we promised you a rain check."

"Oh, I promised Jihoon we'd hang out today," Changwan said to Junu, but he frowned, like he wasn't looking forward to spending his day at the hospital.

Jihoon sighed. "Why don't we catch up another time, Changwan-ah."

"Really? You sure? Thanks!" Changwan spoke so fast, Jihoon had no chance to respond.

"Should we grab food first?" Junu slung his arm around Changwan's shoulder and led him out.

It wasn't until they were gone that Jihoon realized they'd left him to pay for all the drinks.

52

THERE WERE NO answers in Hong Kong.

A call from Yena had confirmed that the monks and spiritualists there had no answers for a gumiho who'd lost her bead. And Miyoung had to perform an acrobatic dance of smooth talk to convince her mother not to return to Osaka, where she would find an empty apartment as proof of her daughter's lies.

"We don't have much time," Miyoung had said. "Wouldn't it be better for you to go to the next place to find answers?"

"Fine," Yena had replied after a prolonged pause. "I don't want you to worry, Daughter. I *will* find an answer."

"I trust you," Miyoung had said before hanging up.

Then, as if from nowhere, a wave of sorrow had struck her. She hadn't expected Yena to find an answer in Hong Kong. But she realized now that a part of her had hoped. With every passing day, with every failed city, Miyoung knew she was that much closer to death.

What would happen to her after she died? She'd always insisted gumiho didn't have a soul, but the idea that she'd just stop existing terrified her. It was so unfair. She'd lived her life walking a fine line, always being careful. Always being obedient. And the one time she'd tried to truly live had been her undoing. And now she was doomed? Was it because she'd been a fool to hope for more out of life?

Walking used to clear her mind, but she'd been stalking the streets for an hour and it had only proved she was weaker than ever. She wiped sweat from her brow despite the chill that still clung to the early spring air.

She paused, letting herself lean against a bus shelter. She'd wandered to her old neighborhood. If she followed the fork to the left, she'd be back at her old house. And to the right, Jihoon.

A crack of thunder sounded overhead.

Miyoung glanced at the cloudy sky. It felt like the heavens were mocking her, or perhaps empathizing with her mood.

Two steps and her shoes were drenched. The rain fell in a heavy blanket, so she barely saw a meter in front of her. No sane person would want to be caught out in this. Yet still she walked.

Stuffing her hands into her pockets, she continued to walk without feeling the chill that soaked through her clothes, her skin, her bones.

"Babo-ya, you never hear of an umbrella?" Words echoed from another time.

Jihoon stood in front of her, his umbrella so large it created a safe haven underneath. "Are you following me?"

"Of course not," she said. It was the truth. She hadn't meant to come here. It had just . . . happened. She moved to go around him. He stepped to the side to block her path.

"This is *my* neighborhood," Jihoon pointed out. "If you're not following me, what are you doing here?"

"How do you know I didn't move back into my old place?"

"Did you?" He lifted a brow in challenge.

"No." Miyoung moved to the other side and was blocked again.

"Did you mean it before?"

This stopped Miyoung in her tracks.

"When you said you'd help my halmeoni, did you mean it?"

"It's why I came back."

"I don't know if I can trust you."

Miyoung nodded and spun away so he couldn't see the tears forming in her eyes. She didn't have a right to be hurt by his distrust. But the movement was too quick, the road too steep, and her legs too weak from hours of walking. They gave out beneath her, and she began to topple over.

Jihoon caught her a millisecond before she hit the asphalt. He held her so close she felt his heart pounding through his shirt. Not so calm after all. Hers sped to match it in a frantic race as the warmth of his body seeped into her.

His breath fluttered her hair. If she turned her head, they'd be face-to-face. So close she could lean in and . . .

Jihoon stepped back, releasing her. They were both soaked through now. His umbrella lay next to them, where it had fallen.

She remembered another rain-filled night when he'd held her close. When he'd looked at her with affection. Now he watched her warily.

"Here." He picked up the umbrella and thrust it at her.

She frowned at the handle, as if it would come alive and bite her. "Why?"

"It's just an umbrella. Don't read too much into it."

"I'm not," she insisted, but her fingers still wouldn't reach for the handle.

"Take the damn thing." Annoyance laced his command. And a blaze of fire spread through her, forcing her limbs up. She thought she noticed a shining line connecting her heart to Jihoon's, then she blinked and it disappeared.

Miyoung gripped the handle, her hand brushing against his.

"I don't want to be like this," he said, still holding the umbrella. "I don't want to hate you."

"What do you want, then?"

"I don't know." He finally let go of the umbrella. "It makes me so mad you're back, but if you leave again I'll hate you even more."

Drops of water fell down his cheeks. She didn't know if they were tears or rain.

"I'm used to people leaving," he continued. "I'm just not used to them coming back."

His words pierced her heart, leaving another hole in the already battered thing.

"Here." She tried to hand the umbrella back.

"Just take it and get out of here."

There was a force in his voice, a heat that arrowed through her, and she felt her hands clenching tighter around the umbrella. A command she could not deny. "I'll return it."

"Tomorrow," Jihoon said. "At the hospital. I'll meet you there after school."

She nodded and walked quickly away, not wanting to look back, but she did. He stood in the same place, drenched, watching her leave.

o o o

The rain had slowed to a drizzle by the time Miyoung walked through the narrow alley that led to Junu's apartment. Each step felt heavy. Like more than just rain-soaked socks weighed her limbs down. She stumbled, her vision blurring, lights flashing behind her eyes. For a second she thought they were ghosts and remembered another time she'd come down this alleyway searching for help. It seemed like a lifetime ago, but it had been less than four months earlier.

She fell to her hands and knees. A discarded shard of glass sliced into her palm and she swore. But even her cursing was weak. She would have lain there, letting the sprinkle of rain cool her overheated cheeks, but a shadow fell on her.

"What a sight," Junu said with a tsk. "Normally I'd rejoice at having a pretty girl sprawled out waiting for me. But I know for a fact this one bites."

Miyoung didn't have the energy to yell at him or punch him, though they were both all she wanted to do right now.

Junu hoisted her up, swinging her arm around his shoulder.

For some reason she was grateful he hadn't thrown her over his shoulder like a sack of potatoes. It was really the small things she'd learned to be grateful for in these final days.

She was unceremoniously deposited in the dry bathtub, where she wouldn't drip on the pristine floor. Junu returned with a cup of bitter-smelling, steaming liquid. He'd probably heated it to warm her chilled bones, and somehow that made the concoction taste worse.

"I don't remember you taking an umbrella when we left," Junu said, holding it up.

"I didn't," Miyoung muttered, pulling off her shoes and pouring the dirty rainwater down the drain.

"Where'd you get it?"

She didn't want to say, but knew that Junu would guess anyway. "Jihoon."

"How chivalrous."

"I didn't want to take it." Miyoung pulled off her socks next.

"Did he use his fox-bead magic on you?"

"Don't call it that." She threw her socks at him and missed. They smacked into the wall, the dirty water splattered everywhere, and Junu winced. He hated dirt in his home.

"He possesses your bead. He could make you do anything he wants. What else should I call it?" Junu asked, handing her a towel.

"Except he doesn't know he has it." Miyoung stepped out of the tub, feeling a little steadier.

"Has that stopped him from commanding you to do things?"

Miyoung fumed, unable to answer.

"See," Junu said.

"I don't pay you to have an opinion," Miyoung said, trying her best to channel her mother. But it didn't work, as she looked like a drowned rat.

"Whether I say it aloud or not, he's dangerous to you."

"And he's in danger, too. I think the bead is hurting him. His mortal body wasn't meant to hold something so powerful."

"You don't feed on the off chance it could hurt him. You came back to help him with his halmeoni. Isn't that enough?"

"Nothing will ever be enough. Even if I had ten mouths to apologize, it wouldn't be enough." Miyoung pushed past Junu.

"Ya! You're dripping," Junu called after her.

She ignored him and stepped into her room. When he tried to follow, she slammed the door in his face. It was childish but it was satisfying. She peeled off her wet clothes, letting them fall with a *plop*, and wrapped herself in a robe.

She dropped onto her bed, slamming her head against the headboard. The pain was one more thing to pile onto the miserable day.

Junu was right. She hated that he so often was. Jihoon had her bead and therefore held a power over her. When he demanded she do something in just the right way, Miyoung felt a fire in her chest. And she was unable to deny his command.

She glanced toward the calendar hanging on her wall. Three weeks until the next full moon and a month until the hundredth day. A countdown had begun the night her mother had attacked Jihoon. The first night she didn't feed. And with each full moon that passed and each time she chose not to feed, she grew weaker and weaker until she'd fade into nothing. She lifted her hand, almost expecting to see through it like a ghost. But other than being a bit paler, it was still there. For now.

Yena wasn't the only one who'd been searching for an answer. Miyoung had visited her fair share of monks and shamans.

She'd come up with her own theories.

There was more than one reason she refused to feed. She believed if she made her bead weak enough, it could be removed from Jihoon on the hundredth day. Right before she faded away forever.

Miyoung wondered again what became of gumiho when they died. Did they really have souls? Or did they just cease to exist?

She had a month before she had to find out.

ISOLATION IS THE enemy of humanity. Loneliness a threat to empathy.

Perhaps this is how the gumiho grew up with hate in her heart. She had not yet taken on the name of Gu Yena. But what she called herself is inconsequential here.

Shunned by her family, she lived alone in a cottage high in the mountains. She fed on the energy of wayward travelers and planned how she would seek revenge on humanity.

As Seoul grew around the mountains that held shrines and temples, the city crept up the mountainsides.

One day she met a man. He had sharp eyes and rough hands. And he made her feel more beautiful than a thousand suitors confessing their love.

He made her regret her solitary lifestyle. He made her icy heart warm.

With him, she allowed herself to dream of a life free of the hatred she'd harbored for hundreds of years.

But for her, love meant uncertainty.

She'd lived for centuries and had learned that humans were not to be trusted with her secret. They would fear her or, worse, use it to manipulate her.

So she lied to the man about what she was. She considered it a small price to pay for love.

But love and lies do not mix well.

53

MIYOUNG HATED HOSPITALS. The ill and the dying seeped gi like a crack in a dam. And right now the temptation to take a taste was too great.

She kept her head lowered and walked down the hall, her footsteps a quick staccato.

"What are you doing here?"

Miyoung winced at the hard voice and lifted her eyes to meet Somin's.

"I'm—" She broke off, unsure what was better, the truth or a lie. Somin's eyes bore into her like she was waiting for Miyoung to reveal some nefarious plan.

"I asked her to come," Jihoon said, walking up the hallway. "And you're late." He directed this statement to Miyoung.

"Why would you have her come here?" Somin asked.

"Somin-ah, *you're* the one who told me to call her."

Miyoung raised her brows in surprise.

The other girl cast a furious look at Jihoon and said in a harsh whisper, "I said to *call* her for closure."

"I came back on my own," Miyoung said, annoyed at being talked about like she wasn't right there.

"Well, then, you can leave on your own. You've done it before." Somin gave Miyoung a hard glare.

"Somin-ah, it's getting late," Jihoon said.

"So?" The girl crossed her arms stubbornly.

"I'm fine," Jihoon said. "You said I needed closure. Let me get it on my own terms."

This seemed to break through Somin's stubbornness. "Call me if you need me."

"Always." Jihoon gave her a hug, and even though Miyoung knew better, she felt jealousy stab through her at the easy affection between the two friends.

Once she was gone, Jihoon gave Miyoung a raised brow, then walked into his halmeoni's room.

She sighed. It seemed there would be no pleasantries traded, just right down to business.

The room was dark with the shades drawn. And the second bed was empty, though Miyoung was sure in the overcrowded hospital that wouldn't last long.

Miyoung took out supplies that she'd purchased at a shaman shop. Not Nara's, and to be honest, she wasn't sure if this place had even been legit. But as she pulled out a yellow bujeok, it sparked against her skin.

"What do you plan to do with that?"

"It's not for her, it's for me," Miyoung said. The talisman made her skin itch, but it was meant to lower her shields, make her weak. She hoped it would allow her to sift the loose gi she'd felt all over the hospital into Halmeoni.

"To be honest, I've never done something like this before." Miyoung lit the incense.

Jihoon watched her carefully over the flame of the lighter. "I'm trusting you here. Against my better judgment."

"I know." She lowered her eyes, unable to meet his anymore.

Then she took Halmeoni's hand and held the bujeok in the other. She opened herself to Halmeoni, searching for her gi. It was even weaker than the last time. A low-burning ember.

She was afraid to touch it. Afraid the taste of it would make the raging beast of her hunger rise up. So instead she tried to find a way to connect that wasn't through Halmeoni's energy.

Poor child. The voice was a whisper; there, then gone like a call on the wind.

She strained herself toward it. The sound of it had felt so warm, so familiar.

Forgive yourself.

She frowned at that.

Miyoung didn't have time to wonder if her mind was playing tricks on her; she could already feel her tenuous hold on Halmeoni's gi wavering. She tried to sift the gi from the sick and the dying into her. It resisted her hold, like a dozen slippery snakes slithering through her hands.

She drove her own energy out, trying to seek the evasive gi sliding through the hospital.

No, not this way, the voice in her head said. *I don't want to live at the expense of others.*

The voice was distant but she could place it now.

Halmeoni? Miyoung gasped in her mind. And her voice echoed as if she were in a dream.

Let go, child. And then she felt like she was tumbling down, down, down. A drop that felt never-ending. Until she could see without opening her eyes. A light so blinding it filled her mind.

Please, let me help you. I need to do this, for Jihoon! Miyoung pleaded.

You don't need to do this to earn his forgiveness. Halmeoni's voice sounded kind, understanding, and it broke Miyoung's heart.

When he finds out what I did . . . Miyoung couldn't finish the thought.

You don't need to tell him. You only need to love him.

I can't, Miyoung replied. *I don't deserve that.*

Child, that's not for you to decide.

And Miyoung felt like she was yanked back. She tried to reach out again, scrambled to find the connection. But it broke with a snap and a flash. And she felt the sting of the severed bond as she opened her eyes to see Jihoon kneeling over her.

"Oh, thank God, I thought you were going to hurt yourself." Worry was etched over his features. Worry for her. It caused a warm glow to settle in her.

"Hurt myself?" Miyoung asked, realizing she was sprawled on the ground. She sat up and rubbed the back of her head. She must have hit it when she fell.

"Yeah, you were jerking around and I couldn't stop you." His hand rubbed at his cheek and she saw the beginnings of a bruise.

"Are you okay?" She touched the purpling skin, and he pulled back, the worry gone and replaced with a stony mask.

"So? Did it work?" His eyes went to his halmeoni's still form, but she thought she felt his disappointment.

She heard Halmeoni's voice in her head still and wondered if that had been real or if she'd just imagined it all.

"No, I don't think it worked." Miyoung decided it best not to tell him what she'd heard in case it had all been her imagination.

"So you can't do it."

"I'll keep trying." She gathered her things.

Jihoon didn't reply; he only sat in the chair she'd vacated and took his halmeoni's hand in his.

You only need to love him, halmeoni had said.

But how could she when she only brought him pain?

o o o

Two weeks passed with no progress. Halmeoni had been right. If Miyoung took the gi of the sick and the dying in the hospital, then she might accidentally drain them, killing them in the process. Then she'd be the monster she claimed she didn't want to be anymore.

So Miyoung scoured the city, finding relics and objects rumored to hold some spark of energy. At one point she spent a whole afternoon trying to see if she could pull energy from an old Joseon vase rumored to have once been a dokkaebi. She'd achieved nothing other than shattering the vase.

And with her energy waning, she couldn't handle the physical demands of searching the whole city for an answer.

Miyoung leaned over the bathroom sink and let the water flow into her cupped hands. She was grateful there weren't many visitors in this wing of the hospital so she could be sick in private. Her mouth still tasted like bile, and her stomach still rocked like she was standing on a boat in the middle of the sea.

Leaning against the counter, she studied her sallow face in the mirror. It was getting worse.

The closer she got to the hundred-day mark, the worse she felt. Sometimes she was so hazy, she felt like she was walking through a dream, one she couldn't wake from. But during moments when the pain was at its peak, she yearned for the fugue-like state.

"Keep it together, Gu Miyoung," she said to her reflection.

"You don't need to last much longer." The pep talk didn't really work, but a part of her figured if she was talking, at least she wasn't throwing up.

She made her way up the hall toward Halmeoni's room. She took a minute outside to straighten her shirt. She rubbed at a small stain, hoping it wasn't vomit, but not completely discounting that possibility.

Finally, she slid the door open and gave a small sigh of relief when she saw Jihoon wasn't there yet. Just Halmeoni and her new roommate, who was fast asleep, with only the sound of the monitors.

Miyoung sat and rested her head against Halmeoni's cool arm. It worried her that the woman's skin was cold to the touch, but the sensors measured out her slow heartbeats, assuring Miyoung that Halmeoni was still alive. For now.

She almost jumped at the buzz of her phone.

Yena's name flashed across the screen and she wanted to ignore it, but remembered her mother's warning not to miss her calls.

"Hello?" The word was hardly out when Yena's shouting voice came through the line.

"You're in Seoul? Why would you go back there without my permission?"

"Because—"

"And to get Junu to *lie* to me with my own money, as if I wouldn't notice the withdrawals in such huge sums?"

Miyoung scowled. "So he told you. Traitor."

"Don't blame this on him. This is all on you and your continuously horrible judgment. Are you with *him*?" Miyoung knew that Yena didn't mean Junu now.

"His halmeoni is sick. I'm helping—"

"Do not go near that boy while he has your bead. Do you forget he could control you if he knew?"

"But he doesn't know," Miyoung pointed out.

"Unless he's a complete idiot, which I wouldn't completely discount as a possibility, he'll figure it out soon. Don't go near that boy, Miyoung."

She almost gave in. The anger in Yena's voice could still cause her to freeze in fear. But she was so tired and run-down from weeks of failure and hunger. She just wanted one thing to hold on to. And though he never seemed that happy to be spending time with her, just seeing Jihoon's face every day was a small boost that kept her exhaustion at bay for a while. So she added some iron to her voice. "You can't tell me what to do anymore, Mother."

Then she hung up.

"That was your mother?" Jihoon asked from the doorway.

54

"YENA IS BACK?" Jihoon asked, stepping into the room.

Miyoung whipped around, holding her phone behind her back as if she were hiding evidence of a crime. Then she lifted her chin, recovering her composure. "My mother is none of your business."

"She is if she hurt my halmeoni. This could be the solution we've been looking for; why wouldn't you tell me she's back?"

"It's complicated." Miyoung's lips pulled down at the corners.

"You said you'd help me."

"Telling you where Yena is wouldn't be helping you."

He could tell there was something she wasn't saying, and it infuriated him that she was keeping secrets when his halmeoni's life was at stake.

"What if she can tell us what she did to my halmeoni?" Jihoon worked hard to keep his tone even, but there was still frustration in every syllable.

Miyoung shook her head fervently. "You can't blame my mother for your halmeoni."

Jihoon couldn't believe what he was hearing. The vehemence with which Miyoung defended her mother. Like she truly didn't think Yena had done anything wrong. His halmeoni had lain in a coma for almost three months, and Miyoung still thought her mother was without blame.

"My halmeoni is all I have. And your mother didn't care about that when she took her away from me."

This seemed to break something in Miyoung. Her fists clenched tightly against her sides. Her face flushed. "Your halmeoni is not in the hospital because of my mother. She's old and mortal. Mortals die. It's what you do!"

Jihoon's vision became a haze. People say the color of anger is red, but his was white. Pure white washing out the world and filling his mind until he thought he'd erupt in a burst of light.

"Of course you'd say that," he shouted. "You have no idea what it's like to have a family. Your mother's a monster and your own father didn't even want you!"

He regretted the words as soon as they were free.

Miyoung's hand whipped out, cracking across his cheek.

She stormed out of the room and Jihoon didn't stop her.

55

JIHOON CALLED MIYOUNG the next day, but she didn't answer. Or, as he suspected, she was screening her calls.

His shift at the CU Mart was a small piece of hell. Stuck behind the counter when he really wanted to find Miyoung and explain himself. He didn't want to feel this guilt, the kind that sat on his lungs like a taunting demon.

"If it's bothering you this much, just go to her house." Somin leaned against the counter, sucking on a yogurt drink.

"I would if I knew where she was living now." Jihoon jabbed at the keys of the register as he wallowed. It wasn't his fault, he told himself for the twentieth time that day. She'd just made him so mad.

"I told you it was a bad idea to let that girl back into your life," Somin pointed out unhelpfully.

"I don't need another lecture." Jihoon let his head drop onto the counter in frustration. He'd hit on a sensitive spot with Miyoung because he knew it would hurt her. That was all he'd wanted in the moment, to make her suffer like he was suffering. His halmeoni had raised him to know better, to be better.

The door to the convenience store opened and he jerked upright. Then he let himself slump again as Junu walked in.

"What do you want?" Jihoon asked.

"I'm pretty sure that greeting is not in the employee training manual."

"I'm pretty sure you're not only here to buy ramyeon," Jihoon retorted.

Junu laughed, then noticed Somin standing in front of Jihoon, legs spread like she was ready to fight.

"And who is your stunning friend?" Junu asked.

"Lee Somin, this is Junu." Jihoon flicked his fingers in the dokkaebi's direction like he was shooing away a mosquito.

"No family name?" Somin asked. "You think you're an idol like Rain or TOP?"

"No, much better-looking," Junu said with a laugh and a wink.

Somin scowled, and for the first time Junu's grin turned down a bit. Jihoon wondered whether it was the first time a girl had rejected his charms. He leaned forward, thoroughly entertained.

"I'm going to be late for after-school study. I'll see you tomorrow, Jihoon-ah." Somin grabbed her hot Cheetos off the counter and, without acknowledging Junu, she left.

Junu's eyes tracked her exit. "Your friend is icy." He paused, then smiled at Jihoon. "I like her."

"Stay away from my friends," Jihoon said.

Junu lifted his hands innocently. "That's not why I'm here."

Jihoon rolled his eyes. "What do you want?"

"I think the question is, what do *you* need?"

"Are you talking in riddles because you're a dokkaebi? Or because you're annoying?"

"I came to help," Junu said. "There's a very angry girl in my apartment. She's been stomping around all day. It's giving me a headache."

"I've been trying to call her." Jihoon sighed. He didn't care that it was Junu. He needed to vent to someone. "How can I say I'm sorry if she won't answer my calls or my texts?"

"Too bad there's no one around supernaturally made to woo women. No chonggak dokkaebi so handsome that girls swoon at his feet."

Jihoon glowered. Was he really thinking of doing this? Taking the advice of someone he hated? "Fine."

"Phone." Junu held out his hand.

Jihoon complied, glaring at the dokkaebi as he typed furiously. "What are you writing?" Jihoon asked, leaning over the counter to see the text.

Junu backed away. "Don't worry. I won't send it without showing you."

Jihoon tried to be patient, but as Junu typed and considered and deleted and retyped, he started to lose patience.

Finally, Junu presented the phone.

The message was a splash of cartoon flowers, hearts, and bolded letters.

"No." Jihoon shook his head emphatically. "I'm not sending something like this." He jabbed the delete button.

"Ya!" Junu protested.

"It doesn't even sound like me. She'll know it was you."

"Fine, then what would you type?"

Jihoon wrote out a quick note: We should talk.

Junu grimaced at the plain message like it brought him physical pain. He made to grab the phone, but Jihoon pulled it away. Junu sighed. "When you just type texts like that, they look flat. You have to add volume."

"Add volume?" Jihoon asked, perplexed.

"Yeah, put a heart or emoji after," Junu suggested.

"No." Jihoon drew the line at putting a winking smiley face in a text.

"Fine, then give it a wave." Junu grinned as he pointed to the ~ symbol.

Jihoon rolled his eyes, but he added the ~ before pressing send.

"Why are you helping me?" Jihoon asked.

"I told you. I don't like to be around grouchy people. It puts me in a bad mood."

"Really?" Jihoon didn't believe a thing out of the dokkaebi's mouth. He was too smooth, too good at lying.

Before he could prod Junu more, his phone beeped. Miyoung's name appeared on the screen. Jihoon lifted surprised eyes to Junu. The older boy gave him an encouraging thumbs-up, and Jihoon smiled back. Then he realized how friendly he was acting toward the dokkaebi and stopped grinning.

He read the message: I'm at Namsan.

o o o

Namsan was a high mountain in the middle of the city. Though there were many restaurants that boasted well-known wang donkatsu along the way, the main attraction was Namsan Tower. A popular place for dates and somewhere Jihoon wouldn't go if he were paid. Except he found himself crammed into one of the cable cars leading to the top. He didn't like how crowded it was; it was giving him a headache. Or maybe that was the result of being anxious all day.

And even after reaching the end of the journey, he still had to climb stairs that led tourists and lovers past food stands. Jihoon glared at the hot dogs on a stick surrounded by fried potato and remembered promising one to Miyoung once. It had been a different Jihoon who'd promised that to a different Miyoung, he thought.

It was hard to find her in the crowd of bodies and he craned his neck back to look at the top of the tower, wondering if he'd have to go up there. He was pretty sure you needed a reservation to go into the restaurant on top.

He took in the landscape at the base of the tower. The fence that ran around the perimeter was covered in padlocks, so plentiful and colorful they created a metal tapestry. Locks also created metallic Christmas trees in the middle of the courtyard.

Walking to the fence, Jihoon had to admit the view was stellar. As the sun approached the horizon, it gave the city a glow. He could mark the patterns of Seoul from up here, where the old tile roofs of the hanoks merged into the newer metal and concrete of the city. Such a contrasting mess to see the old homes that boasted under-floor coal heating and rice-paper walls next to the most modern of skyscrapers. But in this city the dichotomy worked. In this city the dichotomy thrived. It seemed that sometimes opposites did find a balance.

Then he saw her, standing at one of the viewfinders that showed the city below.

He approached her slowly, worried now that she might take advantage of the location to pitch him over the side of the mountain. But he comforted himself in the fact that Miyoung didn't like to make a scene.

"Miyoung."

"Yes?" she replied coldly, as she refused to look at him.

"You said you'd talk."

"I told you where I was. You were the one that wanted to talk," Miyoung corrected him.

Jihoon seethed. His frustration was two centimeters from breaking the surface. It made the low headache brewing pulse, but he took a deep breath and tried again.

"Fine, I wanted to say I'm sorry," he said, then waited for her to accept his apology. She didn't and instead studied the locks that decorated the fence. They were covered in claims of everlasting friendship and love. A beautiful rainbow assortment of promises.

"Did you hear me?" Jihoon asked.

"Yes," Miyoung replied, studying another lock.

Jihoon spun her around to face him. "I'm trying to apologize."

"Why?"

Jihoon blinked in surprise. "What do you mean?"

"Why do you want to apologize when you've made it clear that I'm the reason everything has gone wrong in your life."

"That's a bit of an exaggeration."

"I don't want an apology. Not from you."

"Listen, I shouldn't have brought up your father," Jihoon said. "If you don't let me apologize, I'll never feel right about it."

"Fine," Miyoung said, through a jaw so clenched her cheeks visibly flexed. "I'll accept your apology. Will you leave me alone now?"

Jihoon suddenly noticed how exhausted she looked. Bags shadowed her eyes. Her skin was pale. Her shoulders slumped.

"Excuse me?" A young mother stood behind him. "Can you take our photo?" she asked.

"Sure." Jihoon accepted her phone and waited for her to get two fighting toddlers to stand still. The family huddled together, her husband hugging the three of them from behind. It was a lovely picture of a normal family. Jihoon's eyes slid to Miyoung, who looked anywhere but at the happy unit. Neither of them had ever taken a photo like this.

After Jihoon handed back her phone, the woman asked, "Do you two want a picture?"

"Oh no, we're okay." Miyoung took a step back, like the woman meant to do her physical harm.

"You should take photos, even if it's a first date." The woman grinned. "My husband and I still have a picture from ours."

"It's not our first date." Miyoung's cheeks pinked.

"An anniversary, then?" The woman was persistent.

"You know what, we'd love a photo," Jihoon said to avoid any more questions. He handed her his phone, then stood beside Miyoung.

"You should put your arm around her," the husband suggested, winking.

Jihoon complied. It was easier than the awkwardness of refusing.

"And smile!" the woman chirped.

He did and it felt awkward on his face.

"It seems like a first date." The woman lowered Jihoon's phone. "You two look stiff as boards."

Miyoung glanced at Jihoon, her brows lifted in question.

"Okay, one more." This time, he pulled Miyoung until she was snug against his side. She looked up at him, smiling wryly. Her eyes seemed to say, *Only we could get into a situation like this.* And he smiled back because it was true.

"Perfect." The woman beamed. "You make a beautiful couple."

When the family walked away to enter the tower, Jihoon turned back to Miyoung, who'd taken a few steps away. Her shoulders shook. Was she crying?

Placing a hesitant hand on her arm, he was about to ask if she was okay when he saw her wide smile. She was laughing.

"I swear, Ahn Jihoon, when that woman asked if we were on a date, your face got so white you'd have thought you were being faced by a liver-eating demon."

Jihoon let out a surprised laugh at that. And they fell into a fit of mirth together, holding each other up as it quieted into hiccupping chuckles.

"It's your fault, you know," Jihoon pointed out. "Why in the world would you come up to Namsan, the capital of romance, alone?"

She shrugged, and her eyes fell to his hand still on her arm. He dropped it quickly and a tension rose between them.

"I guess it's always been on my bucket list, and I figured it was a good time to start working on that." She looked out at the city.

Jihoon frowned at the idea of an immortal gumiho having a bucket list.

"Listen, I accept your apology," Miyoung said, her back still to him. "You can go home with a clean conscience now."

Jihoon didn't know how to reply to that. He'd come here to apologize and she'd let him. That was all he'd wanted. Except the guilt that had sat on his chest all day had congealed into something heavy in his stomach. Like he'd done something wrong again.

Still, he could think of no reason to stay, so he started to make his way through the crowd toward the cable cars. Out of habit he pulled his phone out, unlocking it as he walked. The photo of him and Miyoung filled the screen. He stopped and a young couple accidentally bumped into him. He mumbled an apology, his eyes never leaving the photo.

In it, Miyoung looked at him. Her eyes soft, her right hand gripping the front of his jacket. He hadn't even felt it at the time.

The look on his own face felt foreign. He couldn't quite peg the expression at first. Then he realized it was contentment. In that moment, caught up in her arms, caught up in his memories, he'd been happy.

Jihoon wasn't sure what to make of the realization. He knew in his gut that he should still be angry at her. Miyoung kept secrets. He couldn't fully trust her. But he was finding it harder and harder to stay mad.

She'd been honest with him about who she was, what she was. She'd told him she ran when things got hard. But she'd come back this time to help with Halmeoni. That should count for something, shouldn't it? And after all he'd been through, didn't he deserve to be happy?

Jihoon wove back through the crowd. People packed together as they milled the space. Couples holding hands, children running with shouts of laughter. The March air was crisp with early spring, and it felt like the whole city was on Namsan, taking advantage of it.

It took too long to reach Miyoung, when all Jihoon wanted was to be next to her.

When he reached her, he pulled on her shoulder so she faced him.

"Jihoon-ah?" His name was a question that died quickly, eaten by the mountain wind, when she saw his face.

"I'm done." Jihoon let his fingers run through the hair at her temple, soft as down.

"Okay," Miyoung said as he lifted his other hand to cup her face. "Done with what?"

"All of it." And Jihoon let go of the anger, the tension, the fear. He breathed it out in a sigh of relief.

"Okay," she said again. Whispered it, so only he heard.

He leaned in.

She stood still.

He sighed out her name.

She sucked in air.

Jihoon's heart pushed against his ribs, like it needed to be closer to her and didn't care if the rest of him came with it or not. He let his hands slide down her cheeks, ran his fingers over her smooth skin. Her breath shuddered out.

It made him giddy, her show of weakness at his mere touch. It made him feel powerful, a boy who could make a gumiho shiver.

Their lips were a centimeter apart, and Miyoung's eyes filled his vision, dark pools that captured his reflection. He felt like he could get trapped in there and didn't care. He'd welcome the cage.

There was a pull in him, urging him forward. He lowered his head slowly, sliding his hand over her nape.

Then he laid his lips against hers, softer than the brush of wind across skin.

She linked her arms around his neck, pulling him closer.

And the kiss he'd meant to be gentle became heated in an instant. He swallowed her gasp. His hands tangled in her hair. Her teeth scraped against his bottom lip as she pulled it into her mouth. And now he was the one gasping.

The pressure in his chest built until it became a blinding heat that engulfed him. Stars exploded behind his eyes. This time, when he gasped, it was in pain. He stumbled back, his legs shaking, giving way beneath him.

He heard Miyoung yell his name, a garbled sound that mixed with the ringing in his ears.

Then he fell and he fell and he didn't stop until he lost consciousness.

56

JIHOON WOKE TO beeps and whispers, the all-too-familiar sounds of the hospital. He kept his eyes closed to give himself time to gather his wits. As he let his mind adapt, he realized the whispers were low whimpers, like someone holding back sobs.

Jihoon opened his eyes, blinking a few times to adjust to the light. Miyoung's head lay in her arms at the edge of his hospital bed.

"Miyoung?" It hurt his throat just to say her name.

"Jihoon!" Miyoung squeaked, startled.

"I'm fine." He pushed her probing fingers away. "Why am I in the hospital?"

"You started to convulse. It was . . ." She trailed off. "You scared me."

"I'm sorry."

"Don't say that. You shouldn't be the one who's sorry."

He shook his head, but it just worsened the dull pounding that lived behind his eyes now. "I didn't want you to see me like this."

Miyoung couldn't seem to meet his eyes. Tears hung from her lashes, threatening to fall. His throat tightened at the sight. Originally he hadn't wanted her to see one of his episodes because he didn't want her to think he was weak. And now he didn't because she was obviously worried. He hated to worry people he loved.

He frowned at the unbidden thought. Did he still love her?

Then he sighed. Of course he did—only someone he loved could make him as angry as she did.

"Miyoung, come here." He patted the edge of the bed.

She sat precariously on the edge of the bed so she was more leaning than sitting.

With a heavy sigh, he gripped her hand. It felt clammy, shaking slightly in his.

"Don't worry about me. I'm stronger than I look." He tucked her hair behind her ear so he could see her face.

Tears created rivers along her pale skin.

"Don't cry. I promise I'll be fine." He wiped at the dampness on her cheeks and her hand came up to catch his. It no longer trembled.

"It's all my fault," she said again. "My bead is causing this."

"Why would you say that?"

"Because—" She paused, taking in deep breaths of air so quickly, he worried she'd hyperventilate.

"You're scaring me," Jihoon said. "Just say it."

"It's inside of you."

"What? How?" He didn't realize he'd pulled his hands back until they were cradled against his chest.

"You almost died when my mother attacked you. I didn't know if you'd make it." Miyoung stood, creating more distance between them. "Your halmeoni told me to use the bead."

"My halmeoni?" Jihoon's brow furrowed in confusion.

"It started to heal you, but it wasn't enough. It needed more gi."

"Whose?" Jihoon asked, but the weight in his stomach told him he already knew.

Miyoung didn't answer. She couldn't look him in the eye.

"Tell me whose gi."

"Your halmeoni's."

Disbelief spread through him, a wash of ice. He couldn't feel his toes, his fingers, his heart.

"She wanted you to live. It was her final wish." Miyoung's hands folded together, like she was begging him to understand.

"'Final wish'?" Jihoon spat out, anger twisting his gut. "That's why she won't wake up from her coma." Realization splashed over him like a winter wave breaking on rocks. "It wasn't Yena. It was you."

"I'm sorry. It was the only way to save you."

"That's why you came back? Because you felt guilty after doing this to my halmeoni?" Jihoon tried to catch his breath, praying he wouldn't throw up as nausea curled through him.

"This is what I'm talking about," Miyoung said, urgency in her voice. "Having my bead inside you is making you sick. A mortal body was never meant to hold a fox bead."

"You had no right." Jihoon wasn't sure what he was referring to. Trading his halmeoni's life for his. Saving him only to leave him. Coming back and making him love her again.

"Jihoon-ah, I'm so sorry." She reached out, and he jerked back.

"Don't touch me." His chest flared with heat that he would have attributed to anger, except it lingered, a warmth that washed over his ribs and into his shoulders. Then it centered in his chest, directly over his heart, like a ball of fire. If he concentrated, he could almost hear another heartbeat, one that mirrored his own. Miyoung's heart. Her eyes flashed as she brought her hand down in slow, jerking movements like she fought an invisible force.

A memory tickled at the back of his mind: Miyoung saying that a man could control a gumiho if he possessed her bead.

"That's why you came back." He almost laughed at his own

naiveté. "Not to help my halmeoni, but because you need your bead. That's what it's always been about with us. You lost your bead, and you've been trying to get it back ever since we met."

"No." Miyoung shook her head. "I came back for you."

"Stop lying!"

The heat in his heart receded into a dull glow. He closed his eyes, concentrating on his breathing. In, hold, slowly out.

When he spoke again, his voice was low but steady. "You're no better than your mother. Manipulating everyone around you to get what you want." Jihoon didn't know what to feel. He was worried he'd lost the ability altogether.

"Please," she begged, grabbing his arm. "I was wrong. I was—"

"Stop!" It seemed he could still feel. And he was angry.

She fell silent so suddenly, it was as if he'd pressed the mute button.

They sat for a moment, Jihoon still as stone, Miyoung racked with silent tears she couldn't shed.

There was a knock and Detective Hae opened the door.

"Ajeossi." Jihoon said it like a plea for help. He needed someone to make sense of all this for him.

"Jihoon-ah, what happened?" Detective Hae stepped into the room, then stopped when he saw Miyoung. "Oh, I didn't know you had a visitor."

Miyoung hastily swiped her hands over her cheeks to push away her tears and stood.

"You look just like her," Detective Hae whispered, stopping Miyoung in mid-bow.

"Like who?" Miyoung asked, staring at Detective Hae with appraising eyes. A tiger deciding if the man in front of her was prey or foe.

"Ajeossi?" Jihoon asked, unable to understand the recognition he saw in Detective Hae's eyes.

"You look just like your mother." Detective Hae took a jerking step, a person caught in a gravity pull.

"How would you know my mother?" Miyoung's tone implied she'd decided this man was foe.

Detective Hae took a breath and in that beat Jihoon held his. He didn't know what was happening but he somehow knew it was important.

"Because she was my wife," Detective Hae said. "Which means you're my daughter."

57

IT WASN'T TRUE. It *couldn't* be true. Miyoung sprinted out of the hospital, ignoring the shouts of annoyed nurses and patients following her.

Her father was a useless waste of space. Her mother always said he wasn't someone to seek out because she was ashamed of ever loving a man like him.

But Detective Hae was an honorable man. At least that was how Jihoon described him. And he was a detective who sought to save lives.

Was it possible that instead of being ashamed of Detective Hae, Yena was ashamed of them? That they were monsters who killed while the man she once loved was a good man?

There was only one way to find out. Miyoung called Yena.

"Hello?"

At the sound of her mother's voice Miyoung froze. She didn't know how to explain that she felt hurt by Yena keeping so many secrets. But she also needed her mother more than anything right now.

"Hello? Miyoung? Is that you?"

"Mother." The word was a croaked whisper. Miyoung coughed to clear her throat and tried again. "Mother, I need to ask you something and I need you to be honest with me."

There was a long, pregnant pause before Yena replied. "What is it?"

"My father."

"Miyoung, I don't want to—"

"I met him!" Miyoung blurted out. "And he's not a horrible person like you claimed. He's a detective and he seems like a good man. And you kept him from me and—"

"Do not talk to that man!" Yena's voice was a high screech that forced Miyoung to hold the phone away from her ear. "Do not talk to him, do you hear me?"

"So you admit it! You knew he was in Seoul."

Yena sighed. "I only recently found out where he was. This is one of the reasons I told you not to return. That man is not what he seems, Miyoung. Do not go near him or that boy again. Not until I get there."

"But he's my father."

"Promise me!" Yena demanded.

Miyoung hesitated a bit too long.

"Promise—" With a beep the line went dead.

Miyoung stared at her screen, wondering if her phone had died. But it blinked the time of the call at her before returning to the home screen. She tried dialing Yena again but it went directly to voice mail.

She hung up, wondering where Yena was now. Probably in an airport on her way back to berate Miyoung for all of her bad life decisions.

With a sigh, she pocketed her phone and walked without knowing where she was going. She just knew she needed air. And maybe a drink.

58

JIHOON PUSHED OPEN his front door so hard it slammed against the wall. He cursed at the sound as he fought to push off his shoes.

"Wow, you're in a grand mood."

Jihoon wasn't even surprised to see Junu.

"You know, it's bad manners to break into someone's house. Twice." Jihoon finally wrestled his shoes off and kicked them into the corner.

"Where is she?" Junu asked.

"Who?"

"The president," Junu said in a blasé tone. "Miyoung."

Jihoon ignored the worry and his bad mood and pushed past Junu toward the kitchen.

Everything felt a mess. Miyoung confessing what she'd done. Detective Hae appearing, telling her he was her father. She'd left. Just walked out the door without a word. Jihoon knew he should have stopped her, but he'd been so mad. And now he didn't know what he was. He pulled open the fridge and stared at the measly contents.

"What happened?" Junu asked.

"Her father," Jihoon said without looking away from the almost-empty fridge.

"What about him?"

Jihoon closed the refrigerator without taking anything out. "He's here."

Junu's lips twisted into a scowl that looked out of place on his handsome face. "Something's wrong."

"What is it?"

Junu eyed him. It was clear the dokkaebi wasn't willing to part with what he knew. So Jihoon put his cards on the table.

"Listen, I just found out my halmeoni gave her gi so I could live with Miyoung's bead inside me. And it's probably why I'm having seizures. So if something is going on with Miyoung, I kind of have a stake in it."

Junu nodded. "Yena's missing. I can't get in touch with her."

"So?"

"So a gumiho shouldn't be missing. She's the one who makes people disappear."

"I'm well aware of that."

"Yena would never just vanish at a time like this."

"Time like what?" Jihoon didn't like how the dokkaebi spoke in vague circles.

Junu ignored the question. "It's important that Yena is here before the next full moon."

"Maybe Miyoung is better off without her mother around," Jihoon said.

The dokkaebi's expression became sharp, like he had judged Jihoon and found him lacking. "Whatever your feelings are about Yena, she protects her child. Everything that woman does is for Miyoung."

"I don't care what Yena does."

"Oh, you care," Junu said. "You care because you think she took

Miyoung away. You think that without Yena's influence, Miyoung wouldn't have left you."

"It's none of my business if Miyoung chooses her mother over me," Jihoon said stubbornly.

"Miyoung chose you." Junu flicked Jihoon in the forehead. "She left for you. She came back for you. And you sit here like a big crybaby because she has the audacity to love the mother that's always been there her whole life. If anything, you should feel sorry for Yena. You're the one destroying her daughter."

"Now you're definitely not making sense."

"Do the math. You've had Miyoung's bead in your weak human body for almost a hundred days." Junu spoke slowly as one would when explaining algebra to a three-year-old. "If Miyoung doesn't absorb it again and start feeding at the next full moon, she's going to be in real trouble."

"She hasn't been feeding?" Jihoon asked. "If she goes a hundred days without feeding, she'll die."

"Ding-dong-daeng! Tell the boy what he's won!" Junu announced like a variety show emcee, but his showman's smile didn't quite reach his eyes.

"Why didn't she tell me this?"

"I don't know. Maybe she was trying to protect you from the responsibility of choosing your life over hers."

"She has no right to make that choice for me."

Junu chuckled. "You know what? I might not dislike you so much after all."

"What will happen if Yena suddenly appears again?" Jihoon asked.

"Then I'd find a suit of armor because she's very likely to come right over and yank that pretty bead out of your chest."

Jihoon's hand rubbed against his sternum, which suddenly felt sore. "Why are you doing this? Helping us?"

"Because I'm getting paid."

Jihoon rolled his eyes.

"If I can give you some unsolicited advice," Junu said.

"What's this been all this time?" Jihoon asked sourly.

Junu continued like Jihoon hadn't interrupted. "I'd run if I were you. What's the point of sticking around when two gumiho are after you and your only family's a log."

Jihoon's fists came up, wanting to connect with Junu's perfect jaw.

The dokkaebi danced back, lifting his hands for protection, but he gave a saucy grin that proved he wasn't that worried about Jihoon's anger.

"Anyway, you can't say I didn't warn you." Junu slipped out the front door, leaving Jihoon alone with his futile anger.

59

MIYOUNG WALKED THROUGH *the apartment. Her body so cold she couldn't stop shivering.*

She heard water flowing somewhere. Nausea churned through her.

At the end of the hallway, her mother laid in a heap. Miyoung ran to her. Yena's face was twisted in frozen pain, but Miyoung could see she was still breathing.

"Mother?" Miyoung shook Yena's shoulder. No response.

Drops of water fell on her mother's face. Miyoung wiped them away, but they were quickly replaced.

Miyoung realized the water came from her. She was soaked, head to toe, her hair dripping water onto the floor in an off-beat tempo.

And behind her, the rush of water intensified, like a waterfall booming against rock.

Miyoung turned toward the sound.

A bright slash of light emanated from the crack under the bathroom door.

She stood, drawn forward.

With every step, her body trembled until her very bones vibrated with trepidation.

She gripped the knob to the bathroom door but couldn't bring herself to turn it.

A hand covered hers, warming her frozen fingers until her shaking subsided. A red thread connected their wrists.

She looked up into Jihoon's eyes.

"Don't open it," he said.

"I have to." She didn't know how she knew, but she had to go inside and see what was behind the door.

"We'll open it together, then."

She nodded.

Jihoon's hand tightened around hers. The door swung smoothly inward.

At first, she only saw the bright white tiles and gleaming chrome fixtures. The bathtub spigot was on, flooding the room. The water raced toward the drain in the middle of the floor, but it wasn't enough to stop the water from pooling into an artificial lake.

Jihoon walked to the tub, his legs creating ripples in the water.

"Miyoung-ah." Her name echoed in the room.

"What?" She stared at the drain as it created a tiny whirlpool. She broke out in a sweat at the sight of it, afraid the churning water could somehow pull her down as well.

"Miyoung-ah," Jihoon said more urgently.

She tried to reply but something filled her throat. She coughed and water flowed from her lips like a fountain.

Jihoon called for her as the water devoured him.

She tried to swim, but her fear overtook her. She didn't like the water. The current pulled at her limbs, drowning her.

Kicking desperately, she pulled at the red thread connecting her to Jihoon, but it snapped in her hands. She searched and searched, but found nothing. Her muscles gave in to the heavy weight of the water pulling her down.

60

JIHOON WASN'T QUITE sure why he was wandering the streets at 3:00 A.M. He'd woken in a sweat, choking on his own breath like he'd actually been drowning. It was all still so clear in his mind. The hallway, Yena's unconscious form, the flooding bathroom. And he knew now that it was probably not just a dream. With the bead inside of him, he knew he was connected to Miyoung.

This probably meant all of those damned dreams where he begged Miyoung to return hadn't been his alone. Had she seen him then? At his most vulnerable? It made his head hurt to wonder.

This dream made him worry about Miyoung despite himself. The residual anxiety made it impossible to fall asleep again. So he'd taken a walk to calm his racing heart and ended up by the old neighborhood playground. The trees beyond looked like gray statues, guarding the abandoned swing set.

Miyoung sat on the roundabout. He should have been more surprised, but it was almost as if he knew he'd find her here.

"Jihoon-ah!" she slurred out, gripping a bottle of soju. Another green bottle already lay empty beside her.

Miyoung squeezed one eye closed in an effort to more

accurately pour into a plastic cup. Her tongue stuck out the side of her mouth as she concentrated on the task.

"Why are you here?" Jihoon asked.

"Couldn't sleep. Bad dreams." She threw back the soju in one perfect gulp.

"Where did you get that?" Jihoon eyed the extra bottle sitting in a plastic bag with more cups.

"At the CU Mart. That smarmy guy made me promise not to tell anyone he sold me this. I think he has a crush on me. Pyopyo or something." She gave him a drunken grin.

Jihoon would have laughed at Pyojoo's butchered name, but he was too worried Miyoung would pitch off the side of the ride.

"You look like you've been enjoying yourself." Jihoon sat on the edge of the roundabout, dragging his feet on the ground to stop it.

"I'll pour you a glass." Miyoung tipped the bottle against a second cup. Most spilled over the side.

"I'm good."

"Nonsense!" She raised her cup. "We're teenagers. We're supposed to do thoughtless things. Now that I have a father, I should make up all the lost time defying him. Drink," Miyoung said—actually demanded—with expectant eyes. Jihoon sighed and raised the cup. She clumsily tapped hers to his. "Geonbae!"

As she tilted her head back to drink in one shot, Jihoon poured his out.

"Kaaah." She let out the throaty noise in appreciation, or perhaps because she'd heard it on one too many dramas, then held her cup out. When Jihoon didn't move, she shook her hand at him.

"Haven't you heard it's good manners to pour for each other?"

He still didn't move and she sighed, grabbing the bottle herself.

"Fine!" She poured so fast she spilled half the bottle to the dirt below. He counted it as a blessing that she had less to drink now. "I never used to be so impatient. Maybe because I had all the time in the world."

She let out another laugh, her eyes already blurry and unfocused.

"Do you know what it's like to live forever?" she slurred out. That last cup had definitely tipped her over the edge.

Jihoon realized she was staring at him, expecting an answer. "No."

"Well, I was supposed to." Miyoung poured another cup. "And when you think you're going to live forever, things aren't as serious. Missing fathers, strict mothers. People constantly hating you for no good reason. I mean except the fact that I could suck the life out of them." Miyoung chuckled at her own morbid joke.

"Mortals treat everything like life and death. How long it takes to pay at a store is a favorite of mine. They get so mad!" Miyoung gestured wildly with her hand at that, some of her newly poured drink sloshing out.

"And then people get into fights and one of them ends up yelling, 'What's your problem?' Like it's not completely obvious everyone's problem is that they're going to die one day."

Miyoung became somber at that and put her cup down. Jihoon reached for it, but she lifted the cup again before he could take it away.

"Everything in my world was tied to being a gumiho. My mother, my immortality. So it's weird I meet my mortal father now that I'm dying. Do you think it's a sign? That I should just be a human, a *pfft*." She stuck her thumb down to symbolize death.

"Miyoung-ah, is that what will happen to you if you don't feed for the full hundred days?" Jihoon asked. He needed to hear her say it.

She blinked at him, her lips curling down into a deep frown. "You don't actually want to know that."

"I do."

"I'm not sure," Miyoung said. "But yeah, it seems like that's the end game. Gumiho only bring death. Even to ourselves."

Jihoon shook his head. "If you stopped feeding because of me, I don't want the responsibility of it. My halmeoni is already in a coma because of me." And he realized part of the reason he'd been so angry wasn't because of Miyoung's part in what happened to Halmeoni, but because of his. He'd been such a bad grandson and still she'd given everything for him.

Suddenly, it felt like a great idea to drink. He picked up the bottle and poured more into his cup, gulping it down in one shot. He hissed at the burn in his throat.

"If I die, it's not for you. I'm dying for me."

"What is that supposed to mean?" Jihoon wasn't sure if she didn't make sense because she was drunk or because she was Miyoung. Probably a mix of the two.

"I watch my mother and I realize how lonely she is."

Jihoon didn't know where this turn in the conversation had come from. And he wasn't in the mood to give Yena any sympathy. He took another shot and this one went down a bit easier.

"I never worried about the things I was missing out on. Like having friends or relationships. I think I always figured there'd be time for that later. But now . . ." She sighed. "Everything reminds me that my time is running out. I'm weaker now. I have scars now." She traced the white mark on her palm, a twin of Jihoon's.

"My mother told me to make a choice. So I did," she said,

flinging her arms wide, knocking herself off-balance. Jihoon caught her before she fell. She put her hands on his shoulders for stability. "And every day I decide to keep doing this, I know it's what I need to do. Not for you. Not for my mother. *I* made this decision. So it's mine. It's all I have that's just mine."

A pang shot through Jihoon, a tightening of his lungs.

He cupped her cheek lightly. Why couldn't he admit before that he'd missed this? Hearing her voice, running his fingers along her hair, seeing her eyes so close he traced out the pattern in her irises. Blooms, like flowers. He'd missed it all desperately.

"Miyoung-ah." He said her name quietly, his hand moving down her neck. "I didn't—"

"Don't be sorry. We're both sorry all the time. A sorry pair." She chuckled. "I wish things could go back," Miyoung said with a wistful sigh. "Can't we just be Miyoung and Jihoon again? Can't we be okay for five minutes?"

"I think I can do that."

"Good." She smiled sweetly. "Because I'm going to throw up."

She ran to the edge of the playground and vomited in the underbrush.

Jihoon gathered her hair back and held it as she was sick.

o o o

Jihoon carried Miyoung on his back up the sloping streets. Her arms and legs hung from him like vines, swinging back and forth as she drifted in and out of drunken consciousness.

"I'm sorry I sucked out your halmeoni's gi," Miyoung mumbled.

He tensed, unsure if he wanted to talk about that right now. Then he realized most of his anger had evaporated.

"I know how stubborn she can be. If she asked you to take her energy for me, then she probably made it impossible to say no."

"I'm a horrible gumiho," Miyoung muttered. "I couldn't even say no to a halmeoni. Some immortal being I was."

Jihoon chuckled.

Then he shifted to hitch her higher, thanking the stars when he saw his apartment across the street.

"I'm sorry I left," she said. "I thought I was doing the right thing. I didn't want to hurt you."

"No one likes a martyr."

He started up the stairs, his legs wobbling as he climbed.

"You know what I missed the most?" Miyoung whispered by his ear.

"What?" He tried to ignore the tingle along his skin as her breath fluttered over it.

"Being friends."

"Huh?"

"You were my best friend." She rested her cheek against his shoulder. "I miss my best friend."

"I miss you, too," he said, but she'd already fallen asleep.

61

MIYOUNG WONDERED IF someone's brain had ever broken out of their skull. Because even as the fog of sleep still sat over her, she was sure this was going to happen to her. The pounding behind her eyes made it almost impossible to open them. And when she tried, she immediately shut them again with a moan.

"I see the alcoholic is awake," Jihoon said from the bedroom doorway. "Oof, and you look awful." He seemed particularly pleased about this fact.

Miyoung succeeded in opening only her right eye to glare at him. The sun blazed through the windows, exacerbating her headache.

"Haven't you ever heard of curtains?" Her voice sounded like gravel scraping over a pumice stone.

"Yes, but I also don't drink two bottles of soju by myself."

"Was it only two bottles?" Miyoung mumbled, closing her eyes again and pulling up the covers. "I could've sworn it was a hundred."

"Nope, you're a lightweight. Deal with it." Jihoon yanked the blankets away ruthlessly, earning a whimper from Miyoung.

"Come on, I made bugeoguk," Jihoon said, too cheerful for her liking.

Miyoung finally smelled the savory scent of the soup and sat up with her eyes still closed.

She followed him out to the living room. The night before, she hadn't noticed the space, but it looked exactly the same as she remembered. The low, lumpy couch, begging to be sat upon. The kitchen nook was small, perhaps with more dirty dishes than before. Bookshelves still littered with picture frames. And bujeoks fluttering like bright yellow flags along the door frame.

Miyoung sat at the low table, weathered and well-used. It held two bowls of pollack soup. She let the steam hit her face.

"Best cure for a hangover," Jihoon announced. Dipping a spoon into Miyoung's soup, he lifted it to her lips. She slurped up the salty broth obediently. It was a good balm for her sore throat.

"I never knew you could cook." She took the spoon from him and scooped up more soup eagerly.

"I'm more than a pretty face." Jihoon winked.

"Oh good, I see your old sense of humor is intact." Miyoung scowled, but inside her heart swelled.

Jihoon chuckled and started to eat. On the couch was a crumpled pile of pillows and blankets. He must have slept out here and given her his room.

His hair was a mess and his cheek was creased from the pillow. There was a hole in his shirt and his pants were frayed at the hem. He still had a sleepy look in his eyes, but he'd woken up early enough to prepare a whole meal. In this moment, he was the most handsome boy she'd ever seen.

"Thank you." Miyoung couldn't stop staring at him.

"Sure thing," he mumbled, obviously embarrassed at her sudden attention.

"Is it weird that I missed this place? Even though I've only been here once?" The words were out before she thought them through. And with them she remembered what had happened the last time they were here. On the very same couch he'd slept on. A flush rose up her cheeks.

Jihoon coughed nervously, making it clear his brain had gone to the same memory.

"It's weirdly normal to have you here." He spooned up another bite. "I don't know how to feel about that."

"I can leave . . ."

"No, stay. I think it's time we can let the past be the past. I can't stay mad at you forever. I actually realized this because of Junu. Who'd have thought?"

"What did he say?" Miyoung didn't like the idea of feeling gratitude toward Junu, but she had to admit the dokkaebi was fairly persuasive.

"He made me realize I couldn't blame you for loving your mother. I love my halmeoni. I'd do anything for her. And you'd do the same for Yena. I can't be mad at you for listening to her and leaving. I think it was just an excuse, really. When you're so used to people leaving, you start to think something might be wrong with you. It was easier to be mad at you than to feel like I wasn't good enough yet again."

Miyoung didn't know what to say, but she was saved from having to reply by the ring of Jihoon's phone. His eyes moved from the screen to Miyoung, and she knew who was calling.

"Answer it," she told him.

He swiped the screen. "Hello?"

Jihoon listened a moment, his lips pursed in concentration. He answered only in a series of yeses and nos. Which frustrated Miyoung with its vagueness.

Finally, Jihoon placed his hand over the mouthpiece. "He wants to come over."

Her first inclination was to say no. To say he'd had nineteen years to come see her. She opened her mouth to say so. "Yes."

Jihoon hesitated, his brows lifting for final confirmation.

And she paused as well. Did she want to see her father? He'd left her before she could even know him, but he'd looked at her yesterday with such yearning. The look she'd probably dreamed of seeing a dozen times without realizing it.

Jihoon waited patiently, watching her with understanding eyes. She knew she'd regret it if she refused him.

Miyoung nodded, sure of herself now. "Tell him to come over. I want to see him, too."

62

MIYOUNG SAT AT a table in Halmeoni's old restaurant, facing her father for the first time in her life.

Surprisingly, she didn't feel like crying or vomiting, two things she'd been afraid of doing. In fact, she felt completely calm.

Detective Hae, however, fidgeted with his phone though his eyes never left her face. His stare so strong she almost wanted to check if she had something smudged on her cheek.

Detective Hae finally spoke. "I'm sorry. I know this must be hard for you. I wasn't sure if you'd want to see me."

"Neither was I." Miyoung had no desire to make things easier on him.

"So your name is Gu Miyoung now?" Detective Hae asked, and when Miyoung didn't answer, he cleared his throat awkwardly. "It used to be Hae Mina."

Miyoung stayed silent, unsure what to do with this randomly volunteered information.

"I've thought about you constantly since . . ."

"Since you walked out on us."

"Yes." Detective Hae's eyes lowered as if in remorse. She steeled herself against it.

"And now what do you want from us?" Miyoung asked. She

made herself and her mother into a unit on purpose. They were one and Detective Hae was separate.

"I know something's going on that involves Jihoon."

Miyoung didn't reply. She didn't like how familiar the detective seemed with Jihoon and she hated that part of it was jealousy.

Detective Hae sighed. "I know you don't trust me, but I'm worried."

Worried about Jihoon. But not about her. Miyoung wanted to shout at him, ask him why he had left her. A part of her wondered what her life would look like if he'd stayed. Would she have been a better person? Could she have been a better person? Or was she always doomed to her monstrous fate? She'd never know now.

"I thought you were dead," he said. "When I left your mother, there was a fight and you were hurt."

"No, you left before I was born."

Detective Hae shook his head. "No, I was there until you were a year old."

Miyoung frowned; she didn't remember this. If it was true, it meant Yena had lied to her.

"When I was transferred back to Seoul, I heard about the animal attacks and something about them felt familiar. So I looked into it." He trailed off, but Miyoung filled in the blanks. Jihoon had told her about how the detective had been looking into her mother's kills. It made sense now why he'd been so dogged about it.

"I thought I could save her soul once. And now I fear that I've cursed you to a horrible fate by leaving you with her."

"Don't." Miyoung half rose in her chair. "Don't you dare talk as if my mother is the villain here. *You* left. *You* abandoned me. *She* raised me and took care of me and lov—" She broke off, partly because her head was spinning from her rage, partly because she couldn't finish saying the word. She knew Yena loved her, but she couldn't say it aloud. She let herself fall back into her chair, suddenly exhausted.

"Miyoung-ah?" Detective Hae came around the table in two quick strides, but she shook her head before he could reach for her. It hurt to hear him say her name like a concerned father. She wasn't ready to forgive him. All of a sudden, her whole body ached.

"Do you regret it?" she whispered, her words choking in her throat. "Do you regret leaving me?"

"Every day." He sounded so sincere, and she wanted to believe him so badly.

"Are you here because you want to be in my life again?"

"Oh, Miyoung, I can't promise anything without your mother here . . ." He trailed off.

"You should go." She couldn't meet his gaze. She didn't want him to see the tears burning her eyes.

"But—"

"Just. Leave." She bit out each word.

And she waited until the restaurant door closed with a chime before she dropped her head in her hands and let the tears come.

63

"YOU DIDN'T HAVE to knock," Jihoon said as he opened the front door. Then he froze. Instead of Miyoung, Nara stood in front of him, her hands folded, her head bowed.

"What are you doing here?" Jihoon didn't mean to make his voice so flat; it just came out that way.

"I need—" She broke off, tried again, and failed. And her choked attempts softened Jihoon.

"Can I come in?" she whispered.

He hesitated. Despite her small stature and hunched shoulders, he knew how dangerous this girl was.

But she looked at him with such hope it melted the rest of the ice around his heart.

He opened the door wider to let her in.

Nara settled onto the sinking cushions of his halmeoni's couch. It somehow made her look smaller.

"Are you here to see Miyoung?" he finally asked.

Nara shook her head.

"Are you here because you need help?"

She shook her head again.

"Listen, I can't do anything unless you speak."

"She should leave!" Nara blurted out, finally lifting her head to look at him.

He wondered whether he'd made a mistake letting her in. "Why?"

"It's not safe here."

"Why?" The question cracked out with suspicion. "Because you'll hurt her again?"

Another head shake. "My halmeoni. She won't stop until she gets her revenge."

"And she sent you here to do her dirty work?"

"Before, I was doing what I'd thought was right. I was raised to believe that Yena was a monster. That her daughter must be equally evil." Nara held out her hands, like she was trying to offer these words to him as penance.

"And now you've magically changed your mind?" Jihoon asked, his words harsher than he intended.

Nara shrugged and Jihoon sighed. "So what is it that you want now?"

"This time I want to warn her before it's too late."

"So tell her yourself." Jihoon's eyes shifted to the door, wondering how things were going downstairs between Miyoung and Detective Hae.

"I already tried. She won't listen to me." Nara's voice cracked with desperation. "But she'll listen to you if you tell her to leave."

Jihoon hesitated. He didn't want to believe Nara. But he'd learned that it was unwise not to heed such warnings. The last time he didn't listen was when Miyoung told him to run and his halmeoni had paid the price.

"What if she doesn't leave?" Jihoon asked.

"Then she'll die."

Jihoon stiffened. "There isn't a way to stop your halmeoni?"

"She's too powerful. I couldn't stop her even if I tried," Nara said. "Plus, she's keeping things from me now. I think she's found someone else to help her. I heard her the other night on the phone. She has something she's been looking for. She said this is how it should have always been, that the punishment will be ten times worse now. Miyoung needs to leave."

"That's not going to happen."

Jihoon spun around as Miyoung entered the apartment.

"If your halmeoni won't give up her grudge, then maybe I'll need to get rid of the threat." Miyoung's voice could freeze a fire.

"Please," Nara stuttered, "I've come to you in good faith. Please don't hurt my halmeoni."

After a second of frozen indecision, Miyoung replied, "I won't kill her. I don't do that anymore."

"Thank you," Nara breathed out.

"So you came to warn me and you did. Are we done?" Miyoung's face was set in a blank mask. But Jihoon saw the turmoil she hid. Like a storm brewing behind her steady irises.

Nara hesitated, her eyes darting between Jihoon and Miyoung.

"Is there more?" Jihoon asked gently, because he felt like he was standing next to two pressure points that were ready to burst.

"The bead," Nara said. "It's the center of this all. My halmeoni still wants it. She thinks if she can control you, she can hurt Yena."

"Does this mean she's coming after me?" Jihoon asked.

"I think I can do it," Nara said instead of answering him. "The ceremony I did before to take out the bead."

"You said you didn't have enough power," Miyoung replied.

Jihoon didn't need to see her face to know she was worried. He felt it like electricity traveling through the air. Or maybe it was the connection from the bead inside him.

"Not alone." Nara bit her lip. "But I realized this full moon means something."

"No, it doesn't. It's not the winter solstice or the summer. It's not even a harvest moon."

"But it *is* the last full moon before your hundred days. The third since you stopped feeding. Those numbers have significance," Nara said. "It's important to *you*. And that might be more powerful."

"So you're saying you can take out the bead, and Jihoon will be fine?"

Nara's silence answered for her.

"No," Miyoung said, hard and final.

"I can't say for sure it'll work. But I can say it's your best option, the only one where you can have a hope you'll both survive."

"If I make it to the hundred days without feeding, then maybe the bead will be weak enough to come out on its own."

"And if you die while the bead is still in him? How can you know he won't die, too?"

"She's right," Jihoon said. "The bead is making me sick. The migraines, the seizures. The way I see it, things can't stay the way they are now. If we do nothing, the odds are pretty high one or both of us aren't going to make it. I'd rather do something and fail than give up."

Miyoung gave in. "What do we need to do?"

Nara started to speak when Jihoon's phone rang.

He glanced at Miyoung, unsure if the moment could handle such a disruption.

"Answer it," she said. "I need some fresh air to think."

Jihoon picked up with an impatient, "Hello?"

He listened to the formal voice on the other line as his eyes followed Miyoung to the front door. It opened with a blast of cold air.

"What?" he asked sharply. Miyoung glanced at him curiously.

"I'm sorry," the person on the other line said. "I hate to tell you this kind of news over the phone. It's your halmeoni."

64

THE TWO BLACK lines on the white band around Jihoon's arm indicated he was the family of the deceased. He stared at them as he accepted the bows of his halmeoni's doctors, who had come to pay their respects.

Halmeoni's funeral took place in the hospital's jangryesikjang. It was filled with rooms for viewings and memorials, a hallway where every door led to death and grief.

Rooms down the hall hosted funerals of other patients. Some had dozens of wreaths lining the entrance, as if showing the social status of the deceased.

Jihoon stood in a daze beside the portrait of his halmeoni that sat on a table among chrysanthemums and incense. He watched the bows of mourning from each visitor.

"We bow once to the living, twice to the dead," his halmeoni had always told him at his harabeoji's grave. Jihoon's grandfather had died before he was born, so greeting his grave had felt natural. But now, each time a mourner bowed a second time to his halmeoni, Jihoon's heart skipped a beat.

He barely noticed the people who came through to greet him, to eat the funeral food at the tables adjoining the memorial room, to offer condolence money.

His mother stood beside him, greeting each mourner with a demure nod.

He tried to keep up appearances, show that he was a good, dutiful grandson, even as he knew he'd failed his halmeoni. Everything he'd done made her suffer. He refused to be a good student despite her pleas. He went to the PC room after school instead of coming home to help at the restaurant. And she got hurt because of him. She'd given her gi to him. And now she was gone. Because of him.

He glanced at Miyoung, who bustled between the tables of mourners eating the memorial food, clearing dishes and handing out soup. Having her here comforted him, but he didn't know if he deserved it. His halmeoni was dead because of them.

Maybe if he'd swallowed his pride and called Miyoung back, then she would have told him about the bead. Maybe if Miyoung hadn't lied and run away, this could have all been solved. Maybe if she'd let him die like he was supposed to, his halmeoni would still be alive.

So many maybes and none of them worth dwelling on, because the fact was his halmeoni was dead and he wasn't. And he wished with all of his heart that it was the other way around.

65

MIYOUNG SERVED FOOD to the mourners. It was polite for them to eat some before they left—rice, soup, and banchan. She carried around a tray to collect the empty dishes. It was all she could think to do. Even Somin, who served alongside her, didn't protest Miyoung's help.

Beside Jihoon, his mother wore a traditional mourning hanbok, with white hemp tying back her hair. Her pale face was drawn. She greeted all of the visitors while standing beside Jihoon, whose eyes were aimed straight ahead, not looking at his mother and not truly focusing on any of the guests. A boy with nothing left he wanted to see.

It was enough to bring tears, but Miyoung held them back. This was no place for her grief.

After everyone left, Miyoung sat awhile, watching Jihoon and his mother in the receiving room, unmoving statues. Jihoon looked like a supplicant in a church, head bowed, so she could see only the dark crown of his head.

"You can go now," Jihoon said.

His mother didn't respond, her expression calm.

"I said you can go." Jihoon's voice echoed in the empty room.

His mother didn't reply.

Jihoon finally looked up. "Are you not listening to me?"

"She was my mother." It came out quiet, but firm.

"Since when do you act like a dutiful daughter?" Jihoon asked. "Were you acknowledging your mother when you let her work her joints raw to take care of me? Or were you being a filial daughter when you left her to rot in the hospital?"

"Jihoon-ah." Miyoung grabbed his arm. "Stop it."

He shook her off.

"Tell me," he said. "Tell me when you cared about her."

Jihoon's mother finally faced him, her expression cool as a still lake. "My mother and I had a relationship long before you were born. You do not know how I have held her in my heart."

"You speak of her as if she died months ago. She didn't. She's been alive this whole time. She still could be if you—" Jihoon's words cut off, his breathing heavy. Miyoung laid a hand on his arm.

"I'd like to speak to my mother alone," Jihoon said, his face deceptively calm.

Her need to respect his wants warred with her desire to comfort him. In the end, Miyoung stepped out of the room. She hoped she was doing the right thing.

66

"HALMEONI TOOK ME to be exorcised once," Jihoon began conversationally.

His mother stared at him in surprise.

"She thought there was an evil spirit inside me, because after you left I wouldn't eat or sleep. She didn't realize it was because I was doing an exorcism of my own. I was extracting *you*.

"But I was so caught up in how you made me feel that I never wondered if it affected Halmeoni." His words became thick in his throat, but he still pushed them out. "She supported me and worried about me. And I didn't do anything but punish her for it by never living up to what she wanted for me, just like you."

His anger clogged his chest, and he gasped to pull in air. It felt like he was breathing mud. Leaning over, he tried to clear his throat. A fog rolled over his vision.

"Jihoon!" his mother shouted. "Jihoon-ah, answer me."

He couldn't, not even to tell her to leave him alone. He toppled over as his trembling legs gave out.

"Someone call a doctor. Help! My son can't breathe!"

And with his mother's cries ringing in his head, he passed out.

67

JIHOON WOKE SLOWLY to murmured voices.

The alcohol smell of disinfectant filled his nostrils, and he knew he was in the hospital.

" . . . must have been upset, it's understandable with his halmeoni's funeral, but this is the worst attack I've seen yet." Jihoon almost didn't recognize Dr. Choi's voice. The neurologist must have thought it important to attend directly to Jihoon's bedside.

"What are you trying to say about my son?" Jihoon's mother asked. *My son.* His brain and heart latched on to the phrase.

"I didn't think he would deteriorate so quickly. There is nothing wrong with him physically, but tests show his heart continues to get weaker. If this continues, it could be fatal." The doctor didn't mince words. Any other time Jihoon would have appreciated that.

When Dr. Choi left, Jihoon glanced at his mother. She stared at the door, hands clutched to her chest.

He wanted so badly to call out to her like he would have when he was three. Would she come to him? Would she comfort him? And would it only be out of pity because he was dying? The thought made it hard to breathe. Dying. He was dying. He blinked away tears before he spoke.

"You must be relieved to rid yourself of a burdensome son." His voice sounded like the croak of a frog.

His mother spun around, her eyes wide as she realized he was awake. "Jihoon-ah."

"Why didn't you come before?" he asked, his voice a quiet plea. "Why did Halmeoni have to die before you came? You should have known I needed you. You're my mother."

"Jihoon-ah." His name was a sob on her lip. Her grief should have bolstered him. Finally, proof that she cared and all he had to do was die. "I'm so sorry."

"I just wanted you to be there for me," Jihoon said. "That's all I've ever wanted." His body shook with tears. He was too weak to hold them back anymore.

His mother came to him now, her arms warm as they held him. And he finally felt his pride dissolve. He held tight to his mother for the first time since he was a little boy.

o   o   o

When Jihoon blinked his eyes open again, he didn't know how much time had passed. Hours or days.

Miyoung's face came into focus, and he sat up to the sound of beeping machines and humidifier steam. He let himself fall back against the pillows. The mere act of sitting up made him short of breath.

"How are you feeling?" Miyoung asked.

He didn't reply, just stared as she adjusted his blankets, fluffed his pillow.

"Your mother stepped out, but she's coming back." Miyoung spoke quickly, as if to fill the silence.

"You should feed," he said.

"What?"

He took her hand between his. "You should feed."

She shook her head. "We don't know how that could affect you. And after this episode, it's obvious you're too weak. I won't risk it."

"If you don't, you'll die."

"I don't care about that."

"Wouldn't it be better that at least one of us lives?" Jihoon asked.

"No," Miyoung said emphatically.

"Don't you get it?" Jihoon asked, his monitors beeping a warning of a rising heart rate. "I don't want to live anymore. My halmeoni is dead because of me, and my body is giving out anyway. Just feed. Don't be a martyr for me when I don't want one."

"We'll figure out another solution."

"You said it yourself. You're too used to having all the time in the world. But it's not something you can spend in limitless amounts anymore."

"Since it's mine to spend, I'll do with it what I want," Miyoung snapped.

"If you get the bead, you can live forever. Why would you throw that away?"

"I can only live if I kill others. I won't. Not anymore."

"What does an immortal gumiho care about us mere mortals," Jihoon muttered. "We die, it's what we do."

Miyoung winced as he threw her own words in her face. "I don't care about immortality. I care about you."

A month ago, even a week ago, he would have held on to these words like precious sunlight. But he didn't deserve it, not after he'd failed his halmeoni so completely.

"I shouldn't be the reason for anyone's happiness."

"That's not true."

"My halmeoni died before I could prove to her I was worth it. All the things she sacrificed for me, and she died thinking I was a failure. A last-place nobody."

"Jihoon-ah, your halmeoni never believed that."

He let go of her hand and rolled away from her. "Just leave me alone. It's what you're best at."

He shut his eyes until he heard the door close as she left.

68

JIHOON DIDN'T KNOW when he fell asleep. But in sleep he dreamed, a fitful toss of images.

"Jihoon-ah." She was just as he remembered, fair skin, dark eyes, hair as white as the moon.

"Halmeoni. Are you real?"

Halmeoni smiled, the kind that creased the skin at her eyes and made them sparkle. "Whether I'm a spirit come to visit or a figment of your dreams, say what you need to say to me, Grandson."

"I'm sorry." Tears ran hot and thick down his cheeks. "In my next life, I hope I'm reborn as your grandson. Then I can treasure you, and honor you the way you deserve."

"Oh, Jihoon-ah, you can still do that in this life. I hope you can live this life filled with joy. I think that will be a great way to honor me."

"How can I, after what I've done to you?"

"I made my own choices. You don't want to die, Grandson. There's still so much I hope for you to have in this life."

He squeezed his eyes shut, the last of his tears streaming down his cheeks.

When he opened them again, she was gone and he was outside. He blinked up at the sky. He lay in the forest under so many stars that they outnumbered the dark.

"It seems you didn't need me to get into trouble."

Jihoon glanced at Yena beside him, sitting cross-legged in the tall grass. She watched the heavens instead of him. Why would his mind do this to him? Take his halmeoni away and replace her with this woman? "You might love your daughter, but I can never forgive you for what you've done."

"I never asked for your forgiveness. But if you love my daughter, then let her live." There was a pleading on Yena's face, lending a softness to her angles he'd never noticed before.

"I don't want her to die."

"But you want to live, too." Yena's voice became hard.

As she said it, he knew it was true. New tears sprung to his eyes. It swirled the light of the stars until they mixed into a potion of stardust that blinded him. He couldn't look his impending death in the eye and accept it. He wanted to live so desperately it hurt.

"At least when humans die there is an afterlife," Yena said. "Gumiho cannot be promised such things."

Jihoon was silent, unable to answer.

"Miyoung tethers me to my humanity," Yena said softly, her eyes shining. Jihoon blinked. Sitting like this, Yena almost seemed human. "I had a human family once. They betrayed me, tried to kill me. Called me a monster and then made me into one. I thought that I didn't deserve a family until I had Miyoung."

"Is that why you're fighting so hard for her?" Jihoon asked. "Because you're afraid of becoming a monster?"

"I don't fear my own fate. I was betrayed because I thought

with my heart instead of my instincts. I won't let the same thing happen to my daughter."

Yena stood, her eyes black as onyx.

"That's why you must die."

And Jihoon realized this wasn't a dream.

69

MIYOUNG FROWNED AS an automated message told her the voice mail was full. She'd been calling Nara all day, and the shaman hadn't answered.

She shoved her phone into her pocket and glanced out the windows that lined the walkway back to the patient rooms. The sky was cloudy, but she saw, beyond the haze, the full moon.

She clutched the two banana milks tighter so her fingers made small indents in the plastic. Nara would call back. She knew how important this was. Miyoung didn't want to dwell on the trust she was placing in the shaman again.

It's too late, there's no other choice, she told herself.

She stopped abruptly. Pain sliced through her, cold and sharp.

Her heart stuttered, and one of the containers fell from her fingers to splatter on her shoes.

She raced to Jihoon's room, past startled nurses and patients. The rumpled bed was empty. Sheets tangled at the foot like they'd been kicked away. She dropped the second banana milk when she spun to grab the nearest nurse. The woman looked harried, her arms loaded with gauze.

"Where did the patient in room 1696 go?" Miyoung's voice lifted in panic.

"I don't know. Maybe they took him for a scan." The nurse

extracted herself from Miyoung's grip and hurried away, sending curious glances over her shoulder.

"No," Miyoung said to no one in particular, pressing her hand against her speeding heart. No matter what she did, she couldn't slow it down. "Something isn't right."

Lights flashed across her vision and she blinked, worried she would lose consciousness if she didn't calm down. But they wove in and out, stretched across her line of sight.

Somin walked up, eyeing Miyoung suspiciously. "Where's Jihoon?" she asked, staring at the empty bed.

"I don't know." Miyoung squeezed her eyes shut. When she blinked them open, the lights began to bleed together. She realized they were pulsing. A beat like a heart. And it called to her. She knew then that it wasn't just her imagination or the delirium of her weakening state. It was the bead calling to her. The bead leading her. To Jihoon. She let it embrace her, let it surround her. A glow starting in her chest and growing outward. When she opened her eyes, the lights were now a steady line of glittering crimson. She followed it.

The automatic door opened to let her outside, but Junu blocked her path. "Miyoung."

She tried to move around him but he stopped her.

"What?" she asked, exasperated.

"It's Yena."

Dread settled in Miyoung's belly. "What did you do?"

"*I* didn't do anything."

Miyoung narrowed her eyes at his careful wording. "You mean you didn't stop her."

Junu spread his hands out. "I don't get involved in situations that can get me killed."

"You should have stopped her."

"She paid me well not to. And she paid me to keep you here."

"Just try it." Miyoung rocked onto the balls of her feet, ready to fight.

"If she finds out I let you go so easily, she might come after me."

"Then you better run."

Junu sighed, like he'd expected that answer. His hand clamped around her wrist. "I can't let you leave this hospital. And you're in no state to fight me."

Miyoung twisted to free herself, but Junu was right. He still had his superhuman strength, and she was as weak as a child. Still, she had her wits and her desperation. Still cuffed by Junu's hand, she bit the fleshy part of his palm.

With a shout of pain, he let go and she darted past him. But Junu was still too fast and he caught her, holding her in place.

"If you just stop fighting, it'll be easier for you. Let your mother retrieve your bead and forget all of this."

"No!" she shouted, clawing at his arms.

Then Junu let out a surprised yelp and his arms loosened as he was dragged away. Miyoung twisted out of his grip to see Somin pulling Junu back by his hair.

"Let go!" He tried to break free, but Somin's grip must have been like iron because he only screamed again. Tears of pain sprang to his eyes.

"Well, I'm not sure what kind of argument you two are having. But I don't like to see you manhandling my friend," Somin said.

My friend. Miyoung lifted her brows at the words.

"This is none of your business," Junu said through gritted teeth. He was bent low at the waist now, as Somin was so short and refused to let go of his hair.

"That's the problem. I can't seem to keep myself from getting involved in Miyoung's business. I'm nosy like that." Somin shrugged.

"Miyoung? Somin? What's going on here?" Detective Hae asked as he approached them, his eyes taking in the scene.

"Ajeossi," Somin said, finally releasing Junu and shoving her hands behind her back like she was hiding evidence.

"Young man, I think you should get going," Detective Hae said, pushing his blazer back in a way that clearly revealed his badge. Miyoung wondered if he practiced the move to get it just right.

Junu's eyes shifted back and forth between the detective and Miyoung.

"This is not worth what I'm getting paid," he said. "Don't say I didn't warn you." With that he stormed away.

"Is one of you going to tell me what's going on?"

"We can't find Jihoon," Somin said.

"What?" Detective Hae's eyes shot to Miyoung as if for confirmation.

"She's back. She has him."

Detective Hae's face became stony, and Miyoung knew he understood her meaning. "Come on, I have my car."

"Wait!" Somin called out. "What's going on? Someone took him? How do you know?"

"I just do," Miyoung said impatiently. "Wait here—we'll find him."

"How?" Somin demanded.

"I have a way," Miyoung said. The line of red still shone beside her, pulsing with urgency.

"What way?" Somin asked, a stubborn frown settling on her face.

Miyoung glanced at the detective, but he shrugged.

"I can't—"

"I have a right to know," Somin said. "Please." The whispered word was scared, almost desperate.

"Somin, what I'm about to say will sound ridiculous, but it's true and you have to believe me." Miyoung took a breath, then plunged headfirst into her confession. "I'm not human. Not fully."

Somin laughed but sobered when Miyoung didn't join in. "Okay, what are you?"

Miyoung hesitated. She'd never said it outright before, not like this, but she didn't have time to think of the right words. She'd take a page from Jihoon's book and be blunt. "A gumiho. So is my mother. Jihoon said you grew up with him, heard the same stories his halmeoni told. That means some part of you must have believed once. I'm going to depend on that part of you and ask you to trust me here. Jihoon has something my mother wants, and if she has her way, he could die."

Somin stared at Miyoung a moment, her mouth hanging open. It was frustrating that Miyoung couldn't read the other girl's reaction. She looked past Miyoung, toward Detective Hae, who gave a slight nod.

"Okay then," Somin said. "Bring him back safe."

Miyoung frowned. She'd asked for Somin's trust, but she realized now she hadn't really been expecting it.

"I'll make sure Jihoon doesn't get hurt," Miyoung promised.

"And you," Somin said.

"What?"

"Make sure you don't get hurt either."

"Miyoung, we have to go," Detective Hae called from his car. Miyoung jogged to join him and slid into the passenger seat. As the car sped off, she pressed the heel of her hand against her ribs and watched Somin in the rearview mirror until she became a small speck in the distance.

"Where are we going?" Detective Hae said, drawing her attention to the road.

"Turn left up here," Miyoung directed, using the curve of the red thread to guide them.

"We'll get Jihoon back."

"And my mother." Miyoung looked at the detective. He watched her with kind eyes, laying a reassuring hand over hers. And though she hadn't fully forgiven him yet, she gripped his hand. She needed the comfort right now.

"I want her safe, too," Miyoung said. "I want both of them safe."

"We'll do everything we can for them," Detective Hae promised, giving her hand a squeeze. And for a moment she was able to believe him.

70

"ARE YOU GOING to kill me?" Jihoon asked.

"You get right to the point." The light of the moon made Yena's skin so pale she could have been a ghost come to take his soul. In reality, she was a demon come to rip out his heart.

"I tend not to beat around the bush when my life is at stake," Jihoon said.

"I like that," Yena mused. "It's probably surprising, but I never hated you. I just refuse to let my daughter die for you."

"I don't want that either."

"Then you and I are in agreement."

"Are you going to kill me now?" Jihoon asked again. He didn't think he wanted the answer, but he needed it.

"I have to wait."

"For what?"

"For him."

71

MIYOUNG MOVED QUIETLY through the trees, followed by Detective Hae. He was quieter than she'd expected, probably his police training. She was grateful for his presence. Facing her mother would be hard enough; at least she knew there was someone to help if things went south.

"I thought about it," Detective Hae said in a low voice.

Miyoung almost shushed him. It wouldn't do for Yena to hear their approach. But she didn't. "Thought about what?"

"You asked me if I wanted to be in your life now," Detective Hae said.

Miyoung's heart, already so strained from fear, thudded painfully as she waited for him to continue.

"If I could, I would love to have my daughter back. The daughter I loved when she was born," Detective Hae said, and though he whispered, Miyoung heard a trace of tears in his voice. Like he truly regretted all the time they'd lost together.

"I always wondered if my father was a good man," Miyoung confessed. "If maybe that's why it was so hard for me to . . . survive the way I did."

"I try to do the right thing," Detective Hae said.

"I know."

They walked again in silence, but she lifted her fist to knock at her chest. It was suddenly difficult to breathe, like a heavy cloud had filled her lungs.

She couldn't think about the old wounds. She had to concentrate on following the thread toward Jihoon. And to her mother.

If she had to fight Yena to protect Jihoon, could she? If this ended badly, would she be able to move on? She looked at her father's profile and believed for the first time that maybe Yena wasn't all she had.

The thread slowly grew stronger. So bright it lit her path. Miyoung glanced at Detective Hae, but he didn't seem to see the thread. It was only visible to her, a connection to her bead. A connection to Jihoon.

Snaking through the thick trunks, she inhaled the scent of the spring forest. New buds and green leaves. The beginning of something new. But when new things began, that meant old things had to end. She was ready for it all to end tonight. One way or another.

And then, through the trees, she heard a voice and strained to listen. It was clear and smooth. A voice she'd know anywhere. Her mother's voice. They were close.

72

"I'M GOING TO tell you a story." Yena spoke in a melodic flow that would have been soothing if Jihoon's nerves weren't all sparking at once.

"Miyoung used to love my stories. After each, she'd ask me if they were true." Yena sounded like a mother yearning for her lost child.

"Is this one true?" Jihoon asked.

"That's for you to decide after I tell it," Yena said. "There once was a fox who was always alone. Her family had shunned her, beaten her, and discarded her. She grew up and grew smart, learning that those she lived among were not allies but her prey."

The story seemed like every other gumiho tale Jihoon's halmeoni told until Yena said, "Then she met a man."

Yena no longer looked at Jihoon as she spoke. Her eyes reflected the moon, like she read the story from the clear white face of it.

"He was charismatic and handsome. But most of all, he was kind. She never thought kindness was something she craved until she had it. The fox realized there was an ache in her."

Jihoon didn't want to sympathize with the broken heart Yena described. Just the sight of her face reminded him of the night she came into his home and tore it apart.

"This man gave her love, a home, and a child. It was all she could ask for. But when someone gives, they can also take away."

Jihoon didn't want to hear this part. The abandonment that Yena would use to justify her horrific actions. To explain why Jihoon had to die.

"When he found out what she was, he betrayed her to a shaman family that wanted to use her gi to cure their child of the sight. It afflicted the infant so that she saw spirits."

She must be talking about Nara's family. Jihoon wondered if the young shaman knew this version of the story.

"I didn't mean to kill them. Though now I wish I'd killed the old woman, too. If she hadn't gotten away, none of this would be happening.

"I was going to tell him the truth about what I was. Because I was fool enough to believe he'd still love me. But Shaman Kim got to him first. She told him everything that had happened. And instead of standing by me, he let her turn him against me. But that's not the worst of it. He turned against our Miyoung, too. He let Shaman Kim take her."

This was not the story he was supposed to hear. He wasn't supposed to feel sympathy for Yena.

"It was a simple trade. My yeowu guseul for my daughter. They gave it to me like a choice. But that is no choice for a mother."

"You gave up your bead for Miyoung."

"He took my bead and he tried to kill her anyway. Because, he said, she was a monster just like me. He drowned her in the tub and left us both for dead."

73

MIYOUNG COULDN'T BREATHE. It felt like the light of the moon was burning her skin. And her mother's words made her head spin.

This couldn't be right. This story she'd never heard, but it felt so familiar she ached.

When I left your mother, there was a fight and you were hurt. Detective Hae had said that to her and she'd thought he meant something petty, a dispute between spouses. Not attempted murder.

Her world became awash in fog as she remembered her dream. The running water, the flooding bathroom. And she finally saw what was inside. An infant with skin so pale it was blue. The reason she was afraid of water. Because it had already tried to kill her once.

Her head hurt from the memory. There was a shuffle of movement behind her, and she whipped around. Detective Hae stood there, his face shrouded in shade.

"I wish you hadn't heard that."

Pain cracked through her skull and she fell into dark.

74

JIHOON COULDN'T GRASP Yena's story. It didn't make any sense. Detective Hae had tried to kill Miyoung? But he loved her. He spoke of his daughter and wife with longing and regret.

It wasn't true. Yena was a liar; she would do anything to get what she wanted.

"So are you saying that Detective Hae is behind all of this? He's the reason you're going to kill me?" Jihoon needed to keep her talking; maybe if he bought himself time, Miyoung would find him.

"I'm not here to kill you, but to deliver you."

"What?" Jihoon took a step back, looking for a good escape. He knew it would be useless to run; Yena would overtake him in seconds. But he had to try.

He'd backed up a full three meters before he realized she was not following. In fact, she'd stood in the same spot the whole time he'd been there.

"Why aren't you attacking?"

She scowled.

"You said he has your bead," Jihoon said slowly. "So that means he has control over you."

"Such a smart boy," Yena said. "Yes, he was the one who

commanded me to bring you here. And he instructed me not to hurt you."

Jihoon started to flee. Then blinked in confusion at the sight of Detective Hae walking toward him with Miyoung in his arms like a limp doll.

Yena let out a low growl behind him.

"She's not hurt." Detective Hae laid Miyoung in the middle of the clearing, between Yena and Jihoon. He ran a gentle hand over her pale forehead, pushing back her hair.

"What's going on here, Ajeossi?" Jihoon asked. "What happened to her?"

"Many things. But I'm about to fix it all."

"You're insane," Yena said, hatred lacing her voice.

"I'm righting a wrong. One that was my fault. So it falls on me to fix it."

A white figure emerged from the forest behind the detective like a ghost bleeding out of the trees. As she drew closer, Jihoon recognized Shaman Kim, her steps kicking at the hem of her hanbok so it swayed around her.

"Yena, I can honestly say it's a pleasure to see you again." A wide grin stretched Shaman Kim's paper-thin cheeks.

"Your search for revenge is tiring, Kim Hyunsook," Yena said.

"And your lies have finally caught up to you."

Shaman Kim pulled a bujeok from her sleeve. Jihoon jerked back.

"Stand still or it'll hurt more," Shaman Kim warned.

"What are you doing?" Jihoon asked.

"I'm saving you." The old shaman's maniacal grin was that of someone about to taste victory.

Jihoon stayed in place, fear holding him still. This shaman

with her bujeoks and her vendetta scared him more than Yena with blood on her teeth. Because, he realized, Junu had been right. Yena was driven by her love of Miyoung. Shaman Kim was driven by hate.

As the old shaman placed the talisman over Jihoon's chest, he glanced at Detective Hae. "Did you use me this whole time?"

"Of course not." Detective Hae frowned as if genuinely upset by the question. "I was saving your soul from the damnation that comes from association with demons. I know what it's like to fall under their spell, Jihoon-ah. Trust me when I say this is for the best."

Shaman Kim began her dance before Jihoon could ask more. She sang a low, guttural chant. Her body swayed. She held up a white paper and set it aflame. Jihoon remembered his halmeoni talking about this part of the kut, the dances shamans use to commune with the spirits and their powers. White was for the purity needed to connect to the gods.

Ice clutched him. It started at his toes, freezing them so he couldn't feel his feet. Then rose up his legs, turning his veins to shoots of ice.

He gritted his teeth against the pain, so cold it burned. His fingers and limbs bent in wretched agony. He dropped to his knees and the ground rose up to meet him as his body seized.

75

MIYOUNG WOKE TO chants and pain. She wondered if she'd died and lay at one of the twelve gates to the afterlife.

"Miyoung-ah."

Yena stood a meter away, her voice a harsh whisper of concern.

"Where's Jihoon?" Miyoung coughed out. Her chest felt like it was on fire. And she searched for the red thread, hoping it would lead her to Jihoon.

"Miyoung-ah, get yourself together. You have to get out of here."

She finally remembered where she was and what she'd been doing. She lifted shaking fingers to the back of her throbbing head. She hissed with pain, and her hand came away wet with blood from a wound where Detective Hae had hit her.

When Yena saw Miyoung's stained fingers, her eyes flashed. "I'm going to kill him."

"Not if I do first," Miyoung growled, pushing to her hands and knees.

She could just make out two figures standing across the field. She squinted to see them clearly and saw Detective Hae. Then, with a start, the dancing form of Shaman Kim came into focus.

For a second she didn't see Jihoon. Then his body jerked, sprawled on the ground between the detective and Nara's halmeoni.

With a shout of rage, she stood. But the very act of standing made her head spin, as if she'd spent all of her energy on the simple physical task.

"Steady," Yena said, reaching out to hold her daughter.

Miyoung gasped in ragged breaths as she watched Jihoon's body jerk in tormented angles.

"Stop!" Miyoung called out before turning to Yena. "Mother, do something."

"I can't."

"If he dies, then so will I. My bead is still inside him."

"I can't," Yena repeated, and Miyoung finally realized her mother was planted in place, like her legs had sprouted roots that reached into the ground.

Miyoung's eyes moved to Detective Hae as she remembered the end of her mother's story. She'd traded her bead for Miyoung's life. The irony of it wasn't lost on her. Like mother, like daughter, to sacrifice for the ones they loved.

Jihoon let out a cry of pain. And his agony echoed in Miyoung's chest, so sharp and hot that she almost dropped to her knees again. But Yena held her upright.

The moon's glow was a spotlight for their shared torture. Then the pain abated, leaving Miyoung's head spinning as it receded. And she saw that Jihoon was still as well.

Shaman Kim knelt, holding her hands over Jihoon's chest, making figure eights with her palms. Then she pushed her hands down on his belly. He jerked up like a puppet whose strings were yanked forward. The yeowu guseul shot from his lips before he fell back into an unconscious heap.

Shaman Kim picked up the bead reverently, like she was picking up the moon itself.

"Jihoon-ah!" Miyoung shouted. Her cries went unanswered. She glared at Shaman Kim. "Are you happy? To see the pain you've caused?"

"I'll be happy when it's done," the shaman said.

"Why are you involving my daughter in your ridiculous vendetta?" Yena asked.

"Because you killed mine!" Shaman Kim screamed. Her shrill rage sent a shiver down Miyoung's spine. "You took my daughter from me, so I wanted to take yours from you, but this time I've found a way to take your life as well. Who's to know if you even have a heart to mourn her passing. It'd be better to kill you both."

She handed a white paper to Detective Hae. "You must burn it to purify so we can connect to the gods. Call upon your ancestors to give us strength in our purpose."

"Hae Taewoo, don't do this," Yena pleaded. Miyoung had never heard her mother beg before. She gripped her mother's hand. And, for the first time, Yena laced her fingers through Miyoung's, holding tight.

"I have to," Detective Hae said. "I am responsible for all the souls you've both taken in the past seventeen years. I must atone for my weakness. I never should have let you live."

He reached into his pocket and pulled out another bead. This one had a softer luster than Miyoung's, as if it had lost its shine over time.

"At first, I regretted losing you," Detective Hae whispered reverently, staring at the stone. "I tried to order you to return to me a thousand times. You never came. You were too far for me to reach you."

"I'm here now. So let our daughter go."

Detective Hae shook his head as his eyes traveled over Miyoung as well. "You both hold evil inside. I have to save you from it."

"By killing us?"

"In death you will find absolution."

"Taewoo, please, if you ever loved me—"

"I love you still!" Detective Hae shouted.

"It's time." Shaman Kim held out her hand and accepted Yena's bead, wrapping it in a bright bujeok. Then she did the same with Miyoung's. Two perfect spheres wrapped in gold and red.

As Detective Hae set the white paper he held ablaze, Shaman Kim laid out a white handkerchief and placed the stones atop it. Then she lit incense sticks and stuck them in the ground in a circle around the beads.

Shaman Kim began to chant. And with her words she began to sway, her movements becoming long and rhythmic, joining her song.

It reminded Miyoung of that night three months ago, when the shaman had pulled at Miyoung's soul until she thought it would be sucked out of her body.

And as the shaman danced, the moon's light burst through the clearing, a thousand times more powerful than the glare of the sun.

It blinded them all. Turned night to day and cold to fire.

Miyoung screamed, holding Yena's hand tightly. Her wails mixed with her mother's.

"I'm sorry." Yena's agony was painted on her face. Her pale skin reddened, as if she were held over a flame.

"You can't give up," Miyoung said through gritted teeth.

Yena grinned, a feral smile that gave Miyoung hope. "Never."
Then her body shuddered and her hand tightened. Blood seeped
from Yena's eyes, her nose, her lips. And she fell to the ground.

Miyoung tried to move, but her muscles seized, and she fell
beside Yena's prone form.

Flames rose up inside her. Giant licks of agony that scorched
her until she was sure she would burn to nothing.

76

MIYOUNG WANTED TO let the pain take her into the dark. At least then her torment would end.

"If you die, you'll be going against my wishes." The words were an angry rasp from Yena, her eyes closed against the pain. Miyoung almost laughed. Leave it to her mother to command her to live.

"As you wish, Mother."

Miyoung pulled herself up and lurched to her feet, swaying at first. The air sizzled and sparked, an electric energy created through magic and might to hold down a gumiho.

She gathered the last of her strength and charged. With each step, pain engulfed her. It coursed through her like a thousand volts.

Detective Hae's eyes widened at the sight of her, blood and spit foaming at her snarling lips. Each step pulling a scream of agony from her. "You said they wouldn't feel pain."

Miyoung almost laughed at her father's belated concern. But instead another groan of pain escaped.

Fire swept around her, through her, into her.

Pain became her world.

Then a voice called to her. "Miyoung! Fight it!"

Jihoon? Was he alive? Or was he calling her to join him in the world of the dead? Her eyes flew open and found Jihoon's. He lay across the ground. The bujeok pasted to his chest burned as bright as the flames around her, but he watched her calmly.

"Fight it," he said again.

"Seonbae!" Like an avenging spirit appearing from the shadows, Nara leapt into view. She grabbed Miyoung's bead from the makeshift altar on the ground. As Nara cradled the bujeok-wrapped stone, she began to scream.

"No!" Shaman Kim shouted, falling out of her dance.

And for a blissful moment, Miyoung's pain subsided.

Nara lay on the ground, her arms covered in mottled blisters. She cradled them against her chest, tears tracking down her cheeks to pool in the dirt.

Shaman Kim took up the dance again, even as her granddaughter lay burnt and battered at her feet. As her song reached a crescendo, she lifted her hands to the sky. Yena's bead caught ablaze. The bujeok burned away with a flame that arced into the air. And when the fire died, it revealed ash instead of stone.

"No!" It was meant as a shout, but it came out as a whisper from Miyoung's dry throat.

She spun toward Yena and almost fell in shock. Where her mother had lain before, there was now a beautiful fox. Long and lean, with lithe muscles and lush fur. Her nine tails splayed behind her. Like she was reverting to her basic form on her way to death.

Shaman Kim bent to pry open Nara's fingers. The younger shaman moaned in pain.

"Foolish girl," Shaman Kim said with a snarl. She pulled Miyoung's bead from Nara's hands.

"This is wrong," Nara moaned. "We're not murderers."

"You can't murder a demon," the shaman muttered, placing Miyoung's bead back into the center of the circle of incense. It now sat on the ruins of her mother's bead.

"You said it would be quick." Detective Hae stared at the bead, dumbfounded, as if he wondered how he'd gotten there.

"Again!" Shaman Kim said before she took up the chant.

Miyoung stood on trembling feet.

Her forward motion was so haltingly slow that she knew she couldn't make it to the shaman before the kut was finished.

"You said you cared about me." Miyoung aimed the accusation at her father, who still stared at the ash-covered altar.

His eyes lifted to hers, and he winced at the sight of her. "I'm doing this because I care," Detective Hae said. "You are evil things. It is better you are gone from this world, where you can no longer hurt anyone."

"If you're sending me to the afterlife"—Miyoung lurched forward, her voice gurgling on her own blood—"then let me take you with me."

With all of her might she dove, slamming herself into her father's body. He gave a cry of distress as they went sprawling into the altar. She felt the burn of the incense as it dug into her skin. Stars exploded behind her eyes as she slid across the hard-packed dirt.

When she blinked free of the agony, she saw her father crawling across the clearing, reaching for her bead, now set ablaze in the bujeok.

"No!" Miyoung shouted, but she couldn't pull herself up in time.

The streak of color. A low growl. A snap of teeth. Yena, gorgeous and sleek, leapt, her tails fanned out, dancing in the air. Her father let out a howl as they struggled.

The bead was a bright beacon, fire licking through Detective Hae's fingers as he gripped it. Yena's teeth clamped over his fists.

Miyoung watched as her parents fought for ownership of her bead. Like they fought for her very soul.

A light pulsed from them. The clearing became awash in luminescence. It plumed up, encompassing the trees, the sky, the stars.

Miyoung lifted a hand to shield her eyes.

In the middle of the clearing stood a figure. At first a shadowy silhouette that Miyoung couldn't make out. Then, as the light faded, she saw the tails weaving behind her mother, human again, her naked skin glowing in the moonlight.

Detective Hae lay at Yena's feet, a broken form of bent limbs and torched flesh. An unrecognizable body that had once been the man who'd helped create her. The man who'd wanted to kill her.

"You won't ever hurt my daughter again," Yena said. But when she took a step, her legs folded beneath her and she collapsed to the ground with a *thud*.

Miyoung ran, skidding to her knees beside Yena. She stripped off her jacket quickly, throwing it over her mother.

"Mother?" Was that her voice? It sounded so young and afraid. "What should I do?"

"Feed. Live," Yena whispered, tears dripping down her smooth cheeks.

"I can't," Miyoung said.

"Miyoung-ah." Jihoon stumbled over, wincing as he knelt beside her.

She glanced around the clearing, searching for the others, but the shamans were both gone.

Yena held out her hand, in a tight fist. "It seems the human protected it well for you." She glanced at Jihoon as she dropped Miyoung's yeowu guseul into her hand.

The bead grew warm in Miyoung's palm, tapping a beat that matched her pulse—like she held her own fluttering heart. The heat of it swept through her, as if living within Jihoon had stoked the flame so brightly that it could now burn on its own.

Yena's body began to shake so violently it looked like she was about to shatter.

"No!" Miyoung gasped. She cupped the bead over Yena's heart.

Jihoon grabbed her arm, stopping her. "What are you doing?"

"She's dying," Miyoung said. "I have to help her."

"Miyoung-ah." All of the pleading in the world was packed in that one word. "We don't know how this could affect you. You're so weak already."

"It could kill you."

"My bead isn't what's killing me. I could never live in a world where I didn't try to save her."

It looked like Jihoon wanted to argue more, but he nodded with understanding and released her.

Yena had stopped shaking and now lay so still, she could have been carved from marble.

"Don't worry," Miyoung crooned. "I'm going to save you."

She placed the bead on her mother's chest. It beat fiercely beneath her hands, a steady tempo that calmed her.

She concentrated the gi she could gather from within. Not much was required, just a spark to jump-start the bead. It already burned against her palms like a furnace.

It thrummed as a white light escaped from between her pressed fingers.

Yena's body jerked like a person shocked back to life.

"I think it's working," Jihoon murmured beside her.

The bead was so bright in her hands, she feared it would burn her mother to ash before it revived her. Yena's body began convulsing.

"What do I do?" Miyoung asked no one in particular.

"Keep going," Jihoon answered. He pulled off his jacket and bunched it under Yena's neck.

Miyoung pushed on the molten-hot bead with all of her might.

Yena's body shuddered like waves of energy ran through her. Her mouth wrenched open, and her wailing pierced the air.

Then, echoing silence. Yena's body no longer shook. And the bead was gone.

Miyoung watched Yena's face. "Eomma?"

Her mother's eyes fluttered open, and Miyoung let out a breath of relief. "It worked."

Yena's cracked lips tilted into a sweet smile. She gripped Miyoung's hands.

"We'll get you somewhere you can rest, Eomma."

"You haven't called me that since you were a baby." Yena's voice sounded faint, like it was cast from some faraway place.

"I'll call you that every day if you want."

"I'm proud of you, Daughter," Yena said. "I never told you that enough."

"Well, you have a chance to now." Miyoung's tears caught in Yena's hair like falling stars.

"There are so many things I never got a chance to tell you"—

Yena paused to catch her breath before continuing—"because of my pride."

"Why are you talking like this is it? Don't you get it? I did it. I saved you." Miyoung gripped her mother's hand, a desperate fear taking root in her.

"I'm sorry for so many things that I can't make up for now."

"Don't talk like that. Don't talk like you're still dying," Miyoung demanded. "You're scaring me."

"No, nothing can scare my brave daughter." Yena sighed the words. "Miyoung, who are you?"

Miyoung tried to reply, and it came out a sob. She took a deep, shuddering breath and tried again. "Gu Yena's daughter."

"And what does that make you?"

"Smart."

"And?"

"Beautiful."

"And?"

"Strong."

"And loved."

Miyoung felt when her mother's life left her body. Yena's cold hands loosened around hers. Her body let out a final sigh with the relief of letting go.

"No," Miyoung sobbed. "I saved you. I saved you. I saved you." She repeated the words again and again. A mantra she couldn't give up.

Then she did stop. And she wept.

She wept as Yena's body faded to nothing. Not even leaving dust behind, but becoming air and vapor.

77

AFTER MIYOUNG CRIED herself dry, she left the clearing without a glance at the charred remains that were her father. He could be picked at by the crows. She rushed to the shaman shop. Nara would have to help her—it was only right the shamans undid what they'd created—but it had been emptied. Cleared so completely that not even a speck of dust lay on the worn wooden floor. And Miyoung collapsed in the middle of the empty store to weep out her anger and despair until Jihoon found her.

o o o

They placed a placard for Yena below a maehwa tree. The plum blossoms would flower in winter despite the cold. It was a hardy tree, but beautiful when it bloomed. It reminded Miyoung of Yena, so that was where they laid her to rest.

It was a simple ceremony lit by the waning moon. When Junu arrived, they exchanged no words, but Miyoung had no strength to make him leave.

With nowhere else to go, she stayed with Jihoon. His room became her sanctuary where she waited for her death. Her bead had disappeared with Yena's body. And without it she expected to soon join her mother. As she lay with the curtains drawn to block out the sun, she didn't know how many days had passed.

The full moon had marked the ninetieth day, which meant she had ten days of feeling like her grief would consume her. Ten days of mourning before she could go to oblivion.

A fever raged through her like a flash fire sweeping through a forest. She slept through days and wept at night. And every time she woke, Jihoon was there, wiping her sweaty brow or napping beside her.

It was her only comfort, that he'd be with her in the end. Though she felt sorry when she saw the pain in his eyes.

"This has to stop," Jihoon said one day, stomping to the curtains and flinging them open. "You're not dying, Miyoung."

She didn't reply, didn't even move to block out the light.

"Miyoung-ah," Jihoon said, his voice softer. "I don't know what to do for you. Can't you tell me?"

She stared at him, resting her cheek against the pillow, still damp from her tears. "When I die—"

"Don't."

"When I die," she continued, "don't mourn me. Forget me and live the life you should have before I came into it."

"Miyoung-ah." Jihoon sat beside her, folding his legs beneath him. "If you die, then I'll always remember you. That doesn't mean I won't live a full life. People leave us and our lives will never be the same, but if we forget them, then what does that say about how we value them?"

"When did you get so wise?" Miyoung asked.

"When the hundredth day passed."

"What?" Miyoung sat up and the sudden movement made her head spin.

"I didn't want to say anything. I was worried it would jinx it. But yesterday was the hundredth day," Jihoon said. "And you're still here."

"No." Miyoung shook her head, trying to calculate the time, but it was all a blur of mourning and sleep. "That can't be. I don't have my bead. I should be dead."

"Is it really that horrible?" Jihoon asked, a smile tilting the corners of his lips. "The idea that you'd have to live a human life with me?"

Miyoung let out the breath she didn't know had been clogging her lungs. And let herself believe. With it came a lightness as if she'd float away without Jihoon to anchor her to the earth. She laughed and flung her arms around him, hugging him to her.

"I'm alive." Saying the words made her giddy, and she let out another laughing breath. "I'm alive."

"You're alive," Jihoon said, and she heard the answering joy in his voice. They held each other close.

Then she sobered as the weight of the realization came down on her.

"So now I'll have to live without her," Miyoung whispered.

Jihoon squeezed her hands. "We'll both learn to live without them."

Miyoung sighed, remembering Halmeoni. Grief wasn't exclusively hers.

"I don't know how." She sighed, and it shuddered through her whole body to shake her. "She was my everything."

"Maybe it's wrong for us to hold any one person as our whole world. Maybe . . ." Jihoon trailed off with an odd expression. "Maybe it's wrong of us to owe all of our happiness or sadness to one person."

"What is it, Jihoon?" Miyoung asked, frowning.

"Nothing. I just think maybe I owe someone a visit," Jihoon said. "But that can come later. Right now, I'm going to make you soup."

"Soup sounds good." Miyoung smiled.

78

WHEN JIHOON KNOCKED on the sleek metal door, his hand trembled. He closed it until the shaking stopped. He felt back to normal for the most part, but a few residual weaknesses remained. The doctors had assured him it was just the last fading effects of overcoming such an acute illness, though they still had no name for what had afflicted him. He didn't suppose it would help for him to explain the supernatural parts of it. The hospital could just view him as a medical oddity.

The door opened and his mother's surprised face appeared.

"Jihoon-ah," she said, caution in her eyes. "What are you doing here?"

"I have something to say." He paused. On the way there, he'd practiced his speech over and over. But now, facing her, he wasn't sure what words to use. So he blurted them out. "I understand."

"What?" His mother's voice shook with unspoken emotion.

For some reason, that made Jihoon feel steadier. "I understand why you left."

She hesitated, glancing behind her. Then seemed to come to a conflicted decision. "Why don't you come in? I'll make you tea."

It was a step, he thought. But not one he wanted to take right now. He'd gathered enough courage to talk to her, but not to spend time with her. Not yet.

"I'm not staying long. I just need to say something."

"Okay." She folded her hands, waiting patiently for him to continue.

"I understand that when you left, you thought you were doing good for me. I used what you did as an excuse to push people away for too long. It was easier for me to blame you for my insecurities, but I can see it now, how you were right about one thing. Being raised by Halmeoni was the best life for me."

"Oh, Jihoon-ah—"

"I've decided to stop blaming you. I don't want to be angry anymore."

"Jihoon-ah, I *am* sorry for how things ended up."

"Thank you," Jihoon said. "And maybe I'll forgive you. One day."

She gave a small smile. "I hope so."

79

MIYOUNG WAITED IN the bright sunlight. It felt good to be outside. Spring sat heavy in the air, filled with pollen and grass. She took a deep breath.

Her sense of smell had become muted. The same with her vision, her speed, her strength. It took some getting used to.

She didn't feel fully human, but she didn't feel the hunger for energy she once did either.

Miyoung was caught in some kind of limbo, not quite gumiho and not quite human. And though she hadn't told anyone yet, she knew that she was weak even for a human. Recovery had been slower than she'd hoped, but it wasn't something to burden anyone with. Especially because there was no precedent for her situation.

"Ya! You're not pedaling right!"

Miyoung glanced over, holding in her smile at the sight of Somin chastising Changwan as they tried, and failed, to ride a tandem bike.

"Your legs are shorter than mine," Changwan complained as his limbs dragged over the ground to stop them.

"You have to watch my lead," Somin instructed from her front seat.

Junu leaned against the railing. "Isn't the boy supposed to sit in the front?" Behind him the Han River flowed peacefully, the smell of water saturating the wind that blew over Miyoung's cheeks.

"The better rider sits in front," Somin corrected, sending him a glare patented just for the dokkaebi.

A strange truce had formed between Miyoung and Junu. The dokkaebi hadn't disappeared after Yena's death like Miyoung had expected. And surprisingly, it had been Jihoon who'd told her to give Junu another chance.

"It seems like he's sticking around because he needs to make amends," Jihoon had said. "I think we can both understand how that feels."

So Miyoung had begrudgingly accepted the dokkaebi whenever he randomly showed up. Like today, as he arrived with the tandem bike and Changwan.

"Miyoung-ah! Come save me from these boys!" Somin called to her.

She chuckled. "No thanks."

Somin sighed, then gestured to Junu. "Come and take a turn, then."

He sauntered over, a knowing grin on his face.

"You want me to take a turn, sweetheart?" Junu asked.

Changwan was starting to climb off when Somin stopped him.

"No, I think you guys will make a much better pair." Somin grinned, climbing off the bike.

Junu raised a brow, then shrugged and climbed into her seat. "Okay, Changwan, let's show them how it's done."

He took off a bit too fast, Changwan's shout of alarm trailing behind them.

Somin chuckled with Miyoung.

The girls had formed what could only be called a friendship

over the past weeks. Somin had a lot of questions, some of which Miyoung hadn't answered yet, partly because she couldn't. Somin wanted to know the weirdest things, like how come gumiho eat food when they only need gi to survive. Or why gumiho are solitary creatures when they'd be so much stronger in a pack.

Once, Miyoung had caught Somin staring at her.

"What?" Miyoung asked.

"I think you'll age well," Somin mused. "You have the bone structure for it. I guess we'll get to find out now."

It had caused the girls to break out into laughter.

Oddly enough, Miyoung liked Somin's blunt curiosity. In a way, it made her think of her gumiho state differently. Not as a monster, but as another being trying to figure out how to exist in the world.

"You look tired," Somin said.

"Gee, thanks." Miyoung laughed, but she worried about Somin's sharp eyes. "I'm fine, just didn't get a lot of sleep last night."

Somin nodded and let it go. She knew Miyoung still had bad dreams about the night her mother died.

"Do you really not want a turn on the bike? It's kind of fun." Somin grinned and it pulled an answering smile from Miyoung.

"Maybe when Jihoon gets here."

Somin rolled her eyes. "Good luck, that boy is worse than Changwan with hand-eye coordination."

"Heads up!" Junu called as they rode by Somin, a bit too close for comfort.

"Ya!" she shouted, taking off after them.

Miyoung was laughing at the sight when someone clamped their hands over her eyes. "Guess who."

She grabbed Jihoon's wrists and pulled until he was hugging her from behind.

"What are you doing?" Jihoon whispered in her ear.

"Nothing," Miyoung replied, releasing him so he could walk around the bench. "Talking to the sun."

"What does it say?" He sat and swung an arm around her shoulders.

"Nothing much. Just hello."

"Not very talkative, huh?"

"It doesn't need to be," Miyoung said. "The sun and I have a good relationship." She set her head against his shoulder. Her own personal sun, plucked out of the sky.

"You finally got to come to the Han River. Is it everything you thought it would be?" he asked. "Full of magic and unicorns?"

Miyoung snorted out a laugh. "Unicorns don't exist."

"I've learned never to discount the existence of anything." Jihoon winked. "And you didn't answer my question."

Miyoung grinned as she glanced toward their friends. Somin was yelling curses as Junu chased her on the bike.

"It's definitely nothing like I imagined," she mused.

"And?"

"It's perfect." She smiled as the sound of laughter lifted in the air around her.

She linked her hand with Jihoon's.

She didn't know how long she had in this world. A hundred days, a hundred months, or a hundred years.

In this moment, as she watched her friends and held on to Jihoon, she was happy. And she would keep finding her happiness in each moment, until she had no more moments to spend.

EPILOGUE

THE FOREST WAS dark despite the full moon. The branches now held so much foliage that it created a barrier between the earth and sky. The moonlight no longer hurt her, but still, Miyoung was grateful for the protection.

She'd avoided the woods after losing her mother. But she'd missed her safe haven. The memories this place held were both comfort and pain. And now, as she picked her way over twisting roots and through reaching branches, she breathed in deeply. The scent of dirt and wood calmed her nerves.

She loosened her grip on the flowers she carried. She didn't want to break their delicate stems. Was it useless to bring such a token? Yena had hated flowers; she said they made a mess when they died. But her mother couldn't voice her disapproval of such a gift. Not anymore.

Miyoung swiped at her eyes, stinging with tears.

As she approached the maehwa tree that commemorated her mother, she blinked, wondering if her tear-filled vision was playing tricks on her.

She squeezed her eyes shut and opened them again. But it was still there. A dark *X* burned into the tree, still smoking from the ugly brand.

"Miyoung-ah."

She whipped around at the whisper. It had sounded so close, like someone spoke into her ear.

The forest behind her was empty. The shadows of tree branches twisting ominously.

"You are not free."

She spun toward the maehwa tree and stepped back in surprise. The branches reached out, like sharp wooden hands. Grasping at her. She tried to run, but her feet sank into the ground. Roots rose to twist around her legs. Squeezing so hard they cut off her circulation.

The branches took her into their cruel embrace. They bit into her arms. Rough bark rubbing at her skin.

It's a dream, Miyoung told herself. *This isn't real. You have to wake up.*

She tried to push free, but the branches held tight. She tried to kick, but her feet were encased in dirt and roots.

This isn't real, she repeated to herself. But still her heart sped. Tears fell down her cheeks. She tore futilely at her prison until her fingers bled.

As the branches closed around her, she became surrounded by darkness.

"Miyoung-ah. Leave."

"I can't." She couldn't breathe. If this was a dream, why couldn't she breathe?

"If you stay, you'll die."

"No!" She clawed at the branches with bloody fingers.

"You think it's over, but it's not. You think you're free, but you're not."

Out of the darkness a pale face appeared, beautiful and cold. Yena's eyes captured Miyoung's.

·"Eomma," she sobbed out. "Help me."

Yena's lips peeled back, revealing sharp teeth. "Help yourself!"

Miyoung jerked awake, struggling against the tangle of sheets that had twisted around her. As she remembered the dream, she knew that wasn't all it was.

She still felt like she couldn't breathe. She thumped a fist against her chest to clear her lungs. She finally wheezed in air.

Squeezing her eyes shut again, she could still picture her mother's face. Fierce. Cold. Almost threatening.

It was more than just a dream. It was a warning.

ACKNOWLEDGMENTS

So many people contributed to bringing *Wicked Fox* to life. I will be forever grateful to them for helping make my dreams come true!

First, I want to thank my amazing agent, Beth Phelan. You believed in my story even during moments when I thought it was too difficult to bring to life. You also held me to a high standard that pushed me to grow as a writer. Your tireless enthusiasm and amazing insight helped me make a story even I didn't realize I could tell. You have given so much hope to so many diverse creators and I feel lucky every day to have you on my team!

I also want to thank my editor, Stacey Barney. I was a fan of your work long before I was gifted with the chance to work with you. Your faith in my story has given me a boost every time I've had the pleasure to talk to you. I am in awe of your insight. I am inspired by how hard you championed my book. I am one of the luckiest writers in the world to be one of your authors.

To my Putnam/Penguin team, thank you so much for everything you've done for my book!

To my critique partners and beta readers, my story would not be what it is without your amazing help and advice! Liz Mallory, thank you for reading my book when it was pretty much a first draft and I was stressing about querying. You gave me the strength to push forward. Akshaya Raman, you are such a beautiful friend and I am so lucky to have your brain and talent helping me out when I'm struggling with writer's block. Katy Pool, your early enthusiasm for this book meant the world to me. You are a shining star and I am so thrilled you like my story! Rena Baron, you read some of my first-draft chapters, and I cannot thank you enough for giving me an alpha reader boost. Sarah Suk, thank you for being so encouraging about my story and reading it as one of my beta readers!

To Rebecca Kuss, Deeba Zargarpur, Emily Berge, and Alexa Wejko. I've learned so much about writing and publishing from each of you. The last year and a half has been a joy because of the time I've been able to spend with you amazing ladies! I know you all are going to do great things for the publishing community!

To the Speculators: David, Anitra, Dave "Dadvid," Helen, Nikki, and Alex. You were the first big writer group I was a part of and your support helped me push through the anxiety of putting my work out there!

To my ChiYA ladies: Ronni Davis, Samira Ahmed, Gloria Chao, Anna Waggener, and Lizzie Cooke. I am so lucky I had you ladies while I was in Chicago. I miss our ChiYA brunches, but I know you'll always be there to share book and life news with!

To my beautiful friends Karuna Riazi and Nafiza Azad. You are a constant source of joy in my life. Thank you for sharing your stories with me and for always encouraging me in my writing. I am so happy to know you both!

To my writer cult girls, you are all stars in your own right and I adore you all so much! Janella Angeles, Ashley Burdin, Alex Castellanos, Mara Fitzgerald, Amanda Foody, Christine Lynn Herman, Tara Sim, and Melody Simpson. From our Cultreats, unofficial karaoke with pots, Vat o' Wine, and near-death experiences via swan or stove, we've been through so much together! There's no one I'd rather cry at *Hamilton* with. I am grateful every day to have you as friends.

To the authors who came before me and gave me advice and mentorship, thank you! Ellen Oh, your books were the first time I saw a Korean main character in a YA fantasy setting. It inspired me to tell my own experiences with my culture and my identity. Thank you for all the amazing advice and support you've given me along the way! Julie Dao, your grace and intelligence have been a guiding light for me in my path to publication. Zoraida Cordova, thank you for your amazing advice. Our discussions about publishing and debut year have helped me navigate this journey and keep my head on my shoulders (most of the time).

To my friend Meg Kohlmann. Thank you for dealing with my writer (and life) breakdowns as I worked on this book. You are my favorite "daughter" and I'm so glad we got to live in our teeny tiny apartment together! I'm sorry we never got that puppy that you definitely super wanted.

To my best friend and Twitter wife, Claribel Ortega. There aren't enough words to explain how much you've come to mean to me over the past three years. We might have met through our writing, but you have been a friend that has soothed my soul. I am a better person having known you and I am so excited to support your career just as you've always supported mine. I love you!

To my family, I am so lucky to have grown up with such loving people around me. And you have all been there for me. Halmeoni, I love how steady you are as the head of our giant family! Emo Helen, Uncle Doosang, Emo Sara, Uncle Warren, Uncle John, Aunt Heejong, Emo Mary, and Uncle Barry, I couldn't have asked for more supportive aunts and uncles! Adam, Alex, Saqi, Sara Kyoung, Wyatt, Christine, Kevin, Bryan, Josh, Scott, and Camille, you are the best cousins and I love having adventures with you! I love you forever!

To my cousin and friend Axie Oh. You are my hero. I would not be here if not for you. I am inspired by your talent, your spirit, and your sweet sweet jokes. I never had to feel like I was alone in this industry because I always had you. You're my favorite author. I love you, cuz.

To my brother(-in-law), Jim Magiera. When you married my sister, you immediately treated me like family. I never had a brother growing up, but I'm so glad that you're my brother now. You are a fantastic husband to my sister, a great father to Lucy, and a wonderful brother. Thank you for reading fifty pages of my book.

To my niece, Lucy—you can't read yet, but I hope when you can, you might read this book!

To my sister, Jennifer Magiera, you are my person, forever. You have always been there for me when I've had amazing moments, and you've been my rock when I've been at my lowest points (when we've been at our lowest points together). I couldn't have asked for a better sister, best friend, hero, and role model. And I love you very much!

To my parents, Kello Katie and David Young Cho. Every story I have in me started with you. You sparked a love of reading and writing in me that grew into a flame and then a fire so great that it filled my whole being with light. I learned how to be strong when I saw you struggle. I learned how to be compassionate when I saw you with others. I learned how to love because of all the moments you provided us with as a family. Everything good I have in me, I owe to you. I miss you. I love you.

GLOSSARY

63 Building (63 스퀘어) formerly called Hanwha 63 City, a skyscraper on Yeouido island overlooking the Han River in Seoul; it was built as a landmark for the 1988 Summer Olympics

-ah / -ya (-아 / -야) informal name-ending implying the speaker is close to the person they are addressing

-nim (-님) name-ending used when speaking to someone senior in school or in the workplace (or someone of higher position in general)

-ssi (-씨) formal name-ending, often used with peers you are not friendly with; sometimes an elder will use it to refer to a person formally

abeoji (아버지) father

aissi (아이씨) irritated/annoyed expression loosely translated to "darn it"

ajeossi (아저씨) middle-aged man

ajumma (아줌마) middle-aged woman

Apgujeong (압구정) one of the wealthiest neighborhoods in Seoul, located on the southern bank of the Han River

appa (아빠) dad, daddy

babo (바보) fool

banchan (반찬) Korean side dishes, like kimchi

banmal (반말) informal type of speech in the Korean language

bindaetteok (빈대떡) mung bean pancake

binyeo (비녀) traditional hairpins used to fix women's buns, called chignons, and also used as ornamentation

bugeoguk (북어국) soup made with dried pollack strips and radish, said to be a great cure for hangovers

bujeok (부적) talisman created by a shaman or monk, often used for luck, love, or to ease stress (see *Notes*)

Cheongdamdong (청담동) area south of the Han River where many entertainment studios are located; a well-known hub for fashion and K-pop

chonggak dokkaebi (총각도깨비) handsome "bachelor goblin" that is known to attract humans

Chuseok (추석) autumn harvest festival; a holiday held on autumn eve where families traditionally gather in their ancestral hometowns to celebrate with food

ddaeng (땡) variety-show onomatopoeia used to imply a wrong answer

doenjang jjigae (된장찌개) stew made with fermented soybean paste, vegetables, tofu, seafood, and meat

dokkaebi (도깨비) goblin; legendary creatures from Korean mythology that possess extraordinary powers and abilities used to interact with humans, at times playing tricks on them and at times helping them

eo-seo-o-se-yo (어서오세요) common greeting, meaning "welcome," used by shop owners

eomeoni (어머니) mother

eomeonim (어머님) title to address another person's mother, usually to reference a mother-in-law

eomma (엄마) mom, mommy

galbi-jjim (갈비찜) braised short rib dish

geonbae (건배) "cheers," used when drinking alcohol

gi (기) human energy, also known as *qi, chi,* or *ji* in other East Asian cultures

Goguryeo (고구려) from 37 BCE to 668 CE, one of the Three Kingdoms of Korea, along with Baekje and Silla; it was located in the northern and central parts of the current Korean Peninsula as well as the southern and central parts of Manchuria

gu (九, 구) nine

Gwangjangsijang (광장시장) traditional market in Seoul that was the first permanent market in the city

Habaek (하백) the Goguryeo god of the Amnok River; sometimes called "the god of the sea"

Haemosu (해모수) sun god

halmeoni (할머니) grandmother

hanja (한자) Korean word for Han Chinese characters that were adopted from Chinese and incorporated into the Korean language with Korean pronunciation

hanok (한옥) traditional Korean house made with all-natural materials that do not cause pollution, usually wood, stone, and paper

harabeoji (할아버지) grandfather

heol (헐) slang term to express surprise

Hwarang (화랑) "Flowering Knights," an elite warrior group of male youth in Silla, one of the Three Kingdoms of Korea

hyeong (형) older brother; also used for an older male the speaker is close to

janggu (장고 / 장구) hourglass-shaped drum, sometimes called *seyogo* ("slim-waist drum"); the two heads produce sounds of different pitch and timbre that, when played together, are believed to represent the harmony of man and woman

jangryesikjang (장례식장) the building a funeral is held in, often located close to a hospital

japchae (잡채) sweet potato starch noodles stir-fried with vegetables and meat

Jeollanam-do (전라남도) province in the south literally meaning "South Jeolla"; the largest city in Jeollanam-do is Gwangju

jjajangmyeon (짜장면) Chinese Korean noodle dish topped with a thick sauce made of chunjang (black bean paste), diced pork, and vegetables

jjamppong (짬뽕) Korean noodle soup with a spicy seafood- or pork-based broth flavored with gochugaru (red chili paste)

jjigae (찌개) stew

jjimjilbang (찜질방) bathhouse with saunas, showers, massage tables, and areas for lounging and relaxing

kimbap or gimbap (김밥) Korean dish made with rice, seaweed, and fillings such as meat and vegetables; the rice and fillings are rolled into the seaweed and sliced into small discs for ease of eating

kimchi (김치) fermented vegetables, most commonly napa cabbage or radishes, served as a side dish in Korean cuisine

kitsune nine-tailed fox in Japanese mythology

kut or goot (굿) rites performed by Korean shamans, involving offerings and sacrifices, to commune with gods and ancestors; through song and dance, the shaman begs the gods to intervene in the fortune of humans

maehwa (매화나무) Asian flowering plum tree, also called a **maesil** (매실나무) when emphasizing the fruit

makgeolli (막걸리) milky, sparkling rice wine

miyeokguk (미역국) seaweed soup, often served on a person's birthday or to someone recovering from an illness

mul gwishin (귀신) water ghost

Namsan Tower / N Seoul Tower (N서울타워) communication and observation tower on top of Namsan mountain; a popular tourist site that affords views of the city of Seoul and is often a place where couples will go for dates and leave a lock

nappeun gijibae (나쁜기지배) slang term used as a slur against girls; recently, some have started to reclaim the phrase, like CL in her song "The Baddest Female (나쁜 기집애)"

noraebang (노래방) private karaoke room

ojingeo (오징어) squid

Palgongsan (팔공산) large mountain in the Taebaek mountain range

ramyeon (라면) instant noodles

saekki (새끼) slang that loosely translates to bastard

Samcheongdong (삼청동) neighborhood in Seoul with historical sites such as the Gyeongbok and Changdeok Palaces (from the Joseon Dynasty), Cheong Wa Dae (the president's office), and Insadong nearby

samjokgu (삼족구) supernatural three-legged dog from Korean folklore that can see through a gumiho's disguise

Sangdalgosa (상달고사) "tenth month," a ceremony of ejecting spirits from the household performed after harvest during the month of October to ask the house gods for peace and stability of the family and thank the gods for a prosperous year

sansin (산신) mountain god

seolleongtang (설렁탕) beef bone soup

seonbae (선배[님]) someone senior in school or in the workplace

soju (소주) clear distilled alcohol usually made from rice, wheat, or barley

soondae (순대) blood sausage, a popular street food in Korea

suneung (수능) nickname for the College Scholastic Ability Test or CSAT (대학수학 능력시험) given to third-years (seniors) in high school in Korea every November; on the test day, the stock markets open late and bus and subway service is increased to avoid traffic jams that could prevent students from getting to testing

Sungkyunkwan (성균관) the top educational institute during the Goryeo and Joseon Dynasties; its original site is now part of the modern Sungkyunkwan University in Seoul

sunsaengnim (선생님) teacher; **saem** is the abbreviated term for "teacher," often said with affection

tteok-bokki (떡볶이) hot, spicy rice cake

wang donkatsu (왕돈까스) "king donkatsu," a giant breaded pork chop

yeo-chin (여친) slang abbreviation for **yeoja chingoo** (여자 친구), which literally means "girlfriend"

yeot (엿) a variety of hangwa, or Korean traditional confectionery. It can be made from steamed rice, glutinous rice, glutinous sorghum, corn, sweet potatoes, or mixed grains

yeowu (여우) fox, or "foxy" when referring to a woman

yeowu guseul (여우구슬) fox bead

yogoe (요괴) monster, demon

NOTES

- When women in Korea marry, they do not take their husband's surnames, thus the different surname for Somin's mother (Moon, not Lee).
- In Korea, a person is one year old when they are born, and everyone turns a year older at the new year. Therefore, though Jihoon, Miyoung, and Somin think of themselves as eighteen years old, they are actually seventeen years old chronologically. They all turn nineteen years old (Korean age) when the new year passes.
- Bujeoks contain letters or patterns that are believed to carry the power to chase away evil ghosts and prevent calamities. In Korean folk religion, amulet sheets are generally made by painting letters or pictures in red on a sheet of yellow paper. Nowadays, they are made with disassembled and combined letters written as abstract forms on a piece of paper. Bujeoks are often sought out before a big test or interview.